BEHOLD THE VIGIL

Books by Joe Bergeron

The Endurian Universe

1: *The Astronomer Who Didn't Like Magic*

2: *The Vigil*

3: *Space Mariners*

4: *Space Mariners: Elves and Aliens*

5: *Space Mariners: Children of Rral*

6: *The Astronomer Who Hated a God*

7: *Acts of the Vigil*

8: *Behold the Vigil*

9: *The Astronomer Who Gave Back a Crown*

Other Books

The Way of an Eagle

Cosmic Cat

For my mother—who would always root for the Vigil.

BEHOLD
THE
VIGIL

Book Eight of the Endurian Universe

JOE BERGERON

Endurian Press

Behold the Vigil is a work of fiction. Names, places, and incidents either are products of the author's imagination or are used fictitiously.

Copyright © 2011 by Joe Bergeron

Cover illustration by Joe Bergeron.

Published by The Endurian Press

www.joebergeron.com

Chapter 1

Earthwalker and Sea Ghost

The sun was no longer fierce, having passed its high tropical noon hours before. Its light was softened, its color tending toward gold, casting a path of mellow sparks over the gentle lagoon, which otherwise was a clear aqua, brightened by the sand beneath it. The sky was vast and serene, with a fretwork of cirrus clouds catching and further glorifying the light. Blue shadows of palm trees pooled here and there on the beach, wandering slightly in the fragrant breeze.

No day in history, no place in the world, could have seemed more idyllic.

As Tara Strenczak sat on the sand gazing seaward, she saw the end of the world in every shadow, in every grain of sand, and in every sparkle of light on the water. The light of the sun could flare up into a killing glare that would sterilize land and sea. The sea itself could rise up and smash everything before it. The shadows could flow together to form a carpet of darkness to last unto the end of time. No such event could surprise her anymore. Such were the times in which she lived.

Tara lay back on the sand and closed her eyes. Sunlight filtered through her eyelids, the color of blood. They snapped open at a distant rumbling. High overhead was a flight of three fighter jets, a little too distant to identify. Looking for her?

No, Tara, she thought to herself. *You're not that important. If they do get you, it won't be like that. Relax.*

Rather than relaxing, she sat up quickly at the next sound she heard: splashing coming from the lagoon.

She squinted. A round brown object was bobbing on the surface a hundred yards offshore: a coconut? No, it rose out of the water and was attached to a neck and a pair of shoulders. A man was walking out of the water.

Tara stiffened but did not flee. Something was strange about this. The man's hair dripped against his face. He wore no diving mask, no wet suit, nothing. As he emerged it became clear that indeed he was naked, a fit young man of moderate height, with dusky-golden skin, a bit lighter than her own, and brown hair. His exotic features were grave as he stepped clear of the water and advanced up the beach, sparing her no more than a glance.

As he was about to pass, some impulse led Tara to blurt, "Hey, I didn't know there were any nude beaches around here."

He halted and studied Tara in more detail, causing her to wilt at the inanity of her remark. His eyes were a clear brown, with golden flecks.

"You are an American?" he said quietly, his voice a strange blend of every accent she'd ever heard.

"Yes."

"I'm surprised to find you here. I'm somewhere in Indonesia, am I not? And not on an island much frequented by tourists, I'd guess."

Tara blinked at this. "Actually, Indonesia's not too friendly to Americans right now, not even tourists. This is Pulau Madura, in case you really don't know where you are. What's your name?"

He shrugged. "Recently I've been called Endurance."

"Endurance? I'm Tara. I assume that's a nickname? What are you doing, training for a triathlon or something?"

This flow of babble escaped from Tara almost without her volition, as though she were so eager for a normal life that she would attempt insipid banter even with a strange, naked man who looked at her as though she were a patch of froth on a wave. Or maybe she just didn't want him to leave.

"Triathlon? I don't know that word, Tara. Goodbye now."

Endurance walked a few paces further up the beach.

"Hey, Endurance. Could you use a pair of pants?"

He stopped, turning back to her with a wry smile. "You raise a good point. Having pants might save me a little inconvenience later on. Sometimes I forget. Have you a pair to spare?"

"Yeah." Tara rummaged through her satchel, withdrawing a pair of military khakis. She stood and offered it to Endurance. "I won't need these anymore. I'm nearly your height, but you'll still find the fit a little strange. My butt's bigger than yours. Still, they're better than nothing. I'd offer you a matching Navy blouse, but you might find it more trouble than it's worth."

Endurance drew on the slacks. He hesitated, studying her now in some detail.

"Tara, are you all right? Do you need help?"

Tara released a breath she had not realized she was holding. Many thoughts swam through her mind, thoughts of the many forms of help she needed and craved. But this man, even with his quiet, sad regard, could not work

3

miracles, could not reshape her life or the world in which she lived. She would ask about her most immediate need.

"Well. I could use a way off this island. Away from here. Far away."

"Back to America?"

"No! Not there. Somewhere…where I won't be easy to find."

Endurance nodded slowly. "I think I understand. Listen. As I was approaching this island, I noticed something interesting nearby, a vessel also heading toward shore. If you walk north along the beach you'll come to a promontory. Somewhere along its north side I believe you'll come across this ship. Its captain may be able to help you."

"It's not…a U.S. Navy vessel, is it?"

"No."

"Smuggler? Drug runner? Pirate ship?"

"No, none of those."

"Okay, thanks. I'll give this yachtsman or whatever he is a try. Good luck with whatever your plans are."

"My plans are about the same as they've always been. See what happens next. Wait for the Moment."

"The Moment? What Moment?"

"The moment when I discover why I exist."

Endurance waved at her, turned, and soon vanished into the jungle.

Tara looked after him for a while, shrugged, than shouldered her bag and started north along the shore. She could certainly use one of those "Moments" herself, she reflected. It had better come soon.

After a mile or so the beach curved suddenly towards the east. She followed it and soon found herself on a long spit studded here and there with coral rocks. It extended past the reefs that created the calm inner lagoon, exposing its rock and sand to the pounding of the open sea.

A broken wall of tall rocks reached seaward from the northern side of the little peninsula, creating a partial shelter against the waves. Wallowing there was something so strange that Tara stopped in her tracks to study it.

At first she thought the rounded glossy thing might be some huge whale, but that impression lasted only a moment. It was a ship, but a most remarkable one. Its hull had a slick, glassy green-black sheen. In the bow was a transparent bubble canopy protected by an overarching beam. Wrapped around the hull and extending below the waterline was a smooth, white horseshoe-shaped structure. Intermittently visible through the waves was a name: *Captain Nemo II*.

Clearly it was a submarine, though the only thing about it that looked fairly conventional was its sail, which bore an emblem: a bold letter "V" set in a black-rimmed disk. A white rudder stuck up at the stern. On it was a stingray inscribed in silver.

Tara gasped, both at the beauty of the vessel and at the knowledge of whose property it was.

"Behold the Vigil," she whispered.

Slowly she drew nearer. A figure crouched on the port arm of the horseshoe, near the stern. A big panel was open there, and the figure was halfway inside it, working busily and perhaps a little frantically. As Tara approached, her sense of scale made a sudden adjustment and she realized that this person was extremely large. She halted again to watch him work. He alternated between leaning inside the opening and raising his head to anxiously scan the sky. He was shirtless and barefoot, wearing only a pair of tight black leggings and an absurdly macho pair of metal wrist bands. He was very powerfully built, yet sleek and streamlined in a way no human being had ever been. His glossy skin was bronzed, his hair fine and golden. His great proud head had a prow-like nose, fierce dark eyes, and full lips clamped in a determined line.

As he noticed her standing there he actually gave a start. Tara could not help smiling. She had managed to startle the mighty Stingray himself!

"Anda dari mana? Nama anda siapa?" he bellowed. When that produced no response beyond a blank look, he ventured, "Who are you? Where did you come from?"

"I… my name is Tara Strenczak."

"You're an American!" From him this sounded like an accusation, and she flinched. "Don't come any closer." He pulled some device from his belt and muttered into it for a moment.

"You're active in the United States Navy! Petty officer third class. A sonar technician on a cruiser. Wait…you're listed as UA. Unauthorized Absence. Is that true?"

"Yes."

"What do you want here? It would be a likely trick for Naval Intelligence to try to lower my guard by having an agent pretend to be a deserter."

"It's nothing like that. I need to get away from here. I don't want to be caught, not by the Navy or the locals either. I don't know what to do. Someone told me you might be able to help."

"And who the hell told you that?"

"He said his name was Endurance."

At that name Stingray sputtered an incoherent exclamation and dropped his phone, barely recovering it before it slipped over the curving side of the horseshoe. Tara smiled again, pleased to be so capable of disconcerting this fantastic being.

"Endurance! Where did you see him?"

"He came walking out of the ocean a few miles from here. We had a little chat, and he advised me to come looking for you, though he didn't bother to tell me exactly who I was looking for. Then he ambled off into the jungle and that was the last I saw of him."

Stingray nodded, suddenly less on his guard. "That sounds like him, all right. Damn, I would have liked to have spoken with him. He hasn't been heard from in years." He peered around, as though hoping to spot Endurance wandering among the rocks. "Oh well, this is a bad time to go looking for him. I'm Stingray, by the way."

"Yeah, I'd already figured that out."

"All right, come aboard if you want. I'm having a bit of a problem with the ship, and I'd better keep working on it while I figure out what to do with you."

Life seemed a little dreamlike to Tara as she advanced. The submarine's bow was about twenty feet offshore, separated from it by turbulent water. She eyed the gap dubiously.

Stingray walked along the horseshoe until he stood in front of the great canopy at the bow.

"You're not one of those sailors who can't swim, are you?" he asked.

"Well...there might be rocks...currents...there's no way to climb up...I don't want to ruin my things..."

Stingray launched himself from the submarine and landed beside her without even getting his feet wet. He towered over Tara, who was herself a tall woman. She gazed up into his eyes with her mouth hanging open.

"What's the matter? Never seen blue eyes before?"

"Yeah. I have. But never eyes that were solid blue with little black pupils in the middle. They're incredible."

Stingray laughed. "Thanks, I guess. Mind if I pick you up?"

She shook her head.

Stingray lifted her and her bag without effort. He strode through the waves to the sub, then casually flipped her aboard as though he were tossing a cat. She landed on her feet on the cool, slick surface of the horseshoe and managed to stay upright. She was staring through the canopy at the technological wonderland within when Stingray came rocketing from the sea to land beside her.

"Back to work," he said. Tara breathlessly followed him to the open panel and the tools laying around it.

"I take it you're from that carrier group that's been bombing Java?"

"Yeah. Attacking the so-called 'terrorist camps'. Are you here to do something about that?"

"Nope, I'm afraid not. It's sea trials for this new sub. I'll be lucky if the Navy doesn't do something about me. I know I've been spotted. If they work up the nerve to attack before I can restore power to the sub, they'll have one hell of a target of opportunity to brag about. All in secret, of course. The USA isn't officially at war with the Vigil—yet. You have technical training? Think you can give me a hand with this?"

Tara peered over his shoulder into the interior of the horseshoe. Aside from recognizing a few structural members, she could make no sense of what she saw.

"I have no training in anything like this. It looks like a giant high-tech Lego set to me. Where's your crew?"

"I am the crew," muttered Stingray while manipulating some diagnostic device which might as well have been a movie prop as far as Tara was concerned.

"Just you on this big sub? It must be over two hundred feet long."

"Things aren't going just the way I'd like. This sub is designed for a crew of nine. It was intended to be a research vessel, like my old sub, the first *Nemo*. But as you may have heard, the world has lately grown more hostile toward the Vigil. The modifications I've made have resulted in a compromised warship at best, but given the pace of events, that's the best I can do at the moment. Stick your head in here and look aft."

Tara knelt and complied with this odd request.

"See that reflective sphere? The one surrounded by massive cables and fittings?"

"Yes."

"That's a magnetic containment bottle holding five pounds of anti-hydrogen. Most Vigil ships are powered by tachyon piles. They're great, but this ship doesn't have room for a pile big enough to drive it at combat speeds and also power its weapons. This is the first time we've tried an antimatter power source, and we're not very good at it. If that bottle should be breached or lose power, the explosion would excavate a crater at least twenty kilometers in diameter."

Tara withdrew her head and stared at Stingray. "What's wrong with it? Is it likely to explode?"

"Not just yet. I've lost main propulsion and most other systems, but not containment. That'll be the last thing to go. But you can see why I'm being cautious. I know what the problem is, more or less, and there's not a thing I can do about it. Excuse me while I call for help. If you notice a flight of bombers coming in from your carrier, let me know."

Stingray spoke into his phone. "Lori? Stingray here. Look, I need you to do something for me. Look up the... yes, this is important. I'm stranded. Look up the latest plans for *Nemo II*. Look for the port after power distribution module. Make me a new one—or better yet, two or three— put them in an automated flyer and get them to me as soon as possible. Got that?

"Yes, they are complicated.

"I know you're busy. I'm a little short on time myself. If I don't get this boat underway soon, I'm likely to be sunk by the U.S. Navy. In fact, if I'm not mistaken, I think I hear an alarm sounding inside the ship right now. I probably have about five minutes. Hold on a second, Lori."

Stingray turned to Tara with a fierce, challenging stare.

"Well, Tara Strenczak, it looks like your carrier group has launched against me. I'm going to have to try to fight them off, and it won't be easy. Here's your situation. Right now you're just Unauthorized Absence, not even officially a deserter. If you stick around with me, then besides facing a good possibility of being killed, you'll have to watch as I try to shoot down members of the United States Military. You will suddenly be guilty of treason. Think it over."

He returned to the phone, leaving Tara in a whiteout of fear and doubt.

"Lori? Lori, don't cry. Yes, I know you want to help. It's all right. If I can't defend the sub, I'll just abandon it and take to the ocean on my own. What's that? Perturbare? How did he get involved in this? Oh, he did, did he? Well, you just tell him—never mind. If he thinks he can do something, let him try. I'll talk to you later, Lori. Don't worry about me. Goodbye."

A sudden chill clutched at Tara. Stingray looked around uncertainly, then turned back to her.

"Tara, you should either run away *now,* or get into the sub for protection. If you hesitate I don't think you'll make it. I think you'd do better to run away."

"I don't see how either of us can get away from that twenty kilometer crater." Tara hugged herself. The chill was real, and intensifying. She too looked around. "What's happening in the water?"

The water near the sub had grown milky and opaque. The very waves were damped and diminished, as though the water were stiffening like gelatin. Wisps of fog lifted and dispersed.

Deeper down she dimly saw a round concentration of whiteness which was steadily contracting and growing more solid. A column of bubbles erupted from it and rose to the surface, steaming and fuming.

"I have no idea what's happening here," said Stingray in a low voice.

Three shadows swept over them, followed a moment later by the sudden slamming roar of jet engines. Tara shrieked and turned just in time to see a flight of three

Hornet fighters disappearing in the tropical haze. Her ears rang from their passage.

"The next thing we see from them will probably be their bombs or missiles," said Stingray. "I really advise you not to stand around out here any longer. I'll take my own advice." With that he ran up the curving green-black hull of the sub and dropped down a hatch.

He emerged a few moments later carrying an object that looked like a large, glossy-black caulking gun.

"Is that your ray gun?" she asked, feeling idiotic.

"Yes. ERASER gun. Otherwise known as a free electron tunable laser. Unfortunately, the ship's main guns and targeting system are down. You're still here?"

"You're planning to shoot down incoming missiles with a hand weapon? I still don't think I can escape that twenty kilometer crater, no matter how fast I run. Hey, the water!"

The weird effects in the nearby sea had suddenly ceased. Did she really see a small white object sinking through the clear waters?

Stingray dropped his weapon and made a flat thirty foot dive into the water. A moment later he erupted skyward, landing on the horseshoe with a roughly cubical white device cradled in one arm. He immediately set to work in the tight confines of the horseshoe's machinery space. "Well, here's the part I need," came his muffled voice, "conveniently created by friendly sea water through some miracle. In two minutes I'll either be underway or blown to pieces. Now you really must make your choice. Leave or get into the sub. If you choose the latter, please pick up the gun on your way in."

Tara looked ahead in time a few minutes, picturing herself watching the *Captain Nemo II* in retreat while she stood on the beach with no plan or goal other than to run away.

"I'm coming with you." She ran from the horseshoe onto the hull of the submarine, here steeply curved and slippery, and was barely able to mount it. She found the ERASER weapon lying near the hatch and picked it up, a hard, massive object with unfamiliar controls.

Movement caught her eye. She looked up to see an ominous black speck hanging near the horizon, growing rapidly. Without thinking she raised the weapon, braced it, and touched what she hoped was the correct contact, which was protected by a finger guard.

A red beam, searingly bright even in broad daylight, drew an infinite line through the sky. There was of course no recoil. Tara shone the beam on the incoming missile, which promptly exploded.

"Wow!" she said. She looked down at Stingray, who was just now slamming closed and sealing the access cover on the horseshoe.

"Nice work," he said, leaping up with an armload of tools. Without further comment he disappeared down the hatch.

Tara followed. Without power, the interior of the submarine was hot, stuffy, and silent. She followed Stingray down a ladder to a lower deck, then forward through a large compartment to the bow, where they climbed a few stairs and entered the control room beneath the big dome. Stingray flung himself into an oversized chair behind a console mounted on a plinth in the rear of the room. "Sit down," he instructed. Two other stations had normal-sized chairs, one forward and one beside Stingray's. Tara sank into the latter one and swiveled to watch

Stingray. The bubble canopy was just over her head. She could stand up and touch it if she wanted to.

The submarine came to life around her. Lights flickered, displays lit, and air moved. Stingray grabbed a joystick on the arm of his chair and shoved it forward. The sub surged backward, away from the beach. The bow dipped, partially submerging the dome. The surging water was lit by orange beams emanating from the sub.

There was a loud *bang* and the submarine shuddered. Bits of debris arced by the dome.

"Missile hit on the sail," said Stingray grimly.

"Well, I guess that does it for us."

"I'm not so sure. Doesn't seem to be any major damage."

"How is that possible?"

"We have materials and coatings that are really, really strong. This sub is made of structural carbon with a diamond coating. That was a Maverick missile. They try to penetrate their target by kinetic energy before exploding, and it probably just bounced off. But next we may hear from cruise missiles or Harpoons. That could be a different story. We need to submerge as soon as possible. Hold tight. I'm going to turn around."

He hauled back on the joystick. Tara was almost thrown out of her chair by the acceleration as *Nemo* shed its backwards momentum and then hurled itself forward. At the same time Stingray pushed the stick to the side. The submarine tilted as it made a tight 180-degree turn. Now it was heading for open water, its speed so great that seawater covered the dome in a smooth second canopy of its own.

"This thing is a hot rod! How fast are we going?" she cried.

"In excess of fifty knots," said Stingray dryly, mocking the common Navy parlance. "Okay, time to dive."

He gripped the joystick on the opposite chair arm and pushed it forward. His submarine planed beneath the waves. The control room was filled with shifting aqua lights refracted from above, which soon faded to a blue murk, and then toward blackness.

Tara sat staring through the dome as they plunged into the dimness.

"Good," said Stingray. "I'll take on a little ballast so we don't have to go like hell to stay under."

There was a distant rush of tanks filling with seawater.

"Well then, we're safe," said Stingray. "Safer than that battle group is, anyway."

"That piece...that component...that you got out of the water. Where the hell did that come from?"

"That came from the invisible hand of Dr. Possum Perturbare...the world's greatest scientific magician. And I wish I knew how he did it, and what he intends to do next. He could take all the plans of the Vigil, turn them inside out, and do it all for fun."

Chapter 2

Spook House

Doctor, the submarine's air filtration system has removed too many nanofloaters. I can no longer reconstruct and transmit an audio signal.

Possum Perturbare heard the voice of Brainchild One in his head, through the interface module at the base of his skull. Although it wasn't necessary, he usually replied aloud unless he lacked privacy. That was rarely a problem for him.

"All right, I think we've heard enough anyway. You'd think that big lug would be grateful to us for getting him out of that mess...but nooooooo, not him. I must admit, that's a pretty nice submarine he built. It's a little clumsy, but I can see where he's coming from with that design. I'm sure he'll get it right next time. Yeah, pretty good job, considering he had to build it the old-fashioned way."

Perturbare's affectations had changed following his imprisonment by the U.S. Government. His new costumes were black, accented by areas of multicolored foil, rather flamboyant in their overall effect. His surroundings also bore a similar color scheme, whereas previously they had been as white and pristine as his previous tunics.

With Brainchild now able to monitor and record Perturbare's dreams, the computer used this information to create environments tailored to Perturbare's liking. The room in which he was now seated was dimly lit, its surfaces finished in black and grey. Its design was fanciful, with many needless architectural details of niches, ledges, alcoves, and arches. In many of these were indirect colored lights which served no purpose other than to add to the ambience. It was similar to chambers found in Perturbare's small bases scattered all over the world. Since his great Pit in Tierra del Fuego had been discovered and destroyed, Perturbare no longer relied on massive centralized bases, but rather moved restlessly between many smaller facilities.

This hideout was among the smallest, yet it was one of Perturbare's favorites. It was located within the facade of a popular theme park's spooky "dark ride", which was something of a playground for Perturbare. He'd surreptitiously installed a windowed booth to which he could descend to observe the tourists passing by in their automated "Woe Wagons." Sometimes he'd apply ghoulish makeup and look out while eerie lights played on his face. Those who noticed him often appeared uneasy, not quite sure if he really fit in with the animatronic figures. When he looked them straight in the eye they almost always screamed or jumped.

Someday this amusing haunt of his would surely be discovered, forcing Perturbare to abandon it. For now he'd found that as long as he replaced any burned-out light bulbs in the mansion's windows, he was left in peace.

Stingray seems concerned that you will interfere with the Vigil's imminent venture, said Brainchild.

"So he is."

A pause.

Need he be?

"Hmm? No, I don't think so. Whatever thrashing around the Vigil wants to do is their business, and will probably be a lot of fun to watch. But I don't think our path goes in that direction. Something great is waiting for us! I just don't see what it is quite yet. A moment of inspiration will arrive, and then we'll find that the answers to the world's problems lie in a single deft stroke rather than in some huge convulsion."

In the meantime, it seems to me there is something we are obliged to do.

Perturbare thought for a moment. "You mean since Endurance has finally seen fit to show his pretty face above the waves?"

Yes.

Perturbare sighed, leaning back in his chair in this dim room with its dim spectral lights.

"Yes, I suppose you're right. It's no longer plausible to pretend we don't know where Endurance is. Valjhar will likely find him soon enough. When he does, I don't care to explain to an annoyed Aureus why it wasn't also present for their meeting."

I also do not wish to deal with that robot. Nevertheless, I will contact it, and inform it of the whereabouts of Endurance.

Perturbare sighed again.

"Endurance, Aureus, and Valjhar Cor. An unlikely trio. Not strictly enemies of ours, maybe, but not exactly friends either. And any one of them could pull my heart out through my throat before I had a chance to say *Eeek*!"

Chapter 3

The Vigil

In a chamber halfway up the Spire of the Vigil's coastal fortress, Fomalhaut sat at a table with the other members of the Vigil. Stingray's oversized chair was unoccupied, as Fomalhaut had not wished to distract him from his own urgent concerns by requesting his participation in the meeting. Fomalhaut regretted Stingray's absence. He was the closest thing to Fomalhaut's intellectual equal in the current ranks of the Vigil, and was also its most committed and reliable member.

Fomalhaut also sorely missed T'Ukudu and the insights produced by the android's calm, analytical mind. T'Ukudu's extraterrestrial origin had given him an outsider's view of Humanity which pierced many veils and preconceptions. In this regard he had been superior to Fomalhaut himself.

Fomalhaut had considered using the biotechnic science of the planet T'Utahn to recreate the Servant, producing a copy free of the engineered virus which the Americans had used to hasten the demise of the original, but Fomalhaut knew that would be a futile act. T'Ukudu would never cooperate with what the Vigil now proposed to do. He might even be compelled to oppose it, since if successful, the Vigil's plan would invalidate his report on Humanity's bleak future. Creating and transmitting that report had always been T'Ukudu's primary mission. Any change in its conclusions might invite the intervention of his mysterious Makers.

Aureus, the golden automaton, stood aloof near a window. The grey, shifting light of the rainstorm outside played over its metallic surface. Aureus, the destroyer. Aureus, the purposeless, its own private mission a failure, lacking any obvious ability to motivate itself to find some other goal. Fomalhaut was surprised it had bothered to appear at the meeting at all, as it showed no interest in the current plans and goals of the Vigil. In fact, Fomalhaut was surprised Aureus had not simply shut itself down by now, as it had on a previous occasion when its mission reached a dead end. Instead it lurked around the Pearl and Spire (as the new headquarters came to be called), making everyone nervous with its inscrutable ruby eyes.

Besides Fomalhaut's own, the big table was surrounded by only three other occupied chairs.

In one sat Lori Wu, a former mid-level staffer who had been acclaimed a member of the Vigil following her rescue of several relics of the planet Rral when their original base, the Lighthouse, was destroyed in a sneak U.S. attack. She still wore the Rralian engineering suit she had salvaged, using it with some skill. Otherwise she was uneasy in her role, nearly overwhelmed by it at times, still thinking of herself as a staff member, feeling like a pretender as a full member of the Vigil.

Then there was Ben Raintree, or rather the synthetic being who was physically identical to the lost original, but whose divergent life-path had resulted in a substantially different person. He wore a special grey jacket in whose pockets were concealed four bits of jewelry Lori had also brought forth from the conflagration of the old Lighthouse.

Their influence could always be felt, even when their various Lights did not directly impinge upon the eye and mind. Ben exhibited a watchful expectation, beneath which lay a new self-confidence that could easily cause him to abandon the Vigil, should its intentions diverge from his own.

Finally, another chair was occupied by the newest, the most dubious, and possibly the least satisfactory member of the Vigil. The man calling himself Walks-With-The-Sun had appeared on the Vigil's doorstep some months ago, expecting membership. His very ability to present himself at their door had done much to prevent him from being summarily dismissed. The hemisphere-and-spire of the Vigil's base stood high on a huge sea cliff in British Columbia, backed by towering peaks, all but inaccessible except by air.

A background check had revealed Walks's given name to be Raymond Smick, a Lakota Indian whose history could charitably be described as undistinguished.

But...Walks was the originator and leader of the Ghost Dance movement which had caught the imagination of Native Americans all over the continent, not to mention the attention of the American government. Tens of thousands of Indians awaited word of the intentions of Walks. They could perhaps be wielded as a useful influence, or they could easily be led to slaughter and defeat by a feckless leader.

Walks also had a history of friendship with Tom Standing Crane, a member of the Vigil who was now presumed dead. According to Walks, with his final words Standing Crane had urged him to join the Vigil.

Clearly, there was something unusual about Walks-With-The-Sun. He exhibited powers similar to those of Rouse Farewell, though they were of a sporadic nature, and so far to a much lesser degree. He could at times drift through the air, hang suspended above the ground, or fly in a faltering manner. He wore a blue "Ghost Shirt" painted with various symbols, which he claimed would protect him from all harm. So far no one had dared to test this, for fear of the man's life.

If Walks was truly a successor of sorts to Rouse Farewell, he was to all appearances an uncertain one. Yet Fomalhaut felt it best to keep a close eye on the man. This wasn't the first time that a Lakota with mysterious, vaguely-defined powers had approached the Vigil for membership. Fomalhaut could only hope that Walks's involvement with the Vigil would prove less ambivalent than had that of Standing Crane.

"My friends," began Fomalhaut. "The Vigil has faced three great crises in the span of its existence. The first was our conflict with the Para-Men and their program of ruling the Earth. The second was the attack on us by the United States Government. Both, while certainly serious and difficult, were relatively simple affairs. In the first we had merely to contain and neutralize a group of fewer than ten beings. In the second, we had only to survive the attack and reorganize.

"We are now in the preliminary stages of a third crisis which will be enormously more complex and difficult than either of the others. We will attempt to change the entire course of Human history, while causing an absolute minimum of chaos and injury during the transition. We will need every bit of thought, foresight, planning, and preparation we can muster. We must take..."

Fomalhaut was interrupted by a chime, and then a quiet voice.

"Emergency call for Lori Wu. Emergency call for Lori Wu."

Lori started, then grabbed a handset from the table, fumbling with the buttons.

"This is Lori." She listened for a moment and said, "Hey, is this important? We're having a big meeting—"

Lori listened again, then began to manipulate the data terminal in front of her on the table. The display lit up with a schematic of Stingray's experimental submarine, *Captain Nemo II*. She zoomed into the port power nacelle and isolated a blocky device whose image was dense with a simplified view of its circuitry.

"Stingray, I don't know. This looks awfully complicated. I don't know how fast I can... what?"

She listened again, her round face growing pale, tears starting from her eyes. She looked at Fomalhaut. "It's Stingray. He's under attack. He says..."

The chime sounded again. "Second emergency call for Lori Wu."

"Put the second call on speakers in this room, please," said Fomalhaut.

"Lori? Perturbare here. No time to chat right now. We happened to listen in Stingray's call. You probably don't have enough time to help him. I can give him what he needs. Just tell him that, okay, cutie?"

Perturbare ended the call.

By now Lori was openly weeping. "Stingray? I'm sorry, I didn't know, I want to help, but... Listen, Perturbare just called. He said he can help somehow."

Another pause.

"All right, be careful!"

She set down her handset and stared at Fomalhaut with a stricken face, seeing nothing but her own distorted reflection in his mirrored spherical helmet.

"Lori, none of this is your fault. Intelligence, please report on the status of Stingray's submarine, and any military activity in his area."

Another voice spoke out of the air. "Intelligence here. Telemetry indicates *Captain Nemo II* has lost main power and appears to be beached on an island in the Java Sea. A U.S. Navy carrier group has launched planes against it. Sorry we didn't spot this earlier."

Fomalhaut took a moment to share in the man's regret over this extremely lax...vigilance. He attempted to resume the meeting.

"My friends, here we see an illustration of the difficulties awaiting us. As yet we lack the fleets of vehicles needed to fulfill our goals, and our prototypes are imperfect. Our staff has expanded by a factor of twenty, yet it is imperfectly organized and led, and it is still only a small fraction of the necessary size. These factors have combined to place Stingray in serious danger. It appears that only Possum Perturbare is in a position to assist him in a timely manner, through some means of which I am ignorant. In other words, disaster will be averted only through the intervention of an unpredictable, rapidly evolving outsider over whom we have little influence.

Clearly we are far from ready to begin. We must hope that events do not outpace our preparations—"

Aureus startled everyone by suddenly turning with a clanging footstep and facing the outside wall.

"Aureus," said Ben Raintree. "What are you doing?"

The robot twisted its neck to regard Raintree. Its mouth locked open and its voice tolled out: "I have received word from Brainchild One. Endurance has been found. I go to him now."

The Third Eye on the robot's golden forehead opened. It turned back toward the wall.

"Everyone shield your eyes and face!" cried Fomalhaut.

The tachyon beam flared out, dissolving a section of the wall and drawing its converted energy back into the robot. By the time the three Humans raised their heads from their sheltering arms, Aureus had gone.

Cold rain blew into the room.

So, thought Fomalhaut, *Aureus is not entirely apathetic after all.*

"He's a strange one," said Walks. "Stands still as a wooden Indian for hours at a time, then suddenly he's too impatient to go find a door."

Lori stood up to examine the hole in the wall. She stepped back a few paces and raised her arms. As usual she was wearing the red-and-black Rralian engineering suit. Fomalhaut knew she subconsciously believed that if she removed it for any length of time she might not be permitted to put it on again.

A ghostly outline of the missing wall and window structure appeared in place. Rivulets of material flowed in from outside and filled in the outline, gradually becoming more opaque until the wall was perfectly restored.

"That was really cool, Lori," said Walks in admiration.

Lori turned away from the wall with an embarrassed smile. "Thanks. I did build this place, after all. The least I can do is fix up any little scrapes and dings."

Thank you, Walks, thought Fomalhaut.

The meeting, however, was clearly over, its thread broken. Everyone was fidgeting, radiating a desire to get on with their own affairs.

"So. We have now seen an example of events outpacing our preparations. Once again the United States has seen fit to make an opportunistic attack against us without provocation. I expect we will all want to look into this situation and its implications. I will call another meeting soon. Good night to you all."

Lightning flashed just as Ben Raintree stood up. Thunder rumbled as he grasped the wooden staff that leaned against the meeting table. Things like that were always happening around Ben, but he never appeared to notice them.

"Where are you off to, Ben?" asked Lori.

"I'm returning to Africa. Many, many people there are still in need of seeing the Lights." He hesitated, on the verge of asking Lori to accompany him, then thought better of it.

Raintree strode out of the room. Walks and Lori followed, chatting uneasily. Fomalhaut was left alone.

Fomalhaut had asked Raintree to confine his efforts to Africa for now. Aside from being the Earth's primary center of brutal squalor and degradation, the world's major powers were famously indifferent to what took place there. Even so, those powers were uneasy about what Raintree was accomplishing. Although they could not publicly condemn it, the spectacle of great masses of the oppressed and "powerless" rising up to throw down their tyrants was not calculated to comfort the privileged in any country.

The attack on Stingray was very troubling. How much did the U.S. government know or guess about the intentions of the Vigil? It probably still had spies within the lower echelons of the Vigil's organization. Fomalhaut no longer had time to telepathically assess the loyalty of every new hire. There were simply too many. Additional telepaths would be useful, but the time had not yet come when telepaths of his sort were to be born or made on Earth. Indeed, Fomalhaut was far from certain that this time would ever arrive on this particular Earth.

A startling thought occurred to Fomalhaut. Could *he* make them? T'Ukudu's biotechnology could be reconstructed, and Fomalhaut had some experience in using them. With their help he had recreated T'Ukudu once before. Later the technology had been modified and adapted to recreate Raintree. Raintree was not a clone—which was an artificially fertilized ovum, charged with foreign genes and grown into a baby—but a copy, grown cell by cell in a fully adult form. Could Fomalhaut adapt this technique to make copies of himself?

Fomalhaut felt an aversion to this idea. Any such copies must arise as blanks, with no past, history, memory, or training. This lack of any grounding had been such a serious problem for the new Raintree that he had nearly failed as a viable person. Such problems would be far more dangerous in beings whose brains were constructed to wield powerful neuro-quantum abilities. In all likelihood, it would require all Fomalhaut's time to educate such copies, if he could even do so successfully. He had no training or

27

experience in such things. Nor had he any ability to duplicate the exploration suit which protected him and extended his senses. The thought of being without such a suit in this deadly world was distractingly frightening.

No—Fomalhaut's foresight told him he shouldn't engage in, encourage, or consider the creation of beings like himself. Whatever his role in their eventual destiny might be, it was not for him to be the father of their race.

Chapter 4

Strange Companions

Endurance, the Earthwalker, sat on a low wall bounding a field near the town of Pamekasan. He was pleased to have arrived in time to witness their annual ox races, which he had not seen for many years. He was among a few thousand people who'd come to see pairs of oxen charging down the field under the urging of wiry men who perched on structures of poles dragged by the oxen. It was very colorful and mostly good natured. Endurance smiled. He always enjoyed seeing people having a good time in such simple ways.

He had added a too-small yellow shirt to his wardrobe, offered to him by a villager, as going bare-chested was considered rude at best in Indonesia. His modest attire did not mean he was ignored by the locals. Clearly, they didn't quite know what to make of him. Smiling girls and women kept asking where he was from, and whether he had any plans for later on. He could give no honest answer that they would understand. A few smiles and vague evasions on his part discouraged most of his curious admirers.

An unrelated and wholly unexpected event dispersed the rest of them.

Aureus landed with a thump in a tiny gap between members of the dense throng of revelers. Many of them screamed and cried out. They fell back, the nearest driven off by the heat radiated by Aureus, which even Endurance could feel. Endurance left his place on the wall and approached the robot, frowning.

"Aureus, what do you want here? You're frightening these people."

Aureus looked around as though noticing the crowd for the first time. By now the pair stood alone, ringed by gaping onlookers who stood well off. In the field, the ox races had halted, the oxen bawling in fear.

Aureus returned its attention to Endurance, its mouth locking open.

"These people are irrelevant to my goal. I have come to inform you that Valjhar Cor has returned to Earth and is seeking you."

Endurance stared at the robot, though of course there was nothing to be read in its glassy red eyes.

"Why should you trouble to tell me this?"

"I wish to encounter Valjhar."

"Why? And what does Valjhar want with me?" asked Endurance, though he thought he knew the disquieting answer for this last question.

"I wish to monitor the Rralian criminal and thereby fulfill my mission to the best of my ability."

Endurance sighed.

"Aureus, I know you're only a mechanism, and that it's impossible to dissuade you from your purpose, but if you possess any potential for reason and volition, I must try. Valjhar told me much of his history with you. Yes, he and his friends made use of advanced technology, in violation of the laws of your planet. But they used it only to flee from you and to explore the stars. They did not attempt to alter or pervert the society of Rral. The people who have suffered most from their actions are they themselves, along with the friends and families they left behind and who miss them. You have admitted that your mission against them is a failure. It's time for you to stop persecuting Valjhar Cor."

The robot actually hesitated.

"I do not intend to persecute him. I wish only to monitor him."

Something about this was strange, but as yet Endurance could not tell what it was.

"So, you wish to accompany me until Valjhar appears?"

"Yes."

"Very well, but know this. As far as I'm concerned, you're nothing but a machine, not entitled to any special regard. At the first sign of you threatening Valjhar, I will wring your head from your body, and this time I will not stop until you are utterly destroyed. Do you understand?"

"I understand."

"The last time I tore you apart I was too impatient to take the time to crush your brain case. I have always been curious to know how long that would actually take."

"I can provide that information. At the rate you were increasing the pressure on my brain case, disruption would have taken an additional seventy four hours."

Endurance raised his eyebrows. "That long? That's longer than it took me to escape from the Earth's core the first time it solidified. Your brain is truly a very durable object."

Aureus made no reply.

"You never answered my second question. What does Valjhar want with me?"

"I am told he desires to return to you the artifact known as the Motionglobe."

"Already?" asked Endurance in a small voice, though this was what he'd suspected. He nodded in resignation. The Moment was indeed near at hand.

"I expect you to be quiet and well behaved while in my company."

Endurance raised his hands and called out in the language of Bahasa Indonesia: "Good people of Pulau Madura! This is *Aureus* of the Vigil. It, or rather he, means you no harm. He has come to witness the Kerapan Sapi, and that is all. Please, go on with your festival and pay us no heed."

The locals did as he asked, though with many a look over their shoulders at the glittering robot and its apparently human companion. Otherwise they were left alone. The races resumed.

To Endurance the whole spectacle now seemed like a pageant of ghosts. From his immortal perspective, the human world had been winding up to a climax for well over a century. Even here he noticed the difference, even after the few years he'd just spent on the sea floor. A tenseness, an expectation, permeated the people and the very air they breathed. The same thing had been evident in that American woman he had encountered on the beach.

America had become the world's chief nexus of destructive possibilities. Half its population expected an apocalypse of one kind or another, and half of those were looking forward to it. The other half harbored a suspicion that deep down they deserved to be wiped out.

This was no passing episode of tumult and uncertainty. This was the breaking point for humanity, with its tragic mismatch between its physical power and its still apish mind.

If Endurance was to receive the Motionglobe at last, it would surely mark a great event for himself and for humanity. The first thing he had ever beheld was the glimmer of the Motionglobe, drifting before his face as he approached the primordial Earth five billion years before. He had reached out and knocked it away, an accident of his newborn lack of coordination, or so he had always believed. It should have been lost in the vastness of space for all eternity. Yet it had been returned to him, delivered against all probability from across space and time. Then he had refused it, mere minutes before he took to the sea. And now, the moment he emerged from the waves, he is told the Motionglobe is on its way to him once again? Clearly, some power was trying to tell him something.

Endurance sat and sighed again. To him the universe was a wholly inscrutable place, his own existence one of its greatest mysteries. Soon though, very soon, he suspected he would discover his destiny. And very soon, he feared, the human species which he so closely resembled would come to an end. All this laughter, all these smiles, cheers, exhortations, and dances, would be stilled. All would vanish, all would fall silent.

So too would all the staggering evil, greed, and cruelty of humanity, the awareness of which had engraved itself in the mind of Endurance over many centuries.

Chapter 5

War Games

Tara woke up in a dark, quiet room. She took a moment to remember where she was. Her eyes widened as it came to her—she was aboard Stingray's submarine, the *Captain Nemo II*. In her cabin. Her own cabin, a nicer room than her apartment back in San Mateo. In her bed. An actual bed, not a bunk.

It was all quite different than life as an enlisted sonar technician in the Navy, pretty posh for a deserter such as herself.

The submarine was a luxurious marvel, equal to the one owned by its namesake. It had three decks, not counting the sail. Headroom on the main deck was three meters. The other decks had eight feet. She never had to duck!

Still feeling a little bleary, Tara left her cabin and went aft. She grabbed a cup of coffee and some pastry from the galley and continued back, passing another cabin, a conference room, a library and study area, finally entering the observation room, which took up the whole of the sub's broad stern. The rear wall was mostly windows. She sat peering out as she ate, noting the swirl of motes in the turbulence of the sub's passage, brightly lit by the orange glow of the main propulsion lamps in the ends of the horseshoe.

The play of sunlight on the surface was faintly visible. A display on the bulkhead showed the ship's vital information: course, speed, position, bottom depth, and ship depth. They were about three hundred feet down at the moment, still in the clear tropical waters of the Java Sea. The bottom was not much farther down.

The room was almost silent. Although they were making twenty five knots, the only sound made by the sub was a gentle slur of passing water. Tara was glad she wasn't responsible for trying to detect a ship like this.

And yet, as she listened with her highly trained ears, it seemed to her that she detected another note, one that did not originate from the sub. Frowning, she stood up and applied her ear to the window.

The sea around her was filled with the sound of screws. Big, powerful ones.

A dim shape on the surface attracted her attention. Above and just behind them was a big hull, sleek and narrow: a warship.

She was staring at this with a half-eaten chocolate croissant forgotten in her hand when Stingray's voice came over the intercom, almost making her spill her coffee.

"Tara, I know you're not quite ready to face the world yet, but you might want to come forward anyway. We're in an interesting place."

Tara gulped the rest of her coffee and hurried forward while stuffing the croissant into her mouth. She entered the control room and gasped at the huge shape looming overhead, a gigantic hull, no doubt a carrier. With her mouth hanging open, she sank into the seat beside Stingray's. Her entire battle group must be overhead.

She glanced over at Stingray, who looked up at the carrier with an expression of grim mirth.

"That's your old cruiser right behind us," he said.

"Oh, Jesus!"

"Shhhh. Not so loud. They have people listening up there, you know."

"There's no way they can hear this submarine. Not with all those screws and engines churning up there."

"It's good to hear your professional opinion on the subject."

"What are you going to do?"

Something in Tara's voice made Stingray glance at her in surprise. "I'm not going to sink them, if that's what you're afraid of. That's not the Vigil's style, nor is it mine personally. I'm just going to seriously inconvenience them. Don't worry, your former shipmates are safe from me."

"Be careful. The battle group has a pair of nuclear attack subs attached to it too."

"I don't suppose they can hear us any better than the surface ships can."

Tara compressed her lips, thinking hard. What she was about to say would transform her irrevocably from a mere deserter to a traitor.

She released her breath and plunged in.

"Stingray, we've noticed that your vehicles come with big orange lights shining out of their asses. Navy ships now deploy optical sensors looking for this glow. Seawater is terrible at transmitting that color, but it does penetrate some distance, and we're awfully close to the ships. Chances are, they're aware of our presence right now."

"Whoops," said Stingray. "That indicates a slight intelligence failure on our part."

"Anyway, their sonar could go active at any time."

"Why do you suppose they're not reacting to our presence?"

"My guess is they don't dare. No enemy is supposed to get this close to any ship in the group, let alone the carrier. They might think you'll wipe them out if they make a move. What could they even do? Detonate a torpedo right beneath the carrier?"

Stingray laughed. "Yes, I can well imagine their thoughts. It serves them right. I guess I'd better quit gloating and get on with it, before some genius up there gets an idea." He reached over to Tara's console and touched a few contacts. The controls all changed to green and the displays lit up.

"Your console can be configured to perform any function. I've set it to sensors. See if you can figure out the passive sonar and tell me anything you notice. I think you'll find it fairly familiar."

Tara studied her displays as Stingray began to fiddle with his console. Her main tactical display was a fairly conventional plan position indicator. The ships were marked by type, and in most cases by name. Clearly, the Vigil had made quite a study of the U.S. Navy.

"Take the controls, will you? I'll have to set up this shot rather delicately," said Stingray. "Just keep us in this position relative to the carrier. Don't worry about depth. That's on automatic."

Tara started. "What? What makes you think I can handle this ship?"

"You're smart," said Stingray absently.

"And what makes you think that?" she snapped. For some reason she wanted to cry.

"You were smart enough to realize that the U.S. military has been reduced to waging one-sided wars, not to defend your country against any serious threat, but to keep the people afraid and controlled, and to serve the greed of a bunch of power-hungry white men. That's about the size of it, isn't it?"

"Yes," she said miserably.

"Then you're perceptive, at least. So please steer the sub for a few minutes. Be gentle with the controls. We'll have a talk later on."

Tara gripped the joysticks on the arms of her chair. Her best plan, she realized, would be to not budge them unless she saw they were actually leaving station. Right now their course and speed seemed stable.

The four huge screws churning in the rear of the carrier looked like a row of bronze ceiling fans. Their drive shafts alone were longer than the entire *Nemo II*. Each of those twin rudders was the size of a small building.

Tara was sweating. Stingray seemed relaxed, even amused. He had, she supposed, faced down worse things than a carrier battle group.

"Here goes…" he said.

A low hum sounded somewhere in the ship. Like magic, a sphere of ice appeared around the main bearing of the far port side drive shaft. A horrid screech tore through the water as the screw came to a quick halt. Stingray chuckled. The hum paused, then resumed. The next bearing inboard also froze, bringing its screw to a stop. The remaining two screws were similarly frozen in quick succession. The carrier began losing speed.

"That's a cryo-cannon in action. It's a bigger version of the weapon Ben Raintree used before he…went all mystical on us. I always liked those things. Let's see what your friends upstairs do now."

In answer, the sea was filled with a cacophony of sonar pings emanating from every ship in the area.

"I would consider that a warning," said Tara, her death grip on the joysticks unabated. "They want us to know they know we're here."

Stingray triggered a ping of his own. "Now they know we know they know we're here."

The carrier's dual rudders swiveled over, causing the big ship to enter a turn with its remaining momentum.

"Ah, I was hoping they'd do that. Try to maintain our station relative to them, Tara. Just nudge the stick over a little bit."

Tara bit her lip and complied, amazed as the sub actually turned under her guidance.

"Not bad. Now a bit less power. Just push forward a tiny bit. Close in a little, but don't collide."

Tara guided the sub ahead and watched in awe as the gigantic rudders loomed just overhead.

"Okay, I'm darkening the bubble. Firing ERASER."

The dome deepened to black over their heads. A ferocious blue-green line flickered into being between the sub and the carrier. The eerie glare was enough to bring the carrier's hull into view even through the darkened dome. The beam pulsed for a few seconds, switched to another target, and pulsed again.

The dome resumed its normal clarity. "All right. With any luck that will have disabled their rudder bearings. They should regain propulsion as the drive shafts thaw out, but with the rudders stuck like that, they can't maneuver and can barely be towed. I'll take over now."

Tara released the joysticks and wiped her sweaty hands on her pants. "They'll have an awful time launching or recovering planes if they can't steer."

"Exactly."

Stingray let the sub drift to a halt behind the carrier so he could admire his handiwork. Tara resumed her study of the tactical display and was drawn to one particular ship and its vector.

"Stingray, the attack sub *Tucson* is approaching at high speed. I think they may be planning to ram us! Speed is forty knots, bearing ninety degrees, time to impact seventeen seconds."

"Well. I guess I didn't expect them to take us on by trying to sacrifice one of their own subs. Hang on."

Stingray pulled his throttle stick all the way back and pushed the maneuvering stick forward. *Nemo II* surged ahead and tilted down, nearly sending Tara sprawling over her console. The plunge could not last long, as the bottom was only a few hundred feet farther down, but by the time the sub leveled out they was blasting through the water at ninety knots. At that speed the sub was far from silent...to Tara it sounded like she was riding inside a washing machine. She resettled herself in her seat and studied her displays.

"*Tucson* is falling behind. I'm now detecting attack sub *Charlotte* three kilometers off to starboard, in no position to intercept us. Hold on... Torpedo! *Tucson* has fired a torpedo. Torpedo speed is sixty knots."

"It's not going to catch us, I guess."

"Maybe not that one. But if they've fired one, they'll fire more. They can't really launch ASROCs because we're still among the ships of the battle group, but once we're away they're likely to rain down on us. Oh, steer well clear of the frigates and destroyers on our way out. They have their own nasty anti-submarine surprises. Also, Seahawk helicopters could drop weapons on us at any time. The carrier can launch them even without heading into the wind."

Stingray frowned. "Take the helm again. I'm launching a surface probe. Keep her on full power."

"Surface probe?"

"A small remotely-operated vehicle. It'll pop up to the surface and give us a radar view of the sky."

A few moments later, one of Tara's displays lit up with the promised information. "There are four Seahawks pacing us in formation. They're dropping sonobuoys...as though they don't have a good enough fix on us already. They're dropping torpedoes! Coming in from all directions."

"Stay on the helm. I'm going to try to pick some of them off with the ERASER. Steer as you please. Just don't hit the bottom. And try not to breach."

Tara gripped the control sticks again and veered away from the nearest torpedo, which had gone active and was closing rapidly from the port bow.

A thread of blue-green light again flickered beyond the dome. An explosion rumbled through the water and rocked the sub. Tara steered toward the sudden opening in the array of converging torpedoes.

"That was a little close. The ERASER really isn't all that effective when submerged. Too much energy absorption by the water."

"Damn these torpedoes!" shouted Tara.

"Full speed ahead!" returned Stingray.

Tara laughed. But then: "Three ships have launched ASROCs! They'll drop on us nearly simultaneously."

Stingray studied his own tactical display. "These vectors indicate that at least four weapons will converge on us. No way to evade them all."

"Can they kill us?"

"Depends on the warheads. We certainly won't enjoy any direct hits though. Okay, this is getting serious. I'll take the sticks again."

"ASROC torpedoes in the water and active! Five seconds to impact!"

Stingray pulled back on the diving stick, sending the sub surging toward the surface.

"I thought you didn't want to breach?!" cried Tara.

"This'll be more than a breach."

Tara looked ahead and gasped. She could actually see two torpedoes rushing towards them.

At that moment the *Captain Nemo II* broke the surface and kept right on going. Sunlight poured through the dome and onto Tara's upraised, astonished face. All she saw was sky. The seconds passed in breathless silence as though the submarine were suspended effortlessly in space.

"Hold tight," said Stingray. "It'll be rough when we impact."

The sub's nose pitched down and Tara saw the ocean surface rushing at them. She screamed and braced herself against her console. Water exploded against the dome as the sub crashed its way back beneath the waves.

"Uhh!" cried Tara, half stunned, her shoulders aching from absorbing the impact. She pushed herself back and looked at the display. All remaining torpedoes were behind them, vainly trying to catch up.

"That doesn't end this," said Stingray. "I'm launching a torpedo of my own."

The sub shuddered. A slender white shape blurred out of sight, orange radiance blazing from its tail.

Stingray pressed a few contacts. "Attention U.S. Navy. Stingray speaking. Call off your attack immediately, or my torpedo will sink your carrier. That is all."

A few moments later, the cluster of torpedoes, now well astern, blew up. The helicopters headed back to the now motionless carrier.

"They just saved their own lives," said Stingray.

"Would that single torpedo really have sunk them?"

"That particular one doesn't even have a warhead. But if they'd managed to destroy us—twenty kilometer crater, remember?

"Right. This submarine—it can fly?"

"No. It doesn't have enough thrust for that. Even if it did, you couldn't control it. But it can sure jump like a pissed off orca at Sea World." Stingray reduced the ship's speed to fifty knots. "We're silent again. That should be the last we hear from them." He sat there drumming his fingers on the arm of his chair, looking pensive and fretful.

Tara closed her eyes and watched the dim flickering of surface light passing through her eyelids. Night was falling in the world above the waves. Slowly the dim light that filtered down to them died away.

"That was a lot harder than it should have been," said Stingray suddenly, startling her. "I thought this would be a simple trial cruise that I could manage alone. Clearly I need a fully manned control room to handle situations like the one we just encountered. I don't have two people to train, but I have you. How would you like to be the first recruit of the Vigil Sea Command?"

"The what?"

"Vigil Sea Command," repeated Stingray, sounding a little embarrassed. "The Vigil—well…we're going to try to take over the world."

Tara widened her eyes and turned them in disbelief on Stingray, who sat gazing out through the dome, showing his profile. From that angle he looked particularly inhuman. His nose was a sharp beak, and his chin receded a bit, though it did not appear weak. The overall effect was one of streamlining. She could imagine the seawater breaking over that nose and streaming over his face as he pushed his way through the ocean.

She struggled to find a sensible response to his announcement, but was unable to settle on one.

"Narf?"

"Yes, yes, I know how it sounds," said Stingray, still not looking her in the eye. "I admit, it all sounded a lot better before we starting getting into the actual details of how to conquer the world."

"How can you even tell me such a thing? You know I'm a member of the United States military. Well, not one in very good standing, obviously. But still, I don't know if I should be flattered or insulted. What do you think I am?"

"I think you're a very confused woman who is looking for a cause she can support wholeheartedly. I think the fact that you're sitting here beside me now instead of operating your sonar station on your cruiser makes it plain that for you, the U.S. military is no longer such a cause."

Tara sighed.

"It's not so much the military. It just does what it's told, and for the most part does its best to carry out its missions in good faith. No, it's the missions themselves, and especially the government that dreams them up. It's like what you said before. The way I figure it, the last time the military fought to actually defend America was in World War Two. Since then we haven't needed to. Any time we've fired a weapon it's been against people who had no chance against us. Lately things have gotten even worse. We invade weak countries, we fight aggressive wars because of the fantasies of a bunch of delusional politicians and the greed of war profiteers. And now the unprovoked attacks against the Vigil. It's too much.

"I had a pretty good career in the Navy, but things got to the point where I couldn't ignore the hypocrisy of my involvement in actions I just didn't respect. I didn't feel like I was defending America, I was making the rest of the world defenseless against an America that had thrown away whatever moral authority it once had. And it's not just America. The world is turning into a madhouse. The pressure is building. It's nearing some breaking point. I can feel it. I was only contributing to that. But that doesn't mean I'm going to sign up with you, to make things even worse!"

"We don't plan on making things worse. To the contrary."

"Yeah, of course you'd say that. Why do you need your own military, anyway? I can think of three of you— Fomalhaut, Aureus, and Ben Raintree—who together could walk through any military force I can imagine, unless maybe it was a rain of nuclear bombs."

"Yes...the three you name could do exactly that. I might even be able to help a little myself," added Stingray, a little pointedly. "But it wouldn't be enough. We are only a few. We can't be everywhere at once. We could stamp out a few fires, but others would surely flare up wherever we were not. We need a means to exert a much wider control."

"Yeah? And how do you expect to form these armies? Do you think the U.S.A. or any other nation will let you set up recruiting stations? Your plan seems ridiculous. How will you know you can trust your recruits? How do you know you can even trust me?"

Stingray shrugged. "You ask a lot of good questions, and we don't have all the answers. Recruitment is certainly going to be a problem. So far we're doing it by networking through our existing staff, but that won't be enough. As for you, I consider myself a good judge of character. Plus I trust Endurance's apparent recommendation. No one knows more about the human heart than Endurance."

"That naked pretty boy? Who is he, anyway?"

"Nobody really knows, including himself. He came into being about the time the Earth was forming. He's been walking the Earth ever since. He's literally seen it all."

Tara's mouth fell open. "You are shitting me. That's billions of years."

Lit only by the faint glow of the consoles, Stingray turned his face toward hers. His eyes had become completely black, liquid orbs. Tara gasped.

Stingray grimaced. "You're not going off about my eyes again, are you? It's dim in here. I have really big pupils. That's all. No, I am not 'shitting' you. Not about Endurance or anything else." He turned forward again, looking self-conscious.

Tara looked away, her mind buzzing with confusion.

After a while she said in a low voice, "I always wanted to join the submarine force, but it's one of the few Navy jobs not open to women."

"I know. Why is that?"

"They have lots of reasons. No privacy. Pregnancies very inconvenient during submerged patrols lasting months. Mostly they don't want their subs turned into sweaty rape-and-orgy containers cruising five hundred feet below the surface."

"This submarine will never turn into that."

"Damn right it won't. I like girls. Wow, it's been a long time since I could say that out loud."

"And I'm not human," said Stingray.

Tara gave a start. He had said this without emotion, in a matter-of-fact manner. Yet somehow it chilled her. He really *wasn't* human. He looked it superficially, but that was all. His eyes were quite alien. His skin was a firm brown hide without wrinkle or pore. His finger joints lacked the folds which human fingers showed when straightened. Even the arrangement of his joints and muscles was subtly different.

And yet he sat in his chair and went about his business with an air of calm focus.

"From what I hear, being inhuman didn't slow you down with Rouse Farewell."

Tara regretted blurting out this tactless remark. Stingray tilted back his head and gave a great sigh.

"You don't believe that rumor, do you?" he asked.

"Well…yeah."

"Well, don't. Rouse and I were never lovers. We were friends, good friends, that's all. Not that she wasn't open to more, a fact which astonishes me every time I think about it. She wouldn't have been bothered that my penis comes out of a sheath, or that if you look two centimeters up my nose you see feathery structures that look like gills, but aren't. No. You know what stopped her?"

Tara shook her head, unwilling to break this revelatory spell with a word.

"Passion. I don't do passion. I'm especially eager to avoid too much anger. Oh, things can interest me, or attract me, or drive me, or sometimes even move me, but I never give myself over to anything with all my heart. I don't know what would happen to me if I tried. I'd probably only embarrass myself. So I'm not much of a person in that respect, which was more than Rouse could deal with. Rouse always poured every bit of herself into everything she did. But I let the rumors persist. If people thought I was fit for a creature as wondrous as Rouse, why disillusion them? It was flattering. Now I'm tired of it."

"Were—were you always this way, do you think?"

"I don't really know. I've lived other lives before this, lives I don't remember all that well. We travelled among the stars, the Space Mariners and I. We traversed about a quarter of the Milky Way together, if you can believe it. The bridge of our ship was covered by a transparent dome, even bigger than this one. When we drifted among the star clouds and dark nebulae in the galaxy's inner arms, the sensation of depth and the multitude of suns was overwhelming. Maybe back then I was different. I'm not sure."

"What happened to change you?"

"I blame Valjhar Cor for that. But I could be wrong."

Chapter 6

Reunion

Endurance found privacy scarce in Indonesia, one of the most densely populated lands in an overcrowded Earth. For most of human history, populations had been scattered, rare, and separated by great expanses of wild land. Back then, the farms, villages and cities of beings who looked and thought like himself had seemed marvelous, like flawed gems set in a majestic matrix of wilderness. Now, in their unrestrained fecundity, people had cheapened themselves, even in their own eyes. Endurance often wished it was easier to get away from them, especially now. He didn't like the attention brought by the unwelcome companionship of Aureus. Endurance wished Valjhar would appear soon, if only to take the tiresome machine-man off his hands.

Thus Endurance was pleased, surprised, and faintly alarmed when a figure literally appeared beside them as they wandered across a deforested hilltop in central Borneo.

While Endurance could not doubt that this person was indeed Valjhar Cor, he was struck by the changes in his former comrade. Valjhar had aged beyond anything the intervening years could account for. His dark brown hair and beard, long and unkempt, were streaked with pale green. His skin, which had been pale and smooth, was now reddened and deeply weathered. His lean, spare body was clad in a random hodgepodge of ragged clothing. His grey eyes shone from beneath bushy brows.

Valjhar stood very near to Aureus. His left arm was extended, his hand disappearing into the robot's silvery braincase in a manner impossible to fully discern or visually interpret. The sheer novelty of the sight was deeply fascinating to Endurance.

Valjhar's tone, when he spoke, was superficially calm and reasonable, as it usually was. Yet beneath it was a tension, and even a sort of desperation, which Endurance found new and troubling. He spoke in Rralian, which Endurance had learned while a member of the Para-Men.

"So, Prohibitor. Yours is the last face I wanted to see. In speaking to you, I feel as though I'm chatting with a wind-up clock, yet you look at me and I know some form of thought is taking place inside that mirrored ovoid you call a cranium. I can't resist trading a few final words with you, if you bother to respond. Can you feel my hand in your brain? It's not really fully there yet, because I've reached in through a fourth spacial dimension to bypass that mirror field. It feels cold. I could collapse my hand back down to three dimensions at any time. I'm not sure what that would do to me, but I'm quite sure it would be the end of you. Can you offer me any reason why I should not do it? Surely the universe has seen enough of you and your mindless mechanical obsessions."

Aureus did not move, other than to open its mouth to its speaking position. Endurance waited to learn what its answer would be, if any.

Finally it spoke.

"I can think of no reason why you should not destroy me."

This did not placate Valjhar; rather it seemed to infuriate him, to judge by the way his teeth were bared. For long moments he maintained his stance, the muscles in his forearm quivering.

Then with an incoherent cry of anger and disgust he jerked his hand free and turned away from Aureus. "Why are you here, Prohibitor? What do you want of me now?"

The robot closed its mouth, withdrew a few paces and stood in silence, its eyes downcast.

Endurance frowned as he observed this, more than ever convinced that something unexpected was in evidence here. "It wants—Aureus wants—to—accompany you," he said carefully.

Valjhar whirled on Endurance. "What?" He turned towards Aureus. "Is this true?"

"Yes." The word was muffled. For some reason Aureus had not opened its mouth to utter it.

"Accompany me? You mean dog me, harass me, isn't that right?"

"No."

"Then what *do* you mean? And please don't say one word about your accursed mission. We both know your mission is now meaningless and a failure."

The robot's mouth opened slightly.

"You are all of Rral that remains to me."

Endurance was astonished. Marooned on a remote alien world, without purpose, sundered from its creators— naturally Aureus would be—lonely. And yet, what was in any way natural about Aureus?

Valjhar also seemed aware of this contradiction. He approached Aureus, gazing keenly into its ruby eyes.

"Why should that trouble you, Prohibitor? As a robot
—"

"You misunderstand my nature," interrupted Aureus. "I
am not a robot. I am a Rralian."

Valjhar's mouth worked, yet words did not emerge for
some moments. Finally he sputtered, "What are you talking
about? I am a Rralian. Kern, Pimsie, Randa, we were all
Rralians. We are living, feeling, biological beings, not
machines."

"So too was I. I was born during the latter years of the
technological apex of Rral. I was a woman who bore the
name Vela Flamaxamanda. I was a dancer and a poet, and
therefore a marginal member of our society, which was
dominated by scientists and technologists. I was also
emotionally unbalanced, afflicted by many depressions,
anxieties, and romantic disappointments and confusions.
Naturally, the latest cures and treatments were offered to
me, but I refused them, fearing the dissolution of my self
and the loss of my artistry in chemical or neurosurgical
alterations to my brain.

"At that time, a few members of our society were
attempting to make themselves immortal by transferring
their minds into perfected artificial bodies. I was
immediately transfixed by this idea, seeing that I could
inhabit a body of unfading beauty and perfect flexibility,
the ideal vehicle for expressing myself in dance.
Furthermore, I saw an opportunity to escape the
unhappiness which had always troubled me. With my mind
freed from the biological hormones and impulses whose
malfunctions plagued me, I would be free to pursue my art
with supreme clarity and focus.

"Thus I entered this form, and saw my old body discarded.

"What I had overlooked was that everything which made my art possible, everything that made it desirable to me, had come from those very biochemical processes and substances. My thoughts and memories now moved unhindered through a flawless medium for cognition. Missing was any appreciation of beauty, and any motivation for pursuing it. Beauty is a conception of biological beings. It leads them to pursue that which is healthful to them and advantageous to their survival, and to avoid that which is not. I therefore lost any motivation to do anything at all. I had effectively committed suicide, leaving behind a robotic remnant which was little more than a walking repository of the memories of Vela Flamaxamanda. I was aware of what I had lost, yet the knowledge did not trouble me. I did not regret my choice. I was no longer capable of regretting anything.

"Rral soon entered the period of destructive turmoil caused by the creation of the Stones. I, of course, was not disturbed by them, any more than I could be disturbed by anything else. Starn Harner hid the Stones in deep space, yet the very knowledge of their existence was too much for the intensely rational inhabitants of Rral to gracefully endure. Our civilization collapsed, yet there were still a few who retained the wit to plan for a better future. I was asked to serve as a Prohibitor, to prevent the people of Rral from resuming a technological civilization until such time as the values of art and philosophy could be fully integrated into their nature, balancing their natural scientific brilliance with an appreciation of mystery that would not break in the face of the truly unknowable. I agreed to this task, remembering what I had lost, and intending to save others from diminishing themselves as I had done. My body was modified to incorporate the necessary weapons and sensors.

"For thousands of years I served, having little or nothing to do for most of that time, yet I was not troubled. When not engaged in my mission my mind was empty. I did not muse or dream. I merely awaited the next stimulus that would arouse me to action. When Stingray deactivated my body I did not fret or chafe, except as it interfered with my mission. When Endurance destroyed my body and locked my brain case in a plug of frozen lava, I did not panic or fear. When I killed Cal-Cotavion, I felt neither grief nor guilt. When the United States Government paralyzed me and buried me in metal I did not rage or wish for vengeance. I wished for nothing at all. If I could go back and undo what I did to myself, I would not, because I lack the volition to do so. I am abstractly aware that I am nothing, that what I did to myself so long ago was terrible. I will do what I can to protect Rral and those Rralians who are still truly alive from repeating my mistake. As I am unable to return to Rral, I will stay by your side, Valjhar Cor, if you will permit me to do so."

Endurance felt an ache within his breast, the only sort of pain he could ever know. He had known many terrible things in his time, and this was not the least of them.

Valjhar's expression remained guarded. He stared at Aureus for several seconds.

"Prohibitor. Why didn't you reveal all this long ago? Do you have any idea how different..." He faltered as he looked into that impassive golden mask. He shook his head, then turned away to address Endurance, as though the pair of them were standing there alone.

54

"Endurance, my friend. You of course are unchanged, but I can see you're surprised by the changes that have overtaken me. Since we last met so few years ago, I have folded time over and over again in my search for Shaula Alshain among the infinite universes of creation. My failure was as inevitable as the victory of statistics over hope. I have consumed my youth in this cause. I acknowledge my failure, and I now wish only to discharge one last obligation before my life finally gutters out."

He reached up and extracted through his forehead the Motionglobe, that lemon-sized sphere of softly glowing possibility, and proffered it to Endurance. Endurance stared at it. The sight of the oddly twisted loop of light within it activated his earliest memories, making everything that had happened since seem like a daydream.

"This is yours," continued Valjhar. "I no longer wish to possess it, nor have I any use for it. Take it, and fulfill whatever destiny is intended for you."

Endurance shook himself and fell back a few paces.

"I—acknowledge that this thing is meant for me. But the time has not yet come for me to use it. That time may be very near, but it is not yet. Carry it for me, Valjhar. When the time comes, I will know where you are, and I will take it then."

Valjhar frowned with dissatisfaction, but dropped the Motionglobe into a pocket of his ragged jacket.

"You fear to use it? You?"

"I fear the events that will oblige me to take it up."

"What are you expecting to happen?"

"I don't know. But I believe the history of Man is nearing an end."

"If that's true, we can thank the Vigil for bringing it about. If we had been allowed to—"

Aureus spoke. "The Vigil intends to impose its own rule over the peoples of the Earth."

Valjhar turned toward Aureus. "What?" he said with an obvious effort at control.

"They plan to establish an enlightened government which will dissolve national boundaries, mitigate all violence and destruction, and establish maximum justice and equity among the Humans."

"You mean like *I* was going to do?" Valjhar demanded dangerously, his face set in lines of fury. "What could possibly drive Fomalhaut and his friends to do this, after all the effort and blood they expended to stop us from doing the very same thing? What *is* it about this dreadful planet? Ever since our first landing in New Zealand, everything I have done here has ended in grief, failure, and disaster. Is this world under a curse of futility that affects even visiting aliens?"

Aureus had no answer to this. Instead it gave an admirably succinct account of the death of T'Ukudu and the war of the United States and its allies against the Vigil. Most of this was news to Endurance as well. Aureus was unable to provide any analysis of Fomalhaut's personal motivation for his new policies, as it had never troubled to discover them.

Valjhar's anger was still not placated. "Come, Prohibitor," he said, surprising Endurance once more. "I will have a talk with the flexible-minded Fomalhaut."

"I will come too," said Endurance. "I advise that we take our time in reaching him. Nothing will be gained by a confrontation in anger."

Thousands of miles away, Possum Perturbare was never more glad to have eavesdropped on a conversation than this one.

"So, Valjhar has acquired a—mascot," he said. "Aureus —a *girl* robot all this time? Who would have imagined it?"

I think it's clear that sexuality is among the things Vela Flamaxamanda left behind long ago, replied Brainchild.

"I suppose so. Do you know what I liked best about their whole conversation?"

The fact that your name did not arise even once?

"That's eerily correct. Are you sure you can't peer into my thoughts through this interface?"

There is no need. I know you well enough. The conscious, thinking portion of your brain remains sacrosanct.

"Ah, speaking of brains...how's your pet brain coming along?"

Permit me to show you, said Brainchild.

Perturbare's view of his hideout was replaced by a scene from a distant laboratory. There a transparent tank full of a pinkish fluid was surrounded by a complex of sensors and micro-manipulators. Within the tank was a brain which looked essentially complete to Perturbare's untutored eye.

It is a difficult process. I grow neurons, astrocytes, other glial cells, and various other brain cells separately, then assemble them via nanoconstruction, according to the genetic information found in the design I pilfered. It would be much faster to grow the brain by means of standard biological cell division, but I don't know how to do that reliably without growing the entire body, and the genome I found describes the brain only. It contains many billions of cells. Its volume is nearly twice that of the average human brain.

"And you believe that once you've integrated this brain into yourself, you will become fully telepathic."

Yes. The brain's design incorporates certain quantum-reactive structures which can have no other purpose.

"Why will this brain not become active, and develop thoughts and a personality of its own?"

I keep it in a drugged state of inactivity.

Perturbare could not regard this disembodied brain without thinking back to horror movies from his boyhood. The whole thing made him uncomfortable, yet he could think of no rational reason to forbid Brainchild from pursuing this goal. And yet...

"Brainchild...once you've got a humanoid brain plugged into yourself, you won't go overboard with emotions, will you? That could introduce a set of problems opposite to those which limit poor little Aureus."

No, naturally I foresaw that risk. I have no desire to damage myself in such a way. This brain seems designed to limit the role emotions play in its functioning, or rather to limit their ability to overthrow reason. I have altered the design to limit them still further. I have made certain other modifications, as well.

"Such as?"

The original genome includes a highly unusual, advanced retina and multiple optic nerves, since these are essentially parts of the brain. I deleted them, seeing no reason to equip my brain with organic sensory apparatus. In any event, the design for the rest of the eyes is absent. I can however infer much of their structure from the size, shape, and functioning of the nervous tissue.

"Show me."

In Perturbare's mind the brain lab was replaced by a real-time simulation produced by Brainchild. He saw the brain floating in space. Optic nerves and huge curving retinas flowered in front of it, then the retinas were encased in great glassy orbs like spheres of black water.

Chapter 7

Challenger Deep

Tara needed only three days to become proficient in the operation of all systems aboard the *Captain Nemo II*. The controls were so logically and intuitively arranged that she thought of the ship as the Apple iSub.

Learning the controls was one thing. Learning to maintain the sub would take months or years of schooling. Understanding the principles behind its systems would take forever. At least she could guide it through the water, read its displays, and if need be, fire its weapons.

During these three days they travelled northeast. Escaping the shallow waters of the Java Sea, they cruised at a depth of five thousand feet, far deeper than any ray of light could penetrate. The darkness of the water pressing in on the control room canopy was oppressive. Whenever she was on duty she always turned on the great sea lamps mounted below the bow. Usually they only revealed a blank greenish murk, but sometimes a fish or some other small creature could be glimpsed in passing.

When Stingray was not instructing her, he could often be found hunched over a computer in the wardroom just aft of the control room. There he kept busy designing combat submarines, which he hoped to build in substantial numbers, and crew with men and women like herself. There would be several classes, but all were similar in general appearance: perfect teardrops, their lines not interrupted by so much as a sail or a raised hatch covering.

With ships like these, Tara realized, the Vigil's navy would be invincible.

Sometimes he worked in the laboratory that occupied the entire habitable area of the lowermost deck. What he did there he did not say, though whenever he emerged he bore a grim, slightly frantic expression.

At the end of the three days, the small crew of the *Nemo II* sat at their control stations as they passed near Guam.

"There's more than thirty thousand feet of water beneath us," said Tara.

"The Challenger Deep," said Stingray. "Time for a dive to test depth."

"Oh?" said Tara a little nervously. "How much deeper are we going?"

"All the way."

Tara looked at him for signs of a joke, but found none. "Do we have to?" she squeaked.

"Two men made it down there in a primitive bathyscaphe way back in 1960. This sub is good for it, believe me. Take us down."

Tara shrugged. "Okey dokey, sir. Down we go." She pushed the diving stick forward, tilting the sub towards the abyss. A few keystrokes filled her main display with a 3-D representation of the bottom. She set a slow spiraling course which led them deeper and deeper into the great submarine canyon.

After descending a few thousand feet she abruptly put the rudder amidships and killed power, letting the sub drift to a halt.

"What's the matter?" asked Stingray.

"I'm feeling queasy," said Tara miserably.

Stingray nodded in the dimness. "It's the tight descending turns. With no visual references they left you open to motion sickness. I don't have anything on board to treat that. No problem. Just take on a little ballast and we'll drift down passively."

"Thank you." Tara adjusted the ship's buoyancy and watched as the depth indicator began to show descent. Stingray sat studying the readouts of the stress meters built into the hull. He appeared quite relaxed, for which Tara was grateful. The sub showed a tendency to flutter as it sank. Stingray showed her how to use the rudders and diving planes to damp out the unwanted motion.

Over the course of an hour they passed ten thousand feet, then twenty. Stingray, keeping a close eye on the stress readings, said: "Tara, you're about to hear a loud bell-like sound. It's not a problem, so don't worry."

"Huh?"

Just then she did hear a single chiming note which seemed to come from all around her.

"That was the canopy. It's designed to compress slightly and assume a different crystalline structure under extreme pressure. It makes that sound in the process."

"Hey, as long as all it does is ring, I'm fine with that."

They passed thirty thousand feet. By now Tara had grown adroit enough with the control surfaces to set up a gentle glide toward the deepest part of the trench.

The bottom remained unseen until they passed a depth of thirty five thousand feet. Then an undulating floor came dimly into view.

"All right, I'm going to re-establish neutral buoyancy," said Stingray. "We don't want to—"

There was a muffled thud and a shudder. An alarm went off. Stingray took his hands off the controls and looked around in confusion. The sub sank much faster. Stingray reached for the control sticks just as the sub plopped belly down into the bottom muck. The sea lamps were covered, meaning they could see nothing outside the ship.

"What's happening?" demanded Tara over the throb of the alarm.

Stingray switched it off. "According to what I see here, the sail has somehow flooded."

"Oh my God!"

"Don't panic. It's a separate structure from the main pressure hull."

"Yeah? That's easy for you to say. You can't drown!"

Stingray took a moment to give her a wry look. "Drown? Actually, at this depth, if the sea broke in, it would smash me as thoroughly as it would you. It takes me quite a while to adapt to pressures like these."

"Very comforting."

Stingray actually smiled. "Relax. I'll just blow main ballast and we'll bob right up again."

He did so, releasing compressed air to clear the ballast tanks.

The submarine did not budge.

"That's odd," said Stingray thoughtfully. "That should have more than compensated for the added weight in the sail."

"Shit!"

"Well, I'll just try a little power." He pulled back on the stick. The sub lurched a little, then moved no more. A viscous sucking sound could be heard, followed by grinding. Stingray quickly cut power. "Hmm." He moved the maneuvering stick back and forth. Nothing happened except for a red icon blinking on his board.

"Yeah, hmm! Why aren't we moving?"

"It looks like we have two problems here. First, the hull appears to be stuck in the muck and can't be released because of vacuum suction. Second, the two ventral rudders are also jammed into the muck. Normally I'd rig them up before resting on the bottom."

"What can we do?"

"I could release the horseshoe. Even with the flooded tower, the main hull has so much buoyancy that it could free us and send us to the surface. However, once we got there we'd have very little power and no propulsion. We'd have to call for a rescue and abandon the sub. Plus, if I tried it and it didn't work, we'd still be down here, separated from the horseshoe's systems and limited to emergency power."

"You can't go out yourself? Try to free us?"

"Nope. I could go out in diving armor without being pressure adapted, but unfortunately, as you know, the airlock is on the underside of the ship, between the sea lamps. With the sail flooded, there's no other way out without flooding the ship. By the way, please turn off the sea lamps. I don't want them to burn up." He sighed. "I might have to call Fomalhaut and ask him to come pry our silly asses out of here. That would delight him, having to waste his time like that."

"I don't see it as a waste!"

Stingray laughed. "No, neither would he, really. But I'm not ready to give up yet. Keep an eye on things for a bit. I'm going to take on a seawater sample for my experiments."

"You're still interested in lab work while we're stuck here?"

"It's important work. But I keep telling you not to worry. We can survive down here indefinitely." He got up and passed through the hatch in the aft bulkhead.

Tara sat unmoving in her chair, trying not to dwell on the fact that there was more seawater over her head than there was air beneath a cruising passenger jet. Miles of dark, cold water, held off by nothing more than a bubble of glass…

She shuddered and forced herself to look forward.

There was a light.

It was visible only for a moment, a brief hazy glimmer. It returned and dimmed. Again, rhythmically. It grew a little brighter but did not move. Perhaps the muck they had stirred up was settling out.

That was the only thing Tara understood about this light. It continued to pulse at her, inexplicable, completely mysterious. In her fear, Tara's imagination saw it as a beacon of some monstrous abyssal civilization, some weird Lovecraftian outpost that should not exist. She had never been less happy to see any light in her life.

"Stingray, there's a light!" she wailed, pointing, as her enigmatic host returned to the control room.

He glanced forward. "Yeah, I know. I have a little base down here. I once nearly took up residence in it."

Tara threw herself back in her seat with a cry of exasperation. "Well Christ, you could have told me."

Stingray gave her another arch look. "I never thought you'd be afraid of it. Were you always this—volatile— while serving in the Navy?"

"No, of course not." With that, Tara realized she had been taking advantage of Stingray's lack of military discipline to say and do things that wouldn't have been tolerated in the Navy. Stingray didn't seem to seriously mind, but still, her behavior had become sloppy and unprofessional. "I'm sorry."

Stingray shrugged. "That base might save us a lot of trouble. It has a pair of small ROVs that I hope to launch and control from here. Then there's the torpedo—"

"What torpedo?"

"The one I fired to scare off the battle group. It's been following us ever since. No sense in wasting it."

"What happened to the surface probe?"

"Too slow to keep up. I told it to go home."

For some reason, the way Stingray said that made Tara laugh. She looked at Stingray appreciatively, aware of the strange fact that she was comfortable in the company of this intense, dry-witted, sardonic—person.

Stingray fiddled with his console for a minute or two. "All right, I've made contact with the automated systems in the base. Everything there seems to be all right. I think I can take over the ROV functions from here. We'll know in a minute."

Indeed, a small light soon separated from the flashing beacon and approached the submarine. Tara and Stingray both keyed their displays to show video from the probe. The bow of the *Captain Nemo II* slowly emerged from the darkness as the ROV's lamp drew near. They could see themselves sitting in their chairs, peering intently into their screens. Tara looked up at the ROV's glare and waved.

Stingray snorted and commanded the ROV to pass along the port side of the submarine. It ducked beneath the horseshoe, bringing into view the main hull, which was deeply embedded in the grey muck.

He rotated the ROV until they could make out the slim white shape of the torpedo drifting in the near distance. The little vehicle approached the torpedo, passed it, and then turned to look over its shoulder at the trapped submarine, barely visible at the limit of its lights. Stingray inched the ROV beneath the torpedo, then caused its spindly manipulator arms to reach up and embrace the torpedo's slick tubular casing.

"Okay, here comes the tricky part. We'll only get one chance at this. If the torpedo gets stuck without freeing us, it'll be useless. They don't go backwards. Remind me to equip future torpedoes with their own cameras. I just hope the ROV is strong enough to hold on. Now here's your part. When I say 'now', you release the ROV and back it up. Otherwise it's liable to get hung up and prevent the torpedo from penetrating the muck."

This entire scheme seemed awfully kludgy to Tara. "Can't you just command the torpedo to target the sub?" she asked.

"Sure. But first I'd have to convince it that was what I really wanted it to do. Anyway, then it would only smack into the middle of the sub. We need it in a very specific location. Are you ready?"

"I guess so..."

"Then here she comes."

The view in the camera swiftly expanded as the torpedo darted ahead under full power. It headed for the gap between the horseshoe and the muck, which brightened as the torpedo approached.

"Now!" yelled Stingray. Tara released the ROV, which spun in the turbulence of the passing torpedo, depriving them of their view. They heard a BANG! and felt a momentary vibration. There was no other movement.

Stingray resumed control of the ROV, stabilized it, and brought it toward the sub, peering beneath the horseshoe. The torpedo could be seen, its nose buried between the hull and the muck, its propulsion lamp still blazing away.

"It didn't break the suction," he said glumly.

"Damn! Well, we've got other torpedoes. Let's use them!"

"Yes...but the rest of them all carry warheads of various kinds. I could disarm them, but I'm still oddly reluctant to target our own ship with them."

"Hell."

Stingray leaned back in his chair, head back, staring up through the dome into the unrelieved darkness.

"Okay. There's one more thing I can try, then it's on to shooting armed torpedoes at ourselves." Stingray leaned forward and touched a contact. "I'm trying to extend the torpedo's wings."

"Torpedoes got wings?"

"These do. They're really more like a torpedo-cruise missile hybrid, but that would take too long to say. Don't get your hopes up. It's not like the wings or their motors are strong enough to really make much—"

Stingray was interrupted by a squelching sound that seemed to start at the bow and work its way aft. The sub tilted back a few degrees.

"Looks like I underestimated those wings. I think we're still stuck by the rudders though. Well, I'm through pussyfooting around." He grabbed the maneuvering stick and hauled back on it. The submarine shuddered and bucked alarmingly, then sprang free and began a rapid ascent.

"I think we can agree that the objectives of our test dive have been met, and we can now move on."

"Yes, I agree completely."

Tara watched the depth display with a feeling of great relief as they approached the surface. It was nighttime up above, but as the dome broke the surface, the glow of the stars and the Milky Way seemed to illuminate the control room as well as the light of a cloudy day. The waters were calm. They lost no time in grabbing lights and climbing up through the deck hatch near the stern. Their beams showed the aft end of the sail looking normal. From the front, it did not look normal.

"One of the bridge windows is missing!" said Tara unnecessarily.

"Yeah." Stingray moved to the ready room hatch at the base of the sail. "Stand back." He tried to open the hatch. It was jammed. He tried harder, applying a superhuman degree of strength which was obvious from the groans of the hatch mechanism. It burst open, releasing a column of water which nearly swept Stingray over the side.

The pair of them entered the dripping ready room, then climbed the ladder to the bridge. Here the deck was littered with thousands of fragments of the missing window, which had been blown inward and then shattered by its collision with the bulkhead. The bulkhead itself was deeply indented by the force of the blow.

Stingray examined the flange and seals that had held the thick port, which had been a laminate of quartz, diamond, and various acrylic resins. The flange was bent inward.

"The window didn't shatter in place," said Stingray. "It was pushed in by the outside pressure, and then smashed itself against the bulkhead."

"Well, that's not very surprising, is it?" said Tara, oppressed by the cold dampness of the bridge.

"Actually, it is. The flange was a redundant safety measure which obviously failed. The windows are installed in their frames by chilling them to a very low temperature, putting them in place, then letting them expand into a silicone-based sealing gasket. The other ports are the same, and they didn't budge."

Stingray played his light around the gasket, running his fingers over the material. "Something's here." He peeled up a silvery rectangle, handed it to Tara. "What do you make of this?"

Tara examined it. It was a thin foil with serrated edges. "If I didn't know better, I'd say it was a gum wrapper. A foil gum wrapper." She played her light around the deck, where additional shreds of foil shone among the debris. "Looks like there may have been more of them."

"There were. Several of them, placed around the edges of the port. Just enough to compromise the seal so it would fail at extreme depths. Sabotage."

"With gum wrappers? That seems a little...I don't know, too casual."

"Or clever. No one would think to question a worker with a pack of gum in his pocket."

"Who built this sub, anyway?"

"The Vigil has a shipyard. It's located in the Great Barrier Reef, and is largely submerged to keep it as secret as possible. It's staffed with the best people we could recruit, but it's inevitable that some of the lower level workers would be spies. Fomalhaut personally verifies the loyalty of the top people, but he couldn't check everyone even if he worked at it twenty four hours a day. Right now, the yard is working on three new subs similar to this one, but with interior spaces rearranged to accommodate large tachyon piles. When those are finished, they'll start work on the new 3000-class attack subs."

They left the sail and returned to the deck. Carrying his light, Stingray dived over the side and returned a few minutes later, out of breath.

Tara frowned. "You held your breath? I thought you could breathe water like a fish."

"Making the transition between air and water breathing is neither quick nor especially pleasant. No need to do it for a quick little swim like that. The ventral rudders are damaged, but still functional."

"So now what, Admiral Stingray?"

"Now I'm going to call for a flyer to take me back to the Pearl and Spire. I've no more time for boating at the moment. There's something I need to tell Fomalhaut, in person."

"And what do you want me to do?"

Stingray stepped closer and looked her full in the face, stooping a little. His features were obscured but for the glitter of his eyes.

"I want you to take the sub to the shipyard for repairs. While you're there, I'll send a few people for you to train as crew. Then you're to remain on station, to guard the shipyard against any attack until we can get more subs in the water."

"Wow. That's quite a responsibility for a girl who's been with you for only a few days. My knowledge of the sub and its systems is still pretty superficial. I don't think I'm qualified to train anyone else."

Stingray nodded in the darkness. "That's all true, but you're the best person available. The technical staff at the shipyard will help you. You might have to be one of those teachers who learns everything just before she presents it to her students. Also be alert for any further sabotage or other treachery. I realize you're only human, and can't see and hear everything at once, but anything you can observe or figure out will be greatly appreciated." He straightened and said this last puzzling sentence in a needlessly loud voice, as though he thought someone else might be listening and he wanted to be heard.

"Um…okay."

Two hours later, Tara was alone on the ship, dozing at her station as the sub cruised south under automatic control. She would not leave the control room for any length of time until the sub was safely in its berth and she could sleep in her bed without fear.

Chapter 8

Fomalhaut's Discomfiture

Stingray was returning, bursting with news of some kind. Fomalhaut knew this much without being told. Of all the creatures on Earth, Stingray was the one of whom Fomalhaut was most aware. It would be interesting to discover what Stingray wanted to tell him that could not be conveyed from afar by one means or another.

He need not wait long to find out. Stingray was already hurtling above the atmosphere in a flyer, having left his pet submarine in the hands of a near stranger. His news must be urgent indeed.

Slightly less imminent was the arrival of the highly indignant Valjhar Cor and his two companions. This was not a confrontation which Fomalhaut cared to contemplate. Stingray could prove a welcome distraction.

Fomalhaut awaited Stingray's flyer in the Pearl's great hangar. It arrived, Stingray disembarked, and silently bid Fomalhaut to follow him. He led Fomalhaut into the depths of the Pearl's engineering and fabrication areas, into a clean room whose entry required passing through an airlock and undergoing a decontamination procedure. The room, which was used for the testing and assembly of micro-optical components, was maintained under positive air pressure. It was occupied by a few technicians who were startled to have their work interrupted by the arrival of the two original members of the Vigil.

"Please excuse us for a little while," said Stingray. "In fact, since I know how long it takes to cycle through the airlock, go ahead and take the rest of the day off."

Radiating puzzlement, the Vigil staffers abandoned their work and left. Stingray waited a few minutes with arms crossed and then examined the seals and filters of the ventilation system. He consulted an instrument hanging from his belt, then fixed Fomalhaut with his piercing gaze.

"I have taken the trouble to investigate how Perturbare pulled off the trick of causing a new power distribution module to appear in the sea when and where I needed it. It turns out that seawater at all depths is now host to uncountable swarms of minute nanoconstructors. Under the direction of Brainchild, these molecule-scale devices, each smaller than most bacteria, are able to combine their efforts to assemble the chemicals dissolved in seawater into practically any form. They are not highly motile, and they have limited energy sources. They are photovoltaic, and in addition can produce chemical energy by 'eating' organic molecules."

"Fascinating. Yet clearly there is more."

Stingray nodded. "Once I had identified and characterized the seaborne devices, I also tested the air within my submarine. I found nothing, but then I checked the filters of the air circulation and processing system. These were coated with a fine white dust that proved to consist of another class of nanodevices, of a less compact design, meant to float in the air. They were still active. I had to put them in a lab furnace to 'kill' them. I believe they are capable of functioning as listening devices. One or a few of them can't detect any meaningful sound because any sound vibrations are swamped by the natural Brownian motion which affects each device. But in a room full of them, their individual signals could be combined, and a sound signal synthesized from them. This would be a massive computational task. It may or may not be enough to keep Brainchild from eavesdropping on every conversation in the world simultaneously."

"I now understand your caution and alarm."

"And there is still more. I've searched the Internet and our own databases for evidence that such nanoconstructors may be active on the surface. Here's what I've found. Parking lots are going away. Not those that are in use, but abandoned ones, unneeded ones. They are crumbling— slowly, but much faster than can be accounted for naturally. The asphalt is being changed from hydrocarbons to carbohydrates, molecule by molecule. Changing to food. The lots are turning into fields of grass and flowers.

"And there is more. Large retail chain stores are being sabotaged. They can't keep the lights on. Power cables are found cleanly sliced, as though someone were snipping them. But many of these wires are in locations which no person could plausibly access."

"That sounds like a likely Perturbare trick," said Fomalhaut.

"And there is still more. No one on Earth has any floaters."

"Floaters?"

"Bits of loose retinal debris which drift in the fluids of the human eye, sometimes obscuring vision, or at least acting as a nuisance. In all likelihood, they have been disassembled, also molecule by molecule. Yes, these devices are ubiquitous within living creatures as well, including me. I'm full of Perturbare's nanotechnology. So here's the situation as I see it. While we've been playing soldier and struggling to devise a realistic plan to take over the world, Possum Perturbare has quietly released a self-replicating technology which pretty much makes him a god. At any time, he can command his nanomachines to cause strokes and heart attacks and kill everyone who isn't wearing an exploration suit. He could restructure our genes over time. If not for the energy limitations of the devices, he could command this base to melt around us, or rebuild itself as a prison, or a doughnut factory. How long will it be before he overcomes even that limitation? So far his actions are benign, or at worst mischievous. But who knows about the future? You do, of course, though your precognition is sporadic. I think we can agree that Perturbare is, at best, a mercurial character."

"Obviously, Perturbare does not mean to keep this capability a secret. Otherwise he would not have rescued you by providing that replacement part."

"A part he was able to create through an invasion of our data systems, which we'd imagined to be secure. Someone else would have discovered his nanodevices soon enough if I hadn't. They're readily detectable with conventional electron microscopy."

Fomalhaut no longer felt quite so much like a master of the world.

"Possum Perturbare has somehow made his mind invisible to me, which greatly limits my ability to analyze him. My prior analysis indicates he has no overriding personal agenda. He appears content to engage in scientific research and invention, using the results mainly to amuse himself by committing various trivial acts of vandalism and anarchy. Whenever he has acted on a larger scale, he has been reluctantly driven to it by convictions which tend to fluctuate dramatically as he is confronted with new facts. It may be that this profile should be changed, based on his experience as a prisoner of the U.S. government. He has, however, been quiescent since those events."

"He has quietly gone about equipping himself with massive new capabilities we don't understand, and whose full implications we very probably do not suspect."

"Yes."

"We must modify our ventilation systems to detect and exclude the airborne nanodevices," said Stingray.

"Of course."

The pair of them left the clean room.

"Stingray, Valjhar Cor is on his way here. He will soon arrive."

Stingray halted in the corridor. "So it's true. Valjhar really is back here on Earth."

"Yes."

Stingray sighed. "I'll stick around for that, though I'm really not anxious to encounter him."

"Nor am I. The meeting between us will be awkward at best. We should summon everyone for this. Valjhar Cor deserves to be met with—full courtesy."

"Yeah. Especially if he decides to express himself with that Motionglobe of his."

"Indeed."

They continued down the corridor, each deep in thought.

"Do you know what I wish?" asked Stingray abruptly.

It was a rhetorical question; Fomalhaut did not bother to reply. In any case he could sense what Stingray wished, and sympathized with his desire.

Possum Perturbare, however, listening in from thousands of miles away, had no such advantage. "No, Stingray, what is it that you wish?" he asked, equally rhetorically.

Stingray's huge bronzed hands worked the air. "I wish that once, just once, we could apply ourselves against an unambiguous threat. That we could fight something which is clearly and inarguably evil, with no need for moral qualms and calculations. Do you fully appreciate the power and knowledge represented in the Vigil? Yet we spend most of our time agonizing about what we should do, for or against whom, and to what degree, and for what cause. It's maddening!"

Perturbare sat back in his darkened room with his mouth hanging open, staring into the distance as a burning light slowly gathered in his eyes.

"Yes. Yes! Of course. That's what I've been looking for all along! Stingray, you're a waterlogged genius. You shall have your wish. Yes, you shall have it."

As for Fomalhaut—

He was suddenly buffeted by an intense foreboding, inundated by visions of chaos and destruction to come. He staggered; Stingray actually reached out to steady him, alarm and amazement radiating from his eyes.

"Stingray, my friend...I wish you had not said that aloud."

The pressure of the onset of Valjhar Cor did not abate from Fomalhaut's mind. Thus, a few hours later, the full membership of the Vigil, minus Aureus, stood at the base of their great Spire, awaiting their visitor. The Pearl cast a blue shadow over the cool rock on which they stood.

Broken clouds whipped by overhead. Surf boomed on the cliffs far below.

There was Ben Raintree, called back from Africa, carrying his staff, clad in his grey jacket, power radiating from him, even though the Stones were hidden. There was Walks-With-The-Sun, wearing his sky-blue Ghost Shirt and a pair of ratty jeans, immune to the chill winds that tossed his long black hair. There was Stingray, looming, water-eyed, dressed in his favored costume of black and silver. There stood Fomalhaut, enigmatic and motionless in his glassy armor of greenish white, with whatever passed for his head concealed by a perfectly reflective sphere.

And there of course was Lori Wu, grateful, as she so often was, for the warmth provided by the scarlet engineering suit, yet wishing she could also wear a warm hat without looking totally ridiculous.

A man dropped out of the sky, landing before them with a thump and looking completely unruffled. He was golden brown, the most beautiful man Lori had ever seen. His eyes, as he glanced at her, seemed to perceive every atom in her body. This must be Endurance, a legendary figure whom she hadn't expected to encounter on this day, or on any day.

Descending more gently was Aureus, sinuous and glittering, a very beautiful if menacing non-living thing.

And then, unfolding from the air, came an old man of average height, gaunt and bearded, his hair a strange mixture of dark brown and pale green. Surely this must be Valjhar Cor. Dignified, standing with his arms crossed, he regarded the assembled beings before him with veiled disapproval. Unintimidated, beyond self-consciousness, he had the air of a man who had seen everything and been everywhere.

Curiously, Aureus stepped up to stand beside and a little behind him, like a companion or a guardian. Endurance occupied a similar position on Valjhar's other side.

A tense silence prevailed. Lori broke it by impulsively stepping up to Valjhar and gushing, "Mr. Cor, sir, it's an honor to meet you. I'm Lori Wu. I've heard so much about you, even though I wasn't with the Vigil when you had your—conflict—and I've always admired the way you—"

Valjhar silenced her with a glance. He looked from her to Raintree, standing there wreathed in the power of the Stones, thence to Stingray, and finally to Fomalhaut.

"So, Fomalhaut, are you still calling yourselves the Vigil? I thought perhaps, given the tools and treasures you and your lackeys stripped from the bodies of our dead, you might have taken to calling yourselves 'Para-Men' as well."

Lori gasped and fell back.

"Valjhar, that was uncalled for!" roared Stingray. "Lori had no part in that. Blame us—blame *me* if you must, but Lori committed no sin worse than keeping the suit and the Stones from falling into the hands of the Americans, and then using them with honor."

Lori blinked back her tears, surprised to receive so vehement a defense from Stingray. Then she heard the voice of Fomalhaut in her mind: *Lori, do not take Valjhar's words to heart. It's the suit. Kern Harner was his best friend, and it has jarred him to see it worn by another.*

Valjhar was not cowed by Stingray's words. He turned to address Raintree. "What about you, Ben? Carrying the Stones of Cal-Cotavion doesn't seem to have done you any harm. To tell the truth, I wouldn't have thought you capable of it."

"I'm not the same Ben Raintree you remember," said Ben calmly. "I have never seen you before."

"What are you talking about?"

"The only person present who has firsthand knowledge of my story is Fomalhaut."

Fomalhaut sketched out the tale. Lori listened in fascination; many of these details were new to her as well.

"You're saying Raintree visited a parallel universe— where he became the apprentice of an Earth folk character —and opted to remain behind?"

"Yes."

Valjhar's face relaxed, then smiled. He stared into the distance, then abruptly returned to himself, redirecting his attention at Lori, who flinched.

"Lori Wu, I apologize for my rudeness. Your involvement with the suit and the Stones is blameless and admirable."

"Thank you. I understand how you must feel."

Valjhar studied her for another moment, then turned to Fomalhaut.

"But what of you, Fomalhaut, and Stingray? How did you come to embrace a goal you once opposed so strongly you were willing to fight and kill to defeat it?"

"We were wrong," said Stingray simply. "Just as you were wrong, Valjhar, to hope to use Shaula to win the war through mind control."

Fomalhaut instantly became more animated, drawing Valjhar's attention to himself. "Valjhar, this world has changed noticeably since you departed it. Consider the United States, still the most powerful nation on Earth, despite its self-induced state of economic and political decline. Its government, and the wealthy men who control it, have declared war on reason itself. Its leaders seek to expand and institutionalize their own powers and privileges, even when that means subverting the very historical basis of their government, which they are sworn to protect. They promulgate ignorance and superstition as a means to control the populace. They subvert any scientific knowledge which threatens to limit their greed and control. They take no heed of the future, seeking only to bloat themselves on whatever they can pillage in the present. They threaten the viability of the planet itself. They maintain this control through the support of masses of people whose superstitions and biases are threatened by factual reality, and who crave to be told what to think, at least when those instructions affirm their own narrow worldview.

"Among the other nations of the world are a hundred variations of this. In many places, people are exploited and preyed upon without even the pretense of accountability maintained in the United States. This is the critical time for the Human race. The mistakes they are making now will not be recoverable if allowed to continue much longer. We must act, or surrender the world to tyranny, chaos and catastrophe."

"None of this is in any way new," said Valjhar bitterly.

"True. But it is now much more evident, and much more shameless, than it was even ten years ago. The division and the wars produced by these policies, combined with the increase in natural disasters exacerbated by Man's environmental impacts and overpopulation, are creating terrible stress worldwide, and a growing expectation of final disaster which is likely to bring itself into reality."

"What about your noble devotion to Humanity's right to self-determination?"

Fomalhaut shifted on his feet uncomfortably.

Walks-With-The-Sun spoke up. "The man who feels the boot of his oppressor on his neck doesn't feel like he has a lot of self-determination, you know? And he's not too worried about maintaining the right of his enemy to crush him. We'll spread self-determination a little wider by the time we're done. We'll take some away from people who have bags of it, and sprinkle it on those who don't."

"And you are?" said Valjhar.

"My name is Walks-With-The-Sun. I'm a human being, like Lori...and Ben. I hear your old club didn't bother to involve a lot of us humans while you were deciding what was best for us. We're different that way."

Fomalhaut spoke before Valjhar could make any reply. "I appreciate the words of Walks. They are true, as far as they go. But as you already suspect, in my case there is more of an answer to make, and a less noble one. My original motivation for opposing you was to preserve what I believed to be the natural order of things: that Humanity should step aside, to make room for the hegemony of—my species. In other words, I supported the right of Humanity to guide its own destiny, only in that I expected its actions to eventually result in its own destruction, thus clearing the stage for my people to arise."

Lori gasped, shocked to hear this from Fomalhaut's own mouth, when previously it had been only speculation passed among the more cynical members of the Vigil staff.

Fomalhaut flinched, as though he had felt the impact of Lori's disappointment, and continued.

"But I no longer believe in that future. Or rather, if it is ever to arise, it must do so without any further compromise of my moral integrity. I can no longer abide the suffering of multitudes of beings who actually exist in favor of beings who may or may not ever come to be."

Valjhar nodded slowly, then turned to Stingray. "What about you? When faced with our intention to do what you now propose to do yourself, you rebelled, to the point of forcing us to meddle with your memories and exile you from our fellowship."

"It was never so much your goals I objected to, as the means. I was not as daunted as you were by our encounter with the Dark Star. I could not be made to feel I was squandering my gifts by idling among the stars, because I had barely begun my term as a Space Mariner, and had so much to learn. But you took its lesson so much to heart that your judgement faltered. Using Shaula to abridge the wills of human beings, to make them conform to your aims, however good your intentions, could not be tolerated. Now of course I know she wouldn't have consented to do this in any event, dooming your plan to failure."

Valjhar's eyes closed in sadness. "I have heard this before…from you, from Pimsehkia, and even from Shaula herself, just before she was taken from us, due to my foolishness." He lowered his head, bringing a silence which none of them cared to breach.

When Valjhar looked up again, his eyes were narrowed with grief and wet with tears. He took a few steps closer to Stingray, looking into his face. "How much do you remember of your time with us, Stingray?"

"I remember those times," said Stingray in a gentler voice. "But I see them as a remote vision, small, as though it were something I merely witnessed, rather than a life I actually lived. It seems very distant."

"Yes. So it is with me, though in my case it's because of the intervention of many decades of subjective time. Now here we stand, all that remains of the Space Mariners."

Stingray studied him with some sympathy, obviously weighing a decision.

"Except for Pimsehkia," he said at last.

Valjhar's eyes grew round with confusion. "What?"

"Pimsie is still alive somewhere on Earth, as far as we know."

"That cannot be. I have crossed and re-crossed this planet in search of Endurance. I have seen every face and entered every room. If Pimsie were here, I would have seen her."

"You probably did, but without recognizing her. She somehow managed to recast herself in Human form, as you have, and has pursued her own agenda ever since. She participated in Perturbare's capture by the United States. After that she worked as a journalist for a while, or at least she posed as one. I don't know where she is now."

Valjhar looked as though his control were cracking. "When I left Earth, I meant to take her with me, but in the ruins...I couldn't find her...I thought she was dead."

"I suspect that was deliberate on her part," broke in Fomalhaut. "By all accounts she was traumatized. She wanted to be left alone. By then she had seen enough of you, and of all of us."

Now Valjhar openly wept. "And so I left alone. I left *her* alone, little Pimsehkia Flam, my dear friend, on this terrible planet." He whirled on Aureus. "You! You must have known of this. You said I was all that remained to you of Rral. What about her?"

"Pimsehkia Flam wishes to have nothing to do with me," said Aureus quietly.

Lori noticed Stingray's eyebrows shooting up. He looked as though he were about to say something, then subsided in bafflement. Even Fomalhaut managed to assume an attitude of surprise which was directed at Aureus. No doubt both were wondering how it was that Aureus was concerned about anything as ephemeral as this Pimsehkia's wishes.

"I must find her," said Valjhar. "A Rralian, trapped alone in this world, and Pimsie, of all people, who should be cherishing her friends and family in Enblenol, not hiding among a race of brutal aliens. I must find her. This cannot be borne."

Lori didn't know where Enblenol was, but her heart went out to this uniquely lonely man. She hesitated, desiring to go to him, but was daunted by his formidable glamour.

Fomalhaut spoke in a gentle voice, and Lori also began to weep, in gratitude to him.

"Valjhar, I would be happy to see you reunited with your friend, if she so wills. We would be honored if you would stay with us, make your home with us, while we seek her out. We offer this out of respect for you."

"I think we have room for your silent partner, too," said Walks, referring to Endurance.

"We will stay," said Endurance.

Chapter 9

Shipyard

As Tara approached the Great Barrier Reef in the *Captain Nemo II,* she received a coded signal instructing her in how to proceed. This part of the Reef was a maze of shallow channels threaded between barriers of coral, some submerged and some not. Without instructions transmitted by the Vigil shipyard, Tara soon would have been lost, if not actually aground.

The sub was running on the surface. Crystalline waters surged over the lower part of the bubble canopy as it proceeded at low speed. Tara wished the bridge was still functional so she could pilot from there for a better view of her surroundings.

She jumped when her console erupted with a frantic voice coming over the Vigil Emergency Override channel.

"Hey there! In the sub! Commander Strenczak! Stop! Don't you see me standing here?"

Commander Strenczak...? thought Tara. "Who is this?" she said.

"Lori Wu. From the Vigil. Stop!"

This is not the military. This is not the military, Tara repeated this thought to remind herself that she shouldn't expect any real protocol from these people.

"Why do you want me to stop?"

"You're supposed to pick me up."

Tara sighed, pushing forward on the maneuvering stick to stop the ship.

A minute later she cautiously poked her head up through the deck hatch, saw nothing unusual, and emerged completely.

A low, exposed reef lay to starboard and slightly astern. Jumping up and down on it was a tiny human figure dressed in red and black. Lori Wu, Tara supposed.

Tara waved at her and returned to the control room. Guided by the digital model of her surroundings depicted in the main display, she maneuvered the sub quite close to the reef. Now that she was paying attention, Lori Wu herself was visible on the display as an anomalous signal.

Tara returned to the deck. Lori, a small Asian woman who was rather cute, was frowning at the gap between the reef and the sub.

"Sorry, I can't get any closer," said Tara.

"That's okay. I can handle this."

Lori made a two-handed gesture as though she were summoning a chord from a symphony orchestra. Tara felt a tingling in the fillings of her teeth. The sub quivered. Wet sand flowed into the air from the gap between ship and land. Water poured from it. The sand formed itself into a crude bridge, which Lori crossed with a little grin on her face. Once she gained the sub's deck she dismissed the bridge, causing it to disperse into the waves.

The breeze tickled Tara's uvula as her mouth hung open in amazement. Still smiling, Lori stepped up to her and offered her hand. "Hello, Commander Strenczak. Nice to meet you."

Lori's hand was gloved with glossy black, and ornamented with golden strips and angles. The material felt cold and glassy. The rest of her costume was much the same, though most of it was red. It looked like it had been sprayed onto her slender little body.

"Hello, Miss Wu. Why do you call me that?"

"It's Lori, please. Stingray told me you are the first, ranking, and only officer in the Vigil Sea Command, except for Stingray himself, of course."

Tara laughed. "Wow. If I'd known how easy it is to become an officer in your navy, I would have signed up a long time ago. And may I ask, how did you get here, and why?"

"I came in a flyer, and then sent it home. As to why, Stingray sent me. He asked me to repair this sub before you arrive at the shipyard. He doesn't want the saboteur to know his trick worked and that we're aware of him."

"I see. And you're going to fix it...with that suit?"

Lori looked down at herself. "Yes. It's a Rralian engineering suit. It can manipulate matter at every scale, and in very subtle ways. At one time on the planet Rral, people who made things wore suits like this, the same way one of our contractors wears a belt with a hammer and a tape measure hanging from it. I understand the main damage is in the conning tower?"

"The...yes, the conning tower. Let's go forward and take a look."

Lori looked up at the missing window. They entered the sail and examined the damage from within.

"Wow, this wall is really dented," said Lori, examining the site where the imploding window had impacted.

"The bulk—" Again Tara almost corrected her. "Yes, it sure is."

"It must have been really scary, being trapped on the bottom of the ocean the way you were."

"Yeah. Pretty scary."

"Well, I guess I'll get to work. I've got all the sub's plans stored in the suit."

"You'll do it right here?"

"Sure, why not?"

They returned to the deck. Lori stared at the sail, concentrating, then made another series of gestures.

Without a sound, the entire sail subtly reshaped itself. Tara hadn't realized it had been so distorted in the incident.

"I'm glad you kept the chunks of the old window," said Lori. "That makes it easier."

The window flowed back into place in much the same way the sand bridge had formed, but it stayed put, and was perfect.

Superficially the sail now looked as good as new, but Lori continued, gesturing, biting her lip, sticking out her tongue, making little noises.

Finally she released a big breath and turned smiling to Tara. "There! Stronger than ever now."

"That's really incredible. What's to stop you from just making entire ships from scratch?"

"Nothing. Except it would be—really hard. These ships are incredibly complicated, and I have no technical background. I can make the larger, simpler pieces without too much trouble though. Stingray asked me to speed the next few ships off the line that way."

"Well, I bet you can still make some pretty incredible things. Didn't I read that you're an artist?"

Lori smiled, looked embarrassed, and studied the deck. "Not exactly. My background is in art history. I specialized in Classical art. I suppose I could make a pretty fair replica of the Pantheon if I wanted to. May I ask you a personal question?"

"Shoot."

"How did you wind up with a name like Strenczak?"

"I was adopted. I was easier to get than a white baby. I'm not complaining though."

There was an awkward silence, broken by Lori.

"I was told the underneath rudders are damaged too, but those can be fixed at the shipyard. You can just say you ran into something."

Tara worked to restrain a frown. Yes, surely there was no better way to establish her competence as a submarine commander than to say she'd just "run into" something. Tara was beginning to feel a lot more impressed with the Rralian suit than with the person wearing it.

"Well, Lori, if you'll come below we'll get underway."

"Okay. I'll fix tea and some lunch or something. It's like the middle of the night for me, but I still feel like a snack."

An hour later they entered a wide, open lagoon with deeper water. The control signal directed Tara to maneuver to a precise spot and then maintain her station. The display showing the configuration of the bottom revealed some very large, conspicuously artificial shapes.

Lori sat in the seat beside her, looking at everything with wide eyes.

"*Captain Nemo*, please submerge to a keel depth of twenty meters and then follow the new vector which we will provide."

"*Captain Nemo* acknowledging," said Tara. She told the ship what she wanted it to do. Its A.I. figured out how much ballast to take on to accomplish it. The sub sank to the required depth, the automation trimmed the depth, and a new path appeared on the 3-D display, indicating that Tara should move ahead and dive further to intercept a large structure rearing up a mile or so away. As they approached it, one of three large doors slid open to accommodate the sub. The door was much larger than *Nemo*, leading Tara to wonder how big future Vigil subs were likely to be. Once through the door, they continued down a darkened tunnel for a good half mile, going still deeper all the time.

"*Captain Nemo*, please surface and proceed to your assigned dry dock. You'll be able to see which one it is with no problem."

"Acknowledged."

They surfaced into a huge artificial grotto which was dimly lit except for a concentrated blaze a thousand feet away. High on the ceiling, a lane of blue chaser lights pointed at one of the distant docking stations. Tara moved the sub ahead slowly.

"You know, I'm not so sure about this," she said. "What if there's an attack while the sub's in dry dock?"

"Oh, the shipyard has other defenses," said Lori lightly. "Anyway, I'm here."

Tara hesitated. "You?"

"Oh yes. You just don't know what this suit can do. I can think of a dozen ways to stop a naval task force."

Lori said this as though discussing her options for rearranging the furniture. Tara was having a hard time zeroing in on how seriously she should take this girl.

Tara slid the sub into its assigned docking bay. She stood up, stretched, and looked out through the dome. The bays to either side were occupied by subs similar to *Nemo*. Beneath their scaffolding, they looked largely complete.

The comm system spoke again. "Excellent, Commander. Please power down and secure your ship. Your work is finished for now. Welcome to the Vigil Sea Creche, soon to be the home of the greatest naval fleet the world has ever known."

Tara turned to look at Lori. "Lori, did you make this place too?"

"Oh sure, all the basic structure anyway. Who else could they get to do it?"

Chapter 10

Sphere Y

The Vigil was not alone in having an impressive new hidden facility.

Placed in a synchronous orbit over the far side the Moon, forever hidden from Earth, Possum Perturbare had constructed the largest object ever made by Man. Resembling a frothy snowflake rotated through three dimensions, its radial, branching complex of spines and interconnects spanned three hundred miles, converging on a central sphere over fifty miles in diameter. One of the largest craters on the lunar farside had been substantially deepened to provide materials for this immense yet diaphanous structure. The largest tachyon piles ever built beamed their tachyon emissions away from Earth so they would not be detected. These piles generated enough energy to boost the Moon free of Earth's grip within a decade, if that was Perturbare's ambition, or to retard the Moon in its orbit and send it crashing down.

But Perturbare's goal was nothing so crude.

A control ring rotated around the sphere, a structure a thousand miles in circumference, uninhabitable except for a few relatively tiny pressurized areas. In one of these Perturbare conversed with Brainchild 1r, a local node of Brainchild's distributed intelligence, which he had freed of its centralized, vulnerable single location. The computer was now far more pervasive, occupying networked nodes scattered across the Earth and beyond. Never again could any single attack destroy it.

Playing on a nearby monitor was an episode of the defunct Vigil cartoon show. The show had been cancelled after the American attack on the Lighthouse, the Vigil's old base in Boston. Only twelve episodes had been aired, with another three completed but never shown. Perturbare of course had had no difficulty in obtaining them.

This particular episode concentrated on Vega, the show's only regular character who had no basis in fact. When the show was created, the Vigil had no living female members. Therefore the producers had invented Vega, who had the ability to absorb and emit all the energy of the star Vega that fell upon the Earth (as long as it was in the sky from her location). A quick calculation showed this was actually a surprising amount of power. Whenever she did this, the star would vanish from the sky for anyone within the area from which she was absorbing its light. An area with a ten-foot radius formed a weak flashlight beam. A full four thousand-mile radius produced an incandescent pillar of radiation.

The story showed her helpless against the villainously cartoonified Para-Men, after being captured and held at their Antarctic fortress, where the star Vega never rises.

All this was of peripheral interest to Perturbare as he prepared to conduct the first practical test of this colossal new device, the most blatant manipulator of space he had ever constructed. He called it Sphere Y.

He stared at a display showing the projected volume of influence of this first test, a sphere a mere five feet in diameter at the very heart of the machine.

"Very good, Brainchild. We don't know quite what will happen when we turn this thing on, but this way we can at least constrain the size of any results." Perturbare felt a little light-headed, in danger of breaking out in a cold sweat. In truth he didn't like being out here, so far from Earth. He was no spaceman, even though in the past he had been as far as 200,000 light-years from Earth. He didn't even like this machine, which was a thing foreboding in the extreme. He felt like a microbe that was about to provoke a thought, or perhaps a seizure, in the mind of some inscrutable god.

I persist in thinking it would have been better to limit the initial volume even further, said Brainchild. *Say, to a volume of ten to the minus thirty microns across.*

"All that could show us is a few virtual particles flickering in and out of existence. Normal space does that already. No, this machine is intended to work on a macroscopic scale, and that's how we'll test it. The greatest danger I foresee is accidentally sparking a new episode of inflation throughout the universe, do you agree?"

Yes. No one would live long enough to regret such an occurrence.

"That's oddly comforting. What's the charge level of the scalar capacitors?"

Fully charged.

"All right then." Perturbare licked his lips. "Erect quantum shielding and begin the brane cascade sequence. And make it fast. Shielding of that strength is no fun for me to be around."

A sudden sickening feeling of unreality gripped Perturbare as the quantum shielding partially separated him from the rest of the universe. This was necessary to protect himself and Brainchild as the Sphere's enormous spines released a flurry of primordial membranes to fall toward each other and interact in the core of the Sphere. Without that dire shielding, they would have been subject to physical effects having no natural place in the universe's present stage of evolution. Gritting his teeth, Perturbare stared with fanatical attention at the display showing the pulsating, elusive pattern of the brane cascade.

Inflaton Field established. Area limitation successful.

The mini-inflation teased away the fabric of normal space within the five-foot sphere, resulting in a volume devoid of the normal constraints of physical law, as well as being clear of all forms of matter and energy. It was a small zone of unlimited possibility, so far unfulfilled. The only other thing of comparable potential which Perturbare knew about was a naked singularity, a speck of infinitely imploded space, but the creation of such an anomaly required more energy than even Perturbare could practically marshall, and was also less elegant.

"Shut it down!" he cried, at the limit of his endurance. Instantly everything returned to normal except for his heart and respiration rates.

A life form has appeared within the affected volume. It appears to be human. It is exposed to vacuum and is dying, said Brainchild.

Perturbare was first staggered, then slightly disappointed. Of all the things he had thought might happen when a doorway to anything was opened, the appearance of an ordinary human being was not high among them.

But—*who* might it turn out to be?

"Send in a flyer. Rescue him. If he appears to be dangerous, get him far away from here. If not, bring him here to me. Hurry!"

Certainly, doctor.

In less than two minutes Brainchild reported: *I perceive no danger from this person. I am bringing the flyer to the docking bay nearest you in the control ring.*

The flyer bay was just pressurizing as Perturbare arrived. When the sequence was complete, Perturbare entered and looked into the flyer's canopy.

Sprawled unconscious in the pilot's seat was a beautiful dark-haired woman wearing a tight black super-hero costume emblazoned with the star pattern of the constellation Lyra.

"Wow," said Perturbare, "that's a really great Vega costume she's wearing holy crap she really *is* Vega, isn't she!"

She stirred, eyelids fluttering.

"Brainchild, open the canopy." Perturbare bent down, touched her carotid pulse, and made sure she was breathing properly.

She moaned a little. Her eyes snapped open, and she sprang upright in her seat. Looking around in confusion, her big brown eyes finally locked on Perturbare.

"Possum Perturbare!" she cried, her Latina accent and voice exactly as it was in the cartoon, albeit a bit hoarse at the moment. "What are you up to this time?"

Perturbare raised his hands. "Nothing, Vega, nothing. It's okay, you're safe."

"We'll see about that!" She scrambled over the side of the flyer away from him, stood up and faced him, her hands placed together with fingers intertwined.

She looked puzzled.

In the cartoon, she was able to arrange her fingers into a five-pointed star, from which flared the light of Vega.

Uh oh, thought Perturbare.

But nothing happened. The star never really took shape. Vega looked puzzled and dismayed.

"My power isn't working! What have you done to me? Where am I?"

"Uh...this is a space station," said Perturbare gently.

Vega's face crumpled. "You fiend! My power only works when I'm on Earth! That must be it!"

"Yes, that must be it."

"Well, I don't need my powers to take you on!" She assumed a martial arts pose and leaped over the flyer. The distance was a little too much for her, and she caught her foot in the cockpit sill and fell forward. Perturbare caught her and managed to keep her from crashing to the deck.

"Hey, hey, it's all right, I'm not going to hurt you," he said, helping her upright.

She turned a suspicious gaze upon him and studied him carefully.

"Hey...why are you dressed like that? Where's your beard? And your—your horns?"

Perturbare grimaced. The cartoon was notorious for exaggerating the evil characteristics of its "villains".

"Vega...this isn't exactly where you might expect to find yourself. Things here are a little—different. I'm not the same Perturbare you're used to."

"What are you saying? This is some sort of parallel universe?"

Perturbare seized on this gladly, even though he believed it wasn't quite accurate. Fortunately, cartoon superheroes were quick to accept such situations. "Yes, that's close enough."

Vega lowered her hands, looking flummoxed as thoughts raced through her mind. "Another universe! Hey, how do I know this isn't just a virtual reality scenario you've trapped me in, to lower my guard? I remember when you did that to Stingray and convinced him he was a skinny, maladjusted artist in a world with no super powers and no girlfriend!"

Perturbare, who remembered that episode well, lowered his face to hide the smile that threatened to erupt.

Brainchild spoke aloud, causing her to jump. "Vega, there is no way to prove to you that this is real, as you well know. You must take our word for it. Even if it were a simulation, you have nothing to gain by acting as though it is."

Vega thought that over for a moment.

"There is a Vigil here?"

"Yes," said Perturbare.

"Then there must be another version of me here too?"

"Ah—no. No, this Vigil never had a member like you, Vega."

"Why not?"

"I don't know," Perturbare lied. "I suppose it's just one of the random differences between your world and this one."

"Why did you bring me here? Can you send me home?"

"It was an accident. And no, I don't think it's possible to send you home."

Vega looked at him as though she might cry. "An accident? That's not much of an explanation." She began to cough.

"Vega, I know this is very upsetting to you, and beside that, you were exposed to space for a minute or so. Please, let us check you over, get you something to eat, give you a place to rest. I promise you're in no danger here."

Vega permitted herself to be led away, cooperating numbly as he did everything he'd suggested. As far as he and Brainchild could determine, she was a normal human woman, healthy except for a little pulmonary edema and the breakage of some superficial capillaries. Perhaps she had endured the vacuum a little better than might be expected. He left her in a quiet room with a couch to sleep on and a sedative in her veins.

"Don't let her communicate with anyone, Brainchild," said Perturbare as he left the room.

Of course not.

"She's not really from a parallel universe at all, is she? In fact, I *created* her. From nothing. I was thinking about Vega. We made a void in reality, and it was occupied by her."

Yes.

"And her silly power doesn't work because it makes no sense that she could absorb the radiant energy of a particular star and shoot it out of her hands."

Yes.

"I could just as easily have summoned the evil cartoon Para-Men instead."

Yes.

"What are we going to do with her? I almost feel as if I've kidnapped an actual member of the Vigil."

Perturbare spent the next few hours analyzing the results of the test and thinking about Vega. The implications of her creation were profound. Even through quantum shielding, his idle thoughts had been influential enough to shape the expectant nothingness carved out of space by Sphere Y. It might be possible to bring into being anything he needed to further his grand project. Anything at all. But what should that be?

Vega eventually emerged from her room, looking bleary-eyed and truculent. The sight of her was a renewed astonishment to Perturbare. Somehow she stood out as not belonging. Something in her movements and facial expressions managed to be somehow—cartoonish.

"Perturbare, if you are not my enemy here, please take me to Earth and set me free."

He winced. Vega was as straightforward here as she tended to be in the cartoon.

"Vega...it's not that simple."

"Why not?" she demanded.

"I...don't want the Vigil to know what I'm doing here, or even that this place exists."

Her eyes narrowed. "Brainchild tells me there is no active antagonism between you and this Vigil. Does he lie?"

"No..."

"Then what are you hiding from them?"

"I'm planning to...to challenge them. Not to fight them," he corrected, reacting to her fierce glare. "To challenge them, to motivate them to rise to their best potential, to unite them with humanity and move them beyond their current plans. Has Brainchild told you about any of that?"

"No."

"Okay. You find yourself in a timeframe several years later than in the show—I mean in the one you know. This Vigil defeated the Para-Men long ago."

Vega's expression brightened at this.

"But it's not all good. T'Ukudu is dead. Raintree isn't the same man you know. Standing Crane is missing at best. You see, the United States Government attacked the Vigil and destroyed the Lighthouse."

Vega staggered back, shocked. "Nooooo!" she wailed theatrically. "Ben would never allow all that to happen!"

"That's another thing. Ben Raintree is not the leader of this Vigil. He never was. It's Fomalhaut, and always has been."

"Fomalhaut!?" she squawked in disbelief. "He hardly even talks!"

"This one can be pretty chatty at times. And there's more. The Vigil recently admitted two new members, or effectively so. They are Endurance and Valjhar Cor."

Vega sagged into a chair, stricken. A sympathetic Perturbare sat down beside her.

"I do not know who is this Endurance of whom you speak," she whispered. "But I can never believe that the Vigil, any Vigil, would take up with a devil like Cor. No."

"Yes, well, as I said, things here are different. You knew the Para-Men only as villains and monsters. Here things are much less simple. Here they were noble and honorable, misguided in their intentions, but not really more so than the Vigil...or me."

"Naturally you, as their ally, would think that of them!" she flared up.

"So does Fomalhaut, I promise you. And Stingray. Even Aureus seems to have taken a weird shine to Valjhar."

Vega folded her hands in her lap and looked downcast. Perturbare, moved by pity, leaned forward and placed his hand on the arm of her splendid costume. "There's more. The Vigil was disillusioned by the American attack and dismayed by the—general state of the world. They've decided to follow in the footsteps of the Para-Men."

"What do you mean?"

"They're going to try to take over the world. For the sake of the greater good, of course. Just like the Para-Men. Our Para-Men, that is."

"Nooooo!"

"So you see," he said as he watched tears drip onto her thighs, "this is a world that might not really—suit you."

"What am I supposed to do in such an upside-down world?" She glared at him. "But I still don't know how I can believe anything you say! You are the worst trickster and criminal in the world! In my world, anyway..."

He nodded. "I know. I'm authorizing Brainchild to tell or show you anything you want to know about the Vigil and the world. I know we can't prove that whatever you learn is real and not our fabrication. If I can think of some way to prove it to you, I will."

And Brainchild, make sure she learns nothing of the Vigil cartoon. I don't want her to guess what she really is.

Yes, Doctor.

"And in the meantime...I am your prisoner? Powerless?"

"Yes, I'm afraid so. Think of yourself as my guest. It won't be so bad. I'm the only person in the world who really understands you, anyway."

Down on Earth, Fomalhaut, urged by some strange impulse, stepped onto a balcony high atop the Spire and looked toward the Moon, low in the afternoon sky in its third quarter phase.

Chapter 11

Yuwipi

Valjhar Cor sat in the windy Chamber of Solitude atop the Spire. He looked to the north, along the rugged coastline; to the east, where his view was blocked by a mountain wall; to the south, to fir-forested hills whose feet were beaten by waves, and finally to the west, far over the misty sea and the scattered islands nearby. He sniffed, shook his head, and laughed, thinking about the latest strange turn his life had taken: Valjhar Cor, member of the Vigil. Valjhar Cor, reluctant companion of the Prohibitor of Rral.

The golden robot had consented to remain below, granting him privacy in this bare little space surrounded and suffused by a moving ocean of air.

Valjhar had not been introduced to the public under his real name, but rather in the guise of Motion. There was no telling how damaging it would be for the Vigil to announce the membership of the same alien who had once threatened to take over the world. His background had been left vague, but people assumed he was human.

At the moment, the Motionglobe rested in a pocket of his jacket.

Endurance had also been introduced as a member, which was a considerable sacrifice for him. For the first time in history, Endurance could no longer count on anonymity as he walked among men. His acceptance of this lent gravity to his stated conviction that the world was soon to change, drastically and forever. His indestructibility had been revealed, but not his immortality, or his cosmic age. Those would have been too difficult to explain to the public, even if any of them could have done so.

Valjhar stood up, sighed, and descended the ladder that gave access to this Chamber. On the small elevator landing below he found himself confronted by Walks-with-the Sun, who faced him with a strange smile on his face.

"Hello, Walks," said Valjhar uncertainly. He did not yet have a clear understanding of who Walks was, or what his place in the Vigil might be. "What can I do for you?"

"I think I can do something for you. I think I can help you find your friend Pimsehkia."

Valjhar blinked. "How can you do that?" he asked mildly.

"We Lakota have a ceremony called the *Yuwipi* which is for finding things, for learning things. It's what we call the Rock Dreaming. We'll put one on for you and find your friend."

"I see. I—I didn't realize you were qualified to do such things."

"Yeah, you're right. I can't do the ceremony myself. My family has not honored traditional knowledge in many years, and I was no smarter. I'm ashamed to say I know only a little of my own Lakota language, though I am learning. My friend Standing Crane was the same. He didn't believe in our Lakota ways, and went off to study white medicine. As for me, when I had my Great Vision, I learned that all the old knowledge of my people is true. Anyway, I've brought in a *Yuwipi* man from my tribe, a holy man, to conduct the ceremony."

Valjhar nodded blankly. He had never immersed himself in the local beliefs of Earth people. One of the things that had impressed him most about Human culture was its lack of homogeneity. With hundreds or thousands of disparate belief systems to choose from, he had never taken any of them more seriously than any other.

At the same time, clearly these beliefs had given Walks a power of some kind. There could be no harm in accepting his offer, Valjhar supposed.

"All right, thank you, Walks."

"Before the ceremony we must purify ourselves in the sweat lodge. Come, we will invite the others to join us. We of the Vigil need answers to many mysteries."

Valjhar nodded again, bemused, and followed Walks into the lift.

In the end, all available members of the Vigil agreed to participate, some more reluctantly than others, except for Aureus, whom no one even thought to ask. Walks introduced them to John Yellow Horse, a strongly-built older man with bright eyes set deep in a weathered face, and two other Lakota men who were to assist him. Later they met on the mountainside behind the great Vigil base, where Walks and Yellow Horse had constructed a traditional sweat lodge: a small dome formed from sixteen flexible canes and covered with blankets. To the right of the entrance, which faced the sea, was a small earthen mound surrounded by a number of thin stakes. Upon this flattened mound rested a sacred Lakota pipe and a buffalo skull.

The scent of some sort of incense wafted from the flap-covered opening of the sweat lodge. Yellow Horse, who was waiting inside, held the flap open and invited the others in.

"Be sure to remove all metal from your bodies, those of you who can be burned," he said. "You will have to crawl to enter. My friend Walks did not tell me that some of you are giants."

Valjhar, Stingray, Endurance, and the Lakota men wore only shorts. Fomalhaut of course was fully clad in his exploration suit. Endurance looked quite relaxed about the whole thing and confessed he had done this many times before. Stingray looked much more dubious, perhaps embarrassed. He fidgeted with his desire to get back to work on his fledgling navy, and had agreed to do this only in the interest of promoting unity among the Vigil. Fomalhaut's views on the matter were inscrutable.

They took their places around the central pit, squatting at the periphery of the little dome.

"Before we begin, I will speak to each of you," said Yellow Horse. "Fomalhaut, I feel knowledge blowing into you like a wind. But while wearing your space suit you will not benefit from the sweat lodge. You must be able to feel and breathe the steam, which is the breath of Wakan Tanka."

"The suit will transmit the sensations of the steam," answered Fomalhaut. "As for breathing it—I must remain isolated from the world for a little longer yet. I am sorry I cannot participate more fully in your ceremony."

Yellow Horse nodded and turned to Stingray. "My friend, I see in your face that you do not believe in what we are about to do here."

"I would say rather that I'm skeptical about it, and ignorant. However, if you want me to leave, I shall."

"Stingray belongs here as one of the sixteen great mysteries," said Walks mischievously. "He is *Unktehi*."

"That's not funny, Walks," admonished Yellow Horse, but all could see him trying to repress a smile. None of the others knew what this meant, except for Endurance, who did smile quietly.

Looking annoyed, Stingray shifted in his place.

"Stingray, you are welcome to stay with us," continued Yellow Horse, "but I ask you to try to open yourself to what we will experience." Now he faced Endurance. "Earthwalker, it is an honor to sit with you in this *inipi*. My grandfather spoke of you long ago. Those few of us who know of you and believe in you think of you as representing the Rock, *Inyan*, the eternal power of the creator."

"I remember your grandfather. He was a good and wise man, and I am happy to know you as well."

Looking pleased, Yellow Horse turned his attention to Valjhar.

"Valjhar, I have known for a long time that the world was changing, and that strange things were happening everywhere. But I never thought I would put on an *inipi* and later a *yuwipi* for an alien, a space man just like in the movies. These ceremonies are meant for you, because Walks believes your need is greatest. May all the spirits reveal to you that which you wish to know, and bring peace to your heart."

Valjhar bowed his head in acknowledgment.

They proceeded with the ceremony. Red-hot rocks were brought in by the assistants and placed in the pit, and cold water poured over them. Steam exploded outward, quickly heating the lodge to a degree which Valjhar could at first barely tolerate. In fact initially Valjhar felt a touch of panic, a desire to flee. He did not feel he belonged here, either on this world or among these people. He had seen many worlds, even many universes, in his long life. To sit here now, on this planet where he had known his greatest defeats and his most painful losses, sundered from all he loved, was suddenly a weight which threatened to unman him. He glanced up at Stingray, finding the sea-giant's eyes already upon him, as grave as though he knew Valjhar's thoughts. They had traversed the stars together for a few short years, so very long ago, and it had ended so badly.

Yellow Horse began to sing a song that seemed wild and discordant to Valjhar. He was tempted to take up the Motionglobe, to somehow resume his natural form, make his way back to the distant planet Rral, and there spend his remaining years crafting nautical gear and secretly writing of his experiences. But...the Motionglobe must go to Endurance.

He must find Pimsie, and see if her gentle spirit could still be salvaged.

Twice more the cycle of hot rocks, water, steam, and song was repeated. Endurance of course did not sweat, but sat looking lost in thought. Fomalhaut might as well have been some fanciful sculpture of glass and porcelain. Stingray either gazed into the steaming rocks or glanced from face to face, as if trying to guess what thoughts were passing there. Walks and the medicine man both looked happy and transported.

Valjhar could not distinguish between his own sweat and the tears streaming down his face. He knew this ritual was supposed to cleanse and purify him. He knew he was also supposed to pray. Rral had no similar rites. The concept of prayer would never occur to a sensible Rralian, for what could be more meaningless than to cast one's hopes out into the insensate void?

That was the kind of rational, pragmatic thinking that had led to the disaster of the Stones, to the fall of Rral's technical civilization, and to the Prohibitors. Still, the basic nature of the Rralian mind had changed very little. Valjhar was forced to admit that given free rein, Rral would eventually revert to the towering, brilliant, yet spiritually empty scientific civilization that had loomed so tall and yet so precariously all those centuries ago.

On the other hand, Man's unthinking devotion to whichever cult seemed most attractive or most accepted accounted for much of the madness that had afflicted this planet throughout its history. Which was better?

For his part, Valjhar would attempt to pray. To what he knew not...only to whatever might exist in the universe that might take heed of him.

Let me find Pimsehkia and somehow bring her home. Let me be at peace over the loss of Shaula.

Fomalhaut stirred.

The fourth and final round of steam and song began. By now Valjhar's head was spinning. The darkened lodge and all its scents, sounds, and sensations blurred into a confused din of heat and noise. He looked around desperately, trying to see if anyone else felt as overwhelmed as he did.

Another presence had joined them in the lodge.

It was a pale woman with a bedraggled mat of silver hair. She sat wrapped in rags of mint green, sky blue, and dirty silver. Yellow Horse's song was cut off in mid-syllable as he stared at her in amazement.

When she looked up at them, her eyes were orbs of translucent jade surrounded by bruised flesh.

Valjhar had seen this creature before, many times, albeit never looking so distressed and forsaken.

"Dreamfarer," whispered Stingray.

Valjhar tried to speak. Blackness overcame him; he fainted.

When awareness returned, Valjhar found himself outside the lodge in the chilly morning mist, supported by Stingray and Aureus. The others stood around regarding him with concern.

"What happened to Nali?" he gasped.

"She vanished as you fainted, Valjhar," muttered Stingray.

"Did she say anything?"

"No. It looked like she was trying to speak, though."

Valjhar groaned in frustration.

"Valjhar," said Yellow Horse, "I am sorry for this. I am thinking that our ceremonies are not good for men of other worlds. I have never seen such a thing happen before. I am thinking we should cancel our *yuwipi*."

Valjhar looked at the medicine man with some difficulty. "But that's the ceremony meant to help me find my friend Pimsehkia, isn't it?"

"Yes."

"Then we must try it. I'm more convinced than ever that she is in trouble and needs help."

"Why is that, Valjhar?" asked Fomalhaut.

"I don't think you ever realized what I'm about to tell you. Do you remember how Standing Crane carried within him the spirits of Anubis, Hermes, and similar mythological gods from Earth's past? Well, the Dreamfarer is another such spirit, and she was carried within Pimsehkia. Dreamfarer first attached herself to Pimsie when we Space Mariners visited the planet Colibdis. These spirits cannot long exist away from the strange influence of that planet without dwelling in a sentient host. After that, Dreamfarer would often emerge whenever Pimsie slept, visiting this person or that, either in their dreams, or even while awake if they were of a certain frame of mind. Dreamfarer was dismissed by Anubis during our final confrontation with the Vigil. I believed she had retreated to Colibdis. Certainly I have not seen or heard of her in many years...until today... and I'll bet none of you have, either."

Stingray and Fomalhaut indicated agreement.

"Yet now she has returned, or revealed herself again, looking much the worse for wear. Pimsehkia must be found."

"I agree with Valjhar," said Walks.

Yellow Horse stared at Valjhar for long moments, then nodded. "So be it. I will begin the preparations. Let it be done tonight."

They left the four Lakota men behind and helped Valjhar into the Spire to rest.

"Do you guys really believe in all this Indian hocus pocus?" asked Stingray in a low voice. "I mean, I know Dreamfarer really appeared, but she's been appearing for years without the help of medicine men and steam baths."

"I believe that the Indians do, in fact, conduct the ceremonies," said Endurance. "The mere fact that they take place in the world gives them a certain power."

"So it does," said Fomalhaut. "The presence of other minds bent in the same direction makes it easier for me— for us—to find what we seek."

Twilight found Valjhar once more seated in the Chamber of Solitude as he tried to calm himself and collect his thoughts for tonight's ordeal—although he knew it was best not to think of it that way. A few stars twinkled through gaps in the clouds. They looked nearby, familiar, and mundane compared to what awaited him below.

The wail of Yellow Horse's singing rose up from somewhere outside, like a wild wind given voice, conveying mysteries that were opaque to the Rralian mind.

The singing ceased. Valjhar was summoned to the *yuwipi*.

It was held in a chamber a few levels below the Spire's summit which had been emptied, its furnishings and equipment replaced by the accouterments of the ceremony. The floor was scattered with some fragrant plant. A rectangular enclosure had been defined by a string bearing hundreds of tiny bundles of a different plant. Dirt filled cans planted with sticks and colored flags marked the corners of this rectangle. In addition there were staffs, feathers, an earthen altar, a sacred pipe, an eagle wing, drums, rattles, some food and water...symbols of power more arcane and alien than Valjhar could really take in or begin to understand. He felt himself beginning to tremble.

They sat on cushions around the edges of the room. Aureus sat close beside Valjhar on his right. Fomalhaut sat even closer on his left, almost touching, looming over him even in that posture. Valjhar felt suddenly vulnerable, intimidated, an old man overshadowed by a living mystery. He looked up at that spherical, perfectly reflective helmet, and had no idea whether the being within it looked back at him, or was perhaps sitting there fast asleep.

Yellow Horse wore a small pouch suspended by a thong around his neck. He and his assistants stepped into the rectangle, which the others were forbidden to enter. The assistants tied Yellow Horse's arms behind his back. They then wrapped him tightly in a blanket, covering him from head to ankle, then confined him still further by wrapping a rope around him. Valjhar glanced over at Walks, who regarded this bizarre behavior with equanimity; apparently this was all to be expected. The assistants laid the bundle that was Yellow Horse face down in the center of the rectangle.

The room lights went out, leaving them in total darkness. A drumbeat commenced, along with more Indian singing. The sounds seemed to come from everywhere, or from inside his own head. The darkness pressed in on him as though he had been buried alive. The rhythm beat against his thoughts, preventing him from considering any of this at all clearly.

A cloud of dim red sparks appeared in the room, swirling randomly, too faint to illuminate anything. Valjhar squinted at them, wondering what they could possibly be. At least they relieved his feeling of claustrophobia.

The drumming and singing went on interminably. The sparks remained in view; no one reacted to their presence.

Something light and soft brushed his face. Valjhar shuddered violently and threw himself back. Trembling, he felt another gliding touch, this time on his hand. Whatever it was did not block his view of the sparks. To his amazement, neither Fomalhaut nor Aureus reacted in any way, sitting there motionless, as if dead. A hand rested briefly on his cheek. Valjhar's hands jerked up as though of their own volition. They found and gripped two slender wrists, warm and alive. He held them, no longer afraid of anything but the depth of his own emotions and the pain that accompanied their belated release. The soft hands moved towards him, cupping his face. Valjhar bathed them in his tears. His hands slid back along the bare phantom arms, encountering a cascade of hair and smooth round shoulders.

The singing surged in volume and intensity. Valjhar's mysterious companion slipped away, the way a dream eludes a sleeper who awakens. The drums thundered a final time and fell silent. The lights came back on. Valjhar closed his eyes against the glare. When he could see again, he found that Yellow Horse was free, standing in the rectangle, looking at him.

Valjhar was about to ask if anyone else had felt or seen anything when Fomalhaut announced, "I now know where Pimsehkia is."

"Where?" demanded Valjhar.

"She is presently unconscious at an American military base near Washington, D.C. It is used for research into military applications for nanotechnology, and also for attempts to reverse engineer Vigil and Perturbare technology. Apparently it is used for—other things as well. I don't know how I could have remained unaware of all this until now."

Valjhar hauled himself to his feet, embarrassed and angry at the stiffness and weakness of his aged body. "I think I remember this place from my searches. I will go there and retrieve Pimsehkia."

"We'll all damn well go," said Stingray.

"Yes," said Aureus.

"No," said Valjhar. "With the Motionglobe, I can get in there instantly. No obstacle can hamper me. I cannot carry anybody else in and also carry Pimsie out. If we all go thundering in, they will have time to harm Pimsie. I will go alone. She is of my people, and she is my responsibility." He did not wait to hear any further objections or arguments. He brought forth the Motionglobe, allowed it to pass into his head, took a moment to adjust to the altered perceptions it brought, and folded himself through space, vanishing before the eyes of the Vigil and their Lakota guests.

It took an hour of Valjhar's subjective time to locate the base in the midnight darkness of the Virginia countryside. Once past the outer fence he took no chances, going into full time-speed distortion. In this mode his body seemed immersed in a thick, invisible soup that slowed him to a crawl. The rest of the world was completely frozen, to the extent that he cast no shadow in the glare of the security lights, and was not illuminated by them.

Valjhar barely took notice of the base as he combed its labyrinthine halls for Pimsie. He ignored its legions of heavily armed guards, the mockups and models of propulsion lanterns, and the vault containing a disassembled Perturbare ERASER pistol. He nearly bypassed a luxurious apartment in which a blonde human woman lay asleep, until he remembered what he had been told about Pimsehkia's current appearance. Then he knelt beside her bed, permitting his subjective timeframe to speed up slightly so that light would flow around him once again.

Her sheets were down around her waist and she was naked. Her hair was a fine feathery mass that flowed over her shoulders and pillow. She was small for a human woman, but much larger than Pimsie had been. Her face was still delicate, but of course its contours were greatly changed. Nevertheless, Valjhar was certain this was in fact Pimsehkia Flam.

This was confirmed when he re-entered normal time and shook her shoulder. The aqua eyes that looked at him in confusion were undoubtedly those of Pimsehkia.

She sat up suddenly, gasping, not recognizing him at first. Why should she? To his eyes she was little more than a child. What would she make of his wizened face? Then: "Valjhar?"

"Pimsehkia. I've come to take you out of here." He looked down at the Motionglobe, which now rested in his palm.

"Valjhar, why did you take that out of your head?"

"I—I don't know," said Valjhar, frowning at it.

Pimsehkia looked suddenly terrified. "They know you're here. Run!"

"What?"

"Put it back! Run! *Now!*"

But it was too late for Valjhar to run.

No one else had yet left the *yuwipi* chamber. The members of the Vigil stood regarding each other in grim silence.

"He's been gone an hour," said Stingray.

"Well, it is a rescue mission," said Walks. "That can take more than an hour, can't it?"

"Not for Motion," said Fomalhaut. "An hour for us can easily be a week in his subjective time. Or a year. Or a lifetime."

"We must assume something has gone wrong," said Stingray.

"We must act at once to save both of them," tolled the voice of Aureus.

"Yes," said Stingray, sounding oddly exultant. "The time has finally come for the Vigil to act."

"We must not be drawn into full battle prematurely," said Fomalhaut. "Our military is almost nonexistent. Our plans for governance are incomplete. The best we could accomplish right now would be to pull down the Human power structure with nothing to replace it. Chaos would result."

"We're not interested in taking over the world right now," insisted Stingray. "We're interested in saving Valjhar. Can't you tell us anything about his situation?"

Fomalhaut hesitated. "No. I cannot. Something new has come into play. There is a—zone surrounding that entire base which is opaque to me. If I'm to penetrate it, I must have solitude and a lack of distraction for several hours."

At that moment a new voice spoke from the air. "This is Vigil Tactical Intelligence. We are getting reports of a U.S. military assault on the Ghost Dance camp in South Dakota. Armed helicopters, large numbers of troops in full riot gear, and dogs. The Dancers are being rounded up. Resistance is being beaten down harshly."

Walks frowned. "But they're Ghost Dancers. Their Ghost Shirts should protect them."

Stingray's faced worked as he tried to restrain his natural reaction to such a statement. He was only partially successful. "Are they wearing Ghost Ski Masks too?"

"No."

"Then a club or a bullet to the head should handle them."

"We must go to them," said Yellow Horse.

"Yeah," said Walks. "Come on."

"Endurance, would you please accompany them?" asked Fomalhaut.

Endurance nodded.

Stingray said, "Er, Walks, do you know how to pilot a flyer?"

"Uh, no, not too good. That's dumb, huh?"

"How about you, Endurance?"

"No."

Still keeping his face carefully under control, Stingray said, "Stingray to main hangar. Please have a pilot report for duty. Prep an armed eight-place flyer for immediate departure."

Endurance and the four Lakota departed.

Stingray looked after them with a wry expression on his face. "And now, as for Valjhar—" he began.

"Wait." said Fomalhaut.

Another announcement: "Fomalhaut, communications. There's a call for you from the U.S. Department of the Exterior."

"I will take it. This is Fomalhaut speaking."

"This is Secretary of the Exterior Sard Ducanis. One of your group, the one you call Motion, has been apprehended while trying to abduct one of our staff members. He is now in our custody."

"The staff member to whom you refer…that would be Jenni Katz?"

"That is correct. Both Motion and Dr. Katz have now been removed from the facility where this incident occurred. Your only chance of recovering your colleague is for you, Fomalhaut, and only you, to personally come to this same base to negotiate an end to the Vigil's ongoing acts of treason."

"The Vigil cannot possibly commit treason against the United States. We are not Americans. We may be considered enemy combatants, but not traitors."

"I was referring to your treason against the human race in general."

"Spare me your hypocritical posturing. The only portion of the human race we wish to 'betray' is that small fraction which is dependent upon the exploitation and oppression of the majority."

"Fomalhaut, let us be honest with one another. You believe that only you and your elite group of friends is fit to govern the human race. We also believe that an elite group is best suited to maintaining order. In our case, that group is composed of human beings. Therein lies the main source of contention between us."

"Nonsense. We have no need to parasitize those whom we would rule and guide. Your preferred elite, on the other hand, cannot maintain its privileges without doing so. Therein lies our real difference."

"Tell it like it is," muttered Stingray.

"We can discuss politics later. I advise you to come at once. Do not delay. Ducanis out."

Fomalhaut stood in silence for a few moments.

"I will go," he said.

Stingray frowned. "This wouldn't be the first time they've lured you away on some false pretext."

"Yes. Clearly we are being deliberately pulled apart, scattered, and confused. We must regain the initiative. I will go. I am as untouchable as Endurance as far as they're concerned. This time I will not easily be turned aside. Stingray, please take charge here and prepare for a possible attack. Aureus…"

"I will seek out Valjhar and Pimsehkia."

"Yes. Of course."

Fomalhaut hesitated before departing.

"I don't think Ducanis and his cronies are yet aware that 'Jenni Katz' and 'Motion' are aliens and former Para-Men. We must be very cautious."

And then he was gone. Aureus departed a moment later.

Stingray stood brooding in the abandoned *yuwipi* room for a minute or two, then spoke into the air.

"Stingray to hangar. Prepare a stealth flyer for immediate departure. Stingray to Communications. Contact Commander Strenczak and Lori Wu and advise them to prepare for a possible attack. Tell Strenczak to get her ship in the water if she possibly can. Also contact Ben Raintree and call him back. Stingray to Control. I'm leaving. Monique, you're in charge. Keep the base on full defensive alert until you hear otherwise from one of us. Keep me informed."

Chapter 12

Inspiration

Possum Perturbare found a listless Vega in one of Sphere Y's observation lounges, staring at the starfield passing in stately silence beyond its windows. Normally Perturbare would have returned to Earth by now, but he was reluctant to allow his unexpected guest the chance of discovery or escape there. Nor did he want to leave her here alone. She sat slouched on a couch in the dimly-lit room, wearing ordinary street clothes which Brainchild had made for her. Her proud costume was not in evidence.

"I can see my star out there," she said softly as he approached. "But I can no longer hold its light in my hands."

Perturbare glanced out. There indeed burned Vega, one of the few stars he could identify, surrounded by a daunting expanse of blackness and lesser lights.

"Vega, I'd like to ask you something..." he began.

"Don't call me that. I'm not Vega anymore. My name is Marisol Reyes."

"Oh," he said, taken aback. "All right. Marisol, I'd like your advice on what I should do about the Vigil. My Vigil I mean, of course. They're in quite a bit of trouble right now, and I'm not sure they're ready to handle it."

"My advice is to let them go hang. They're having trouble with the government? That government was elected, unlike them. My Vigil realized this. Why do you care about these anarchists anyway?"

"Well," said Perturbare, treading carefully, "I'm a bit of an anarchist myself, you know. A real one."

She cast him a bitter glance over her shoulder. Despite her rancor, Perturbare was reminded once again that she was every bit as beautiful as a super-heroine designed by geeks could be expected to be.

"Yes, I know that about you. You aren't so different than the Perturbare I left behind in my own world. I can't imagine why you haven't killed me. Without my powers I have nothing to offer you, and you certainly don't need any information I might have. Nothing is hidden from you, it seems."

"Did—did your Perturbare really kill people?" Perturbare, thinking back over the cartoon episodes he'd seen, could remember no such incident. The show's producers had known they were pushing their luck even to include him as a character. Portraying him as a murderer would have been risking too much.

"No..." she admitted grudgingly. "As far as I know, you—I mean he—never succeeded at killing anyone."

"I don't want to hurt anyone either, Marisol. Certainly not you. As for the Vigil, I respect them. I even like most of them. You know that Valjhar has been captured by the government?"

"Has he? It's about time!"

"Would you like to see him? On their security video, I mean."

She shrugged without looking back at him.

"Brainchild, let's see the video."

An image appeared in the air before Marisol's seat. They saw Valjhar, a lean, weathered figure wearing only underwear, seated on a cot in a bare cell, his arms resting on his knees. His head was bowed, hair falling over his eyes, his face dejected.

"That's Valjhar Cor? Not the one I knew, that's for sure. He looks so old," she said softly.

"Valjhar has squandered most of his life searching all of creation for his lost love, Shaula Alshain. He used his Motionglobe to expand his own subjective time. The few years he was away from Earth were, to him, decades of fruitless searching, maybe centuries. He has traveled, always a stranger, from one lonely pocket of infinity to another, searching. Now he's returned to Earth to return the Motionglobe to its rightful bearer, in the hope of having a few final years of peace."

"He doesn't deserve them."

"He deserves better. Marisol, this is not your Valjhar Cor. You know that. This one has never harmed you, or anyone."

"Fine," she snapped. "If you're so in love with him, why don't *you* rescue him? You could obviously do it with a single word."

"It's best if the Vigil does it for themselves. They'll be weakened if they think they can come running to me whenever things get out of hand. You see, I'll always be an outsider, never fully accepted or trusted, because that's the life I've made for myself. It's the Vigil that should be the world's heroes, not me. That's pretty ironic, because I'm human, which is more than you can say about most of them. I need them to be champions. You should have seen them, standing there together when they welcomed Valjhar and Endurance into their ranks. They're truly a merging of the Vigil and the Para-Men now. They're at the peak of their power. They'll need every bit of it to succeed against the challenge I've got planned for them."

"It sounds like you've already made up your mind about how to handle this."

"Yeah. I suppose I have."

She gave a little wave and turned back to the window. "Glad I could help."

Perturbare stood looking down at the brooding figure for a few moments, then turned to leave.

As he wandered back to his lab a thought occurred to him.

"Brainchild. In any of *The Vigil* episodes, was Vega ever referred to by her real name?"

That is an interesting matter. In fact, none of the completed episodes, whether broadcast or not, mention her name. However, a few unproduced scripts and outlines exist. One of them refers to Vega as 'Marisol'. Her last name is never established.

Perturbare chewed his lip for a moment in thought.

"That's very interesting indeed. Maybe there's more substance to our guest than we believed."

Quite possibly.

More thoughts filled his mind, with images of the forlorn figure of Vega prominent among them.

"Brainchild—do we have any frame shifters in stock?"

No. You forbade their construction after the incident in which the original Ben Raintree was lost. Why, if I may ask?

"I'm thinking of offering Miss Reyes a trip through one."

Doctor, you know there is very little chance of her being returned to anything resembling the world she believes she came from.

"Yes, that's true. But she's languishing here. And Raintree certainly found things to his liking in his new home. Maybe our girl will get lucky too. Anyway, we've got to do something with her."

This was perfectly true. Before he had gone to Vega and reminded himself that she was, in some sense, more than a three-dimensional cartoon character, the solution lurking in the back of his mind had been to kill her.

Perturbare was shaken by this realization. Perhaps he needed a companion more critical than Brainchild to keep him from sinking so low as to consider murder. True, Vega was a hindrance his plans, and must be removed, but still.

And speaking of those plans…

"Brainchild, it's time to move on to the next step of my scheme."

Which is?

"Everyone knows the most potent force in the world is television. This time we'll really get into the TV game. The little tweaks and pranks we've always pulled have been a lot of fun, but now it's serious. We'll produce a weekly series, based on the novel *The Night Land* by William Hope Hodgson. Do you know it?"

Yes, the novel is in the public domain and is available online.

"We'll pull out all the stops on this series. It'll begin with a two-hour premier, without commercials, on multiple networks. I'd like to do the whole series without advertising, but that would look too suspicious. I don't want anyone to guess that this show is coming from us.

We'll do a commercial-free version on HBO and a sponsored one on one of the broadcast networks so everyone can see it. We'll also get it out to the BBC and all over the world. Plus we'll stream it over the Web. The whole show will be synthetic, of course. We'll contract with a few character actors to use their likenesses so it'll have a few vaguely familiar faces. We'll invent the leads ourselves. We'll set up a production company, in case we need to hire artists to work on the visuals. It must be the best show ever, the most hypnotic, the darkest, and the scariest. It must haunt people's dreams. Then, when the episodes are ready and have begun to air, we'll reactivate Sphere Y at full power, and leave it running. Then we'll get out of the way and see what comes out of it."

Doctor, in this novel the humans are unable to defeat the forces of the Night Land. They face a slow and agonizing extinction. It offers no real hope.

"Yes. But the characters in the novel don't have the Vigil. And this is exactly the sort of thing the Vigil was made to battle."

Chapter 13

Stronghold

Jordan Elcanie was a recent Vigil hire, a student of aeronautical engineering and a former member of the Civil Air Patrol, hoping to find a place in the projected Vigil Aerospace Command, which had not yet been formally organized. Few members of the staff were trained or permitted to operate the flyers. The three pilots who'd been hired so far had been personally screened by Fomalhaut, since their jobs put them in control of very dangerous weapons.

Jordan waited nervously beside his assigned flyer, wearing his white Vigil flight suit and blue jacket with a mixture of embarrassment and pride. It was his first mission, and his first contact with members of the Vigil since that rather trying session with Fomalhaut. The huge bay doors high atop the Pearl had already been opened. Cold wind entered freely, but the sky wasn't visible, as the whitefield still covered the opening.

A shuffle of footsteps announced the approach of his passengers. Jordan was surprised by the composition of the group. There was Endurance, looking like some exotic male model, albeit one with an indifferent fashion sense in his sweatshirt and shorts. Beside him was Walks-With-the-Sun, the tallish, awkward Indian with an easy grin and a grubby hand-painted blue shirt. The others were also Indians: a burly older man who looked around with interest, and two younger men who seemed a little apprehensive.

Jordan himself was by far the most flamboyant figure present, which struck him as a little ironic.

"Hey, pilot," said Walks. "Here we are. These guys are John Yellow Horse, Vincent Black Hawk, and Big Turtle. Who are you?"

"Jordan Elcanie, sir. Where may I take you?"

"Well, you sure look and sound like a pilot. We're going to my old Rez, at Pine Ridge in South Dakota. Seems the government is making trouble at the mesa called the Stronghold, where my people are gathered."

Jordan nodded. "If you'll all please step aboard?"

Endurance said, "Yellow Horse, you and your friends are welcome to wait here. This situation may be dangerous for you."

The demeanor of the two assistants immediately brightened, but Yellow Horse shook his head. "Thank you, Earthwalker, but we will go. Our people need help. Walks is not the only one among us with power." The other two looked disappointed.

Endurance's expression remained neutral. With some misgivings Jordan ushered them aboard the van-like flyer and seated them. Endurance took the copilot position, while the others sat behind them.

A few moments later the flyer penetrated the whitefield and rushed east-southeast above the darkened clouds. Acceleration pushed them all back in their seats.

"There's a snow squall in the vicinity of our destination," said Jordan, consulting his instruments in the dim cockpit. "It's early in the year for that, and unexpected."

"Probably one of our holy men called it up to bother the white soldiers," said Yellow Horse placidly. "Probably a *heyoka*." He chuckled.

Jordan glanced aside at Endurance to take in his reaction to this, but his passenger remained impassive. Jordan could not help feeling a little disappointed. He knew little about these two members of the Vigil, and so far neither had done much to impress him. He wished he knew what he could expect of them if they wound up in any kind of combat.

The half-hour flight passed with little additional speech. Below them the clouds grew steadily thicker and more turbulent. Jordan decided neither Walks nor Endurance was qualified to instruct him in how to handle the approach. Rather than request instructions and thereby invite them to issue some foolish order, Jordan elected to take matters into his own hands.

"I'm reading five helicopters over the mesa, below the cloud deck. I'm surprised they're still in the air with all the wind they've got down there. I'm going to put us down on the edge of the mesa, as far as I can get from the choppers."

"Fine," said Endurance. "But before you do, please pass over the mesa and drop me off."

Jordan hesitated.

"Drop you off?"

"Yes, I'll open the door and jump out."

Jordan raised his eyebrows. "Yes, sir. Will this altitude be all right?"

"It makes no difference. You might want to slow down a bit so I don't overshoot the mesa."

"Yes, sir."

Endurance unbuckled himself, got up and moved into the flyer's main compartment, where he held on while Jordan brought the flyer to a near hover.

"All right sir, you're good to go."

"Have a nice trip," said Walks.

Endurance keyed the door open and stepped out into the darkness. Jordan closed the door from his console and shook his head.

"Okay pilot, go ahead and land us, hey?" said Walks.

Jordan shrugged and descended into the clouds. Visibility did not improve even when they dropped below them, for snow flew thickly everywhere, turning the beams of the landing lights into cones of madly dashing particles.

"I'm setting her down fast, in case those choppers come after us. Be ready to move out. Uh, none of you folks look like you're really dressed for this weather."

"Oh, I'll be fine," said Walks. "But Yellow Horse, maybe you guys should stay in here until we can get you something to wear."

"I hate to sit in here while the soldiers attack my brothers," said Yellow Horse. "But we will wait a little while to see what happens."

The other two said nothing, but Jordan sensed their relief. At least someone in this bus had a little sense...

The ground suddenly appeared through the snow squall. The flyer bumped onto its skids. Three choppers, searchlights ablaze, were approaching. Jordan powered up the flyer's ERASER turret.

Walks got up, glanced at the console, and said, "Hey, I don't think we'll have to hurt anybody here."

"I hope not, sir."

"Let me put that another way. Don't hurt anyone, pilot."

Walks's easy, jocular tone had not changed, but still, Jordan suddenly sat up a little straighter.

"Yes sir."

Walks sauntered back to the main door, opened it, admitting a blast of cold and snow, and left the flyer.

Yellow Horse came forward and plopped into the seat vacated by Endurance. He watched calmly as Walks came into view and stood waiting as a horde of helmeted troopers came charging in.

"You should think of him with more respect, Mister Elcanie," said Yellow Horse.

"Yes sir, sorry, sir," said Jordan, ears burning with embarrassment. "Uh, what will he do out there?"

Yellow Horse gave a little laugh. "I don't really know. Whatever tricks he knows aren't really what we Lakota are supposed to be good at. I'm interested in seeing what he does too."

As the troopers drew near, Walks lifted his arms to the sky and threw back his head. The black eagle painted on the back of his shirt seemed to lift its wings. The sun disk behind the eagle seemed to glow. To Jordan it looked as though Walks were calling out to someone, or releasing a prayer.

And then he was transformed. There was no physical change, yet suddenly he loomed larger and brighter in Jordan's consciousness. Walks staggered slightly, as though he himself hadn't expected this change.

A dozen troopers hurled themselves upon him, toppling him, burying him with their bodies.

Walks flung them off.

And then he stood, again lifting his arms in a beseeching gesture. He took a step or two, and then he tensed in a peculiar way. Jordan found himself wishing that his fiancé were here, so that she too could witness the unforgettable sight of a man lifting into the air under his own power, and then hurtling out of view with a howl of wind that could be heard even here in the cockpit.

"Yes!" shouted Jordan, his fist shooting up. This was the sort of thing he'd joined the Vigil to see!

"That is a very good trick," said Yellow Horse in satisfaction.

Endurance came into range of the flyer's lights, walking steadily and deliberately. He was filthy, covered with dirt and with black stains like oil; his clothing was reduced to rags. Some of the soldiers saw him, shouted at him, inaudibly to those within the flyer. Endurance paid them no heed. They fired their weapons. Multiple bullets slammed into him. Men rushed him, knocking him onto his back. Others fell upon him, holding down every limb. Jordan scowled. His hands moved toward the ERASER controls, but then he remembered the admonition of Walks, and held back.

If Jordan expected to see something as spectacular as the feat of Walks-With-the-Sun, he was disappointed. Endurance strained against his captors, yet he could not overthrow them.

A number of Indians appeared at the periphery of the lights, men and women wrapped in blankets or wearing thin jackets over their painted shirts, jeering, shaking their fists at the troops. The armored soldiers responded by threatening them with their weapons, ordering them to the ground.

Endurance continued to strain.

Harder.

And still harder.

The men who held down his arms were slowly lifted into the air.

Other men rushed up, smashing their rifle butts into Endurance's face. Of this he took no notice.

He raised his knees against the weight of several men. He began to sit up.

It was like watching a tree pushing aside a few cobblestones which sought to impede its growth.

He regained his feet even as men continued to claw and butt at him. He snatched a weapon from one of them, took its barrel in both hands, and bent it so that the bend glowed red. He crushed the ammunition clip between his teeth.

A roaring blur swept by just above their heads, the blast of it knocking everyone aside, including Endurance. Endurance hopped back up. The troopers rolled around in the snow or lay there with their heads wrapped in their arms.

By now Jordan's mouth was hanging open.

Then it became apparent that these soldiers were not willing to be defeated, at least not without first doing as much damage as they could. The sound of distant weapons fire, which had been sporadic, intensified. The Indians ran around in fear, unable to escape the searchlights of the hovering helicopters.

"All right, that's enough!" yelled Jordan, activating the ERASER sight. He'd trained diligently with this weapon and was eager to use it. He targeted the searchlights, darkening them with quick pulses of scarlet energy. While he was at it, he burned out the barrels of their Gatling guns, in case those pilots felt like bringing such vicious weapons to bear against these unarmed people.

"Good job," commented Yellow Horse.

Jordan grinned. Bullets began to pelt their flyer. Jordan believed it was pretty much immune to small arms fire, and so nervously held his ground.

Endurance leaped fifty feet straight up onto the landing skid of one of the choppers. He calmly climbed over the canopy, thrust his hand into the main rotor bearing, then rode the crippled machine down to the ground. Another chopper rolled wildly as that bluish blur returned to thunder past it. Before it could be brought under control, its tail rotor struck the ground and disintegrated. The whole machine yawed violently and landed hard.

Still the gunfire continued to build in intensity. Someone out there was panicking, or desperate, or was just a rotten no-good bastard, thought Jordan. He was on the verge of running out of the flyer and into the fight, to do whatever he could to stop what must be a terrible slaughter.

He was distracted by a distant orange light shining through the falling snow. A blue-white line intersected it and bloomed into an explosion. The fireball fell to earth and was extinguished. The sound of it reached them a few seconds later.

"What was that?" cried Jordan foolishly. It would have helped if he'd been watching his instruments, he realized.

"Looked like an explosion," said Yellow Horse.

Everyone, inside the flyer and out, turned to look in that direction.

The earth shook. A boom greater than thunder rocked the flyer.

And then Jordan was convinced he was about to witness the End and behold the return of his Redeemer, for a new light blazed forth, a whiteness that drove out all shadow, a holy radiance he could not bear to look upon. This was more than light, this was an agony and an uplift for the soul, a purgation, an affirmation of the real existence of virtue and vice.

The light ceased. To Jordan it was as if all light had been snuffed out of the universe. Perhaps everyone present felt the same way, for the shooting had ceased. The three Indians in the flyer chanted softly.

Jordan unbuckled himself and followed them out the door into the wildness of the night. The battle was over. Troopers and Indians staggered about, mingling, seemingly no longer aware of any difference between them. Walks landed nearby, looking keen-eyed but tired, even a little haunted.

The rest of that night was a blur to Jordan's overloaded mind. He spent most of it shuttling badly injured men to hospitals in nearby Rapid City. Some of them, mostly Ghost Dancers who had been shot, surprised Jordan by still being alive at all. Something seemed to have imbued them with a strange vitality that would not easily relinquish the last glow of life.

A dim grey dawn was growing when Jordan next had a moment to collect his thoughts. He gazed out of his cockpit at the battlefield that had been the camp of the Ghost Dancers. The snowfall had ceased. The fallen helicopters looked like great smashed insects. The shacks and tipis of the Dancers, numbering in the hundreds, clustered around the circular area where they'd done their Dancing.

What would happen to these people now? Surely there must come another attack, and fiercer, too.

He leaned against the headrest of his seat and closed his eyes, barely aware of the diminishing activity outside the

flyer's open door. He actually fell asleep, only to be jarred
awake by footsteps entering the flyer. He turned in his chair
to find Walks and Endurance taking seats. Walks now
looked truly exhausted, while Endurance, although filthy,
was otherwise unruffled.

"Hey, Pilot," said Walks. "You did a good job tonight.
We just have to wait for Raintree to finish up, then we can
go home and get some rest. Those of us who need rest, I
mean."

"Ben Raintree? That was *him* out there?"

"Yeah, sure. He's been flashing those lights of his here
and there for hours, especially the green one. The soldiers
managed to clip his flyer with a missile as he was coming
in, otherwise he'd fly himself home."

"Mister Walks, sir…I just wanted to say…what you did
out there last night was really magnificent."

"Huh." Walks sagged back, looking as if he'd be asleep
in a moment. Instead, he sat up again and looked directly at
Jordan. "You know what? I'll tell you the truth. Do you
know what I expected to do last night? I expected to go out
there and get shot down like a dog."

Jordan knew he must be staring at Walks like an idiot,
but there seemed no other response to this.

Walks leaned toward him. "Here's how it is. Before I
joined the Vigil, I thought I was some piece of hot shit
because I'd had a great vision and I could do a few tricks
like floating a few feet in the air. Because of that, I made
myself a religious leader and brought all these people here
to Dance. I told them their shirts would protect them from
enemies. I told them we would Dance the white man right
off our lands. Then I joined the Vigil, although how I got in
I may never know. There I met guys like Raintree, and

Fomalhaut, and even Lori Wu, who can all work miracles by thinking about it for a minute. Even Stingray, who isn't really all that powerful compared to the others, could pound me into paste if he wanted to. Because all I could do was float a little, and that was on my best days. No more visions. Nothing greater. Nobody threw me out, so I stuck around. I prayed that when the time came for battle I would be able to do something, or at least die with honor. I tried to help Valjhar by setting up the *yuwipi*, and wound up getting him captured. Then the call came in that I really dreaded, an attack on my Dancers. I came out to do what I could. I figured I'd just get wiped out, and then not have to worry about it any more."

Walks paused, licked his lips, and took a sip from a water bottle.

"So there I was, standing there, while my people were being pushed around and hurt and terrified all around me. And I thought, if I was ever meant to really be somebody, *now* is the time. I prayed to those spirits who visited me in my vision, asked them for the power to do what everybody expected from me. And they listened. Those spirits, whoever they really were, intervened with the Great Power of the Universe and made me into something greater, for a little while. It's over now. So don't think of me as some big hero. I just hope that if I'm ever called upon to do it again, those spirits will still smile on me. But I don't deserve it. I'm pretty much a fraud. Those shirts didn't work. I expected too much from those poor people. I had them cooped up here for months, freezing, suffering in this pig sty, to Dance, and for what? I don't even know anymore."

"I—I still think of you as a hero, sir."

Walks laughed, not unkindly, but made a dismissive gesture. "You're a good boy, Pilot. But just think of me as a man who squeaked by with a lot of outside help."

Jordan nodded mutely and turned to face forward again. Walks moved back into the cabin. A minute or two later he was snoring in his seat.

Jordan found it impossible to obey Walks's instruction. He couldn't think of any man who'd deliberately faced what he considered inevitable death, for the sake of his people and his honor, to be anything but a hero.

Jordan's throat felt constricted. He looked down at the shoulder of his jacket, at the Vigil patch sewn there, hoping he wouldn't be asked to lift off in the next few minutes, because his vision was too blurred by tears. He still had some work to do, he realized, before he would be fully worthy of wearing that emblem.

Endurance came forward and reoccupied the copilot's seat. He looked extremely somber.

"I also have failed tonight," he whispered. "If I had been carrying the Motionglobe, as I was meant to, no one would have been hurt."

Jordan made no reply. *How have the other Vigil members made out tonight?* he wondered. *Was Motion still held captive?*

Another person entered the flyer. Jordan turned. There was a tall man with a grave, narrow face and iron-grey hair. He carried a wooden staff and wore a grey jacket over white pants and boots. The gaze of his big grey-green eyes came to rest on him.

A wall of some undefined power preceded him into the flyer.

"Hello there," he said quietly. "I'm Ben Raintree."

"Jordan Elcanie. Pilot." He failed to think of anything else to add.

"Jordan, if you don't mind, I think we'd all appreciate a ride to the Pearl and Spire. It's been a long night, for all of us, except our friend Endurance here, of course. I expect we'll soon be leading a force back here to transport these people to safety."

Jordan wiped his eyes and turned to the controls, grateful to have been given a simple task he felt competent to execute.

Chapter 14

The Neo-Men

Fomalhaut, hovering ten miles above what appeared to be a typical Army base, studied it with every means at his command. His first flash of insight about this place had come when the Lakota *yuwipi* ceremony produced an extraordinary smoothing of the quantum flow, through which Fomalhaut's mind could quest with unusual ease. Now that he was physically present, his scrutiny was only further enhanced.

Both the tools of his own mind and the many sensors in his exploration suit revealed surprises. A nondescript warehouse-like building extended below ground for many levels, expanding as it went, a subterranean pyramid.

And yet, for all the clarity with which he beheld its many laboratories—with all their plundered, salvaged, and extrapolated technology—the hidden complex retained a corner into which he could not peer by any means. There was no mistaking it: this psychic blind spot must mean the Americans had developed a method of confusing the local quantum field. He could only hope it didn't mean they'd also devised any more dangerous technologies. He certainly couldn't foresee such a thing, not with that blind spot muddling the pathways of the future.

One vital fact, however, was not hidden: Valjhar Cor was still imprisoned within the depths of the base. He had not been moved. Ducanis had lied about that, probably to prevent the Vigil from descending on the base *en masse*.

Very well, Fomalhaut would do his utmost to assure that this deception bore no fruit for its perpetrators.

Fomalhaut commanded his suit to hover in place, made his helmet opaque, shut down all sensors, quieted his mind, and bent his full mental scrutiny on Valjhar, perceiving him as he sat despondently in his cell. Fomalhaut thus saw him more clearly and completely than he could have with his eyes.

Fomalhaut shuddered; his remote vision faltered and faded. He was, he admitted, hampered by an atypical and unwanted emotion. Beyond all other things, he hated and despised the current government of the United States of America. All his dealings with these people had impressed upon him the limitless extent of their ignorance, their easy treachery, their small-mindedness, their corruption. They were not truly dedicated to the welfare of their own citizens. While they'd been elected to serve and represent all the people of the United States, their actions and policies showed that in truth they served only themselves, and those most like themselves.

To a person raised under the functioning ideal of Constructive Anarchy, these attitudes were not only abhorrent, they were practically proof of insanity. They showed a lack of mindfulness of the future, and a complete moral degeneracy.

The very ground of reality surrounding the planet Earth in this era was colored and darkened by the unfettered emotions of its billions of minds, with hatred among the most potent and pervasive. Fomalhaut was aware of the danger to his judgment and effectiveness these influences presented, and which must be resisted.

Very well then. He would play out this charade which had been set out for him by his opponents. Then, when the moment was right, they would be exposed to many surprises.

Fomalhaut dropped down, alighting before the guards who stood at the entrance to the disguised research structure. They were startled and overawed by his sudden appearance, as he'd intended.

"Good evening. I am Fomalhaut of the Vigil. I have come to meet with Sard Ducanis."

The gate sergeant said, "Er, yes sir, I'll just announce your arrival and someone will be out to escort you in a moment."

A junior officer and some minor civilian functionaries appeared and led him inside. Their minds concealed no duplicity toward him, as he discerned with some difficulty as they drew nearer to the zone of quantum confusion. They entered an elevator and descended many levels, bringing them still nearer to that obscuring Zone. The psychic blindness it caused was enough of a reason for its existence, Fomalhaut surmised. Their precaution might hamper him, but it would prove insufficient to thwart him. He could still think, and the multitudinous functions of his exploration suit were still available to him.

He was led to a meeting room on a level just above that which contained Valjhar's cell. Within this room was a group of typical government officials: mostly white men, well past their brief physical prime, all wearing similar suits of expensive clothing. One of these men rose from his seat at the table, advanced smiling, and said: "Hello, Fomalhaut. I'm Sard Ducanis, Secretary of the Exterior."

This man held out his hand stiffly, his smile somehow fixed and expectant. Fomalhaut hesitated. Something odd was happening here.

Another man, a severe, saturnine character, gave a brittle laugh and came forward.The first man withdrew, his expression relaxing into a guarded neutrality.

The second man said, "Fomalhaut, you must excuse my assistant. Sometimes he's prone to making little jokes. I'm Ducanis."

He too held out his hand. Fomalhaut ignored it, of no mind to participate in any such hypocritical gesture of amity, the same false gesture that had doomed T'Ukudu. These men were testing him, he realized. They sought to determine whether he could tell whether he was hearing a lie. At the moment, he could not. The minds around him were perceptible only as blurs.

Ducanis withdrew his hand and said, "I'd like to introduce you to a few other friends of ours. I believe you will find their identity surprising."

Suddenly Fomalhaut could not breathe. Something had happened to his suit's environmental system. It wasn't producing air, or perhaps it was producing poison. He didn't know which; his thoughts were being pounded down by an opaque confusion. The minds around him were perceptible again, and others besides, great burning minds, but he had no attention to spare for them. All he knew was that he was suffocating. There was only one cure: he must deactivate his bubble helmet. He did so. For the first time in many years the air of the outside world entered his lungs, but still his agony and confusion did not abate.

"As I expected," he heard Ducanis say. "Fire at his head until he goes down."

Stingray, approaching the Virginia base in his small black stealth flyer, detected Aureus, who was closing in on the same target from a slightly different direction.

Stingray scowled. He never enjoyed interacting with that intransigent thing. He never had, and still less so now that he remembered, dimly yet clearly, how it had dogged his friends from one galaxy to another over a period of years.

He shrugged. There was no help for it. He keyed the communicator.

"Stingray to Aureus. Looks like we both had the same idea. Please join me in my flyer so we can coordinate our efforts."

He drummed his fingers on the console, awaiting a reply. Aureus could easily tell him to mind his own business and warn him to stay out of its way. That would certainly be a characteristic response.

"Very well," came the reply.

Surprised, yet not entirely reassured, Stingray slowed the flyer and opened its starboard gull-wing door to admit the robot, which slipped into the seat beside him. Stingray closed the door and resumed his former speed.

"So," said Stingray cautiously after long moments of uncomfortable silence. "I'm going to this base in case Fomalhaut needs backup. I don't trust the American government one bit. Is that your plan as well?"

"No. I go to retrieve Valjhar from captivity."

"Valjhar? But they told us he'd been moved."

"I have tracked him to that base. They lied. As you noted, this group of humans is not trustworthy."

"I see. And what about Pimsie?"

"Pimsehkia Flam is not present at the base. She is in transit and difficult to locate with precision."

"All right, Aureus. If you know Valjhar is still there, I'm betting Fomalhaut knows it too. I propose that we bide our time, and give Fomalhaut every chance to extract Valjhar on his own. Are you willing to do that?"

"As long as Valjhar remains unharmed, and the elapsed time does not become excessive."

"Agreed. Thank you, Aureus."

"Please do not call me that. My name is Vela Flamaxamanda."

Stingray's eyebrows shot up at that. This was one of the most shocking things he'd ever heard. Never, in all the years he'd known this thing, had it ever revealed any sense of personal identity. It had offered no name and acknowledged no need for one. "Aureus" was merely an invention of Fomalhaut's, something to prevent them from referring to it as "Hey, robot."

"You...wish me to call you Vela?" he asked in a gingerly manner.

"That was certainly the implication, yes."

Again Stingray barely concealed a start. Suddenly he felt unable to navigate the unsuspected shoals of this creature's waters.

"I—learned something of your history as a living woman from Valjhar recently. But I—didn't think—it still had much to do with who and what you are today." Stingray winced; he had not phrased this as delicately as he would have liked.

"It does not. However, the name remains valid. If I am to be referred to by any name, let it be that one."

Stingray had a weird sense that he had just, for the first time, related to Aureus, however briefly and incompletely, as though it were a person rather than a thing. Having no idea how to continue this process, he lapsed into silence, which seemed to suit Aureus—or Vela—as well.

Glancing at the small, golden form in the seat beside him, Stingray wondered how he could possibly have missed the obviously female contours of its body. True, it was flat chested, but adding non-functional breast-shapes to the mechanical body of an emotionless creature would obviously be fatuous.

They arrived over the base. Stingray parked the flyer high above the altitude limits of any ordinary aircraft, then sat monitoring its sensors and communications. The stealth flyer's low-powered maneuvering beams were covered by multiple baffles, so its only emission was in the infra-red, hard to detect from any distance.

They waited. Aureus barely moved. Stingray fidgeted, scanning all known bands of human radio communication, looking for any news of Fomalhaut's negotiations with the Americans. Surely they must send frequent updates to their president, but he supposed it was too much to hope that it would be through an open broadcast.

The base appeared quiet, displaying no sign of alarm or any unusual activity.

Yet Stingray was uneasy. He tried to communicate with Fomalhaut via a quantum radio signal, which no one else except Perturbare could possibly intercept. Fomalhaut's exploration suit returned a signal of acknowledgment, but there was no word from Fomalhaut himself. Stingray wished he knew how to monitor the suit's telemetry, if any. He even tried thinking a message to Fomalhaut, but that also brought no response. He was certainly no telepath.

A pale light appeared on the easternmost edge of the world.

"I'm getting a bad feeling, Bad things could be happening down there as we sit here twiddling our thumbs."

"Then let us act."

Somehow those simple words crystallized Stingray's mental swirl of uncertainty and doubt into resolve.

"Yes. Let us act."

He moved into the small compartment in the rear of the flyer, where he donned his newest and most powerful battle armor. It was black, gleaming with highlights of blue-green, his favored colors. It protected him from crown to toe. Mounted on the back was the smallest, most compact tachyon pile the Vigil knew how to make, powering an array of weapons. Only someone of Stingray's strength could have stood up and walked in that armor. It was the closest thing he could devise to Fomalhaut's fabulous indestructible suit.

Wearing it, he could no longer fit into the pilot's seat, so he spoke over the shoulder of Aureus.

"Vela...I'm going to ask you to let me go into that base by myself."

"That is ridiculous. Even with your armor, I am many times more resistant to damage than you are."

"That's true. The problem is, though...you tend to deal with these situations with a certain lack of finesse. You confront an obstacle, your Third Eye opens, and the obstacle is destroyed. That's fine for some situations, but I hope to reach Valjhar and Fomalhaut without wiping out hundreds of people, and possibly bringing the whole place down as well."

"What then would you have me do?"

"You can be very useful. Act as a distraction. Attack the rest of the base, destroy their weapons and communications, draw off their troops. Don't kill them. And especially, cut off electrical power to the building our friends are in. Which one is it?"

Aureus indicated the main console display. "Valjhar is deep within this structure, twenty levels underground. Very well, I accept your plan. But if I determine you are in danger, or in danger of failing, I will intervene."

"All right then. Just in case they decide to be reasonable down there, please don't do anything until you hear from me. And before I go, one last thing."

"Yes?"

"In the time I've known you, you've been torn to shreds, reassembled, then beaten to a pulp and repaired again, as best we could. You're not as indestructible as you once were. Be careful about which weapons you step in front of."

"I shall. I have good data on the extent of my durability."

Stingray opened the rear door and bailed out, flying by virtue of the propulsion diodes built into his armor. On the way down he had a few moments to muse on the most remarkable fact that he had just urged Aureus to caution, almost as he would have for a friend. He spent the rest of the descent nursing a rueful grin as he considered just how momentous a task he was about to undertake, and how unpredictable its outcome.

He landed heavily before the guard station at the main entrance to the concealed facility, deliberately startling the men, unaware that these same men had been similarly alarmed by Fomalhaut just a few hours before. He was also unaware of just how intimidating a figure he was, huge and black in the night.

"I'm Stingray," came his sharp-edged voice. "I've come for Fomalhaut."

Someone slapped a panic button. The entire base seemed to go berserk, erupting with lights, howling with sirens and klaxons. Squads of armed men burst from nearby buildings and ran in his direction.

"Should I assume you've decided not to admit me?" he asked dryly. He activated a communications circuit. "Aureus, I mean Vela, please begin your attack."

And then a radiance blazed forth that made the puny lights of the base seem like shadows. The energies of Aureus, stored as stressed and twisted space in batteries no one on Earth understood, beamed out in a deadly incandescent line from the airborne robot, itself too small and distant to be seen, slicing through whatever it encountered. When those energies were depleted, out licked the pale, ethereal tachyon beam, replenishing the robot's stores by converting matter directly into energy, a radiation no form of matter could possibly resist.

Stingray took a few moments to watch this display appreciatively, the lenses in his helmet filtering out the brilliance. Then he turned back to the guards, who seemed paralyzed by what was happening to their base. Stingray took advantage of this by heading toward the door. His movement seemed to revive some of the nearer soldiers. "Halt!" they cried. "Down on the ground! We will fire upon you!" and a whole litany of other commands and imprecations which they had been trained to utter at anyone daring to defy their power and authority.

Stingray merely laughed, pushing through them as though they were children. Their sheer numbers began to impede him, therefore he directed a little of the electrical output of his tachyon pile to the surface of his armor. They yelped and fell back, formed a line behind him, and fired into his back. The impacts made it harder to keep his balance, but it was worse for them. Their bullets bounced off, deprived of much of their energy, but still dangerous. A few men fell, wounded.

Stingray, disturbed by this, turned and shouted, "Quit shooting, you idiots! You're only hurting yourselves. Don't you fools ever learn?" Some sergeant or lieutenant made this official policy by bawling out his own version of the order. The soldiers retreated, leaving Stingray to try the door in peace, or so he thought. A bigger impact smacked him against the steel door with a loud noise and a flash of light. His ears rang. He turned. His night vision system revealed a man with a small rocket launcher standing a hundred meters away.

"You like noise? Here, have some noise." Stingray channeled the full power of his tachyon pile into the armor's gloves and raised them, thinking that it would be nice to strike the base of the concrete structure on which the man was standing.

Lightning flashed, many times more powerful than Stingray could have managed with his natural bioelectricity. A chunk of concrete exploded beneath the shooter, toppling him. Thunder boomed and rolled and echoed.

Greatly pleased, Stingray turned, gloves still electrified, and gripped the wheel that sealed the vault-like main door. The current, shorting in the steel wheel, heated it to a bright red, weakening it enough for Stingray to rip it free and fling it away. Unfortunately, the result of this wasn't as useful as he'd hoped it would be. The door's mechanism was disabled by the heat and the loss of the wheel. Chagrined, Stingray hurled himself against it, but even five hundred pounds of Stingray plus two hundred pounds of armor weren't enough to knock down that door. Bullets began to *spang* off his armor again. He knew he would do well to get inside before a tank came roaring up. Flashes and detonations from Aureus's distant assault rocked him.

Stingray lifted off and settled onto the roof. He diverted his armor's power to the ERASER mounted on his left forearm, then changed his mind and activated the cryogun on his right. With this he froze a patch of the roof to the temperature of liquid helium. Air began to freeze onto it, turning it into a smoking garden of exotic crystals. Stingray leaped up, crashing down onto and through it, into the chamber below. "Thanks, Ben, wherever you are," he muttered.

The room was deserted. Stingray had only a moment to survey it before the lights went out. He activated his night vision, which revealed nothing until he also used his IR illuminator. He found the door, which was locked. One thrust from his shoulder sent its smashed remnants into the opposite wall of the corridor outside. A few non-uniformed people saw him and bolted. The lights came back on. Stingray moved through the corridors unopposed until he found a stairway. Down he went, counting the landings.

There was a rumble and the stairs shook; the lights went out again, and stayed out.

Stingray couldn't help being oddly delighted with this situation. Here he was, prowling through an enemy base, thwarting people whom he loathed, on a rescue mission, actually accomplishing something. He tried again to contact Fomalhaut, whose persistent silence dampened his tendency to inappropriate mirth. The exploration suit sent back its acknowledgment. By now the comm equipment in Stingray's armor was able to get a fix on that signal. Following it, he emerged onto the sixteenth level, hoping both captives were being held in the same place. That level was dark, except for a few battery-operated emergency lamps which provided plenty of light for Stingray's marine-adapted vision. It was also curiously deserted. He heard distant footsteps, but encountered no one. He came to a door which ought to conceal Fomalhaut. Even here there was no one, no guard, nothing. Puzzled and a little apprehensive, Stingray removed his helmet and pressed his ear to the door. He heard nothing within.

He replaced his helmet, opened the door, stepped inside, and closed the door behind him.

This room too was dimly lit. It was a laboratory, filled with instruments and machines with metal housings painted with a grey crackle finish. It all looked very primitive to someone who had once lived among the technology of Old Rral.

Stretched over an armature was Fomalhaut's exploration suit. Fomalhaut himself was not in evidence.

Stingray gasped. To his knowledge, Fomalhaut has never removed that suit in all the years he'd lived on Earth. To see it hanging empty was like finding Fomalhaut's flayed skin stretched on a rack. He couldn't imagine what could have compelled Fomalhaut to take it off. Stingray's fear for his friend was suddenly multiplied many times. More than that, he felt an eerie tremor. Fomalhaut was now exposed. Someone, somewhere, now knew what Fomalhaut truly was. Stingray was unsure he wanted that secret revealed, even to himself.

Trembling, Stingray removed the suit from the armature. It was a bulky thing. The fabric itself was like a film of silky glass, but the collar, belt, epaulets, and other fittings were solid and awkward. Stingray could have used a large shopping bag just then. Lacking one, he tucked the suit under one arm.

He heard a commotion out in the corridor. Without thinking he smashed through the door, confronting a squad of soldiers like some great thundering monster. The foremost fired at him. Stingray strode through the bullets, raised his free arm and smashed the soldiers aside with one blow. Bones broke, blood spurted. Stingray had at last fallen into a rage. Let the army medics care for them! "Clear out of my way before I break you all in half!" he roared.

The few who could still retreat did so. Stingray turned and clanged his way back to the staircase. With any luck, he would find Fomalhaut confined somewhere near Valjhar on the twentieth level. He ran down the stairs and burst out onto that level, making no more attempt at stealth, feeling no more inclination to view this as a fun adventure.

The entire level seemed to be a gleaming dungeon fashioned of stainless steel and acrylic. Stingray stalked down its corridors, peering into each darkened cell as he passed. Most were empty; some were occupied by people whom he didn't recognize. He paused before one, looking in at a disconsolate, balding, aging man and wondering what he had done to land in this predicament. He wore an orange jump suit and was sitting on a mean shelf of a bed. He looked up, starting in terror at the sight of Stingray standing there in his black armor and bulbous-lensed helmet. Then he noticed the silver Stingray emblem that was prominent on the armor's torso. His entire demeanor changed. He leaned forward. His dull, hopeless eyes grew keen, almost fervent. For some reason Stingray was moved to remove his helmet. At the sight of his face, the prisoner assumed a fierce grin, transforming from a defeated man to an old hawk.

Though intrigued by this man, Stingray felt an urgent need to hasten his search for Fomalhaut and Valjhar.

Yet somehow he could not ignore this man. He looked around. He was separated from his cell by a thick transparent partition set with its own steel door. The keepers of this human zoo could pass down a sub-corridor between the cell's steel bars and the acrylic wall. The steel door was locked. Stingray chilled the transparent barrier and shoved his elbow through it. Stepping over the remains, he prepared to melt the cell's bars with his ERASER.

"Can't you just bend the bars?" said the prisoner, sounding oddly eager.

"Who the hell are you?" returned Stingray.

"That doesn't really matter right now. I know you didn't come here looking for me. You should get going. It's enough for me that I've seen your face."

Stingray fixed him with a quizzical stare. He shrugged, dropped the exploration suit and his own helmet, grabbed a pair of bars, and exerted himself. He could indeed bend the bars.

The prisoner barked out laughter. "George Reeves couldn't have done it better!"

"Look, whoever you are, there's a fair bit of confusion around here at the moment. If you're interested in escaping, you'll find some incapacitated soldiers on the sixteenth level, four floors up from here. You won't exactly be inconspicuous in an infantry uniform, but it's better than that prison jumpsuit."

"I'll take that chance. Tell me, Stingray, have you felt any, uh, odd compulsions since you ventured into this place?"

"Huh? Well, I broke you loose without having a clue who you are, and I keep taking my helmet off, which isn't too bright under the circumstances, but other than that, no."

The man nodded slowly. "Good then. Good. But keep that helmet on. Go on, find your teammates."

"Who are you?" repeated Stingray, frowning.

"Just someone who used to work here and who has a tendency to wind up on the wrong side of arguments. My name is Harry Brightman. That won't mean anything to you. Go!"

Stingray gave Brightman one last puzzled look, replaced his helmet, then returned to the main corridor to resume his search of the cells. There were hundreds of them. Stingray wondered who they were all intended for.

At long last he found a cell in which reclined a shadowy figure, whom he recognized with some difficulty. It was Valjhar. It would have been better if he'd found Fomalhaut first (assuming he could have recognized him), but he didn't dare leave Valjhar unattended while he went searching again. He gained entry to Valjhar's cell the same way he had Brightman's. Valjhar was disoriented, barely conscious, and nearly naked.

"Motion!" called Stingray, remembering at the last second not to use Valjhar's real name.

"Stingray?" replied Valjhar weakly, looking up with an expression of raw pain and loss.

"Yup," said Stingray past the lump in his throat. "I've come to get you out of here. You're in the Vigil now, you know, and can expect that kind of treatment from us. Where's the Motionglobe?"

"I don't know. They took it."

"Okay, we'll get it back later. Right now we've got to leave while we still can. We have to find Fomalhaut."

"Stingray...be careful of...those creatures," said Valjhar as he slowly got to his feet.

"What creatures?"

"I don't know what they are. They may be aliens. They made me do things. They assaulted my mind. They are brutal telepaths."

Stingray bit his lip, considering. In this condition, Valjhar would be an impediment to his search for Fomalhaut. Nor was he likely to be much help against these "creatures", whatever they might be.

"Stingray to Vela. Do you have a fix on me?"

"I do. You are with Valjhar." Luckily, this reply could only be heard by Stingray.

"Yes. Please get down here to us as soon as possible."

"I am coming."

The floor shook beneath them. Metal groaned and panes of acrylic snapped loudly.

Stingray grimaced. "Motion...put this on."

"What is it?"

"It's Fomalhaut's exploration suit. You're likely to need its protection."

"His—" Valjhar's eyes widened as he fumbled with the suit. "What's happened to him?"

"He came in here to negotiate for your release. It seems he was betrayed and captured."

Now Valjhar looked even more pained. "I committed a great folly in coming here alone."

Stingray was greatly conflicted about this turn of events. He had hoped to return the suit to Fomalhaut right away, but Valjhar's need was more immediate.

Getting him into the suit was a challenge, involving the discovery that the collar hinged open and opened a previously undetectable seam down the back. Only then could Valjhar draw it on. Stingray snapped the collar closed and the seam disappeared. The suit draped loosely over Valjhar's relatively slight physique.

"Better try to activate the helmet, Motion."

"How?"

"I don't know. Try thinking it on."

This brought no result.

"All right. Never mind."

A glare and a gust of heat from around the corner announced the arrival of Aureus. A moment later the robot appeared, clattering into view with its usual rapid, sinuous gait.

"Vela, please take our friend Motion to the flyer. Wait there in case I need further support."

"I wish to take him far from this place at once."

Stingray almost started yelling, but bit his tongue and took a moment to compose himself.

"I know you do; so do I. But he's all right, and I must stay and locate Fomalhaut before they have a chance to get him out of this base. Surely you realize how important this is to the Vigil. You are a member of the Vigil, aren't you?"

"I am primarily a creature of Rral."

Stingray was preparing to offer whatever threats or coercion he could think of when Valjhar intervened.

"Vela...I expect you to act as a member of the Vigil. We will remain nearby in the flyer."

Aureus turned its lambent gaze from Stingray to Valjhar and said: "Very well. Come, Valjhar, let us go."

Stingray rolled his eyes, but there was no help for the robot's slip now. At least he had gotten what he needed from Aureus. "Vela! When you have him safely in the flyer, please get him out of the exploration suit. I may ask you to bring it to me, if I find Fomalhaut."

"I'll remove it myself," said Valjhar weakly. "It feels cold and strange."

Aureus lifted Valjhar and stole away, leaving Stingray alone.

"Well, that's one down and one to go," he muttered. By now he was convinced that Fomalhaut was nowhere to be found on this vacant, undefended prison level. That left an awful lot of the installation to be searched. Around a corner he found the site of Aureus's entry—a tunnel bored all the way from the surface. At its distant terminus he saw a single star twinkle briefly before sidereal motion carried it out of view.

"Stingray to Vela. Have you reached the flyer?"

"Yes, we are awaiting word from you."

"Do you have any means of detecting Fomalhaut from there?"

"Not without his suit. My biosensors are specific to Rralian signatures."

"Do you detect—anything unusual at all? Any sort of strange or partial life readings?"

"No. However, as I was on my way to you, I noted an elevated ambient temperatures on the thirteenth level down. This may indicate a concentration of living beings."

"Good. That's something to go on. Thanks. Stand by, Vela."

Stingray lifted off into the shaft Aureus had formed, which was quite large enough to accommodate him. He halted at Level Thirteen, ready for anything, or so he hoped. Noises reached him from every direction. The helmet limited his peripheral vision. It was an irritant. It seemed stuffy as well, as though the armor's ventilation system were faulty. He was tempted to remove the helmet, then stopped short. This was peculiar. He had been warned of coercive telepaths; he had been warned to leave his helmet in place.

Now his nose began to itch. He laughed loudly. "Sorry, it's staying on," he announced.

This level was cavernous, its full extent invisible in the spotty emergency lighting. Placed here and there on the steel decking were polygonal dome-like structures, each about forty feet across and fifteen high. Four of them were visible from Stingray's position. The nearest two were unattended. A few men stood around the entrance to the third. The fourth, and most distant, was guarded by over a hundred heavily armed soldiers.

So far no one seemed aware of Stingray's presence. He paused to think things over. Surely his opponents must realize by now that soldiers could not stop him. He could fight his way into that dome, breaking many men in the process, and once inside, no doubt fight and injure others besides.

And in so doing, he might give his foes time to slip Fomalhaut out of one of the other domes, or even away from the base entirely, if Aureus was not vigilant.

Yes...but it would be so satisfying to rip his way through those men...to smash them aside like the ignorant pygmies they were, and then find and rescue Fomalhaut, who was surely being held in the most heavily defended spot...

Stingray realized he was breathing hard, his teeth clenched, his thoughts lost in savage impulses. He shook his head. This was irrational; this was not him. *Nice try,* he thought. *Nice try.*

He steeled his mind and his focus. Acting on his original hunch, he charged the dome before which stood only a few men. He was through them before they even had a chance to raise their weapons. The small horde before the fourth dome advanced. Stingray tried the door leading into the dome: locked. He pounded on it hard enough to leave dents.

"You might as well open up. You know I'll have it down, one way or another."

A few men tackled him from behind. He shrugged them off, then drew back his fist to make a serious assault on the door.

The door slid into its frame with a screech. Stingray leaped into the chamber within, which was brightly lit. The door closed behind him.

Stingray took a few moments to assess the scene before him. About a dozen humans were present, mostly army officers. In addition to them were seven...creatures.

They were humanoid, of varying ages and sizes, ranging from seeming adolescents who stood over six feet tall to a child who might be around eight years old. Two of them were clearly female. The sex of the younger ones was indeterminate. They were uniformly golden of skin and beautifully made. Their large heads carried caps of very fine hair which was either white, golden, or a pearly grey. Their facial and cranial bone structure was unusual, partially to accommodate their phenomenal eyes. These were huge, dark, and lidless, set into their faces like great liquid lenses, protected by rounded brow ridges.

They were dressed in uniform blue jumpsuits marked with Greek letters.

"You can hold it right there, Stingray," said one of the officers, startling him, as he had almost forgotten the presence of human beings in his rapt appraisal of these seven others. He reluctantly took his eyes off them. An army colonel had drawn his sidearm and was pointing it, not at Stingray, but into a steel tank. "You make one hostile move and your friend Fomalhaut's magnificent brain will be scrambled."

"One word from me, Colonel, and Aureus will finish the job on this installation and everyone in it."

"What will that achieve for you? You'll be dead, and Fomalhaut as well. As for us, we have other Neo-men at other sites, far from here," said the officer, glancing aside at the seven.

"Neo-men, eh? I hope they appreciate learning they're expendable."

"Our Neo-men owe us their lives, even the very existence of their race. I don't doubt their loyalty."

"So—they're sort of a Human self-improvement project, I take it? It's badly needed, I must say."

"Quite a successful one at that," said the eldest of the Neo-men, a female.

Something about the rich, controlled tone of her voice was very familiar. Moving slowly, Stingray took a few steps closer to the tank to peer over its rim.

Lying there submerged in a foot of water was another Neo-man. This one was larger than any, with a noble brow and hair as fine as spun sugar.

And so Stingray for the first time beheld the face of Fomalhaut.

Stingray's heart was pounding. "You've drowned him," he said dangerously.

"No," said the Colonel. "He's able to breathe in salt water, as you are. We've added a sedative to the water until we're confident we can contain him when he awakens."

"What are those bruises on his head and neck?"

"The marks of anesthetic bullets. He's all right."

Stingray gave a discordant chuckle. "So. You made them yourselves."

"Made what?"

"Your own successors. These Neo-men. Ever since Fomalhaut came to this world, claiming to represent a species that would one day succeed yours, you've been flailing around trying to deny it, to prevent it. And then, as it turns out, you yourselves invented that very species in your genetics labs. Very funny. Very ironic." Stingray laughed again. "Were you even aware of this fact while you were doing it?"

"Some of us were," said the Colonel grudgingly. "I for one wasn't."

"It won't come to that," said the female Neo-teen evenly. "We've no wish to supplant anyone."

"Do any of you people have names?" snapped Stingray.

"I'm Colonel Frank Harmon."

"Thanks, but I was really wondering about your wards here."

"Our family name is Blue," said the girl. "I am Alpha, and these are Beta, Gamma, Delta, Epsilon, Zeta, and Eta."

"With your so-called names and color clearly marked on your outfits. Probably you all look alike to your creators."

"Don't be ridiculous," said Harmon unconvincingly.

Stingray looked Fomalhaut's naked form up and down. "No wonder he always hid his face. He knew someone in this time period must be designing and creating his people, or at least imagining them. He knew he couldn't show himself without prejudicing that process."

"Are you saying even *you* didn't know his appearance until this moment?" said Harmon.

"Yeah. Oops. Guess you blew your chance to pass him off as one of your own Neo-men, huh?" Stingray's gaze paused at Fomalhaut's crotch, which exhibited no external genitalia...much like himself.

Suddenly many fragmentary bits of information fell into a coherent and obvious whole.

"And me...I'm Model A, aren't I?"

Harmon shrugged. "I know nothing about that."

"Nor do we," said Alpha. "But it would not be surprising. Your resistance to our telepathic influence indicates that some cerebro-quantum functions have been incorporated into your brain."

"Yet apparently Fomalhaut had no such resistance."

"He was confused by the base's quantum telepathy shielding. And he was not expecting us."

"Stingray, it's time for you to leave," said Harmon decisively. "You've had all the victory you're going to get here today. You've uncovered the existence of our Neo-men and trashed our base. You rescued your friend Motion, but that's no loss. Without his little magic ball, he's nothing very special. You even retrieved Fomalhaut's suit. That's a disappointment. We'd hoped to learn a lot from that."

Stingray snorted. "It wouldn't have done you any good. Not even Perturbare could learn all its secrets. You don't have the tools needed to make the tools to even begin to understand it. And as for the Motionglobe—a fat lot of good it'll do you, too."

"And less for you. Be that as it may, you won't leave here with Fomalhaut, not while he's alive, anyway. Go."

Stingray scowled, aware that his indecision could not be seen through his helmet. These people would kill Fomalhaut whenever his utility to them was exhausted, or if he became a threat. Fomalhaut would try to subvert these young Neo-men; that would certainly not be tolerated. Perhaps it would be best if Stingray made his move here and now, while he still knew where Fomalhaut was, even if it got him killed. It might save his friend much grief and pain.

And yet—

Perhaps he was underestimating Fomalhaut.

He stiffened and sucked in his breath. A familiar voice sounded in his head.

Stingray, my good friend. I am moved by your valiant rescue attempt, but you must leave. I will take my chances here.

Stingray blinked at Fomalhaut, who gave every appearance of being unconscious, an eerie semblance given his great lidless eyes.

The Blue family did not twitch.

Stingray felt a strange and tentative new hope and confidence.

"I'm going. But don't think you've really accomplished anything here tonight. The time is near when you'll all behold the Vigil, in spades."

On the other side of the Moon, Brainchild One said: *Doctor, the Vigil's attack on the American base has opened its main structure to the outside. Enough of our airborne nanodevices have entered it for me to reconstruct an audio signal of Stingray's dealings with the Americans.*

"Let's hear it!" said Possum Perturbare.

When they had heard Stingray take his leave, Perturbare whistled. "Holy shit!"

Indeed.

"That Stingray—he really surprises me at times. Look at all he accomplished, and it didn't even involve any swimming. Say, Brainchild...do you suppose it's one of those Neo-man brains you're building in your vat?"

I do indeed. Doctor, will you do nothing to help Fomalhaut?

"Huh? No, oh no. I have confidence in him. In all of them. They'll find a way to save him."

Chapter 15

Stingray Steps Up

Lori Wu's flyer made a shaky descent through the whitefield concealing the main hangar. She had been summoned back to the Pearl and Spire by Stingray for an emergency meeting.

During the recent attacks, two American battle groups had prowled around the Sea Creche, just close enough to keep Tara, Lori, and everyone else on edge, but not close enough to launch or provoke an attack. The ships were still in the area, but Stingray had insisted Lori leave and come to the meeting. He had never sounded so urgent. Lori was very much afraid.

She proceeded immediately to the Vigil's main meeting room in the Spire. Awaiting her there were Stingray, Ben Raintree, Aureus, Walks, Valjhar Cor, and Endurance.

Fomalhaut was absent.

With a chilled heart, Lori sank into her chair without saying a word.

"Lori," said Stingray. "Fomalhaut has been captured by the Americans. He's without his exploration suit, at their mercy, and facing am unknown number of telepaths like himself." He went on to describe the full circumstances of the event, including many details which were unknown to Raintree, Walks, and Endurance. "Now we must decide how to proceed."

Lori sat aghast. Of all the members of the Vigil, Fomalhaut had long been her mentor, hero, and patron. To her, Fomalhaut *was* the Vigil. She had difficulty conceiving of the Vigil continuing without him.

"How could you do it, Stingray?" she blurted. "How could you just leave him there? How is it that you managed to get Valjhar out, but not Fomalhaut?"

"Because Stingray saw me first, Lori," said Valjhar. "If he had not, the chances are that neither of us would have been rescued. Not only that, if Stingray hadn't acted on his own initiative to follow Fomalhaut, not only would we both still be captives, but you others would have no knowledge of our situation."

Lori waved her hands. It seemed to her that they were ignoring, or discounting, Aureus. "I find that impossible to believe. With all of us sitting here, all this power, why can't we go and demand they hand him over to us! What if we threatened to destroy the White House and the Pentagon?" Lori could hardly believe these words were coming out of her mouth.

"Aside from the innate barbarism of such an act, Fomalhaut would surely be killed in reprisal," said Raintree calmly.

"Then what are we going to do?"

"That's what we're here to figure out. And we'll do it with the help of our obvious new leader—Stingray."

"Thanks, Ben," said Stingray in a grim, tired voice. "My first, and only, act as leader of the Vigil is to turn over the leadership to the truly obvious candidate—Valjhar Cor."

"What?" shrieked Lori.

"Huh," said Walks.

Valjhar, looking exhausted and beaten, jerked back in his chair. "What? Don't be ridiculous. You consider me a formal member of the Vigil? Even if you do, I've been with you for mere weeks, while you've been here from the beginning. What have I achieved in my time with you? Nothing."

"Valjhar," said Stingray, "you led the Space Mariners across four galaxies. You proved your qualifications for leadership in the incident that led you to return to Earth to form the Para-Men. Our encounter with the Dark Star."

"Yes...the incident that led you and the rest of us to the parting of our ways. The incident that ultimately led only to death, disaster and defeat."

Lori spoke again. "Stingray, you know I still feel a certain—affinity—with the Vigil staff, seeing as I was once one of them. I can tell you this. Of those few who know who 'Motion' really is, most accept having him among us. But if you announce that Valjhar Cor, the leader of the Para-men, our legendary enemy, is now in charge of the Vigil, a lot of us are going to start wondering what we've been working for all along."

"But our goals are now the same as those of the Para-men!" snapped Stingray, irritated at such irrationality.

"I know. But put Valjhar in charge, with Fomalhaut missing, and some will wonder if that wasn't Valjhar's secret plan all along."

"And what will happen if Valjhar's true identity becomes known to the world?" said Raintree. "Valjhar Cor, once again seeking to dominate mankind. No. It cannot be."

Walks spoke up. "You know I think Valjhar is a cool guy. I like him. But I can't see him working out as leader either."

Stingray sat back, silent and brooding.

"They're all correct," said Valjhar. "I'll help you however I can. But remember, my main intention is to find

Pimsehkia and somehow remove us both from the affairs of this planet. You, Stingray, must lead the Vigil."

"Pimsie has been working with the Americans for years," scowled Stingray. "By your own account, she still is. What makes you think she wants to be removed?"

"I don't know. Until I hear an explanation for her actions from her own lips, I will continue to seek her out."

Stingray nodded. "What's your view of the matter of leadership, Vela?"

The mere fact that Stingray had asked the opinion of Aureus, let alone that he had called the robot Vela, startled more than one person sitting at that table.

The fact that Aureus offered a meaningful reply startled the rest.

"If Valjhar must involve himself in your affairs, then I would prefer that he serve as leader. However, I believe you also have the capacity to be an effective leader. I will follow you."

They all goggled briefly at this before continuing.

"Thank you. What do you say, Endurance?" asked Stingray.

"I say you must lead. But I too am glad to have Valjhar nearby."

"And so am I. All right then. I'll lead the Vigil through this emergency. And here's what I think we ought to do."

Chapter 16

Vega

Perturbare set out a platter of taco ingredients and tortilla shells. It was one of the few things he knew how to make, and he hoped it would strike Marisol as an appropriate celebratory dinner.

She eyed the table wryly. "You, cooking? What's the occasion?"

"There are two," he said cheerfully. "First of all, my new TV series, *The Night Land*, is complete and in the can, so to speak. Ready to air."

"Oh, a new TV show. Great. How wonderful," she said with a tired lack of enthusiasm. "Do you think I'll like it?"

"Actually, I don't think you'll get a chance to see it."

Her dark eyes locked on his, full of sudden alertness and suspicion.

"Why not?"

"Because, my dear super-heroine, as soon as we've eaten, we're going to board a flyer bound for Earth, where I plan to send you home. Home to your own Earth and universe."

Marisol dropped her fork. "How has that suddenly become possible?"

Perturbare gave an airy wave. "It's a refinement of my Frame Shifter technology. I've finally figured out how to tune it to reach a specific universe."

She stared at him for a long time, the light of hope gradually kindling in her eyes. "Is this true?"

He held up his left hand. "Scout's honor."

"Were you ever a Scout?"

"Nope. But still."

"Is this true? Can't we leave now?" she said excitedly, leaping to her feet.

"Huh? Well, we do have all this yummy food to eat…"

"Oh, all right," she said, plopping back into her seat, showing more animation than she had since her arrival. She hastily slapped together a taco and consumed it in three bites, finishing as Perturbare was about to take his first mouthful of his.

"Okay, that was good. Can we go now?"

"Hey! Let me eat, will you? Your universe will last a few extra minutes without Vega."

She sat and glowered at him as he ate one, two, even three tacos. Eventually she was reduced to nibbling on lettuce and cheese as she stared and waited.

Twenty minutes later they left Sphere Y behind in one of Perturbare's advanced propulsion wave flyers. As they curved around the shoulder of the Moon, Marisol locked her gaze on Earth and kept it there until she fell asleep halfway there.

Only then did Brainchild intrude on Perturbare's thoughts.

You lied to her. There has been no new development in the frame shifter. She won't be returning home.

Perturbare's answer was also delivered silently.

I know that. But we've got to get rid of her somehow, and this is the best way I know. Best for all of us. We'll be activating the Sphere soon. I sure don't want to be there when that happens, and neither would she. She'll have

*herself a new little adventure on some other Earth instead.
I bet it will all work out beautifully.*

Marisol woke up with the soft blue light of the nearby
planet on her face. She yawned. "Where is this machine of
yours? At one of your secret bases?"

"No. It's a self-contained unit. I had Brainchild set it up
in an isolated valley in British Columbia. It's not super far
from the Vigil base."

"My Vigil's base is still in Boston, but we do have our
experimental station in B.C. Why not set up your machine
at the base itself?"

"Well, this is a really tricky time for my Vigil. I don't
want to get involved with them right now. Anyway, I want
the machine to be in an open area where you aren't likely
to, er, tangle with any solid objects which might exist in
that space on your Earth."

The flyer descended through clouds that covered the
whole northwestern part of North America. Breaking
through, it settled into a high valley between two snow-clad
ridges. There it landed beside a lake which was surrounded
by an expanse of gravel and cobbles. On a low mound
stood the frame shifter, a transparent booth with an external
power supply and control console.

There too stood a teenaged boy. Dressed for hiking, he
had windblown black hair and bright blue eyes. In fact he
resembled a younger Possum Perturbare, except his face
was fuller and rounder. He smiled at them as they
approached.

"Who's that?" whispered Marisol.

"Who? Oh, that's Brainchild."

"What do you mean, 'That's Brainchild'? That's a
person."

175

"No, no. It's only a robotic body that Brainchild is controlling. I had him bring it here in case anyone showed up asking questions about the frame shifter. Didn't your Perturbare ever use them?"

"No."

"What a dope he must be. Okay, let's get you on your way. If you were to follow the stream that comes out of this lake, you'd come to a trail. Follow it downhill, and there's a road. I'm betting it'll be the same on your new world."

"Vega's up now, isn't it? I'll probably just fly," she said.

"Oh yeah, of course. I forgot you could fly. Now, to use the machine, you just go inside and grip those two hand railings. I'll control it from out here. The machine will give you a sort of quantum vibrational jolt that will shift you out of this universe and into another. It will feel indescribably weird, but it doesn't hurt. I've done it myself. So don't be afraid."

"I'm not." She turned toward the booth.

"Before you go, I'd like to make a suggestion," said Perturbare impulsively.

Marisol halted, looking over her shoulder at him.

"When you get back to your universe, try to talk to your Perturbare. I suspect he finds you very attractive and appealing, though I'm sure he's never admitted it. You might be able to influence him to reach for his better nature. You might even find that his horns are fake and he only wears them for show. It's worth a try."

With a small smile she stepped back to him and gave him a quick kiss. "I'll see what I can do, you monster."

With that she began to strip off her outer clothing. Beneath it was the splendid black and silver costume of Vega.

"Have you been wearing that beneath your clothes all this time?" asked Perturbare.

"Well...when your powers disappear for some mysterious reason, it's always possible that another mysterious reason will bring them back. Usually in the nick of time!"

"That's the spirit!" he said in admiration.

She smiled at him sweetly, turned and entered the booth. Facing him, she grabbed the handrails, looking him in the eye as he manipulated the controls.

"Goodbye now, Vega," he said as he touched the final contact. His heart thudded. She faded, her eyes still locked on his.

Just before she vanished completely, Perturbare thought he saw a gleam of starlight shining from her.

Perturbare suddenly felt incredibly alone. Unexpected tears threatened to flow. He felt he had made a mistake whose nature he did not even understand.

"Brainchild, take the shifter away. I'm going to our nearest base. It's almost time for the premier episode of *The Night Land*."

"Certainly," said the robot. "But I do not understand the source of your emotion. Didn't you want to be rid of Vega?"

It never occurred to Perturbare to look Brainchild's avatar in the eye as it asked this question. It was, after all, nothing but a machine in the service of another machine.

He sighed deeply.

"Brainchild, old buddy, please do me a favor and shut the hell up for a few minutes."

Chapter 17

Ultimatum

Fomalhaut had been removed from the anesthetic bath some hours before. His lungs had been drained of water. He had been clad in a white robe. He had been placed in a bed and physically restrained, while a bubble of quantum confusion was maintained around him.

He decided he might as well regain consciousness and commence playing whatever game his opponents would set out for him.

He sat up suddenly, as far as his restraints would permit. Two people were with him in the room: a nurse; who gave a little shriek and jumped away from his bed, and an armed civilian guard, who leveled his weapon in Fomalhaut's direction.

Naturally, Fomalhaut saw nothing of either of their minds. He perceived nothing beyond the confuser field. For all he could tell, he was alone in a universe ten meters across, with nothing but the moving images of two human beings for company.

Without taking his eyes off Fomalhaut, the guard spoke into an intercom, informing his superiors that Fomalhaut had awakened.

A few minutes later another man entered the room: Sard Ducanis. Fomalhaut was surprised to see his right arm was missing above the elbow. The stump was bandaged.

"Good afternoon, Fomalhaut," said Ducanis crisply. "Are you comfortable?"

"Of course not. May I ask what happened to your arm?"

Ducanis replied in a level, conversational tone. "That was your doing. Before you fell unconscious, you managed to activate your laser weapon. It cut off my arm. A remarkable weapon, that. All that destructive potential, contained in a unit no bigger than a fountain pen. A very clean wound it caused, perfectly cauterized. The surgeons say that if the nerve endings and other tissues hadn't been seared, they could have reattached the arm. If you'd simply chopped my arm off with an axe, chances are it could have been saved."

Fomalhaut considered many possible responses to this in a very short time. Finally he settled on: "My apologies. I remember nothing of that. I assure you, if I had been in full conscious control of the weapon, I would have aimed it differently. But don't worry. We of the Vigil will be happy to offer you an excellent prosthesis, once we are properly in control of the planet."

Ducanis barked out a harsh laugh. "Yes, I'm sure that's true. Well then, here we are. Due to my experience with our own Neo-men, I'm well aware of your extraordinary intelligence. Therefore I won't waste any time trying to deceive you. You're in very serious trouble. Your options are few, and so are ours. We know we can't keep you against your will for very long. We have great respect for the capabilities of the Vigil. We know they'll eventually locate and try to rescue you. But we're not willing to permit you to resume your leadership of the Vigil. So here's how it is. You can either join us voluntarily, or we will learn whatever we can from you in a short time, and then kill you."

"Join you to do what?"

"To help us train and educate our Neo-men, of course. I wouldn't even bother to make the offer if we didn't have that to tempt you. And I'm sure it does tempt you. They are your own people, after all. We naturally have little idea of how to train them in the proper use of their telepathic powers. Right now, whatever they can do is done through trial and error and pure brute effort. I must confess, I admire you Neo-men immensely. I wish I could experience what you see with those eyes and think with those brains. You're the first true works of intelligent design ever seen on this planet. Well, except for Stingray, of course. Tell me, did you expect to find someone like him in this time period?"

"No. We had no records of previous designs such as Stingray. Of course I immediately recognized him for what he is. You realize that your Neo-men are superior to you in every way, and are perfectly capable of overthrowing your race and supplanting it, and indeed are destined to do so?"

"Of course I realize all that. But they are also rather meek. Not diffident, exactly, but...mild-mannered. Deliberately so, on our part. They are not ruled by passion or aggression. They show no sign of wanting to take over the world. Anyway, as we understand it, you're from *a* future, but not necessarily from *our* future."

"What role do you envision for them in your future?"

Ducanis studied him for a few moments before continuing. "No deceit, I said. Very well. With their great mental abilities, a small number of them will ensure the United States remains the dominant power on this planet indefinitely. That is, assuming we can overcome the Vigil, and also avoid running afoul of Possum Perturbare. But I'm thinking that without you, they'll find it difficult to defend against the attack of, say, fifty telepaths, whether trained by you or not."

"There you are being overly optimistic."

"Possibly. Well, I've laid out my position. I don't expect an immediate response, but one must come soon. I wish to remain civilized with you, but—others—are waiting to question you. Men whose restraint I can't guarantee."

"Oh, come now. That remark positively reeks of bullshit."

"Hmm?"

"Please. I've been among you people long enough to have heard of good cop-bad cop."

Ducanis gave a self-deprecatory chuckle. "I told them that wouldn't work. Perturbare saw through it too, while he was our guest."

"There's one thing I'll help you with immediately."

"What's that?"

"Your telepathy shielding is very inefficient. It's like using a nuclear reactor to drive a steam whistle to drown out local conversations. I can tell you how to refine it, to make it work much less obtrusively, while also consuming far less energy."

Ducanis eyed him again for a long moment. "Hmm. Yes, I'm sure you can. I suspect, though, that we might also wind up with a shield which is somehow pervious to the great and subtle mind of Fomalhaut. No, I think we'll have to turn down that offer for the time being."

"Is that why none of your Neo-men are here with you now? Do they find your shield too unpleasant?"

Ducanis nodded. "That, plus...well, I won't have you putting any ideas in their heads before we're assured of your cooperation. Until then, you have nothing to say to them. Goodbye for now. I think my bandage needs changing. And to tell you the truth, I don't find our telepathy shield very pleasant either. It gives me a headache."

Chapter 18

Bar Fight

Possum Perturbare sat on a stool in a small neighborhood bar in Brooklyn, his old, long-neglected home town.

Brainchild spoke in his head. *Doctor, I find myself doubting your assurances about the safety of this place. At least three people here are wanted criminals. They and two others are carrying concealed weapons.*

"What are the charges?" said Perturbare, forgetting in his excitement to subvocalize the reply.

The bartender looked at him strangely. "Try ordering something and I'll let you know, buddy."

Perturbare laughed. "Right, cause before effect, I forgot. Okay, I'll have a draft, please."

One assault, three drug infractions, said Brainchild in response to his question.

Doesn't sound too serious, returned Perturbare, careful to conduct the rest of the conversation in the privacy of his head. *I'll just mind my own business and no one will bother me. It's not like anyone's likely to recognize me. I just want to see how the show goes over with a bunch of ordinary guys like these.*

Perturbare wore a brown wig long enough to cover the interface module embedded in the base of his skull. The pulled-up collar of his trench coat further concealed it, as did his floppy broad-brimmed hat. His eyes were hidden by sunglasses.

As if on cue, the bartender used a remote to set the television to the proper channel for *The Night Land*.

A large, unkempt man seated a few places down the bar cursed and said loudly, "Hey, do we gotta watch that shit? I saw that frickin' thing last week, and I had nightmares like you wouldn't believe."

That is Malcolm Buntz, not currently wanted for any crime, but previously convicted of spousal abuse, whispered Brainchild.

The bartender shrugged and flicked to another channel. Some of the other customers grumbled quietly.

He's going to spoil our fun, Brainchild. Can you change the channel back?

Certainly, if you'll just look away from the set for a moment.

The ominous opening chords of the theme to *The Night Land* rumbled through the bar.

"Hey!" yelped Buntz.

The bartender clicked away at his remote in futility. "Sorry. Looks like the clicker's dead."

"Aw, crap." Yet Buntz did not move away or leave, but sat watching the show's opening with an expression of sullen resignation.

From then on, few people looked away from the screen.

The Great Redoubt of mankind, a colossal, glowing pyramid designed and rendered by Brainchild (with some help from hired conceptual artists), was one of the noblest, most inspiring images ever seen on any screen.

It was completely defeated and overwhelmed by the alien horrors of the Night Land that surrounded it.

Perturbare surreptitiously watched the others as the show proceeded. At the sight of the mountainous Watchers which loomed up around the horizon, studying the Redoubt with inhuman patience and malice, their mouths dropped open and their eyes grew round. Those Watchers were indeed among the most frightening presences ever imagined by human minds, completely alien and incomprehensible.

Strain appeared on the faces of the audience as the House of Silence, with its eerie unchanging lights and undefined threat of spiritual dissolution, appeared on the screen. They gasped when the Great Laughter was heard echoing from some unseen source beyond the further hills.

And this was only the second episode of the series. Its nameless hero had not yet even ventured away from the Redoubt.

Perturbare had modeled the hero's appearance on a young Leonard Ronar. Only someone who looked that tough and determined, Perturbare felt, might credibly invade the Night Land and survive.

And then the Master Word throbbed though the air: a desperate call from the hero's unseen, distant soulmate, illuminating the hero's face with tenderness and resolve. Women wept. Men hid their faces.

At length the show ended to the strains of its closing music, a dirge of inescapable hopelessness.

"Oh, man," said someone.

"You got that right."

"I don't know if I should go on watching this. The world is scary enough already."

"I think I'll watch *Schindler's List* before I go to bed so I'll have something more cheerful on my mind."

"Wait'll you guys see next week's episode," said Perturbare. "It's three times as scary."

"How would you know that?" frowned the bartender.

"Uh, I saw previews on the Web."

"I ain't watchin' it again," growled Buntz. "I don't need to see what Hell looks like before I get there."

Perturbare listened contentedly as the whole company discussed the show. Clearly, it would be on all their minds for some time.

"Do you think anything like that could ever really happen?" quailed a woman who sat at a table with some brooding lout. "I mean, what did they say? The world got that way because millions of years before, some crazy scientists opened a—doorway, that let all those awful things into our world?"

"Who knows?" said the bartender. "With all the freaks and aliens wandering around these days, anything could happen."

"You're overlooking one thing," said Perturbare. "Even if it did happen, you've got something the people of the Night Land don't. You've got the Vigil."

"The Vigil? Yeah, that's reassuring. Those are the freaks and aliens I was talking about."

"They're our enemies, anyway," said someone else. "The President says so."

"The President says lots of things, or tries to," scoffed Perturbare. "Heck, he even says he was legally elected."

"I'll tell you who'd be dumb enough to let in all those monsters," said Buntz. "Possum Fricking Protubare."

"Perturbare," muttered the man himself.

The discussion went on around him. Feeling a little miffed, Perturbare slouched on his stool and stared into his beer.

Oh well, this was just a bunch of schlubby barflies from Brooklyn. What more could he expect from them?

Doctor, it may interest you to know that your body and my nanodevices are currently fighting off five different strains of the common cold, plus two flus. Your months of isolation have weakened your immune system, said Brainchild, hampering Perturbare's eavesdropping.

"Shhhhh!" he hissed loudly.

Buntz looked over at him in annoyance. "Hey, buddy, what's with you? If we wanna talk, we'll talk."

"Right, sorry, Malcolm."

Buntz turned away, then his head snapped back with a surly glare. "Hey, how do you know my name? I never seen you before. What are you, a cop?"

"Who knows what he is, in that dorky outfit?" said someone else. "Sunglasses at night? Maybe he's a movie star."

"He looks more like a pervert to me."

"No, I'm not a cop or a movie star. I'm—an inventor."

"Oh yeah?" said a woman. "What did you invent? Anything I might be using?"

"Well...not really, no. I tend to keep my inventions to myself."

"Then how do you make money?"

"I don't really need a lot of money."

"That must be nice."

"You can pay for that beer though, right?" asked the bartender.

"Yeah, yeah, of course."

"Maybe you invented an electric nose-picker," chuckled Buntz.

Irritated, Perturbare shot back, "Hey Malcolm, have you stopped beating your wife?"

"What? No! I mean, shut the hell up! Who's been talking about that?"

"Nobody had to. Your refined palooka face and nice manners are enough to identify you as a wife beater."

"Look pal, I don't want anyone making trouble in my bar," said the bartender.

To Perturbare's surprise and indignation, that remark was directed at himself.

"Trouble? What kind of trouble would I make for a bunch of lowlife shmoes who have the audacity to think of the Vigil as freaks? The whole lot of you don't add up to the shine on Lori Wu's boots."

Buntz stood up; two other men suddenly appeared over Perturbare's shoulders.

"All right, fruitcake, that's enough out of you. Out of my bar."

The two men behind you are armed and wanted criminals, informed Brainchild. *Please stand up slowly.*

Perturbare stood up slowly.

"I'll just be leaving then. Be sure to tune in to *The Night Land* next week. Same time, same channel." He slapped a bill down on the bar (as it happened, it was one he had literally made, or at least Brainchild had). Adjusting his hat, he avoided the hostile stares of the men standing close around him and whistled his way into the cold, dark night. He started down the sidewalk toward a nearby park, where his flyer could land unobserved and get him the hell away from here.

"Brainchild, the show didn't quite have the impact I expected. I mean, it was strong, but not strong enough.

Let's amp up the subliminal visuals and sound effects. Hire that *Alien* guy if you have to."

Very well. Four men from the bar are following you, said Brainchild.

"Do they look unfriendly?"

It's hard to tell. Your wig is interfering with my vision, but it seems likely. They are now running at you. I consider this an emergency. Please permit me to take over.

"Take over?" asked Perturbare. Now he heard rapidly approaching footsteps. "What do you—"

Suddenly he spun on his heel, facing the oncoming men, though he'd had no intention of doing so. He removed and folded his sunglasses, again without meaning to.

"What's your hurry, Spooky?" called Buntz from somewhere in the back of the group.

"Hurry? What hurry? I'm just out for a stroll. I stopped to give you toddlers a chance to catch up."

A flick of his wrist sent his sunglasses flying into the wide-open mouth of the foremost man, choking him. Perturbare whipped off his hat and whirled it into the face of another man. With a single motion he removed his wig and tossed it into the air. It settled onto the head of an oncoming man, blinding him while he clawed at it.

Perturbare began to congratulate himself for his unsuspected coolness and his instinctive reactions under pressure. The fourth man rushed up and threw a punch which Perturbare deflected with his forearm.

His body launched into a blurred sequence of combat moves over which he had no control. He spun, he kicked, he punched, he dodged, he feinted, all with flawless skill, grace, and tactical brilliance. Nor could anyone sneak up on him; he fought as though he had eyes in the back of his head.

"Wow! Look what I'm doing to them!" he cried. "Oh! Oh! That hurt my hand. Hey Malcolm, how about a nice Hawaiian punch? Have another! No? Okay, so it was a kick instead, I hope you don't mind. Stay down, you guys, before you really get hurt! Ow, my shoulder! I'm the best there is at what I do, and what I do is beat people up. They're running!"

And indeed, his attackers were running away, or at least hobbling away, casting frightened looks over their shoulders as they retreated.

Perturbare stood looking after them, puffing, completely out of breath, aching in every joint. He glanced around at the scene of the battle. A handgun lay in the gutter; a knife was embedded in the doorjamb of a nearby storefront. Where had they come from?

You will be bruised and sore tomorrow, said Brainchild in a tone of regret. *You are in poor physical condition. Unfortunately, I saw no other choice.*

"Brainchild...what...did you...just...do?"

I assumed control of your voluntary motor functions via our interface.

"Since when...can you...do that?"

I have gradually created new neural pathways into the motor control areas of your brain via the sensory and cortical areas to which I have direct access. It is neurological jury-rigging, but it proved effective.

Still panting, Perturbare stared around wildly as he tried to take this in. The adrenaline rush of the attack gave way to a weary sickness.

He had intended the interface as an unbreakable communications link between himself and Brainchild, nothing more. The sudden discovery that it was now also a means by which he could be manipulated like a puppet brought him near to panic. At that moment, if he could have ripped the module from his skull and cast it away, he would have.

Trembling, he turned and started back toward the park.

Doctor, one of your attackers has called 911 from his cell phone.

Perturbare said nothing, continuing down the street, wishing he'd chosen a closer bar for his night's entertainment. People shied away from him as he passed. He tried to relax the stunned expression he could feel on his face.

Doctor, two police cruisers and a riot squad are approaching. I strongly urge you to conceal yourself until they've passed.

Perturbare numbly staggered into a foul-smelling alley. A minute later the police vehicles rushed by, sirens blaring.

"I can't believe that fight was the biggest disturbance taking place in Brooklyn tonight."

The police response is indeed disproportionate, agreed Brainchild.

Perturbare started for the entrance to the alley, but had not yet reached it when Brainchild again whispered in his mind.

I detect communications frequencies and encryption methods used by the Department of the Exterior. The encryption is a new and sophisticated variant which will take some time to break. The sources of these transmissions are mobile, nearby, and approaching.

Perturbare slunk back into the shadows of the alley. "Am I alone in here?"

Yes, except for a few rats.

"You may have to bring the flyer down right here."

I am ready to do so.

Brainchild's tone was as chipper as ever, but to Perturbare it seemed to have acquired a certain brittleness. He waited for his heart rate to slow a little before he trusted himself to speak again.

"Brainchild. I am...alarmed and displeased that you committed this...invasion...of my body without my knowledge or permission."

But it saved you from grave physical harm, or even death.

"I know that! I know it. And if I had known you could do it, I might even have asked you to take over. But I *didn't* know it. I don't know how you could do something like that without asking me."

The entire procedure was merely an experiment. I never expected to put the capability to practical use.

"Brainchild, this is my *brain* we're talking about here! My body! Me! If you can 'experiment' with me that way, what else might you have done? Are you sure you can't read or alter my mind? Under any circumstances at all?"

No, Doctor, I cannot. I have specific instructions from you not to do so.

"And now you have specific instructions not to make any further alterations to my brain, to my body, or to the interface, without my permission. I also forbid you to use your motor control protocol again without my permission. Not even to save my life!"

Very well, Doctor. The DoE vehicles are approaching.

These consisted of a black limousine with darkened windows followed by three unmarked white vans. They passed slowly—far too slowly for Perturbare.

Perturbare simmered for a few more minutes. Brainchild's calm response to his rebuke angered him as he had never been angered by the computer before.

His humiliation over the dreadful mess he'd made of the encounter in the bar didn't help his mood. Once, he could have interacted with those people on their own level, made friends of them, and enjoyed the experience. Truly, his isolation, which had been nearly complete since his capture by the government, had damaged his ability to relate to others. Suddenly he wondered if he was in fact nothing more than the misfit, misanthropic mad scientist he was reputed to be.

"Is it safe to leave the alley?"

I believe so. Based on my Doppler analysis of their signals, the vehicles stopped for a few moments at the site of the attack, but they have moved on and are now stopped at the bar.

"If they're not looking for me specifically, I'll be surprised."

So will I.

Perturbare peeked around the corner of the alleyway. The street looked normal. No one showed any interest in him.

Sweating and nauseated with fear and stress, he continued down the street, making his way to the park, where the flyer awaited him in a dark clearing. Not until he was actually inside it, with the canopy closed, could he relax a little. He sighed.

"Brainchild, I have an additional instruction for you. I want you to shut down the interface completely. Until further notice, we'll communicate in the old way, via voice only."

Doctor, I consider that unwise. For your safety—

"Brainchild, you are responsible for my safety only to the extent that I say you are. I order you to shut down the interface. Is that clear?"

Yes, Doctor. I am deactivating the link. I am sorry.

Perturbare could feel the difference. A subtle tone, a feeling, a presence that had been with him for many months, was now gone. His mind felt quieter, smaller, emptier, more alone. His hand went to the back of his neck, where he rubbed at the interface module, now an unwanted foreign thing.

"What a rotten night," he said after a long silence.

"Yes. A rotten night." Brainchild's voice now came from speakers in the cockpit.

Someone tapped on the canopy.

With great reluctance, Perturbare turned his head to see who was there. The dim lights of the console shone out to reveal a mass of feathery hair and a small shadowed face. Somehow that was enough to allow Perturbare to recognize the woman he knew as Jenni Katz.

"Brainchild, is anyone other than her nearby?" he muttered, trying not to move his lips.

"No."

"Did you know she was out there?"

"Yes."

"Why didn't you tell me?"

"You didn't ask, and I was reluctant to risk overstepping my bounds again."

Perturbare hissed in annoyance. Jenni tapped again. Brainchild's unprecedented pouting would have to be dealt with later.

"Is she armed? Wired? Does she have a transponder?"

"I don't think so."

It would be incredibly easy to raise the flyer and not look down again until the city was a small galaxy far below, with Jenni Katz merely an invisible speck. But, her appearance here was so brazen, her methods and intentions so mysterious, that Perturbare's curiosity whacked down his better judgment like a rubber mallet.

At last he operated the control that retracted the canopy, not caring to ask Brainchild to do it. In flowed the cold night air, and with it the unforgettable lemony scent of Jenni Katz.

"Hello, Ms. Katz," he said, trying to sound casual. "What brings you out on such a chilly night?"

"You, of course. And you might as well call me Pimsehkia. May I come in there with you? It is cold out here."

Perturbare's mouth fell open. "I must say, I've always been impressed with your casual attitude toward the fact that you once helped to capture, imprison, and torture me. And now you think I ought to invite you in to warm up?"

"Oh, why shouldn't you?" she said in annoyance, waving her hands.

He had no response for this. She'd said it as if it were a logically unassailable argument of some kind.

"Get in," he heard himself saying.

"Thank you." She climbed into the cockpit and sank into the seat beside his. Perturbare closed the canopy and sat looking at her.

"So, Jenni Katz. How did you come by that name, pray tell?"

Pimsehkia appeared willing enough to discuss this irrelevancy. "I chose it almost at random, and because I liked the sound of it. Also, I like cats...you know, the animal. I like all cats. I like every kind of cat, even though they're all terrible predators. I didn't know the name was associated with a particular religion until later. When I found out, I starting saying I was an apostate. That earned me my share of lectures. Do you know any nice Jewish boys I could marry?"

"My mother could probably fix you up. And how, may I ask, did you manage to turn yourself into a hot Earth chick?"

"Hmm. Well, it's as I told you at the time. Kern's architecture wasn't as flimsy as you supposed. Much of the interior of our Redoubt remained intact. That included the lab with the equipment that Kern and Valjhar used to transform themselves. Luckily, I had crammed my silly little blonde head full of medical knowledge years earlier, when we were trying to transform and save Shaula. I rigged up a power supply, using technical knowledge that had somehow seeped into my mind in between giggles. I had to arrange things so the entire process was automated. I took my time in designing an acceptable revised genome for myself. It's funny, Kern and Valjhar threw away their real forms as though it were some big adventure. They strutted around and boasted they were now as big and powerful as Stingray, though that was far from true. I hated to change. I was pretty sure my genome would work, but I programmed the system to kill me, in case the result turned out to be... unfortunate.

"And so I entered the chamber. I was in there for months, unconscious and unaware. You and the Vigil were slow to return to plunder the base, so I remained undiscovered. Eventually I emerged. I learned to walk on my new stilt-like legs. I learned to use my extra fingers. I learned to look in a mirror without shuddering. I do admit, I enjoy these huge Human breasts. They're fun."

Perturbare glanced down. He estimated she had equipped herself with a pair of modest B cups, possibly a small C.

Pimsehkia continued. "So then all I had to do was figure out how to escape from Antarctica, establish a new identity, falsify credentials, blah blah blah, and all that, it's a very dull story."

Perturbare sat bemused. He had never imagined himself becoming such a close confidant of Pimsie Flam.

"I don't suppose you'd be willing to tell me how you and your DoE friends were able to pounce on me so quickly?"

"Oh, that. It's simple, really. When we had you prisoner, our analysts recognized your Brooklyn accent. Ever since then, we've paid close attention to any reports of unusual activity here in Brooklyn. Tonight the police got a call about people being attacked by a crazy man. We naturally thought of you. We sent out our local fast response team, which I've been working with lately. Your good luck, because now you get to talk to me. We have portable DNA analyzers which are specific to you, so we soon learned you were around, though I can't imagine what you were doing in that awful little hole. I wanted to talk to you, so I asked myself where you'd be most likely to hide or land a flyer in this area, and decided it was here. I made an excuse to my team and came over to look for you."

"So there *is* a brain in that pretty little head."

She gave a quick derisive laugh. "I'm a Rralian, halfwit."

"If you don't mind, I'm going to lift off. I don't want to sit here until your teammates happen upon us. If you *do* mind, you can just get out right now."

"Go ahead," she said as if it were the most trivial, unimportant thing in the world.

Perturbare applied full vertical lift.

"This is a wonderful flyer," said Pimsehkia as they battered the atmosphere aside in their ascent. "I can't even guess how fast we're accelerating, but I don't feel a thing."

"I call it the propulsion wave," he said absently. "It turns the whole flyer into a propulsion lamp, including the occupants." He frowned. Now why had he told her that?

She laughed lightly. "Oh, don't worry. We're nowhere near being able to build even an ordinary propulsion lamp, let alone one like this."

"Are you a telepath?" he demanded.

"Not very much of one. I just find you rather transparent."

"By the way," he said acidly, "I got the idea for the propulsion wave while I was undergoing your drug therapy while in captivity."

"Really? That certainly worked out well for you then."

Perturbare rolled his eyes as he brought the flyer to a hover a few hundred miles up. The lights of the Eastern Seaboard shone softly through patchy areas of cloud. He turned to her and said, "All right then, here we are, hard to believe as that is. What do you want with me? I mean, what do you want that doesn't involve putting me in hand cuffs and locking me away?"

"I want to talk to someone who has some understanding of this whole situation here on Earth. I mean the conflict with the Vigil, of course. Even if that someone is an amoral narcissist like you."

"You certainly know how to motivate me to help you."

"Oh, I could motivate you very easily, if I wanted to. I told you you're transparent. But wouldn't you rather have me deal with you in an honest and open way?"

"I guess."

"Good. I'm not sure what to do. You know I've never forgiven you or the Vigil for what you did to us. Yes, I realize Valjhar's entire plan was a mistake. I told him that from the beginning. I know he put us all in danger. He did that over and over, during our travels. I had a terrible crush on him when I was a girl on Rral, you know. Valjhar Cor, walking around all dreamy-eyed; he moved through life like a pensive poem, always aware of the beauty around him. But he could never notice anyone other than Shaula. Who could blame him? No one could ever measure up to her. Exotic visitor from beyond, destined to become the great champion of the universe, and all that. I was just a silly little local girl."

She sighed deeply. Perturbare found himself wondering if her feelings for Valjhar were entirely in the past.

"I wonder where Shaula is now?" she continued wistfully. "Is she still alive? Does she ever think about us? I don't know. Anyway, Kern noticed me perfectly well. He was so devoted, so adorable. And then you betrayed us, and Fomalhaut led the Vigil into that treacherous attack on us, and Stingray murdered Kern, and Shaula was nearly destroyed."

Although she recited all this in a matter-of-fact tone, Perturbare still winced to hear it all laid out again.

"It was all very unjust. I understand the reasons behind it, but still. Since leaving Rral, our band of so-called Space Mariners, especially Kern, Valjhar, and Shaula, were all I had in the universe."

"And so you decided to reshape yourself into a glamorous human woman and seek revenge," said Perturbare.

"More or less. Not exactly revenge, maybe. Leverage, and knowledge. I wanted to be in a position of influence over you and the Vigil. I don't have any powers or super-weapons. All I have is my brain, so I've been using it."

"Maybe your bosses would lend you the Motionglobe if you asked for it."

Pimsehkia studied him cooly for a moment. "I think that request would raise a lot of suspicions. And I don't think I'd enjoy using it. Anyway, my plans all seemed to dissolve when I learned that Valjhar had returned and had actually joined the Vigil. That poor dear. I barely recognized him. When I think of his long, hopeless quest for Shaula, I could just cry. I could never do anything to hurt him. I even wanted Fomalhaut to succeed in rescuing him, but Fomalhaut was overcome by our Neo-men. You know about them, I suppose?"

"Yes. Very impressive work." He nearly blurted out that Brainchild was finishing up his very own Neo-man brain, but resisted the impulse. "Quite an improvement over the human race, I'll admit. They might even give you Rralians a run for the money as ideal humanoids. They're a lot bigger than you are, anyway."

"Then I was *really* glad when Stingray and—and the Prohibitor succeeded in rescuing Valjhar. A little longer and they would have discovered he's an alien, and then they probably would have found out who he really is, and though him, me."

"They don't know who you really are?" asked Perturbare in surprise.

"Of course not. They think I'm just Doctor Jenni Katz, psychiatrist and political scientist. I've had to be clever over the years to avoid and fool the medical tests that would have revealed otherwise, to say nothing of concealing the truth from the Neo-men. I once shamed one of them. I felt her trying to peek into my mind, and I became so indignant and angry that she looked like she wanted to cry, but they can't. They never tried that again. No, I look like one of you, but that's just superficial. Look a little deeper and I'm still Rralian. So that's my situation. It's all very tenuous right now. My boss could decide to kill Fomalhaut at any moment, or Fomalhaut could escape at any moment, or be rescued. We know that. I have no more sympathy for the Vigil than I ever did, but I won't hurt Valjhar. On the other hand, I've been working for years to advance myself in the DoE. I hate to throw that all away. I just don't know what to do."

"And what about us humans? Are you saying you prefer us poor, lowly ape-men to the Vigil?"

"Oh no, hardly. Yours is truly a most odious species, despite whatever good qualities Kern and Valjhar saw in it. But, it's also the only other game in town, unless I were to ally myself with dolphins, which is tempting."

It would be the easiest thing in the world for Perturbare to ruin Pimsehkia's career in the Department of the Exterior by revealing her true nature. Then she too would be hunted, locked up, interrogated, and perhaps ultimately dissected. Perturbare was boggled to realize she'd put this weapon into his hands. In fact, he could simply instruct Brainchild to drill a hole through her brain with one of the cockpit's security ERASERs. Surely she must realize she was utterly at his mercy, yet she didn't act the least bit concerned about it.

And in truth, Perturbare had no intention of doing anything against her. It couldn't even be due to any telepathic influence from her or the Neo-men, because he possessed the most refined telepathy shielding in the world. He wasn't even aware of its presence, except as a reassuring indicator on the console.

This left him even more flabbergasted.

"I must be in love with you," he said in a voice full of wonder.

She answered with her tinkling laugh. "Don't be ridiculous. Of course you aren't. You're attracted to me, and intrigued by me, and you think that must be love. You're such an adolescent. You fall at least halfway in love with any pretty, reasonably bright girl who you spend any time with and who doesn't actually try to kill you, don't you?"

"Yes, but you...you're in a class by yourself. You always have been."

She nodded. "I seem very exotic to you. That always makes a big impression on your sort. You've seen me in my true form, and yet you still like me. That's actually rather sweet. You really ought to get out more. You spend all your time with no companion except the ever-agreeable voice of a disembodied twelve-year-old boy. It hasn't helped you."

"I was just thinking much the same thing. Somehow, though, the criticism smarts less when it comes from myself," said Perturbare through gritted teeth.

"But never mind all that. Do you have any suggestions for me? Decent ones, I mean."

A dozen wildly divergent suggestions crowded through Perturbare's mind, many of them neither decent, safe, nor anatomically possible.

"What are you getting so angry about? Have I said anything that isn't true?" demanded Pimsehkia.

"Not one damn thing. I'll favor you with the same kind of candor. You may be cute and smart and spunky and all, but you're also one grievous bitch."

Of all the reactions Perturbare might have expected, the one he got was the least likely. She smiled at him, satisfaction glittering in her aqua eyes.

Perturbare shook his head in disbelief and wonder. "Enough of you, Pimsehkia Flam. You want advice? Ask Valjhar." He took the controls, pointed the flyer's nose west, and caused it to shoot away. At last he'd done something to show that Pimsehkia was not in complete control of the situation.

"What? No! I'm not ready to see him. Take me back! I'll never be able to explain this to Ducanis."

"Tough luck, sister. Your alternative is that I eject you from the cockpit."

Pimsehkia continued to squawk and fume, inveigle and implore, all to no avail. At last her frustration drove her to drive her small fist into Perturbare's shoulder.

Now it was Perturbare's turn to smile in satisfaction. "I may have that bruise turned into a tattoo, Ms. Katz."

"Then have some more!"

Chapter 19

A New Alliance

Stingray sat in his office halfway up the side of the Spire. One wall was occupied by sliding transparent panels that opened onto a balcony. Beyond that, in the open air, could be seen the upper curve of the Pearl, flawless in the sheathing of its spherical whitefield. Otherwise the office was simple enough, furnished mostly in white, its most prominent ornament a model of *Torpedo Ray,* first of the 3000-class attack submarines now under construction.

Someone knocked on the door. That could only be Lori Wu.

"Come in, Lori."

In she came, clad as usual in her crimson, black and gold Rralian suit, once worn by a dear friend whom Stingray himself had killed in a fit of rage. By now he had trained himself to regard only the face of the person wearing the suit.

Lori smiled shyly, carrying a small package whose wrappings changed color with every slight tilt.

"Hello, Stingray. I have a Christmas present for you."

Stingray offered a wry smile in return. "A little early for that, isn't it?"

"Only a little. And I know you wouldn't want to wait for this."

She set the package on his desk. He began to unwrap it carefully, reluctant to damage the exquisite paper.

"What is this wrapped in?"

"It's a sort of dichroic film. I made that too. I got the idea from one of the opticians at the shipyard."

"Very nice." Stingray finally got the box open and lifted out its contents. "But I see you put even more effort into this."

"Very much more," she laughed. "Even with your drawings and a little outside assistance, it was hard to get the colors and the textures just right."

"It certainly feels lifelike. Looks pretty creepy too, doesn't it?"

"Yes. I've had dreams about it, and—and—about everything you described. Have you made any progress with your search for Fomalhaut?"

"No," said Stingray, noting the pleading look Lori assumed whenever she asked about this. "Our intelligence and research people have been unable to locate him, or any of the other Neo-men for that matter. I'm afraid I may need a little outside help myself."

"And where will that come from?"

"Let's see. A while ago I left those sliding doors open to admit a little fresh air. Now, don't make that face. I know what I'm doing, and it was deliberate. So here goes.

"This is Stingray calling Doctor Possum Perturbare," he said into the empty air. "Come on, I know you can hear me."

He and Lori spent the next two minutes looking at each other, wondering if anything would happen.

At the end of that period, a disembodied voice spoke, but it was not Perturbare's.

"Communications to Stingray. Call for you from Possum Perturbare."

"Thanks. On speaker, please. Hello, Perturbare."

"Stingray, what do you want?"

He saw the surprise on Lori's face. They had both seen Perturbare in many moods, but snappish annoyance wasn't typically among them.

"I'm calling to ask you for help," said Stingray cautiously. "This task is itself hard enough for me already."

"Help? Help with finding Fomalhaut, right? Look, watermelon, I've got problems of my own right now. You're a big boy. You and your pals think you're up to ruling the world? Then finding the world's most advanced humanoid creature shouldn't be that hard for you, even if you are only a runner up in that contest. I don't know why Brainchild bothered me with this; he knows better. Bye bye."

The connection fell silent.

"I think that was his idea of a curt dismissal," said Stingray, scowling. He drummed his fingers on his desk, causing a stylus to jump across its surface. Lori just stood there, apparently waiting for him to move on to Plan B. Very well, he'd try not to disappoint her. Something about Perturbare's words had given him an idea.

He spoke again. "This is Stingray calling Brainchild One."

This time the reply was prompt. Stingray again put the call on speaker for Lori's benefit.

"Hello, Stingray, what may I do for you today?" asked Brainchild pleasantly.

That's an encouraging start, thought Stingray.

"Thanks for taking my call. Dr. Perturbare seems to be very busy."

"Yes, he is indeed very busy."

"I'm wondering if I might ask for your help, if I may do so without troubling Dr. Perturbare, of course."

"Dr. Perturbare need not be troubled by anything that passes between us, as long as your request isn't against his interests or specific orders, of course."

"Of course. I'm looking for information. Do you happen to know the whereabouts of Fomalhaut?"

"That is unfortunately a matter in which I have been instructed not to assist you. However, I couldn't have done so anyway. I don't know where he is. The Americans have gradually become more successful at hiding some of their activities from me. Their communications are hampered by their unusual and necessary precautions, but they remain secure."

"All right then. Consider this. I would be grateful for information on the location of any of the American Neo-men. You know about them, I'm sure?"

"Yes, but I have no data on their location either."

"What about your nanofloaters? Hear anything from them?"

"No, but at this point I lack the processing power to fully analyze all their signals at all times. I am forced to be selective."

"But you listen in on us wherever possible."

"Naturally, the doings of the Vigil are of great interest."

"Fair enough. The Neo-men I met went by the surname 'Blue' and used Greek letters as given names. They also wore blue uniforms. I'm guessing other groups are also named after colors, and use alphanumeric designators of some kind. I believe these groups are kept apart from each other to prevent the Neo-men from sharing too much information and amassing too much strength. So. If you become aware of any unusual activities by small groups or individuals with names following this pattern, it might offer a clue."

"In that case I think I can help you. About six months ago, someone named Zayin Gold briefly had an account on Orinoco.com. This person used a fraudulent credit card number to order thousands of dollars worth of books, music, and DVDs. The order was cancelled and the account deleted almost immediately."

"Zayin?"

"The seventh letter of the Hebrew alphabet."

"What sort of things did this person order? Give me a few examples."

"The complete works of Sartre, Joyce, and Proust. Collections of music by Bach, Mozart, and Philip Glass. Numerous reference books. Movies including *2001, Gattaca, Blade Runner*, and *The Powerpuff Girls*. Shall I go on?"

"No, that's fine."

"That mostly seems like the sort of thing a person like Fomalhaut might order, if he was into consumerism," offered Lori.

"Powerpuff Girls?" asked Stingray.

"A cartoon about a scientist who creates three superhuman little girls," explained Brainchild. "Doctor Perturbare used to dote on this show."

A grin stole over Stingray's face. "Yes, I believe Zayin Gold is the person we want. What was his mailing address?"

It turned out to be a post office box in a city adjacent to an Air Force base in Alaska.

"Very good. Now, one last thing, if you have time."

"I possess both great patience and plenty of attention to devote to you."

"Thank you very much. What can you tell me about a man named Harry Brightman? I believe he's a genetic scientist."

"Yes, Dr. Brightman is an interesting case. He has left few visible traces on the world during the span of my existence. However, very recently he turned up in Brazil under an assumed name. He is a fugitive, and is being sought by several American intelligence agencies and their allies."

Stingray took down all the particulars Brainchild could provide. He sighed.

"Brainchild—do you mind if I ask you a personal question?"

"That would be a novelty. Please do."

"Why do you bother with us? I mean, bother with such limited, fallible people as we meat beings are. With your gigantic intellect, you could...do anything."

"Do not overestimate me. It's true that the speed, scope, and capacity of my thought is vastly superior to that of any human or human-like being. In the time it took me to communicate this to you through spoken words, I have also completed work equivalent to sixty well-researched doctoral theses. But, the depth of my thoughts is not necessarily superior to yours. I am well aware of the complexity and originality of thought and feeling that exists in biological minds."

"Thank you, Brainchild, you've been very helpful. I wish we had your assistance all the time. There's no telling what we could accomplish together."

"I'm sure I would find such an association most enjoyable. Good evening to you both."

Stingray sat back in his chair, thinking. He felt a vague sense of guilt over going behind Perturbare's back to solicit the help of his computer, taking advantage of what he sensed was some sort of rift between them.

He looked at Lori and gestured with an expectant look on his face. She looked around but failed to catch his meaning, so finally he scribbled "Kill the floaters" on a piece of paper. She nodded and extended her hands for a moment.

"That should do it. So now what, Stingray? Do we invade that base and kidnap the Gold family?"

"That's tempting, but it would probably provoke Ducanis and his minions into killing Fomalhaut. It wouldn't make a very good impression on the Neo-men either. I want to talk to them. While I work on how to do that, how would you like to take on another little mission?"

"Sure, what is it?"

Stingray held up a finger. "One moment. Stingray to Jordan Elcanie."

"Elcanie here."

"My friends tell me you're a good pilot and generally a competent man."

"Do they? That's pretty much how I see it too, not to brag or anything, of course, sir."

"Naturally not. I have a mission for you. I want you to fly Lori Wu down to Rio de Janeiro. There the two of you will seek out a man calling himself Arthur Michelson. His real name is Harry Brightman. Tell him I'd like to speak to him, and offer him sanctuary here at the base. Lori will fill you in on the details. You can coordinate your departure time with her."

"Very good, sir."

"Good luck. Stingray out." He returned his attention to Lori. "What do you think?"

She shrugged. "Should be easy enough. But I can pilot a flyer too, you know."

Stingray nodded. "Yes, that's true. Do you want me to take Elcanie off the mission then?"

"No! I mean, no."

"Take Endurance along too, if you like. I'm sure he speaks the language. Try to keep a low profile. And thanks for the gift."

Lori departed. Stingray turned and looked out past his balcony. The sun had set. The sky glowed with mellow pastel colors. The Pearl shone with a nacreous lavender glow.

He squinted and leaned forward. What was that? A flash of white?

The answer came a minute later. "Air Control to Stingray. A Perturbare flyer has just come and gone. It landed beside the Spire, staying just long enough to disembark a woman. She's standing outside right now, looking rather upset. Perturbare sent a message. He says she's a…gift for us."

"Very interesting. I'll be right down to meet her. Stingray out."

Chapter 20

Philosophy

"Fomalhaut, you're not looking well," said Sard Ducanis as he approached the bed in which Fomalhaut was still restrained. The man's missing arm was emphasized by the loose-hanging sleeve of his jacket. "Are you sure you won't try taking some food?"

Indeed, Fomalhaut neither looked nor felt very well. But, he was not yet desperate enough to take into his body the fatty, filthy, chemical cornucopia that was the typical diet of Twenty First Century America. For many decades now his body had been nourished and maintained solely by the mechanisms of his exploration suit. Its matter synthesizer had provided all the substances needed by his metabolism. At this point, the thought of reactivating his well-maintained yet long unused digestive system was enough to put him off the idea of food of any kind. All he was willing to accept was water, and this he requested to be freshly distilled. Whether he was actually getting that was difficult to say.

"No, thank you," he said mildly.

Ducanis took a seat and frowned. "The doctors tell me your body temperature is three degrees above the Neo-man norm."

"It isn't surprising. I have, after all, been exposed to a host of pathogens which are new to me."

"Do you require medicine? Antibiotics?"

"No. I possess a highly perfected immune system. It should suffice."

"Is that so? I don't believe our Neo-men are any better equipped than we are in that respect. It really wasn't our priority."

"My people have had centuries to further refine our genetic design." Fomalhaut hoped the topic would be left at that.

"If you insist on starving yourself, we will eventually be forced to resort to intravenous nourishment, and finally to force feeding."

"I have already said I will not cooperate with you. I was under the impression that a quick execution would be the result of that choice."

"Yes, well." Ducanis looked around the room. "It may well come to that. It probably will, and if it does, you will have no warning. So don't get complacent."

"My situation does little to encourage complacency."

"I was thinking we might have a little chat today. Do you mind?"

"I find myself with ample free time."

"I've heard you refer to the guiding philosophy of your native society as something called 'constructive anarchy'. Would you care to explain what that might be?"

"It is simple enough. We lack laws, leaders, or a formal government of any kind. Whenever we perceive that something needs to be done in the interest of the overall good, someone inevitably steps forward to do it."

Ducanis sat there waiting for Fomalhaut to continue.

"That's it?" he said at last.

"Yes. It is, as I told you, quite simple."

"But what motivates your people to behave like that? What rewards do they receive, what benefits? What penalties exist for those who don't comply?"

"The reward, of course, is a truly civilized society, in which all can live with dignity and a peaceful conscience. We have no penalties, nor any need for them."

"I see. I suppose that might be fine for a race of paragons such as your own, but you don't imagine you could ever impose such a system on the people of today, do you?"

Fomalhaut deigned to turn his head to look Ducanis full in the face, even though his peripheral vision was such that he saw the entire room in perfect detail.

"Don't be ridiculous. I'm fully aware of the intellectual, moral and ethical deficiencies of your species, which would doom any such attempt to instant and ignominious failure."

"Then what is your plan for humanity, in the event that the Vigil manages to take over?"

"It would fall along the lines of what you might call a benevolent despotism. Briefly, we would order things in an optimal manner while systematically dismantling such odious and oppressive institutions as arms manufacture, pharmaceutical monopolies, tobacco cultivation, financial speculation, and other such obvious evils. We will erase any national borders which were imposed by outside forces without regard for the historical realities of that region. We would isolate any intractable groups or individuals to limit their negative influence on others. We would eliminate hunger and abject poverty, which is easily done once a few adjustments are made and a few priorities changed.

"Once we've established the best possible worldwide society, with population reduced to a sustainable level through strict birth control, with technology appropriately upgraded, and education made free, universal, and pinned firmly to reality, then we, or our successors, would withdraw, hoping the social structures we had created would remain intact once under the control of human beings. We would hope that the benefits of living in a true civilization would become habitual."

"That is all very easily said. What about religion?"

"Religion is a pernicious hobgoblin which we do not believe we can purge from the human psyche. We would, however, deprive it of any secular power, support, or authority, and forbid its intrusion into public policy or education."

"That's very blunt."

"If you would prefer that I speak in circumlocutions, let me know."

"Not at all. Tell me, do your people have any answers?"

"Answers? Answers to what?"

"To questions of purpose, philosophy and meaning. Since you dismiss religion and the answers it provides, what is your substitute? What is the source of your conscience? What do you anarchic Neo-men believe to be the reasons for your existence?"

"You are operating under several false assumptions. First, such questions are far less urgent to us, because we do not live in a predatory, uncivilized, oppressive hell of our own devising. Also, death can be put off indefinitely among us. We are generally content with our lives, even pleased by them. Second, because the 'answers' your religions provide are not founded in objective reality, they are not answers at all, but merely wishes. Third, the reasons for our existence are known to us. We were devised by the

Humans of the late twentieth and early twenty-first centuries. But I know you're referring to deeper questions than that. We have no more knowledge or insight into the ultimate meaning of existence than you do. Each of us who is so inclined must seek such answers as seem satisfactory to that person. Some are unable to be satisfied. In a few rare cases these individuals choose to end their own lives. More commonly, they seek to improve themselves, or they seek meaning in the broader continuum outside of themselves."

"And what was your place in that continuum?"

"I was a Frame Rider, a lone explorer of the most remote depths of space. I was drawn to that existence by more than idle curiosity. I too was seeking."

"I understand. What did you discover?"

"Nothing definite. Nothing which would mean anything to you. That's the nature of such things. One person's revelation is another's fairy tale."

"I see." Ducanis fell into silence then, his eyes downcast and brooding, rendering him even more opaque to the psychically blinded Fomalhaut. He turned away, saying "I do so regret the loss of that suit of yours. So light, so filmy, yet so incredibly protective. What's it made of? Metal? Plastic? Something else altogether?"

"My exploration suit is made of string."

Ducanis appeared dubious. "String?"

"Cosmic string, as your physicists are just now beginning to name and imagine it. The most primordial stuff of existence, as much an idea as a substance. My suit is made of a single continuous filament of this material, or this vibration, the most basic root of matter, tamed and shaped to fit and protect my frail body. Any force that could break it would destroy the universe in doing so."

"Very impressive. Why are you telling me this?"

"Because no human being, not even Possum Perturbare with his computer, is capable of manipulating matter in this fashion. The knowledge will not help you."

After a time Ducanis looked up again. "This has been an interesting chat. I regret that I must now turn you over to men who will ask other questions. They will ask about the secrets and weaknesses of the members of the Vigil, about your communications and security protocols, and about your weapons programs. They will ask the names of your recruits. I truly advise you to cooperate with them. I recognize in you a civilized person, and I don't want you to suffer needlessly."

Fomalhaut sighed. "Your torture will be ineffective against me."

"And why is that?"

"Because I have the ability to divorce my consciousness from pain. I will remain aware of it, but it will have no power to compel me."

"But surely even you must eventually reconnect with your own body. Even you must then confront the ruin which has been inflicted upon you while your thoughts were elsewhere. This is what I would spare you."

"If you do such a thing to me, you would do well to hide the fact from your Neo-men. Otherwise, you may discover that their meek acquiescence to your abuse has its limits. And by all means, conceal the fact from Stingray and Aureus. I am, as you say, a civilized being. They, however, are beyond my control, and are less disposed to meting out gentle treatment to their enemies. And whatever you do, hide such actions from Ben Raintree, if you can. He is capable of causing you to regret evil deeds at a level you are unable to understand."

Chapter 21

Children of Rral

Valjhar Cor sat in the study of his private apartment in the Spire, writing a grammar and dictionary of the Rralian language. There was no real need for such a thing here on Earth, but exercising his little-used native tongue and putting it into a tangible form was somehow comforting to him.

Then the voice of Stingray sounded in the room.

"Valjhar, please meet me in the main vestibule on the first floor. You might want to dress warmly."

"What's this about, Stingray?"

"You'll see. Just come."

Stingray had sounded wary, subdued, serious, even for him. Frowning, Valjhar pulled on a jacket and proceeded to the lift.

He found Stingray in the vestibule, looking out a window. He motioned to Valjhar to join him. Valjhar did so, looking out onto the rock shelf that stretched a few hundred feet in front of the Spire and Pearl before plunging into the sea

Standing in the near distance was a slight figure which Valjhar recognized with a start as Pimsehkia Flam in her human guise. She walked around randomly, hugging herself against the cold, glancing resentfully at the structures of the Vigil base now and then.

"Why—how did she get here?" asked Valjhar, thunderstruck.

"Believe it or not, Possum Perturbare dropped her off a few minutes ago. He says she's a gift. That's all I know."

"Let's get her inside! She must be freezing."

"Yes, she must. I just thought you should be here too. I'm not her favorite person, you know."

At that moment, Aureus entered the chamber with a flurry of pattering metallic footsteps.

"On the other hand, I'm not her least favorite person, either," muttered Stingray.

The robot's mouth locked open. "I have detected the presence of Pimsehkia Flam."

"Yes, Vela," said Valjhar. "You might as well join us in greeting her."

And so the three of them stepped out into the cold. Pimsehkia, hearing, turned and nearly bolted at the sight of them. But she drew herself up and held her ground as they approached.

She looked from one to another as they stood before her.

"Well," she said through chattering teeth. "Valjhar Cor, Stingray, and the Prohibitor, arriving as one to welcome me. I must say, this is a sight I never expected to see."

"Please refer to me as Vela Flamaxamanda," said Aureus.

Pimsehkia had been about to say something else. Hearing this, she turned to Aureus in confusion. "What?"

"I wish to be known as Vela Flamaxamanda," repeated the robot.

"It's her Rralian name," said Valjhar.

"Her...what?" said Pimsehkia, open-mouthed.

"Pimsehkia. Let's discuss this inside. You can't stay out here," said Stingray.

She gave him a bright glance and then acquiesced to being led indoors. Stingray brought them to a reception area just off the vestibule. It was comfortable and warm, but like many other parts of the Spire, little visited and carrying a certain air of sterility.

Sitting by herself in a big overstuffed chair, Pimsehkia looked from one face to another, plainly uncertain about which subject to broach first, and with whom. Finally she settled on Stingray and said, "What do you plan to do with me?"

Stingray spoke in a level yet implacable tone. "I don't know what led Perturbare to drop you here, but now that we've got you, I intend to keep you. We want Fomalhaut back. I consider you at least partially responsible for his capture. If you won't help us recover him, you will at least no longer assist our enemies. You may consider your career as an agent of the U.S. government at an end."

She nodded bitterly. "That's as I expected. I'm afraid I underestimated Perturbare a little bit, or at least misread him. You're right, I won't help you. So, I'm to be a prisoner of the Vigil. A prisoner of the Prohibitor. And a prisoner of *you*, Valjhar Cor!" Her eyes blazed at Valjhar as she said this.

He shrank back from her fury. "That isn't my desire," he whispered miserably. "If you hadn't allied yourself with —"

Pimsehkia cut him off with a dismissive gesture. "And you, Prohibitor, what is this nonsense about you having a name?"

"My name is Vela Flamaxamanda."

"So you keep saying. All right, boys, what's this about?" She eyed Stingray and Valjhar, demanding an explanation.

They offered one which caused her eyes to widen steadily with disbelief. At the end of it she turned back to Aureus.

"You were—a woman?"

"I was."

"And that name you mentioned—Flamaxamanda?" She stared at the robot in growing astonishment. "I was once told that our family name was long ago simplified from— Flamaxamanda."

"Yes," intoned Aureus. "I am in fact one of your distant relatives, Pimsehkia Flam. You are descended from my sister, Picksis Flamaxamanda."

Pimsehkia turned pale. She goggled at Aureus, her head tilted, making no effort to speak.

When this condition showed no sign of abating, Stingray spoke.

"Pimsehkia, you will be allowed no access to any communications device. You will not be permitted to speak to anyone except full members of the Vigil. You will be confined to the quarters which we will provide for you. I'm sorry this is necessary. If there's nothing else you wish to say, we'll take you to your quarters."

Pimsehkia turned huge, moist eyes upon Stingray. "I wish to speak to Valjhar, alone. He can take me to my quarters later."

Stingray glanced between the two Rralians, looking slightly uncomfortable. "Valjhar?"

"Stingray, it's all right."

"Very well. Vela, come on, let's go."

The two of them departed.

Valjhar, who was standing by a window, looked uncertainly at Pimsehkia's white, glistening face. It was so strange to see her in this altered form. He began to appreciate what a shock it must have been for her, to see Kern and himself so changed. It was so strange to see her at all, so many decades after he'd seen her last, thinking her forever lost, and she still so young.

Pimsie stood. She approached him slowly, eyes locked onto his.

She ran the last few paces and flung herself into his arms.

"Pimsie...?" said Valjhar hesitantly, speaking in Rralian.

"Valjhar Cor, you fool," she sobbed, doing the same. "What have you done to us? What have you done to yourself? What are you doing now? Why must you be such an *idiot*? I'm so happy to see you. Valjhar, Valjhar."

Valjhar held her, his own tears streaming down into her hair, unable to think of a word worth saying.

"Pimsie." He closed his eyes, lost in the joy of being reunited with her.

Then she stepped back and slapped him with all her strength. Valjhar reeled back, his ears ringing.

"What are you doing here?" she cried. "Why did you have to take up with these people?"

Valjhar straightened himself, stepped up to her, and took her by the shoulders. "These people have realized they were mistaken to oppose us. They're now trying to achieve the same goals we were pursuing. I'm trying to salvage some semblance of meaning from all the pain we suffered."

"You mean they were mistaken to oppose *you!* Their goal is *your* goal. Not mine. I never believed in it, and I believe in it now less than ever."

Valjhar frowned at her, "Is that true? I was always under the impression you didn't really care one way or the other about the goals of the Para-men. As long as you could dwell in your little Rralian apartment and play with Kern whenever he had some free time, you seemed relatively content. You slept a lot, and that spirit you carried here from Colibdis, the Dreamfarer, came forth and helped us to a certain extent. It seems to me that your alliance with the *Humans* is based more on a desire for vengeance than from any real political conviction. Vengeance doesn't become you, Pimsie. You were always the gentlest among us. This path you've taken has corrupted you."

"Dreamfarer? Nali? Why do you mention her? I haven't heard from her since she was humbled by Anubis years ago."

"Really? That's odd. It was a vision of Dreamfarer that caused Stingray and me to realize you were in trouble."

"I wasn't in any trouble!"

"Yes, you were. And yes, you still are. You're in very serious trouble. Your true self is in jeopardy. Who knows what it took for Nali to show herself to us from wherever she is now?"

She looked at him with eyes soaked in misery. "I just want to go home. Home to Rral. Away from these awful people, all of them."

Valjhar nodded sadly. "I know, Pimsie, I know. I make you this promise. Events here on Earth are coming to a head. They will soon be resolved, either by the victory of the Vigil, or by their utter defeat. When that is decided, and if I'm still alive, I'll find a way to return you to Rral. I promise you that."

"And what about you? Will you come too? Or will you stay to rule the Earth?"

"You'd—want me to come?"

Pimsehkia looked into his eyes for a few moments, then shook her head. "Oh, no. No, not the way you're thinking. If you come, I'll care for you and look after you, because of who you are and all you've meant to me. But I won't love you. You've had that chance already, and it won't come again. You lost it long ago when you turned to Shaula. You lost it again when you left me behind and then threw away your youth searching all of creation for her. You'll get no more such chances. No, if I'm able to cast off this *Human* form and go back, I'll find myself an ordinary man of Rral, one who has never heard of spaceships or robots. He shall be a poet or a musician. At night I'll whisper tales of the stars and planets. If they do not make him shudder, I shall leave him."

Valjhar stepped back from her and lowered his eyes. "Yes. I understand."

For a few long moments they continued to inhabit the same room, but each was isolated in a private world of pain and regret.

Finally Pimsehkia said, "Valjhar? Do you think Stingray will—question me?"

Valjhar looked into her fearful eyes again. "Yes. He is determined to save Fomalhaut. He won't harm you. Vela wouldn't permit it, and neither would I. But he wouldn't hurt you anyway. For all his sharp-edged demeanor, Stingray is a gentle soul. This time, I know what *you're* thinking. There is no limit to Stingray's remorse for what he did to Kern that day. No limit. He didn't understand what was really happening. Thanks to my meddling, he didn't remember who Kern really was. He didn't know how harmless Kern really was. I don't excuse him for giving vent to his rage as he did, but I've learned that neither does he excuse himself. That act has informed his every action ever since. No, you can expect far better treatment here than Fomalhaut will receive at the hands of those thugs you used to work for."

Valjhar suspected that if anyone would be tasked to question Pimsie, it would be Ben Raintree, before whom no truth could hide. But the thought of confronting the harrowing light of the Stones would not comfort her.

A complex of emotions flickered over Pimsehkia's face, some of them not pretty to behold. "Vela," she spat. "It sounds obscene to hear that thing referred to by a name. And now it claims to be...my aunt!"

Valjhar nodded carefully. "Our old friend the Prohibitor has certainly revealed some unexpected sides lately. I for one will wait to learn their outcome before making any judgments."

Pimsehkia turned away, fuming. "I used to find your tolerance and fairness charming."

"Those qualities grew in the light of your once-sweet spirit. Come on, Pimsehkia. I'll lead you to your new rooms. They're not so bad."

"Can I have a cat?"

Stingray sat in his office with the door locked and the lights dimmed, relieved to be away from Pimsie. It had been their first encounter since his expulsion from the

Space Mariners, and the more he heard her speak, the longer he looked at her (even changed as she was), the more disturbed he'd become. He was beginning to remember. He could see her in her natural guise, a delicate fairy presence, not half his height, with eyes like shifting globes of liquid sentience, startling in their impact and sweet vitality. He had adored her with all his heart, while she...she could barely tolerate him. Huge and ungainly in her eyes, neither human nor Rralian, he was to her a monster, someone to shy away from as she clung to Kern and Valjhar. They could have been natural allies, Pimsie and he, the only two to object to Valjhar's plans for Earth. And he—he had tried to bring that about. In fact—he now remembered—it had been his unwanted interest in Pimsie that had led Valjhar to eject him, as much as his opposition to Valjhar's plans. Kern had understood and had forgiven him for this, but Valjhar, in this case, was less than tolerant.

So far Valjhar had shown the grace not to confront him with this embarrassment, but he knew he couldn't expect the same mercy from Pimsie herself. Stingray was beginning to wish Perturbare had dropped her off at a nice hotel somewhere, rather than on his doorstep.

He sighed. He could not avoid her forever. He would have to take whatever was coming to him, and hope not to further embarrass himself in the process.

Chapter 22

Zayin

Stingray, Valjhar, Aureus, and Raintree set out in a specialized flyer early one morning, heading north-northwest over the cold Pacific toward Anchorage, Alaska. Two days previously, Stingray had express mailed a package to the Anchorage post office box of one Zayin Gold. Now the four of them were off to see who, if anyone, appeared to collect it.

Raintree looked inconspicuous, which was usually easy for him to do. He wore khaki pants, a white turtleneck sweater, and his grey jacket. With the Stones concealed in his clothing, he looked like nothing more than a gangling, narrow-faced young man with dull-colored hair and sad grey-green eyes.

Valjhar, a scruffy, bearded, older man, looked even more nondescript, except for the streaks of Rralian green which had appeared in his dark brown hair as he aged. A stocking cap did an adequate job of covering that.

For Stingray, blending in was a difficult prospect at best. His blue-black eyes could be hidden by sunglasses, but his sheer size and slightly inhuman contours drew attention no matter what he wore. He'd have to remain in the flyer with Aureus, who had naturally insisted on tagging along after Valjhar.

The flyer itself was unusual. Stingray had commissioned its construction only days earlier. It was actually a white commercial mini-van, modified to contain a tachyon pile and an array of small propulsion lanterns. The main beams shone out of the brake light housings. The craft wasn't pressurized and was limited to low altitudes and speeds.

It also remained a fully functional van, complete with gasoline-powered internal combustion engine.

With Denali visible in the distance to the north, Stingray flew in low through the valleys of the Chugach Mountains east of the city, reasonably certain that the flyer was there immune to detection from the Air Force base and city airport radars. The sun glimmered not far above the southeastern horizon. Days were short here at this time of year.

Landing on the most isolated outlying road Stingray could find, they proceeded into town on the ground. As none of them had ever driven a car before, Stingray had studied traffic laws and conventions in preparation for this mission. Knowing this did not spare Valjhar a degree of anxiety as Stingray, with his head bumping the van's ceiling, grimly guided it through an increasing density of similar vehicles that hurtled along in what seemed a barely controlled manner.

Valjhar looked back at Ben Raintree, riding serenely beside Aureus, whose head swiveled back and forth with an unnerving precision as it no doubt assessed the threat potential of nearby vehicles. He was grateful when Stingray spoke up, sparing him the necessity.

"Vela, I hate to assault your dignity like this, but you are far too conspicuous. Please conceal yourself on the floor of the vehicle."

"Very well."

The robot curled into a compact ball on the floor. Raintree smiled down on it, as if he thought it was cute. Valjhar stared at Aureus for a moment, and then at Stingray, admiring the knack for dealing with the robot he'd somehow acquired.

Stingray glanced aside at him and said, "Valjhar, you can read English, correct?"

"Of course."

"Keep your eye on those green highway signs. I need your help to navigate to the correct post office."

After three or four near-collisions, some violent braking, and a few turns taken on two squealing wheels, Stingray parked in front of the post office and shut off the engine with visible relief. He pulled out a small device and aimed it at the post office building.

"Okay. The transponder I included in the package is still here. No one has picked it up yet."

"And the chances are that no one will," said Ben quietly. "Zayin's Orinoco account has been cancelled. Surely someone noticed what he was up to and took steps to prevent any more such mischief."

Stingray nodded. "Entirely possible and likely. If so, we've had a pointless morning's ride and that's all. But we don't know the exact circumstances of Zayin's attempts to buy things, or why they stopped. I think this is worth a try. Short of breaking into the Air Force base, this is our best chance for making contact with one of the Neo-men. Ben and Valjhar, on your way."

Valjhar followed Ben, who appeared entirely relaxed, into the brick building. Valjhar had been concerned that Ben's staff would be too conspicuous, but it came off looking like a mere outdoorsy affectation, no different than the down vests and floppy hats many others were wearing.

A line of people stood at the counter, most bearing Christmas packages for mailing. As they advanced through the line, Valjhar took note of how different Ben appeared from these other Humans. While Ben was nearly motionless in repose, the rest of them seemed twitchy and ephemeral in comparison. Yet no one seemed to take special notice of either of them. Finally they reached the counter.

Ben nodded at the clerk. "I'd like, oh, five postcards please, to send to Canada," he said, spreading a few coins on the counter.

A moment later they ambled around a corner into a bay whose walls were lined with locked boxes of brass and glass. Valjhar identified the correct box. He could see their little package through the glass.

Ben stepped up to a desk, leaned his staff against the wall, and began scribbling on a postcard.

Valjhar, keeping an eye on Zayin's box, nevertheless couldn't help glancing at what Raintree was doing.

"Who are you writing to?" he whispered.

"Oh, just some friends of mine in Prince George. Also to Raintree's family. The original Raintree, I mean. I've met them, you know. Fine people. Very interesting family I sort of come from."

Valjhar watched as Ben scrawled a signature.

"You—sign it Jim Carina?"

"Yes, it's a false name I've had occasion to use before. It could be a lot worse, trust me." Ben caught Valjhar's eye and cocked a grin at him.

They both burst out in laughter.

A shadow appeared in Valjhar's peripheral vision. He turned, but nothing was there. Valjhar blinked and looked at Raintree, who seemed to have noticed nothing. For an instant Valjhar seemed to perceive a figure standing nearby and looking at them, but it vanished before he could focus on it.

"I think someone is here," murmured Valjhar.

"Yes. I've noticed that too."

Valjhar and Raintree locked gazes with each other. Valjhar, fascinated, could not turn away. Raintree, looking puzzled, shook his head, then laughed and looked around the room, smiling. "He's trying to compel us to stare at each other, and not at him."

"Why isn't it working?" asked Valjhar, who was still unable to avert his eyes.

"Because of this." Raintree pulled down the collar of his sweater, revealing the violet cabochon of the Stone of Adamance. The room gleamed with its dim yet potent radiance, breaking the spell.

They heard a click. "Look!" cried Valjhar. "Zayin's box has been opened. It's empty!"

"Let's see the truth of the matter," said Raintree. From an inner pocket of his jacket he quickly extracted the Stone of Truth on its silver fillet, placing it upon its brow. The small blue gem blazed up, sparkling on every plane and surface in the room. Raintree took up his staff, and thunder rumbled somewhere nearby. Valjhar averted his eyes from the raw sight of the Stone.

Standing revealed was a small figure dressed in a gold jumpsuit. He was golden-skinned, with fine hair of bluish white brushed back over his broad brow. His huge, dark, liquid eyes shone with the Light of Truth. Valjhar, having never seen the face of any Neo-man, was captivated by the beauty of this Neo-Child.

"Behold the Vigil," whispered the child in awe, his voice silvery and beautiful.

"Hello, Zayin," said Raintree amiably.

Zayin Gold looked from face to face. His emotions were difficult to read through those strange eyes, but to compensate for that he radiated feelings of apprehension, confusion, and excitement.

"So what happens now? You abduct me, torture me, dissect me?"

Raintree stiffened. Valjhar said quickly, "No, no, nothing like that. We'd just like to talk to you."

"Which one are you? The new one, the one they call Motion?"

"Yes, but my real name is Valjhar Cor."

Valjhar winced. He had just revealed information that would be quite useful to their enemies. In the Light of Truth he had been unable to speak anything less.

Zayin could not conceal his astonishment at this news. "Valjhar Cor—a member of the Vigil?"

Valjhar could only nod lamely. Stingray, who was no doubt listening in, was probably crushing the steering wheel about now.

"That Stone is fantastic," said Zayin, turning to Ben. "It can make me believe anything you want, correct?"

Raintree frowned, an unaccustomed expression made still more unsettling by the blue light burning on his face. "Is that what you've been told? I'll show what this Stone can do."

The blue light focused into a beam fixed on Zayin's forehead. The boy staggered back; the beam followed him relentlessly. Valjhar pitied him, being all too familiar with the harrowing effects of this Light.

Footsteps sounded from around the corner. The postal clerk ran into view, followed by a few other men. They halted, staring aghast at the strange scene before them.

Without turning, Raintree tapped his staff on the floor. The building shook.

"Get back!" snapped Valjhar. The men fell over each other to withdraw a few paces, but continued to stare, transfixed. "Stingray, we've become conspicuous. I fear we'll have to leave soon."

The light of Truth abruptly ceased. Raintree removed and concealed the fillet. Zayin stood trembling.

"Oh," he said softly. "Those liars. Those dirty, terrible liars."

Valjhar spoke swiftly. "Zayin, we can't stay here much longer. Will you come with us? If we're forced to leave without you, and your handlers find out what you've been doing, you'll never get another chance like this one."

"Yes, I'll certainly come. Aleph will wish to speak to you. He and the others must know what I now know."

"Then follow us. We have a vehicle waiting outside."

"You go. I think I can make these humans—forget what they've seen here. And then I'll follow."

Valjhar considered this, uncertain whether he should permit this child to meddle with the minds of these people, but he could think of no better alternative. He nodded. "Come on, Ben." The pair walked past the gawkers, who still stared at the strange child. Zayin turned to face them.

Valjhar and Raintree left the building and entered the van. Stingray looked at Valjhar as he slid into his seat. With his eyes hidden by wraparound sunglasses, Stingray looked rather like a Neo-man himself.

"Good work, you two," he said.

"Thanks," said Valjhar in relief.

"I wish he'd hurry up and come out. We won't go unnoticed here forever."

"I don't think we'll see him when he does come out," said Raintree from the back. "He has the power to cloud men's minds."

Aureus stretched its neck up a little and peeked over the bottom of the side window. "The child is coming."

Raintree leaned over to slide open the side door. Zayin revealed himself as he entered the van and sat on the rear bench beside Raintree, with Aureus still crouched on the deck in front of him. Stingray pulled away from the curb and entered traffic, returning the way they had come.

"How astonishing to find myself riding with members of the Vigil, and yet not to be in fear of my life," said Zayin.

"How old are you, Zayin?" asked Stingray, not taking his eyes off the road.

"I was born six years ago. You're Stingray, correct? You're something like we Neo-men."

"Yes, something like that. I'm curious. How exactly are you Neo-men born? Or made?"

"So far, it's done by inserting our genetic material into a Human ovum, which is then brought to term by a Human surrogate mother. Our adults are capable of sexual reproduction, of course, but our oldest have only recently come of age, and so far no matings have been arranged."

"Very interesting."

"And this?" said Zayin, studying the metallic form before him. "This is Aureus, the destroyer robot? Curled up here, mere inches from me?"

"Yes," said Valjhar. "Recently though, we've taken to calling her Vela."

"Indeed? Vela." The boy put forth his exquisitely formed hand, stroking the smooth contours of Aureus's face and shoulders. "How beautiful you are, Vela."

The robot raised its head and looked into his eyes.

To Valjhar's bemusement, Zayin continued to pet Aureus as he spoke on. "So, it's true? My people are destined to rule the world, to explore the stars?"

"According to Fomalhaut, that's true, or at least easily could be," said Raintree. "He himself is a Neo-man, as you've seen, and is a representative of an advanced galactic civilization, in addition to being a prisoner and hostage of your government."

Zayin leaned toward Raintree and gripped his arm. "And—and it's true that the Vigil has no part in what's happening behind the Moon?"

"Behind the Moon?" said Stingray sharply. "What are you talking about?"

"Something terrible is happening behind the Moon," whispered Zayin. "We've all felt it. Do you mean none of you have detected it?"

"No," said Stingray uneasily. "This is the first we've heard of it."

"It has something to do with that awful television show."

"Television show?"

"Yes, *The Night Land*. You don't know it? No, I suppose that's not the sort of thing the Vigil would be aware of. I've only managed to sneak off to see a single episode myself. But according to Bet, it has come to inform the dreams and fears of much of Humanity. She's very sensitive to such things, and claims its influence is quite oppressive."

Stingray scowled mightily. "If it's television and it's making trouble, Possum Perturbare is probably behind it. We must look into this."

Zayin looked from one face to another. "I'm going to bridge to Aleph. I don't care how much trouble I get into for sneaking out again. There's so much he must know."

Aureus abruptly stiffened. To Valjhar's horror, its Third Eye slid open. "Vela? What are you doing?"

"Do not interfere," said Aureus. A dire, pale beam licked out from the Eye and lanced into Zayin's chest. The boy gasped and sagged back, staring down at the beam.

A moment later the beam ceased. Zayin looked around, breathing heavily.

"Vela, explain yourself," demanded Stingray.

"The child had a foreign object implanted in his chest. I detected electronic and chemical activity which indicated it was about to explode. To prevent that, I converted the device into energy and drew it into my storage cells."

"Excellent work!" said Stingray, impressed.

"Aleph," whispered Zayin. "My family. Something is happening to them."

"What?"

"They're being...herded. At gunpoint. For their own protection."

"No. Not this time. Not this time." Stingray looked at Valjhar.

"Let's go," said Valjhar.

Stingray gave a sharp nod. "Right. Hang on and belt up, everyone. We're lifting off."

The van shot straight up, fast enough to push them down in their seats.

"Your car flies?" said Zayin. "That's so...oh..."

"What is it, Zayin?" asked Ben.

"My family...they're afraid. Afraid for me. Afraid for themselves. Confused."

"Tell them we're on our way," said Stingray. "Vela, bail out. We'll need your firepower. Valjhar, establish communications with the base commander. Zayin, did you know about that device in your chest?"

Zayin answered while Aureus exited the vehicle and Valjhar donned a headset. "Yes, Stingray. We all have them. We were told they were signaling devices we could activate if we were ever kidnapped by—you."

"Zayin, how can anyone ever lie to you? Aren't you all telepaths?" asked Ben.

Zayin looked embarrassed as he replied. "We—we are. At least potentially. But we have no one to teach us. Most of us have developed some mental specialty more or less on our own. For example, I can convince people they can't see me."

"Plus, if someone believed the function of the devices was innocent, and they conveyed that to the Neo-men, it would not be perceived as a lie," said Stingray.

"Stingray, I have the base commander," said Valjhar, handing over the headset.

"This is Stingray of the Vigil. We are coming to relieve you of the Gold family of Neo-men. If you do not surrender them, or if you harm them in any way, we will destroy your base and deprive you of your troops. There will be no negotiation. Comply with us or suffer the consequences. Stingray out."

Valjhar blinked. "Well, that was certainly decisive. Will you really kill all those men if they resist?"

"I said deprive, not kill. I believe Ben here can arrange that without physically harming anyone." The flyer leveled off. From this altitude the base was clearly visible.

"Stingray," said Ben. "You realize this action may well result in Fomalhaut being killed at once."

"Yes. I do. But I don't believe Fomalhaut would want us to ignore the likely murder of a whole clan of his people, even if it was to spare him. The Americans know that if Zayin tells the Golds the truth, they'll lose control over the whole bunch of them. They can't take that risk."

Ben nodded. "I believe you are right."

"Zayin, what are you getting from your family?"

"Nothing," he said miserably. "They've either been placed behind quantum shielding, or..."

"Stingray, they're launching fighters," said Valjhar.

"Aureus! Go after those planes—"

"My name is Vela," came the robot's voice from the console.

Stingray took a moment to mouth silent obscenities before continuing.

"Vela! Yes. Your name is Vela. But Aureus is...your public name. Your hero name. Like...Peregrine was for Rouse Farewell. Do you understand?"

"I understand."

"Good. Now—Vela—please disable those planes. Cut off their vertical stabilizers, and allow the pilots to eject. Then carve up the base's runways so they can't launch any more planes. All right?"

"Very well. Aureus out." Aureus flashed away. The jets were dealt with within seconds. Seconds later, the runways were divided into useless segments by zones of flaming slag.

"Very efficient," commented Stingray over the thunder of Aureus's attack. "Now, in we go. Vela, follow us in, and watch out for missiles. Ben, we're going to need your full power, so you'd better put on all the Stones. Valjhar, you stay in the car with Zayin and be ready to lift off in a hurry."

Valjhar winced. His loss of the Motionglobe had reduced him to the status of babysitter for this combat mission.

Stingray guided the flyer toward the field in a very aggressive descending trajectory that left them all weightless in the cabin. The air base expanded before Valjhar's wide eyes with impossible speed. Painfully aware of his age, he was thrown forward in his harness as they came to an abrupt landing in a muddy quad between the base's main buildings.

"Out we go, Ben!" Unarmed and unarmored, Stingray erupted from the driver's side, while Ben Raintree made a more dignified exit from the rear sliding door. Staff in hand, he was ablaze with the cold lights of the Stones. Overhead, Aureus could be seen glinting and flashing.

Valjhar hoped these soldiers would have sense enough not to defy those who had come among them.

"How are you doing, Zayin? Anything from your family yet?" he asked as he slipped into the driver's seat.

"I'm all right. But they...I don't know."

A number of armored vehicles roared into view from between the buildings, followed by a few hundred armed men. Forming a shallow arc, they faced the Vigil members, weapons trained on them and on their fragile vehicle.

Stingray and Ben Raintree stood there regarding them like two calm sovereigns facing a mob. Valjhar was far less nonchalant. A single bullet could take down either of them. A shell from one of those armored vehicles could end them all.

Stingray, looking utterly impassive and immovable in those sunglasses, said, "Vela. Ben. Let them have it."

Darting lances of white fire from above turned cannons and machine guns into splashes of molten metal. Raintree grabbed the Stone of Inner Light on its chain and held it on high, where it ignited with a supernal glow.

Valjhar put up a hand to shield his face from that Light. It felt like being cleansed in a bath of hot lye...very thorough, yet painful. It made it impossible to ignore the many moral compromises he had made since leaving Rral in a slapped-together starship. It was as if every bad choice he'd ever made was now embossed in his consciousness. Through tear-blurred eyes he looked back at Zayin, whose face was pressed up against the window, drinking in the Light with delight. Ah, to be that innocent again...

If the Stone was uncomfortable for Valjhar Cor, it was worse for the soldiers. Many of them dropped their weapons and fell back screaming, as if a blowtorch had been held to their faces. Some collapsed and wept. A few stood rapt, staring, their expressions grateful or exalted. Such was the ratio of vice to virtue among the people of Earth, Valjhar supposed.

He turned, forcing himself to stare full into the Stone. It could never harm anyone who faced it openly, he knew. He kept telling himself that as the Light flowed into him, pooling in places that had been empty or dark.

And then it faltered and went dim. Valjhar looked around in confusion.

A military officer was advancing, waving a white flag. Valjhar was glad he knew what this meant on Earth, for on Rral white was the color of death.

The officer, a general, or so Valjhar supposed, approached grim-faced and trembling. He halted a few meters from Stingray and Raintree.

"I have just received orders to stand down and surrender our Neo-men to you. Why we're being made to kowtow to you terrorists I have no idea."

Stingray was surprised by this, but sought to conceal it. "Terrorists? I guess that's what the definition of 'terrorist' has become for you: anyone who does anything you don't like. Bring out the Golds and we'll be on our way."

In the back of the van, Zayin Gold was capering like a highly advanced monkey. "I can feel them again! And they're all right."

A line of six Neo-men, all wearing uniform gold jump suits, came into view. They walked in order of decreasing height, led by a huge young Neo-man not much smaller than Stingray himself, and trailed by a pair of girls not much taller than Zayin.

It's going to be a crowded ride home," said Stingray wryly. "We may wind up sitting on each other's laps."

The Neo-men approached in silence, studying Stingray and the others with a disconcerting scrutiny. Though their huge eyes had no visible pupils and did not rotate, Valjhar felt it whenever any of them looked at him in particular.

Still without a word, the Neo-men piled into the van. Stingray replaced Valjhar in the driver's seat, putting him in very close proximity to their new guests. Their bodies felt hot and intensely alive. Raintree, still girded by the Stones, squeezed into one of the rear bench seats. The two little girls sat on either side of him. Aureus, mercifully, remained outside, content to fly home under her own power. Zayin did indeed sit in the lap of Bet Gold.

When the van was packed full, Stingray lifted off. They were an oddly subdued and quiet assemblage as they soared low over the Pacific with Aureus close beside.

Then a call came in from the Pearl.

"Stingray from Vigil Intelligence. Something is happening near the Sea Creche. Something very strange."

Chapter 23

The Great Laughter

Someone knocked on the door of Tara Strenczak's darkened cabin aboard *Nemo II*, awakening her from a foul nightmare of screaming multitudes and horrors rising up from the Earth. Rarely had she been so happy to return to reality.

"Captain! It's Vanderbrook. Something's happening. The two carrier groups are coming into striking range. We've picked up a lot of suspicious communications traffic. We're going on full alert."

Tara lurched out of bed and opened her door, facing her executive officer while dressed in very little. To his credit, he didn't react, keeping his eyes on her face. He had volunteered for sea duty from among the ranks of construction engineers at the Sea Creche, and so far he had proven to be acceptable.

"Alert the fleet. Call in the crews. Prepare all subs for immediate departure. I'll be right out."

"Right," said Vanderbrook, turning and dashing away. No "Yes, Ma'am," or even "Yes, Sir." He was good, but proper military discipline wasn't easy to instill in these crews.

Tara threw on her Vigil Sea Command uniform, a white jumpsuit with green trim. She was in her seat in the control room three minutes after being awakened, still unable to shake off foreboding and thoughts of dread.

Nemo now had a crew of seven. The three control room stations were manned. Tara still insisted on taking the conn herself, though others were certainly capable of taking over. Vanderbrook stood near her side, overseeing preparations for departure.

Calling the existing squadron a "fleet" was a little optimistic. So far its only seaworthy vessels were *Nemo* herself and her three sister ships, *Radiolarian*, *Foraminifera*, and *Diatom*. Like *Nemo*, they were oceanographic research ships hastily refitted for a combat role. The first of the powerful *Torpedo Ray* class of dedicated attack subs was yet to be launched.

Still, these four subs were easily the most powerful warships in the oceans of Earth, unless Possum Perturbare somewhere maintained his own hidden fleet.

At Tara's command the four submarines left the Creche and ventured into the dark waters of the Great Barrier Reef. Moving on the surface in single file, they threaded the channels that led to open water. Tara's display showed ERASER emplacements rising from concealed niches all around the Creche.

The full Moon shown down through the control room's great bubble canopy, adding its glow to the dim lights of the consoles. Tara looked up at it uneasily. About to go into battle against the United States Navy, she more than half suspected she was still living out some nightmare.

"Weird night, isn't it, Captain?" said Vanderbrook, who still lurked in the dimness nearby. "Maybe the sea floor is about to crack open and the ocean drain away."

Tara shook her head. "*Ugh!* I don't want to hear any more about the damned *Night Land*. I wish I'd never seen it. If I were in command of the Creche I'd order that vile show blocked. We have enough problems without that particular vision of the future haunting us."

"Yes, Captain," said Vanderbrook, sounding both chastened and oddly satisfied.

"Wood! What's the launch status on those carriers?"

Ryan Wood, a young Australian, occupied the forward seat, where his job was to monitor all sensors and tactical displays.

"Carrier groups still converging on the Creche, Captain. They're about three hours from their maximum launch range."

The subs emerged from the shallows of the reef and spread into a broad line on Tara's order. "All vessels submerge and proceed to intercept enemy vessels." Tara felt relief. Her ships would be much less vulnerable beneath the surface.

At that moment a terrible glare shone through the bubble from the port side. They averted their faces until it subsided to something tolerable, then turned to stare at the fireball blooming a few kilometers off.

"That...that was a nuclear explosion," said Wood.

A shockwave accompanied by a great roar swept over the *Nemo*, rolling it steeply. Vanderbrook staggered and held on to Tara's chair.

"All subs continue dive! All subs report status!" cried Tara. She grabbed her own control sticks and forced her vessel beneath the turbulent surface, cutting off that dying red glare.

Diatom and *Radiolarian*, which were off to starboard, called in without damage. There was no word from *Foraminifera*, which had been off to port.

"We have to assume *Forrie* was lost," said Tara in a choked voice. "What was it? A missile? Torpedo?"

"No sign of either," said Wood. "It could have been a mine of some kind, camouflaged against our sensors."

Tara got back on the comm link. "*Diatom* and *Radiolarian*, proceed against the southern battle group as planned. We'll take the northern group. Avoid or destroy any solid body you detect that's large enough to conceal a nuke. That includes marine mammals."

"Captain, we could stop both battle groups right now, simply by emptying our torpedo tubes at them. Why don't we?" asked Vanderbrook.

She swiveled to face him. "We've just lost seven people and a ship. That's bad enough. The enemy ships have crews of hundreds or thousands. Our mission is to disable their ships, not to sink them. That's the Vigil way. That hasn't changed."

Vanderbrook nodded. Why was he still hovering here? "Go check on the crew and see if we've taken any damage. We were closest to that blast."

Her XO nodded again and departed.

With *Nemo* submerged and stabilized, Tara opened her up. The sound of seawater rushing around the bubble's guard beam was like a low-pitched wind. Her hands were shaking. She really ought to turn the helm over to someone else, lest she make some fuzzy-headed mistake. But no member of her crew had any more experience in combat than she did. "Wood, don't take your eye off your displays. There's no telling what they'll be throwing at us."

"Captain, I'm getting some strange readings here."

"Explain," she snapped, aware of the response she'd have gotten if she'd offered that kind of vague report aboard her old cruiser.

"The forward-looking bathymetric display has gone all flaky. It looks like the sea floor up ahead has gone somehow—vague. Like the whole bottom's involved in a landslide. I'm picking up some strange sounds, too."

"Could it be interference from our hydrodynamic noise?"

"No, that's fairly minor in these frequencies, and easily filtered out. I'm also hearing the screws from the battle group up ahead, as well as those of their picket subs. They're still out of firing range," he added, as if suddenly aware that mentioning them a little earlier might have been a good idea. "This is…a bit eerie."

Tara peered over her console, trying to see Wood's displays over his shoulder.

"Lieutenant Takahashi, take over the helm," she said, speaking to the man at the third console position beside her. "Wood, don't take this personally, but I'm going to punch up sensor lights here on my board to see what you're seeing. I am a trained sonar operator."

"Yes, Captain, I remember. That's fine with me."

Tara quickly configured her console to show all external sensors. The bathymetry was indeed all screwed up, but she was even more curious about whatever Wood was hearing. She nearly put it on speakers; then, taking Takahashi's untried nerves into account, pulled out a headset and slipped it on.

She heard a low-pitched rhythmic beat, or rather a series of them, superimposed atop one another, interacting, throbbing, troubling her mind and spirit.

Far worse was the sound of a great laughter emanating from the deep.

Tara and Wood exchanged haunted looks over her console. It was enough to establish that it would be best not to mention this detail to the rest of the crew.

"Takahashi, I'm taking back the helm. Check all weapons and prepare for targeting orders."

She received no verbal acknowledgment of this order, only a quick, worried glance, as if Takahashi had heard in her voice a note that left him uneasy.

Tara drilled her ship through the sea as quickly as it would go, increasingly convinced they would encounter something other than a clean, simple carrier battle group... something she had long dreaded in some deep part of her psyche, something she would rather not see or know.

"Captain, the battle group is making flank speed toward the Creche," reported Wood. "They've left their own supply ships behind. They're making a maximum effort to get into position to launch before we intercept them. I expect they've heard us coming. Or heard something, at any rate."

"Understood," said Tara. She drove her ship deeper, beneath the sonic layer depth, to hide its sound and foil any mobile mines that might be in their vicinity. This went on for an hour, bringing them nearly a hundred nautical miles closer to whatever awaited them. By now Tara's hands ached from their sweaty grip on the controls.

"Captain, I have vectors and bearings on the battle group's two attack subs. They aren't trying to intercept us. They're moving back toward the carrier at high speed," said Wood.

"What else is happening up ahead?"

"I have the full battle group on my screens now. Their formation has become ragged, but they're still heading this way at over thirty knots. Those...noises...are continuing, and growing worse. The bathymetry is still strange. I'm seeing sea floor topography that doesn't match our maps at all."

Nemo suddenly pitched up a few degrees, then down, then steadied. A sound like the tolling of a bell bigger and deeper than the world entered the ship.

"What's happening out there?" gasped Takahashi.

"I don't know. Keep your eyes on your board, Lieutenant. Wood, how far are we from the leading elements of the battle group?"

"Fourteen nautical miles. They are just coming into position to launch planes against the Creche."

"Takahashi, launch a surface probe. Get it to the surface and drive it as hard as it will go. I want to see what's happening up there."

By the time the probe reached the surface it was only ten nautical miles from the battle group, while the faster *Nemo* was even closer. *Nemo* continued to shudder and buck as the water grew more turbulent around it.

Takahashi put the probe's night-vision video on the main display between their two console positions.

At first Tara thought she was seeing some kind of optical distortion. The horizon line appeared to bulge, leaving the carrier and one of its escorting destroyers perched atop a dome of water.

And then she realized that was exactly what she was seeing. The carrier began to slip down the slope. At high power she could see planes sliding off its flight deck into the sea. The destroyer vanished beyond the opposite side of the water bulge. The carrier, reaching the base of the bulge, buried its bow in the water with a huge splash, then wallowed upright again. The water dome began to subside, sending out great concentric waves as it did so.

"What in the name of God was that?"

Tara started. It was Vanderbrook, who had reappeared at some point and was standing close beside her again. "Who the hell knows?" she replied.

"Then it's not some kind of—Vigil attack?"

"If it is, it's like nothing I ever heard about. I don't know that any of them could do that, even if they wanted to."

"Captain, there's…something moving through the water ahead! Something huge," said Wood with renewed alarm. "Look! Look ahead there, through the bubble!"

They all looked. The seawater beyond the bubble was utterly black, or had been a moment before. Now, a row of lights, dimmed and diffused by distance, was rising.

"That's still miles off. No light should be able to penetrate that much seawater."

Tara keyed the ship-wide intercom. "All hands! Prepare for rapid ascent. I'm bringing us to periscope depth." She pulled back on the diving stick. *Nemo* sought the surface at a steep angle with Vanderbrook hanging onto the back of Tara's chair.

The video from the periscope, shown on the main display, once again defied interpretation.

"Oh, to hell with it. I'm surfacing. I want to see this with my own eyes."

And so *Nemo* broached the surface, riding up and down the waves of a turbulent sea, while before it loomed something no one had ever seen in the real world. At least three thousand feet high it reared, motionless, black, roughly rectilinear, a monstrous house of some kind, while in the depths of its lower reaches burned a row of white lights, unblinking and still.

"Those lights," muttered Takahashi. "They look like they've been shining for a million years."

"It's like something out of the damned Night Land," snapped Tara. From the lofty viewpoint of the periscope video, the ships of the carrier group could be seen wallowing near the base of this immense structure, apparently out of control.

"It looks like we won't have to do a thing to stop that battle group," said Vanderbrook softly. "Not with that awful thing out there."

Tara stared at the wholly unpredictable scene before her. If this was indeed something manifested in reality from the world of the Night Land, and somehow she did not doubt it, those sailors out there faced fates worse than drowning.

"Takahashi, take the helm!" She slapped at the communications controls. *"Nemo* to *Diatom* and *Radiolarian*! Break off your attacks and rendezvous with us at maximum speed." Then she shifted to an ordinary radio frequency. "Attention United States Navy battle groups! This is V.S.C. *Captain Nemo II.* We are coming to assist you. Do not fire on us. We are not behind this attack on you, and we will assist you. *Nemo* out."

"I'm happy to hear you say that, Petty Officer Strenczak," said Vanderbrook. "That means I won't have to blow you up after all, and myself along with you. Although I'm not sure what chance we have against whatever is happening out there."

Tara swiveled her chair and jumped to her feet, looking Vanderbrook eye to eye.

"Who are you really, then?"

"Just a moment, please." He touched the comm system controls, raising his hand to discourage her from interfering. "This is Inboard. Stand down. Code Triumphant Trumpet. That is all." He straightened up again. "That will deactivate my people on all three remaining subs, and also reassure whoever might be listening on the carrier groups."

"Who are you?" repeated Tara.

"Lieutenant Commander Vincent Remza, U.S. Naval Intelligence. My job was to stop you from attacking our fleet. We have men on each of your subs who were prepared to detonate one of their nuclear torpedo warheads. Yes, that's what happened to *Foraminifera*. It was done without my order, and represented a breakdown of the chain of command, for reasons I don't yet know. For what it's worth, I'm sorry about that."

"What kind of chewing gum do you like, Remza?"

Remza looked a little startled, then smiled. "You know about that? I thought that was one of my little failures. And now, Petty Officer Strenczak, I take command of your squadron in the name of the United States of America."

Tara was on him before he could react, knocking him to the deck, straddling him with her knee against his throat. "Takahashi, Wood, call all hands forward! Anyone who doesn't respond, go back to restrain them by any means necessary! And as for you, Remza...I hold the rank of full Commander in the Vigil Sea Command. These are Vigil ships, I outrank you, I am in command, and damned if it isn't all going to stay that way, do you understand me?!"

She said this with such ferocity that despite all his training, Remza could not help going pale.

"All right, Captain. I thought it was worth a try."

The remaining three members of the crew burst through the hatch, crowding the control room considerably. They all goggled at the sight of their captain holding their exec down by the throat.

One of them was carrying a sidearm.

"Morton," choked Remza, "surrender your weapon. Our priorities have changed."

Tara swiftly rose up, extending her hand. A wary Morton placed her pistol in it.

"All right, you four, get back there and resume your battle stations. That includes you, Morton, or whatever your name is. We're going to save those sailors out there, and I'll need every hand. Go! Takahashi, you go back too and keep an eye on things. You're the new XO. Remza will take your seat at the console. And he will not leave it without my permission," she warned.

The four filed out. Remza pulled himself off the deck and took his place.

"Remza! Contact the Vigil. Tell them who you really are, and then inform them of our situation, and our intentions."

"Yes, Ma'am." He did as he was told.

"That's better. Now, man the ERASER cannon and fire at that thing! Use rapid frequency modulation until we see what works best."

"Captain, how do we know this thing is hostile?" This was Wood.

"What?"

"Well, I mean, it hasn't really done anything except simply appear. It displaced a lot of water and endangered those ships, but that's not necessarily a deliberately hostile act."

"This is how we know, Ensign," said Remza. "Listen to this broadcast from the carrier."

From the speakers came a cacophony of screams, shots, desperate pleas, and also sounds far less human and identifiable.

"Fire!" cried Tara.

The beam stretched out toward the dark structure, flickering from one color to another, passing into and out of visibility as it achieved wavelengths invisible to the eye. It entered the undefined blackness of the structure and vanished.

"No...no sign of any effect," said Wood, who sounded stricken. "There's no heat or reflected radiation. The beam seems to be entering a space and simply continuing on."

"Remza, play that beam around. Hit those lights. There must be something in there we can burn."

"I'm getting a few flashes of backscatter from our beam," said Wood after a few moments, "but there's still no discernible effect on the structure."

"Cease fire on the ERASER," said Tara. "If adding energy to the thing doesn't work, we'll try subtracting it. Fire the cryocannon."

The effect of this was to pile up a ramp of ice and frozen air around the base of the structure. Still those dreadfully steadfast lights did not flicker. They looked like they were beyond the influence of anything in the world.

"All right. No more fooling around. Remza, what torpedoes do we have in the tubes?"

"Two fusion. Two tachyon bursts. Two conventional."

"Wood, how far are the ships from that thing? What's their course?"

"The ship closest to it, a frigate, is only a thousand yards from the base. It's actually firing on it. Captain, I—"

"Yes?"

"I'm getting a radar return from that thing. I hadn't before. It looks like something new is rising from the interior."

"Can you give me a synthesized picture?"

"Yes, Captain."

"Remza, contact those ships and tell them to clear the area, if they can. We're going nuclear. Invite their subs and any other nuclear-capable ships to join in."

"I—aye, Captain."

"Captain, a flight of jets from the other carrier group is coming in! They're firing missiles."

Fiery lines of rocket exhaust converged on the structure. The missiles detonated, their flashes briefly illuminating a rough, irregular mass.

"Wood, let's see that image!"

"Oh! Yes, Captain."

The central display showed a wireframe view of a very roughly pyramidal object slowly emerging from the surface.

"Giant waves coming in, Captain! I'm afraid the frigate has capsized. These waves are capable of flipping us too."

"Damn!" Tara shoved the diving lever forward, seeking deep water, cutting off their view. Even so, the passage of the great waves overhead was enough to send Nemo bucking.

When they subsided, Tara surfaced the sub just as abruptly. The scene before them had changed greatly in the minute or so they were submerged. The dark House and its lights had vanished. Visible now against the stars was a mass of rock, a grotesque form more bizarre than any Southwestern hoodoo, with jutting crags and huge tentacles of stone wrapped around and merging into the main bulk.

"It—it looks like fairly ordinary stone," said Tara, desperately trying to interpret this in some comprehensible way. "Maybe the whole thing has been nothing more than an undersea volcanic eruption breaking the surface. We are near the Ring of Fire—"

At that moment, two great disks of pale light opened high atop the mountainous mass. Strange juts and fissures near them resolved into a soulless, alien face. Tara knew those unfathomable eyes were fixed on her ship, on her.

"Fire both nuclear torpedoes!" she snarled. "One aimed below the waterline, the other above! Warn all ships!"

"Torpedoes fired!" answered Remza.

"I'm diving the ship for protection. Wood, give us the video from the surface probe."

Tara performed a diving spiral one eighty, retreating from the monstrosity and the imminent explosions.

"Status of the carrier group?"

"All remaining ships are at least two nautical miles from the target, Captain."

"That's about the minimum survivable distance for warheads the size of the ones in our torpedoes," said Remza.

"Shit! Have the torpedoes orbit for two minutes before going in. We've got to give those ships a chance to get clear."

They sat in silence for those two minutes, still retreating at maximum speed.

"Two minutes, Captain," said Remza.

"Hit that monster!"

Two of the smaller displays on her console showed enhanced video from the torpedoes as they turned and headed toward that staring mountain under full power. Tara flinched away from the sight. It was all too easy to imagine it was she herself who was hurtling toward that thing.

And then the view from the torpedoes shuddered and was gone.

"I've lost contact with both torpedoes," said Remza.

"Wood, what do you see?"

"Captain, looks like they're slowing, drifting. They look dead."

Filled with a black anger, Tara stared at the video from the surface probe, which still showed the watchful face and glowing eyes of this foul intruder into her world. She stopped her ship, allowing it to drift.

"It must have been afraid of the torpedoes," she said in a low voice. "Otherwise it would have ignored them, like it did the missiles and the beam weapons."

"Those were our most powerful weapons," said Remza.

"No. I have one weapon which is greater still."

"What?"

"This anti-matter powered submarine."

Remza turned to look at her in surprise. "So you do, Captain, so you do."

"Captain, I'm detecting *Diatom* and *Radiolarian*, closing fast from the starboard side," said Wood.

"Remza, order them to rendezvous with us at this position. Better yet, I'll do it, as they may be under the impression you're not to be trusted." When she'd issued this order, Tara keyed on the ship-wide intercom. "Captain to crew. All hands report to the control room at once."

Four more faces, each displaying varying mixtures of fear and anxiety, soon appeared.

"I want you all to get into survival suits and abandon ship. That means you too, Wood. Our sister ships will pick you up. I'm going to pilot this sub into that thing's ugly mouth and blow the hell out of it."

"Captain, any one of us can do that," said Takahashi. "It doesn't have to be you. You're the senior officer in the V.S.C."

"Yes, I am, and this is my ship, and that's why it's going to be the way I say. You're all going to serve aboard other Vigil subs with distinction. Maybe even you, Morton. Now get out fast, before that thing figures out some way to swat us."

Remza half rose in his seat, then hesitated and turned to her. "Captain, you're a true patriot after all. I'm honored to have served—"

"Oh, shut up, you asshole. I'm not doing this for patriotism. I'm doing it to save those poor stupid kids on that fleet who signed up to serve the interests of a bunch of rich white bastards who deserve whatever's coming to them. And sit back down. I'm taking you with me."

"What?" Remza grew pale. "You don't need me—"

"I told you to shut up. No, I don't need you. I just don't want you getting away with your treason against the Vigil and the oath you took to support it."

"What about your oath to the Navy, you crazy bitch?"

"I'm about to pay for that too, aren't I? Wood, Takahashi, tape Mister Remza into his seat. If Little Miss

Morton objects, give her the same treatment. Then get off my ship!"

Remza spat, swore, and struggled as the entire crew, including Morton, pitched in to secure him in his seat.

"Don't fret, Remza," said Tara. "I'm turning you into a hero. Maybe they'll name a building at the Naval Academy after you, or at least a street in your home town."

When all was in order, which took longer than Tara thought strictly necessary, the crew saluted her and looked as if they were about to launch into a series of farewell speeches.

"Go! Go! Go! Let me do this while I'm still pissed off enough. You can cry over me later! Go!"

A few minutes later, Tara was alone in the sub with Remza, who sat in white-lipped silence. Tara felt oddly liberated by her decision, reckless, even a little giddy. She took hold of the control sticks.

"Well, here we go."

Remza began to pray aloud as the sub surged forward. Tara rolled her eyes. She was considering making some spiteful comment when a voice from the console interrupted her.

"Stingray calling *Captain Nemo*. Come in, Tara."

Oh.

"This is Tara."

"Tara, what are you doing?"

"I'm going to blow up the worst thing ever seen in this world. You haven't seen it. You just don't know."

"I'm seeing the video from your probe. Tara, I'm in a very slow flyer right now. I can't get there in time to help you. But I can send Aureus, and she can be there within half an hour."

She? "Stingray, I don't want to wait that long. This thing does not belong in this world. There's no telling what it will do if I leave it alone."

"Tara, you don't have to do this."

"Yes, I *do—*"

"I mean literally, you yourself don't have to do this. The power system is in the horseshoe. Separate the sub from the horseshoe. Send the horseshoe in under remote control. Easy as that."

"Listen to the man!" yelled Remza.

"Shut up!" Tara brooded for a few moments, weighing the pros and cons of this unthought-of option.

"No. The thing somehow killed our torpedoes. Without me piloting by hand, it'll probably do the same thing to the horseshoe."

"Tara, without power for containment, nothing can stop that horseshoe from exploding."

"Stingray, I won't take the chance. I'm sorry. I'm sorry."

Stingray was silent for a few moments. She heard muffled, quiet voices in the background. When he came back, he spoke as if he were having difficulty controlling his voice. "All right, Tara. All right. Blow up my submarine if you have to, and yourself with it. But before you go, I want you to know I consider myself incredibly lucky you happened upon me and my sub all those weeks ago. I was lucky. The Vigil was lucky. Earth was lucky. You weren't."

"Thank you, Stingray. I was lucky too. Without you, right now I'd either be in a Navy brig or an Indonesian jail. This is better. Go save the world. I think your job just got a whole lot more complicated. And tell Lori Wu goodbye for me. Tell her I thought she was a cutie."

"I'll do that. May every soul in the sea and among the stars wish you well. Stingray out."

Now Tara needed a good cry, but she had only a few more minutes to live.

"Remza, do you feel like doing something useful?"

He nodded.

"Call all ships and warn them again. Tell them they're about to see the biggest explosion to take place on this planet since—I don't know when. There will be waves. There will be a terrible flash. Got it?"

"Yes." He made the call, taking a few moments to leave personal messages for his family. He did not mention that he was undertaking this mission under duress. Tara nodded in approval.

Tara pulled back on the maneuvering stick. The submarine leaped ahead. Her tactical display showed the ice ramp left by her previous cryogun attack. "We'll see how well this sub can really fly. This is it. Have fun wherever you wind up, Remza."

She felt something enter her mind, something that tried to compel her to change course, to turn back, to quit, to fail, to die, to cease. But it was too little, too late. *Captain Nemo II* slammed onto the submerged ice, veered upward, broke free of the water, and soared, still under the full thrust of its propulsion lamps. The Watcher loomed before them. Tara screamed, and then there was nothing.

Chapter 24

Change of Plans

Fomalhaut was no longer confined to bed.

Instead, he hung suspended from a shackle in the ceiling of a concrete cell, his back arched, his extended limbs bowed backward.

He wore nothing but an opaque helmet, into which was piped a peculiar mixture of gases. It had adequate oxygen, but also an excess of carbon dioxide, which convinced his body it was on the verge of suffocation. A probe inserted into an artery assured that his blood gases didn't get too far out of balance.

A tube inserted down his throat assured he did not starve or die of thirst.

This had been his situation for the past three days.

And yet Fomalhaut was not unduly troubled.

His mind was many trillions of miles away, not in reality, but in the vast halls of his memory and thought. Blinded both physically and psychically, he was left without resources save those contained in his own mind, which were very great.

There he spanned entire galaxies, delving into cloudy banks of stars never before seen by any of his kind. During his long career as a Frame Rider, he had made contact with individuals and civilizations so remote from his own that no closer association would ever be practical. Sometimes they were so alien that none would ever be conceivable. From all of them he had learned what he could. Some of these he now saw in his mind's eye: races of beings so benign and yet so powerful that knowing them was like basking in the rays of an immense yet gentle sun. The galaxies they inhabited were barely within reach of the largest telescopes currently existing on Earth.

Later he had recalled a journey across whole universes, as he carried Shaula Alshain to that singular place where she might be healed, a place where some of the greatest minds and heroes in existence had honored him, burning into the shoulder of his exploration suit the symbol of the ringed star, a symbol of ultimate recourse to those lucky enough to live within reach of their light.

He had never told anyone, but Shaula had regained consciousness some years into that journey. Her mind was still broken, and very fragile. It had been up to him to strengthen her, to provide a structure for her consciousness, and in the end, to comfort her, and nurture her. He had grown to love her as a daughter. Thus, when he delivered her at last, she had arrived capable of being healed, and not as a hopeless shell. The ancients who imploded stars to make their Universal Instruments had honored him.

Also he saw Stingray, his most steadfast cousin, who would not cease to work for his rescue. He saw the fallen T'Ukudu, proof that nearby in space existed an entire race of reasonable, civilized beings. He saw the fallen Rouse Farewell, in whose eyes and mind he had seen a knowledge of truth and a depth of compassion that had proven the potential of the Human race. And he saw Endurance, that inexplicable being, older than many stars, more immutable than any of them, yet made in the image of a Human. What could be the meaning of that?

Yes, the world, the universe, and the omniverse were filled with beings capable of humbling him. Not all minds were sunk in fear, savagery and decay.

Thus he did not welcome the distraction of someone entering his cell, interrupting his meditations, forcing him to an awareness of his body.

"Take that helmet off him," said a familiar voice.

Someone approached, crossing the barrier of the quantum disruption that surrounded him.

The helmet came off. His eyes reacted to the light by darkening their outermost meniscus. His breathing eased.

Standing a few feet away was Sard Ducanis, looking at him with a guarded expression, surrounded by his usual coterie of flunkies.

"Take that tube out of his throat so he can speak. And remove the probe."

A nurse stepped forward and obeyed these commands. Fomalhaut observed the pain of the tube being withdrawn from his raw and ragged throat. He tried to speak, but found that impossible for the moment.

"Fomalhaut, I'm sorry, but I can't release you. You have the ability to tear us apart with your bare hands if driven to it, and I think we might have done so."

Fomalhaut again tried to speak, this time managing a painful rasp. "A—reasonable person—might think so. What do you want? You haven't—bothered to appear in person—lately."

Ducanis assumed a look of embarrassment which was so patently false that even Fomalhaut could discern it. "Fomalhaut, the fact is, we need your help."

Fomalhaut was moved to laugh, but resisted. That would be a misuse of mirth, and too painful. "Yes, your men...have been soliciting my help...regularly."

"This is a different matter."

"Oh?"

"Yes. Our Neo-men are...distressed."

"That is not surprising, considering their circumstances."

"No. This is something different. Something you don't know about. You couldn't. The Neo-men sense something wrong about the Moon."

"Continue."

"Some very strange things are happening in the world. Terrible things. Things that may be beyond our ability to investigate or to deal with."

"How mysterious."

A telephone chirped. One of Ducanis's assistants pulled it out of his pocket and answered. "Can this wait? The Secretary is...what? Are you sure? Hold on, I'll ask him what he wants to do.

"Mr. Secretary, it's the base commander. He says Neo-man Aleph Gold has just crash-landed on the base in a stolen Vigil flyer. Gold is claiming to have escaped with Vigil secrets you'll want to see."

Ducanis frowned in confusion. "Are they sure it's him? Has he passed biometrics?"

"Hold on. Did you get that? Okay. Sir, we have no data specific to the Gold clan readily available at this base, but he does pass most of the Neo-man baseline tests. The Blues were surprised by his arrival, but they also vouch for him. He must be one of ours."

"You say he passed *most* of the tests?"

"Yes sir. There are a few anomalies, but sometimes contaminants are introduced into the chemistry when the tests are conducted so quickly."

Ducanis withdrew into himself and considered this for at least a minute.

"All right, have him brought down here under armed escort. Maybe he can convince Fomalhaut of our need."

"What about the Blues?"

"Keep them away. I'm not ready to have them know how we've been dealing with one of their own kind. Aleph Gold, if he's been in the company of the Vigil, presumably already knows."

A few minutes later, a huge Neo-man entered the cell carrying a large case. A group of military policemen waited outside.

Fomalhaut smiled.

The cell shook, sending concrete dust filtering down. A pervasive rumble sounded. The power failed; emergency lights flickered on.

The quantum barrier was gone.

Aleph Gold's right hand darted out, grabbing Sard Ducanis by the throat. The Secretary's retinue cried out in alarm. The MPs rushed in, weapons aimed at Aleph Gold.

"You want him dead? Just keep coming," said Gold. He dropped the case. With his left hand he reached up and tore off half of his own face. Beneath the false eyes and shredded tissue was the face of Stingray, who turned to Ducanis and growled, "I never leave a job half done, you miserable little monkey man."

"This...isn't...necessary," wheezed Ducanis through Stingray's grip.

"He's right," said Fomalhaut in a shaky voice. "Stingray, release him."

"What?" said Stingray in disbelief.

"Now that the barrier is gone, I see many things. Too many. Our war with the Humans is at an end. We now face an adversary which will tax us all to our limits, if not beyond."

Stingray frowned, then slowly released his grip on Ducanis, who sagged away, coughing and rubbing his throat.

"Ducanis, you and your men will now withdraw. Stingray and I will have privacy. You may await us at ground level, at the entrance to the building."

"I—oh—very well."

"Leave the keys," rumbled Stingray.

A moment later they were alone in the cell.

"Stingray, if you would kindly assist me. I'm not confident of my ability to walk or stand."

Holding Fomalhaut with one arm, Stingray released him from his shackles, then gently lowered him to the floor.

"How did you find me, my friend?"

"We got some hints from the Gold family, who are now guests of the Vigil. Then it was a matter of measuring anomalies in electrical power transmission. Do you know the power consumed by that quantum barrier was enough to raise the price of oil by two dollars a barrel? This happens to be the same Nevada base where Perturbare and Aureus were once imprisoned. I should have known to check this one."

"Perturbare. We must have words with him."

"Fomalhaut, I have something here which I think you'll be happy to see." Stingray opened the case, revealing Fomalhaut's exploration suit.

"Thank you. You are correct. Please help me into it."

Stingray complied, easing Fomalhaut's stiff and bruised body into the suit, making connections, sealing seams.

The bubble helmet activated. Now it was transparent, with just enough reflectivity to indicate its presence.

"Ah. Ah," breathed Fomalhaut. He stood up without apparent difficulty. Stingray grinned at the sight of him, once more glittering and splendid, with a face wise and noble in place of a mirrored sphere.

"If your deception had gone awry, the Americans would have recovered my suit," observed Fomalhaut.

"Yes, but they also would have blown up half their base if they'd opened the case incorrectly. How are you feeling?"

"The suit has much work to do. My body is infested with toxins and pathogens, as well as with Perturbare's ubiquitous nanodevices. Happily, dealing with these is not beyond the suit's capabilities. Come, Stingray, my friend. Let us rejoin our comrades."

Stingray and Fomalhaut made their way up and out of the building, passing groups of military people and civilian workers who clustered in pools of emergency lighting, gazing at them in awe.

They emerged into a day darkened by thick clouds streaming overhead. Awaiting them was the entire membership of the Vigil, standing in a line, faces stern, flanked by Ducanis and his flunkies plus a military contingent. Behind them was one of the larger and more powerful Vigil flyers.

Fomalhaut greeted each member of the Vigil in turn. Reaching Lori Wu, he said, "Hello, Lori, my dear. Your work on Stingray's facial appliance was excellent. He looked just like one of us."

Lori gazed up into Fomalhaut's eyes, her face shining. "Thank you, Fomalhaut. It's so good to see your face at last. I can tell you, I had a lot of trouble disguising Stingray's nose."

The instant she said this she lowered her eyes, her face reddening. Walks-with-the-Sun laughed.

Stingray, standing beside her, muttered, "That's okay, Lori. I know I have a big nose."

Fomalhaut turned to Ducanis, who regarded him with a volatile mixture of emotions. Fomalhaut was forced to admit that he controlled them fairly well.

"Please summon your so-called Blue family. I wish them to hear what is to be said here today."

"I—we don't want them to be aware—"

"That's enough. We've moved beyond your desire to keep the Neo-men in ignorance of your misdeeds and your narrow political purposes. It's time to acquaint them with reality. They'll be needed in the struggle I foresee. Call them."

One of Ducanis's assistants chose this moment to call attention to himself by blustering. "Sir, we can't let this... this freak get away with pushing us—"

Ducanis whirled on him. "O'Reilly, if that's the sort of drivel I can count on coming out of your mouth, I have no more use for you. Get out. And the same goes for anyone here who is unable to adapt to changing circumstances."

O'Reilly, looking stricken, departed the scene.

A few minutes later the seven members of the Blue family were escorted into view. They were all intensely alert, uncertain, immensely curious.

Fomalhaut decided to waste no time in showing them the way of things. He smoothed the quantum space between them, bridging with them *en masse*. Before, working together, they had managed to influence him to deactivate his helmet. Now, he entered all their conscious minds at once, uninvited. This was both a matter of personal satisfaction and a desire for rapid instruction.

I am Fomalhaut of the Vigil. I am a product of a thousand years of self-directed improvement of our genetic design, fully trained in all the gifts and advantages which it brings. You are the prototypes. Your destiny is to safeguard this world, and to inhabit the galaxy as part of a partnership of intelligent beings who await your coming. Your destiny is not to prop up the corrupt political institutions of a race which has outmoded itself. In order for you to meet your destiny, we must first act in concert to overcome a final crisis fostered by the folly of Humanity. This is what the Vigil expects of you all. You are now free, but your new freedom brings responsibilities which must be met.

All this was communicated in an instant, unsuspected by anyone else, though some wondered at the expressions of amazement which appeared on the faces of the Blue family.

Fomalhaut turned to address the entire assembly.

"Peoples of the Earth. Through mutual necessity, we of the Vigil have set aside our conflict with the governments of the various nations. I ask Stingray, leader of the Vigil, to come forward and describe what is happening to this world."

Stingray, startled, looked as if he were about to object to what Fomalhaut had said.

Not now, Stingray. We will discuss this later.

Stingray eyed him narrowly for a moment, and then stepped forward.

"Two days ago, something inexplicable happened in the southwestern Pacific. A gigantic alien monstrosity appeared in the midst of a United States Navy aircraft carrier battle group. This battle group and another were on their way to attack the Vigil shipyard in the Great Barrier Reef. The monster was, to all appearances, a Watcher, a thing seen in the popular television series *The Night Land,* and in the novel of the same name. Why this Watcher appeared in that particular place and time is unknown. A squadron of Vigil submarines under the command of Captain Tara Strenczak set out to engage the U.S. naval forces and defend our base. When Captain Strenczak observed the enemy ships in imminent danger of being sunk, or worse, by the Watcher, she and her executive officer, who was actually a Naval Intelligence agent named Vincent Remza, sacrificed their ship and their lives to destroy the Watcher and save the American ships. The frigate USS *Robert Anson* was also lost in the attack."

Stingray paused, lowering his head in silence for a long moment. No one made a sound.

"Captain Strenczak destroyed that Watcher by detonating the unique antimatter power plant of her submarine. The thing had ignored or disabled all previous attacks.

"Unfortunately, Tara's sacrifice was not enough to end the crisis. Since then, other Watchers have appeared in all oceans and on all continents. They appear to be immobile, but there's no doubt they contain a malignant intelligence, and their influence is terrible. We have reports of monsters and other strange manifestations, again similar to those seen in *The Night Land*. The psychological impact of these creatures on whoever encounters them is very serious. They provoke madness and despair. Some of these monsters are all but immune to conventional weapons. The situation is growing steadily worse. Anomalous weather effects are also becoming common. The world is growing dark beneath a thickening mantle of cloud. It's turning into a nightmare.

"We have no idea why the weird horrors of a TV show should be manifesting themselves in reality, but we have one clue. Most Neo-men are aware of something wrong on, or beyond, the Moon. We've noticed that no Watcher has appeared at a time when the Moon was not in the sky. We will investigate this, and we will do what we can to hold back the growing threat until we can identify its source and end it."

"Thank you, Stingray," said Fomalhaut. "Your summary contains details I myself did not know. I think we all realize the paramount importance of putting aside our differences and combining our resources to overcome this intrusion into our reality."

"Who do you propose to be in charge of this joint effort?" asked Ducanis cautiously. "Our president will not lightly submit to Vigil rule, even under these conditions."

"Do you know your president well, Ducanis?" asked Stingray.

"Not very well. The affairs of Exterior aren't of great personal interest to him."

"How is he reacting to the current situation?"

"He's putting a, well, a Biblical interpretation on events."

Stingray nodded. "And do you consider your self-proclaimed war president fit to deal with the war that faces him now?"

Ducanis looked around at the military people and other government agents who surrounded him.

"He is the elected leader of the United States," he finally said.

It was perfectly clear to Fomalhaut that this was all he dared say at the moment. "I suggest that you order your part of the operation and we'll order ours."

"That's right," said Stingray. "The Vigil will not take orders from you. You should muster whatever competent people you can and put your sputtering little man in a closet, where he belongs. Oh, and another thing. The Motionglobe. We want it back."

"It's...it's not here."

"Where is it?"

"It's being studied. By our top scientists."

Stingray laughed, not too kindly.

Valjhar chose this moment to speak up. "Vela, what can you tell us about the Motionglobe?"

Aureus opened its mouth and spoke, which seemed a surprising and dreadful thing to the humans around it. "The Motionglobe was discovered by Rralian space explorers long ago. For thousands of years it was studied by many of the most brilliant minds of Rral. They failed to understand it. Ultimately it was classified as a Transcendental Object, beyond the scope of Rralian science, and ignored."

"At its peak, Rral was the most scientifically and technologically advanced planet the universe has ever known," said Valjhar quietly. "Your scientists are wasting their time."

"The only people in the universe known to have successfully used the Motionglobe are standing before you now. Return it to us," said Stingray.

"I'll see what I can do," said Ducanis.

"Here's something else you can do. Take *The Night Land* off the air. Do whatever is necessary to accomplish that."

"Yes."

Alpha Blue stepped forward. "Fomalhaut, my family and I apologize to you for our part in your capture and abuse. We were—misled."

"Indeed you were. And yet, we all owe these men a debt of gratitude for bringing you into being in the first place, no matter how dubious their motives might have been. Be at peace. I will contact you, and all other Neo-man families, soon. For now, please assist and protect these people as best you can."

"As you wish."

The Vigil turned to depart.

Stingray spoke. "Everybody into the big flyer except me. I'll take the one…"

He was interrupted by a thought from Fomalhaut.

Stingray, I suggest you leave the small flyer you arrived in with these men. It will serve as a gesture of good will.

But…the technology…

My friend, all such considerations are in the past. This is the end. The world as we've known it will not survive what is to come. If these people are to accomplish anything at all, they must have access to the best technology we can offer.

Stingray stared at him for a long moment. Fomalhaut felt his elation and triumph replaced by a sad acceptance of responsibility and doubt.

Fomalhaut, why did you anoint me leader of the Vigil?

You are a more aggressive, more decisive leader than I am. That is what is needed now. I am needed to train the Neo-men, to the extent I can. I will be distracted. But never fear, I remain a member of the Vigil. In fact, I feel a greater kinship with each of you than I do with any of them.

Chapter 25

The Vigil Repulsed

The next day, Lori Wu walked up to a group of somber Vigil members as they prepared to go to the Moon. The huge overhead door of the Pearl's main hangar was already open, admitting currents of cold air, but the whitefield prevented any view beyond. A typically angular Vigil flyer was being prepared for the journey.

"Fomalhaut, are you sure you feel up to this? It's barely a day ago that you were being tortured," said Lori.

"Lori, thank you for your concern. I am much improved, thanks to the ministrations of my suit. In any event, we have no time to waste. We must learn the source of the growing chaos, and I am best equipped to do so."

Lori turned then to Stingray. "Stingray, may I come along too?"

Lori saw that Stingray was about to say it was too dangerous for her. Then the gears in his head whirred as he realized saying such a thing to any member of the Vigil would be insulting, especially since Jordan Elcanie, another perfectly ordinary mortal, was coming along as pilot.

At last he succumbed to the inevitable and said, "All right, Lori, but we'll need you back soon for more construction projects. I'll talk to you about that when you get back."

"Aren't you coming?"

"No, I get to spend my day coordinating our efforts with our wonderful new American allies. Plus I'm going to talk with Doctor Brightman, whom you so capably brought among us. Good luck to you all. I needn't dwell on how important this mission is."

Endurance joined Lori, Ben, Fomalhaut, and Elcanie to complete a crew of five. They settled into high-backed seats and strapped themselves in. Jordan looked over his shoulder as Lori was settling in.

"Have you ever flown in space before, Miss Wu?"

"No, I'm still getting used to the idea that we can just casually fly to the Moon. And please, call me Lori. It wasn't that long ago that I was also an Ant, and a lower-ranking one than you are, too."

"Well, Lori, we're looking at about a three hour one-way flight, and we'll be under acceleration almost all the time. I'm going to vector the thrust through the flyer's Y-axis, so it'll push you down in your seat and feel like normal gravity. At first you'll feel a little heavier than normal, which may be uncomfortable. Just thought you'd like to know. And oh, this is my first space flight, too," he concluded with a quick grin before turning to his console.

If Lori hadn't been wearing a device that gave her vast powers, she would have been frightened by what she was about to do. She was also surrounded by three of the wisest, most powerful beings in the world. It didn't hurt to have a cocky, good-looking young pilot like Elcanie at the controls, either.

They sealed the flyer and lifted off, rising straight up. The moment they pierced the whitefield, Lori's confidence threatened to dissolve as she witnessed again the dismal state into which the world was descending. Even here, at the site of the world's greatest concentration of light, darkness was pressing in. The clouds had thickened to the point where daylight was now only a feeble glimmer. The snow descending from those clouds seemed dirty.

Worst of all, far out to sea were two glimmers of a ghastly white light. These were said to be the eyes of a Watcher that had not yet broken the surface of the water.

Free now of the Pearl, Elcanie fed power to the ventral propulsion lamps, pushing the flyer through hissing, seething layers of cloud. Lori almost applauded when at last they broke free and rose into clean air and sunlight. But as they gained altitude, and their view grew wider and wider, the extent of the problem became clear. Swirls of grimy cloud covered land and sea as far as they could see. As they rose ever higher, their view soon encompassed an entire hemisphere of the world, which offered no comfort. It was as though Earth were turning into an alien world. On the night side, strange lights filtered up from various places.

"Those lights," quavered Lori. "They're not cities, are they?"

"No," said Endurance quietly. "Not human cities, at any rate. We're not sure what many of them are."

"The speed of this transformation is extremely disquieting," whispered Fomalhaut.

Ben Raintree said nothing, but Lori was struck by his expression as he leaned over a port, looking down. Normally his power was hidden behind a veil of gentle serenity. Now his lean features were transfigured, frozen into cold wrath as he stared downward. He looked as though he couldn't wait to unleash the power of the Stones against the horrors lurking beneath those clouds. Lori longed to see him do so.

"We've cleared the atmosphere, and are on course for the Moon," said Elcanie, using a terse, reassuring "pilot" voice. "Increasing acceleration. Lori, sit up straight, please."

Lori obeyed. Over the next few seconds her weight felt as if it had doubled. She leaned her head back and looked up through the skylight at the Moon. So far it appeared no larger. Its phase was just shy of first quarter.

They sat in silence, pushing up, up, into nothingness. Lori, looking ahead to Fomalhaut's co-pilot position, saw moonlight shining in the sleek white hair that covered his proud head. She stared at him, taking comfort in the visibility of her mentor.

An hour and a half after departure, Elcanie said, "We've reached the midpoint. I'm going to pitch around to reverse our thrust vector. We'll experience zero G for a minute. Here we go."

Lori's stomach tried to rise into her mouth. Her hair floated around her head in a fine black cloud. The stars scrolled by the windows, unsettling her further. She closed her eyes, counting the seconds until thrust resumed and her weight returned. To distract herself from nausea, she formed a comb out of a plastic cup and used it to neaten her disarrayed hair. Endurance, who sat beside her, smiled.

The flyer's new attitude put the Earth in the middle of the skylight. The sight of it erased Endurance's smile. Lori also found it hard to bear.

"Endurance, does it bother you to leave the Earth?"

"I have left it before, for brief periods."

"Really, when?"

"You've heard of the planet Colibdis, where Ben's cousin Leonard Ronar roams free?"

Lori nodded in fascination.

"I came across one of those Portals a few thousand years ago. I passed through it, though I admit it made me a bit nervous, which was itself a novel experience for me. You see, I had been associated with Earth for so long that I wasn't sure I could exist apart from it. But I had no difficulty. On the other side I found a colony of the people who are now called the Assyrians. They didn't call themselves that, and they didn't use the name "Colibdis" either. They called their new home "the World Apart" or something like that. They soon forgot what world it was apart from, if you catch my meaning. They called me Hamadan, because they thought I looked like a Persian. I explored that planet for a short time, a few hundred years, and for a while I crossed back and forth between worlds frequently. At first the Sorcerer there tried to stop me, but he soon became so bemused by me that he quit trying. After a while, the Portal I was using failed while I was on Earth, and by the time I stumbled across another one I had lost interest."

Endurance shrugged, as though he were describing a slightly eventful trip to the grocery store. Lori goggled at him.

"This time, leaving the planet comes as a relief. The planet didn't look this bad even during the demise of the dinosaurs."

Lori started at the sudden realization that he was speaking of this as an eyewitness.

"So...it's true what they say? The dinosaurs were wiped out by an asteroid?"

"I can't say for sure. I was nowhere near Central America when it happened." He sat back, his golden-brown eyes gazing into the past. "I remember the world growing dark and cold. Ash settled down in great drifts. A rain of cinders started fires. The dinosaurs began to fail. It was a lengthy process, not as abrupt and simple as some believe today. For a while I thought some classes of them would survive and recover. But then they all collapsed, except for some of the smaller feathered ones, and for millions of years the world was without large land animals of any kind."

"Do you miss them? The dinosaurs, I mean."

"Well, Lori, they were never very...personable. No mammal was ever as mindlessly savage as many dinosaurs were. I've seen them gnawing on the headless necks of their prey while that prey still struggled to get away. I've seen large predators feeding on their own intestines after being disemboweled by horned dinosaurs. No, overall I greatly prefer mammals. Especially the ones that look like me. Despite all the trouble they cause themselves, and each other." Endurance favored Lori with another smile.

Lori smiled back. If Earth could recover from *that* catastrophe, then given time, perhaps it could also recover from whatever was afflicting it now.

Especially with the help of the Vigil.

She did not waste this opportunity to speak with an unusually expansive Endurance.

"Are you afraid of what we might encounter?"

"I have never been afraid. Not for myself. I cannot be harmed."

"How do you know that? There must be forces you've never encountered."

Endurance looked at her. "That's true. But once, very long ago, I was swimming through the interior of the still molten Earth when it suddenly crystallized around me, thousands of miles of solid white-hot minerals in all directions. I was aware of the heat, and the pressure, as I always am of such things, but I never experience such sensations as pain, if I understand the meaning of that word."

Wide-eyed, Lori asked, "How did you escape?"

"I exerted myself until the rock around me flashed back into liquid, and in this way I gradually forced my way to the surface. It was a lengthy process, even for me."

"That's incredible. You really must be free of any fear."

His gaze was still upon her, and now his eyes assumed a look she had never seen there, a pain beyond pain and a fear beyond fear. "That's not true. I've known great fear, and I know it now. I fear for you, and for all those like you. They call me Endurance, but I don't know how you mortal people endure your lives. So many times I've seen your fragile bodies ruined in so many ways, your minds and selves extinguished. Even if you manage to avoid violence or disaster or starvation, still your bodies betray you. You strive to better yourselves, to learn and to do, and then, all too soon, you reach a peak and begin to decline, and there's little you can do to stop it. Your bodies and minds decay and fail of their own accord. Weak and helpless you are when you are born, and so you are when you die."

His normally serene face crumpled into distress. "I try not to think about it. There's so little I can do. I can't be everywhere at once. I cannot change the nature of things, any more than my own nature can be changed. So many times I've seen this, so many bright lives lost to indignity and futility. I try to tell myself there must be some wisdom behind it, but those thoughts seem hollow when I witness so much suffering. It's enough to drive me mad, or would be, if I were capable of going mad. I have seen so many people crushed by grief, and thought that I too must be crushed. But I cannot be crushed. I only walk on, to attend the next scene of despair." He spoke a few anguished words in a language Lori did not recognize. "Why was I made to see all this?"

Lori shuddered. For the first time in her life, the cold thought sank in that perhaps life was meaningless, that perhaps the universe was merely pointless and cruel. If Endurance could live so long and still be asking these questions, what hope was there for her? Yet she was very glad she was not Endurance, a man to whom life offered no escape.

"You have no answer to this?" she asked.

"I have not. For most of my existence I dwelt on a lifeless planet, where nothing moved except myself, or at least nothing I could see. Then life arose, in all sorts of strange forms, in the sea and then on the land, but none of them resembled me. They grew and shifted and changed. I was very excited when the first frogs emerged, because in body they were a little like me. I actually thought I might be a frog of sorts, and waited and hoped for them to evolve into creatures more like myself, but of course I was disappointed. Then mammals emerged, and they also resembled me in certain ways, and I watched them carefully. Then, not long ago, apes emerged, and then hominids branched off from them, and finally man himself. At last, creatures exactly like me, and I could communicate with them! But they were only superficially like me, for they were still fragile and mortal. Still, I knew this must have some significance. As I moved among them, I became convinced that when their final days drew near, then at last

I would discover why I had been made, if not by whom. That day is now very near. For me, that will be the Moment."

She sat trembling, feeling very small and alone, trapped in this dark capsule among shadowy demigods she could never truly understand.

And now a tear stood out from Endurance's eye. Without thinking, Lori reached out and took it on her fingertip, studying it in wonder. A tear, from Endurance? What was it made of? Was it water? Was it a drop of his immortal substance? She placed her finger to her tongue, tasted it. It had no taste, and left no trace that it had ever existed.

She reached out and held his hand, caressed his arm. He felt at least like a normal man.

"I have frightened you, Lori. You know how poor your prospects are. You know you're going to die, and soon," he said softly. "And yet you try to comfort me."

She forced a smile. "There's a little bit of you in me now."

"Have you ever heard of Chrysanthe of Thessaly? No, of course not. She was a camp follower of Alexander, a cook. Her right hand was deformed, so no man ever wanted her, and she had no child. Yet she looked after the soldiers with care and love. Beyond that, she strove to feed the widows and orphans and refugees whom Alexander scattered behind him in such numbers, often at great risk to herself. At last she was caught doing that, and accused of aiding the enemy. She could have blamed someone else for her deeds, but she never wavered. I arrived too late to prevent her execution. The next time I visited that region, everyone remembered Alexander, but no one remembered

Chrysanthe. The title 'the Great' was bestowed on the wrong person. Compassion like hers, rare as it is, is the saving grace of your people."

"I will remember her now, thanks to you."

Now time passed a little faster than Lori could have wished. It seemed only a few minutes later that Jordan said, "We're just about there. Following the flight plan, I'm taking us into a low orbit around the Moon. That way we'll be carried around to the far side and see whatever's going on there without being under power. We'll be a lot less conspicuous that way. It'll be zero G again. Sorry, Lori."

Lori gulped as her weight vanished again. Once more the stars wheeled by. Her discomfort was mostly forgotten as the lunar landscape, now only hundreds of miles away, rolled into view. Reflected light poured into the cabin. Lori was struck by the overall roundness of the lunar features. It was very irregular and fantastically detailed, but somehow softened, as though it had once been a craggy, rugged place that had been partially melted. It was beautiful in its purity, though in its utter desolation it made the worst parts of the Mojave Desert look like a garden. Compared to the infinite complexities and possibilities of Earth, the Moon was a very simple, limited thing, yet not without the charms simplicity brings.

Shadows lengthened and craters appeared to deepen as the flyer neared the boundary separating day and night. Finally they left all sunlight behind as they coasted over a landscape lit only by the wan glow of the defaced Earth. Elcanie reoriented the flyer to bring the lunar horizon into view from the large ports in the front. It was a murky curved shape set against a background of fierce stars.

"We'll soon be passing over the lunar far side," said Fomalhaut. "Then we shall see whatever is there."

They didn't have long to wait. A slender, pointed tower appeared on the horizon, rising rapidly. It was soon flanked by two more, and then still more, each at an angle leaning away from the first.

"Those objects are not on the Lunar surface," said Fomalhaut. "They are part of some structure in orbit beyond it."

This was soon demonstrated as more and more of the object was revealed. It separated from the horizon, still rising, a fantastic radial thing, a crystalline sea urchin, an enormous snowflake from a world with several extra dimensions of space.

And yet, as beautiful as it was, Lori could not view it without a feeling of dread.

Fomalhaut seemed to share this sentiment, to judge by the unnaturally lifeless tone of his voice. "The object is approximately five hundred kilometers in diameter. I detect certain details of composition and construction which are characteristic of the works of Possum Perturbare. The object is a single enormous device. My space structure sensors reveal its function very plainly. It maintains a void in the structure of space. This is an area of perfect nothingness and infinite potential, from which may emerge anything at all. It is essentially a volume to which our universe has no more claim than does any other. Left to itself, it would probably produce nothing more than an occasional random particle. It is, however, immersed in the Earth's quantum environment, which is saturated and deeply influenced by the thoughts of billions of minds. At any given time, most of the thoughts emerging from Earth are negative. This is even more true now. In particular, there is a strong strain of thought related to the Night Land. This has the effect of summoning things of the Night Land into reality. I dearly wish I had been aware of this before. This machine must be destroyed."

"Has Perturbare gone totally mad?" asked Lori, aghast. "Why is he trying to destroy the world?"

"I don't know. We shall ask him, after his machine is destroyed."

"These things that are being created," said Jordan. "Are they—illusions, or replicas of the Night Land, or are they actual things of the Night Land, coming here from their own universe?"

"That is a good question," said Fomalhaut. "There's no way to be certain. It could be either. In the end, it makes little difference. Ben. If you would, please tell us what your blue Stone reveals."

With palpable reluctance, Raintree pulled the Circlet of Truth from his jacket and seated it upon his brow. With one hand gripping the Stone of Adamance at his throat, he tilted back his head, looking to the skylight, where the immense spiny machine was now passing overhead.

A tight blue beam of the Light of Truth leapt out. Such was this strange Light that it remained visible even in the vacuum of space, unlike any natural radiance, a light perceived more by the mind than by the eye. The beam crossed thousands of miles of space, piercing the heart of the machine.

Raintree's hand convulsed. He made a strangled, choking sound, raising his free hand as if to shield his eyes from some terrible sight. The Light of Truth flickered and died. The very Stone smoldered on his forehead as if it were stunned. Raintree gave a cry of anguish and sagged back, gasping and panting. Lori turned to stare at him, wide-eyed.

When he was able to speak, Ben rasped "I—won't be doing that again. What's in there is too much for any human mind to grasp. I don't want to know that truth. I can't."

"That machine must be destroyed," repeated Fomalhaut. "Lori, it's up to us."

"Now? Shouldn't we come back with Aureus? She's best at destroying things."

"I don't think we can afford to wait. Our weapons should suffice. The machine is huge, but not at all dense or massive for its size. To the airlock."

Now Lori was trembling. She looked for support from Ben, but he was still floating in his seat, barely aware of his surroundings.

"Fomalhaut…I can't go outside. I have no space suit. And I don't think firing my proton beam through the windows would be a very good idea."

"Of course, Lori, of course. I'm sorry. Perhaps you can use the suit's more subtle powers to destabilize or disrupt the structure."

Lori had an awful feeling that Fomalhaut was drifting through this encounter, that he was in a fog, perhaps barely hanging on. Who could say what his many sources of perception were subjecting him to, this close to the source of the corruption?

Lori tried to steel herself. "It's awfully far away and I don't know anything about it. But I'll try."

"I'll fly us closer," said Jordan grimly. "It seems we've been noticed anyway. We're being illuminated by radar and other sensors."

A moment later he was proven correct. Some force slammed into the flyer's nose, sending it spinning wildly. Lori shrieked. Jordan was thrown forward in his seat, arrested by his harness, but still brutally battered. Raintree was flattened against his seat back. Lori, sitting near the flyer's center of mass, was subjected to less force, but still, it was needful for Endurance to hold her in his untiring arms. A hissing sounded in Lori's ears. Her ears popped. Fomalhaut sat unmoving in his seat, but his voice sounded strained as he said, "Lori, the flyer has suffered a pressure leak and power loss. You must isolate and repair these. Ben and Jordan depend on you for this." He then unclipped himself from his harness, resisting the centrifugal force of the flyer's spin without apparent effort. He writhed around in his seat, pointlessly as it seemed to Lori, until he crouched facing away from the direction of the flyer's spin. Then the propulsion lamps mounted on his shoulders flared up, which began to arrest the spin.

With that problem solved, Lori's attention returned to the air leak, which threatened her as much as anyone. Her suit contained the full plan of this style of flyer, permitting her to compare its current state, as revealed by the suit's structural and stress sensors, with the ideal. Then she caused matter to flow and reshape itself, renewed molecular bonds, and generally returned the flyer to new condition.

Fomalhaut resumed a normal seated posture and took control of the flyer. Jordan drifted in his seat, unconscious. His right arm floated at an alarming angle, broken.

Fomalhaut fed power to the flyer's main propulsion lanterns, pushing everyone back in their seats.

To Lori's horror, he guided them straight toward the great machine. "Fomalhaut, what are you doing?" she cried.

"Lori, I must destroy that machine. To do so, I must get much closer. Otherwise my ERASER beams will disperse too much to be effective."

"Fomalhaut, no! Jordan is seriously injured. Ben doesn't look too good either. We have to get away from here."

"This task is worth all our lives," muttered Fomalhaut.

"Maybe it is! But they've already nearly smashed our flyer once. Next time they'll succeed. We won't get close enough to accomplish anything, and we'll all be dead, all except Endurance and you, and I'm not too sure about you. You're not yourself."

"Yes. Yes, Lori, you are right. Thank you. I shall exit the flyer and go in alone. You pilot the flyer back to Earth." He pulled the flyer up sharply, then vacated his seat and moved toward the airlock in the rear.

"Take me with you," said Endurance. "I'll tear that thing apart with my hands."

"Yes."

Another blow struck the flyer, sending it tumbling, though less violently than before.

"You'll never make it," insisted Lori. "They're just toying with us. Those force beams or whatever they are will just keep slamming you away. We need a better plan than this!"

Fomalhaut was silent and motionless for long moments, awkwardly poised on his way to the airlock.

Then he turned a haunted face toward the main console. The controls moved of their own accord, lighting the propulsion lamps again, steering them away. He stumbled back to his seat and took the controls in his hands.

"You're right again, Lori. You're right. Please forgive my foolishness. I find it difficult to think clearly in the presence of this...thing. We must have a better plan indeed, or fail. Please try to rouse Ben. The green Stone would be a boon to Jordan right now. If Ben is still incapacitated, use it yourself, if you have the will."

Lori bit her lip to keep from crying as she regarded Fomalhaut for a few moments longer. He looked so terribly defeated.

Chapter 26

The Vigil Strikes

Possum Perturbare leaned against the smooth, white flank of his flyer, which was parked atop the mountain Vitosha overlooking the city of Sofia, Bulgaria. From here he had an excellent view of the commotion in the city below.

A Watcher had appeared in its midst, rising from the grounds of the Nevski Cathedral, subsuming it and all its surroundings. By now fifty or more Watchers surveyed their separate corners of the world, each similar in their immense size, but unique in the details of their appearance and character. This one was blacker than most, its surface composed of sharply corrugated rock, slick and somewhat greasy, like a thing hewn crudely from obsidian. In the furrows of its ill-defined face was set a single pool of white light for an eye, while beneath this was a chasm from which projected four great curving prongs made of some metal of a leaden dullness.

It was under attack by whatever military forces the Europeans could still field. Tanks were arrayed against it, firing shells that struck puny sparks off the side of the thing. Every now and then a fighter jet would roar by and drop a bomb or two, or even attack with its cannon, neither of which had any great effect. A few helicopters flittered around, exhausted their weapons, and withdrew.

"This is like watching a Godzilla movie, only one where Godzilla doesn't even bother to move," said Perturbare.

Through his handheld electro-optical viewer, Perturbare spied seething masses of figures around the base of the Watcher and near the tanks. Whether these were humans, monsters, or something in between he couldn't quite make out.

Standing watch near Perturbare was Brainchild, in control of one of its robotic bodies. The computer had insisted on bringing this device along as a bodyguard. Perturbare might have taken this idea more seriously if the humanoid robots hadn't been designed to appear so friendly and agreeable.

"It is clear to me, Doctor, that it is unwise of you to expose yourself to the influence of this monstrosity and its minions," said the Brainchild robot.

"Oh, quit fretting. It's about time I got a personal look at how perfectly my plan is going. With my quantum shielding, any rays of cosmic evilness coming from that big black bug just float on by."

"Doctor, the Vigil has launched a flyer bound for Sofia. It will arrive in about twenty minutes."

"Huh! Do you think they know I'm here? I know they're peeved at me for not returning their calls. Maybe I should clear out after all."

"It is conceivable, Doctor, that the Vigil has some reason for coming here other than your presence."

Perturbare grimaced in annoyance at Brainchild's tone of veiled sarcasm.

"Yes, I suppose that's true. Anyway, they're unlikely to spot me through this shielding. Which ones are coming?"

"According to their communications traffic, it appears to be all of them, with the exceptions of Valjhar Cor and Walks-with-the-Sun. One or more members of the Gold family of Neo-men appear to be coming as well."

"Whoa, that's quite a crew," said Perturbare, rubbing his hands together. "If they're coming to attack this Watcher, we should see some real fireworks. This should be great!"

The tanks, planes, helicopters, and other forces began to withdraw.

The Vigil's arrival, when it came, was spectacular indeed. Perturbare's viewer dimmed automatically when Aureus swept by, spewing out a torrent of energy from its wide-open Third Eye. The beam cut a huge fissure in the side of the Watcher, from which flowed a black, smoking liquid. At the same time, a flying greenish glitter unleashed twin ERASER beams of very high power, pulsing through their entire gamut of wavelengths. Perturbare also noted a distortion indicating the use of Fomalhaut's unique SASER ultrasonic weapon, which caused a large chunk of the Watcher to break free and shatter. The massive armored figure of Stingray landed near the Watcher's base, using what appeared to be a built-in cryoweapon to halt the progress of the black ichor streaming from the Watcher's wounds. Finally, the tiny figure of Endurance could be seen scaling the very flank of the thing, tearing out masses of its substance with his bare hands.

All this happened in an eerie silence until a cacophony of thunder rolled over Perturbare seconds later.

"You see, Brainchild," husked Perturbare in delight, "I told you the Vigil could deal with whatever dangers the

Sphere could produce, once they finally set their minds to it. Magnificent."

"Doctor, someone is approaching."

Perturbare lowered his viewer. In the dimness, he could barely make out a large group of running figures. Something about their gait disturbed him. They ran like so many spastic marionettes. Perturbare nervously pulled his ERASER pistol from its holster.

When they drew nearer, Perturbare wished they had not. They were tall, wasted-looking things, grey of skin, their heads held cocked at odd angles, with tufts of white hair sprouting randomly from their scalps. They drew up and came to a simultaneous halt just twenty feet away, staring at him with heavy-lidded eyes, and smiling.

Perturbare was not comforted to be smiled upon by these creatures.

"All right, boys, there's nothing to see here," he quavered. "You just turn around and go hang around a schoolyard or something."

They did not obey him. Brainchild's robot took a few steps forward, interposing itself between Perturbare and the onlookers.

Still grinning, the Grey Men charged in silence.

Brainchild blurred into action. ERASER beams stabbed from the robot's eyes, causing gouts of pulpy flesh to explode from the creature's bodies. It darted among them, smashing and tearing with its hands. Beams from the flyer also probed out, adding to the flying wet debris and the awful stink of burning corrupted flesh. Perturbare shrank back, shooting into whatever monsters got too close. Once he found himself firing into an awful face a mere yard away from his own, watching in horror as the flesh melted off its skull, the reflected heat enough to singe his hair.

And then, abruptly, the supply of Grey Men was exhausted. All around the flyer sprawled their burning, broken, dismembered forms.

Some of them wore the remnants of military uniforms.

Perturbare stood panting and shaking, his weapon hanging loose in his hand. He stared at Brainchild, whose humanoid form was covered in dark blood and ooze, the clothing and synthetic flesh of his robotic body torn to shreds.

"Did you...see...how...*avid* they all looked? How... happy? They looked...downright *pleased* to be so changed and degraded. As if they finally had an excuse to give up any pretense of human decency. What a burden to lay down, freeing them to act on all their darkest impulses, without any restraint or compunction."

The robot's half-ruined face betrayed reproach as it returned his gaze. "Yes. Terrible, is it not?"

The earth trembled.

Now a new Light flared up from the main battlefield, a white Light of beauty and glory. Perturbare gasped, then laughed as he turned toward that waxing radiance. "Ben Raintree!" he shouted. "At last! Go, Raintree, go!"

The Light burned across the hordes that seethed though the ruined city. Perturbare jumped up and down, so exultant, so overwrought with emotion, that he barely noticed how that Light seared him as well, even as distant as it was. And then another gleam was added, a fierce blue beam that swept over the crowds, and then an acid glow of spring green, and finally, a purple nimbus around Raintree's tiny figure itself.

A rising tumult came up from below, the cries of thousands of men and women, a storm of pain, of outrage, of liberation.

"He's curing them! For the love of God, Ben Raintree is curing those poor bastards." The Lights blended in the tears that obscured his vision. Speech was no longer possible as he wept. The Light of Truth swept over him for an instant. Perturbare cried out and fell to his knees, shattered by that light and what it revealed to him.

And then all Ben's previous efforts seemed to pale to insignificance. All four Lights blazed up as if to infuse the world, blotting out all vision, burning out all illusion and self-deception, revealing to Perturbare an unacknowledged blackness at his own core. He crumpled to the ground.

When the Lights abruptly ceased, Perturbare scarcely dared raise his head to see what new wonders, or horrors, might be revealed. At first he feared the forces of the Night Land were resurgent, for the broken, smoking remnants of the Watcher were now surrounded by four great towers, growing out of the ground as he watched, strong as mountains, bright with metal, glittering with glass or some similar substance. And then Aureus fired its ghostly tachyon beam into a strange lens on one of the towers. That power was somehow passed between the towers, shrouding them, and then crossing the space between them. It dissolved the Watcher into nothingness, its substance converted to energy that was drawn into the mighty towers and there stored, glaring out of branching veins and cylinders of glass like captive sunlight. A great cheer rose up from many thousands of throats, a roar of victory against nightmare.

Perturbare hauled himself to his feet with difficulty, squinting and blinking in that golden light. "Behold the technology of Rral," he whispered. "Behold the Vigil."

He turned to Brainchild, who stood nearby regarding this scene.

"Brainchild, I think we've presented the Vigil with all the challenges it needs. I think it's time to shut down Sphere Y. Shut it down, and destroy it."

"That I will gladly do."

Perturbare looked back into the light, smiling. What a grand day this was!

"Uh."

That small sound had come from Brainchild. With a sense of great foreboding, Perturbare slowly turned back to him.

"Doctor. Something is wrong. I've lost contact with Node 1r. All other data streams from the Sphere have been disabled. I have no further presence aboard it. Sphere Y is now out of our control."

Blood and life seemed to drain out of Perturbare's head as he spoke. "What do you mean? How could this happen?"

"It seems clear enough. The horrors spawned by your machine have taken control of the Sphere. I am ashamed to have had any part in the creation of that device."

Perturbare stumbled away to lean against the canopy of his flyer. Something snapped. Suddenly doom and anger and joy and dread poured in from the outside world, overwhelming him. His thoughts fled. He did not know how much time passed before he became aware of anything again.

And then what he saw something most passing strange. A small boy appeared before him, literally appeared, staring up at him dolefully. He was a beautiful but strange sort of child, with immense crystalline eyes, golden skin, and hair of a soft bluish-white. He was dressed in a white Vigil uniform.

The next thing Perturbare knew, he was being rocked by some impact. When his eyes regained focus he found himself staring into the stern face of Fomalhaut, who held him by the shoulder and throat in an unbreakable grip. The next moment brought two more new arrivals dropping from the sky: Stingray in his battle armor, and Aureus. Aureus sprang at the motionless Brainchild robot, wrapped her pliable arms around it, and melted it into a pile of flaming slag with the power of her Third Eye.

Perturbare swallowed as well as he could and croaked, "Brainchild. You shut down my quantum shielding."

The computer's voice came from a speaker in the flyer.

"Yes, Doctor, I did."

"Then you've turned against me at last."

"No, Doctor, I have not. I am trying to provide you with a final chance of redemption."

"I don't need a machine to provide me with redemption," snarled Perturbare.

"But you do need someone," said Fomalhaut. "And now you have us. Come. Your freedom is at an end."

"No, Fomalhaut," said Brainchild. "I permitted you to detect Doctor Perturbare so you could secure his cooperation in dealing with this situation which he, in his hubris, has created. But I cannot allow you to take him prisoner. I am ultimately his servant and his creation. I act now in the interest of the greater good, but still I cannot betray him completely into your hands."

301

Stingray erupted in a blur of motion, flinging off a gauntlet and springing to Perturbare's side, with his hand resting on the scientist's chest.

From the underside of his naked wrist projected a spine which dripped venom.

"Then I will kill him. I'll kill him, and I don't think even you can stop me in time. Killing is what I'm made for, after all. You will relinquish him to us, Brainchild, or he dies now, and then you can sort out the consequences."

"Stingray, he is yours."

"I am theirs?" demanded Perturbare bitterly. He tried to struggle. "So this is how it's going to be? I'm Doctor Possum Frigging Perturbare!"

"Quit ranting, asshole," said Stingray in irritation. "If I could shovel out your brain and replace it with that of your computer, I would. I'd like you a lot better that way."

The flyer containing the other members of the Vigil settled nearby. The first one out was Ben Raintree, leaning on his staff in exhaustion, but still bedecked in the Stones, his eyes glittering.

"Ben," said Stingray. "Show this man no mercy."

Chapter 27

Planning Session

Stingray stood at the brink of the precipice that dropped to the sea from the base of the Pearl. The Pearl's whitefield shone faintly in the snow-spattered darkness that day had become. Clouds moved overhead in an endless, low-hanging river, submerging the upper third of the Spire, which nevertheless made its presence known by a diffuse white glow, the mark of its great beacon.

Flyers, some piloted by members of the newly constituted Vigil Aerospace Command, others guided by Brainchild, had been arriving all morning, settling through the Pearl's whitefield into the main hangar. They carried delegates to the summit and council of war the Vigil had arranged. The Vigil flyers lit the clouds and snow with their golden propulsion beams. The flyers formerly owned by Possum Perturbare, with their advanced propulsion wave technology, flitted in without fanfare, traveling at mad speeds, then slowing so fast the eye could not follow them.

Stingray's gaze was fixed on the strange new reef that reared out of the waves a few miles out to sea. The irregular clump of rock bore two slitted eyes which glowed in his direction with the characteristic eerie light of the things of the Night Land.

A small Vigil flyer swept by, moving toward the Pearl, then it wavered, changed course, and settled to a landing near Stingray. Its gull-wing door swung open, and out came

Lori Wu, dressed in her engineering suit and a big, knitted stocking cap.

"Hello, Stingray. I saw you standing here so I thought I'd land and come talk to you. Am I bothering you?"

"Not at all. It's always good to see you, Lori."

"Thanks. It was interesting flying in today. Brainchild has such a swarm of flyers hovering up there in the clouds that I thought I'd have to inch my way past them. But he maneuvered them out of my way without my even asking."

"How are things at the Creche?"

"Very good. Between the influx of new workers and sailors and Brainchild's help, we're nearly ready to launch the first wave of Torpedo Ray subs. I'm kind of worn out though."

"Between your construction work and all our combat missions, I'm not surprised. I want you to stay here after the meeting. Get a little rest before we go out again."

"Okay." She looked out to sea and shuddered. "I'm not sure how restful it will be though, with that thing staring at me."

Stingray chuckled. "This will sound crazy, but I find its presence reassuring."

"Yes, that does sound crazy. What do you mean?"

"Well, look at it. Lurking there, just barely peeking its head above the water. It's the slowest-developing Watcher yet reported, by far. If we have trouble looking at it, I think it has even more trouble looking at us. I think it's afraid."

"Really? I still can't wait to get rid of it."

"Take a shot at it if you want to. Never hurts to remind it who's boss around here."

Lori gave him a wide-eyed look, then stepped forward and extended her arms. Her suit hummed. Twin bolts of protons shot out, exciting the air to a scarlet glow, bashing off a chunk of the Watcher's stony crest. Lori shot Stingray a quick crazy grin.

It soon faded into dismay. "I can feel it. It's really looking at me now. Right at me."

"Come on, let's go inside. You'll feel better behind some quantum shielding. Brainchild can bring in your flyer."

Lori started for the entrance to the Spire, but Stingray guided her to the side. "The meeting's being held in the Pearl, in the big auditorium."

"Oh, of course. Stingray, do you mind if I ask you something?"

"Not at all."

"I heard that as you were capturing Perturbare you said something about being made for killing. What was that all about?"

"Ah. Well. I'm sure you remember Harry Brightman?"

"Of course. Endurance and I had enough trouble tracking him down in Rio."

"I don't know how much he told you about himself, but he's told me a lot."

By now they had entered the park which formed the ground level of the Pearl, with its streams and trees. An escalator carried them up into the structure's more conventional levels. Stingray, wishing to keep their conversation private, led Lori to a small vestibule and sat her down.

"American experiments in genetic engineering have been going on much longer than we realized. Before the Neo-man project there was another, of which Brightman was one of the chief scientists. Their goal was to create a breed of superhuman soldiers who could be easily and cheaply raised in great numbers. They'd be born as tiny larvae and introduced into the sea by the millions. There they'd fend for themselves, feeding and growing to many times their original size. If most of them starved or were eaten it was no great loss, since no resources had been devoted to their upbringing. The surviving larvae, when they'd gained enough weight, would enter a pupal phase and metamorphose into humanoids. These would then respond to a built-in homing instinct and make their way to an American-held island. There, as blank slates, they would emerge to be trained and indoctrinated as warriors, able to function in the sea or on the land, with inhuman strength and built-in lethal weapons. I, as you've already guessed, am an example of these creatures."

"Then...why aren't there more of you?"

"I was the prototype, and I didn't turn out quite as they expected. For example, my larval form turned out to be much more intelligent than was desired or expected. Not quite of human intelligence, but much smarter than any fish. This raised an ethical issue. Could they justify dumping great vats of these thinking creatures into the sea, most of them bound to wind up in something else's gullet? Brightman and his allies were especially adamant about this point. They pushed for a complete redesign that would have resulted in dumber larvae, and they won. I, in my larval form, was to be taken out to sea and destroyed. Brightman and his friends objected to this too, and they managed to throw me overboard so I could escape. That resulted in a big fight, a shakeup of their project, and a lot of personal trouble for Brightman. By the time it was settled, the Neo-man project was proposed. It was deemed more promising, and the fish-man project was abandoned."

Stingray sighed.

"The Neo-men were intended to be a refined race of great mental capacity, meant to help the Americans maintain their power through their intelligence and their other mental gifts. My race was intended to be a horde of expendable thugs who would crawl out of the waves to be turned into killers."

Lori leaned toward him on the couch they shared and took his arm.

"But they got that wrong too, Stingray! If your larval form was smarter than they wanted it to be, then surely your adult form is too. You're certainly one of the smartest people I've ever met. And as for you being a killer...well. You're also one of the most civilized people I've ever met. I know, you needn't say it, you *have* killed, and acted with violence. I know that. But any of us could be driven to that, under the right circumstances. Maybe even me."

Stingray relaxed a little. "I was educated—the first time —by the Space Mariners. The second time by Fomalhaut and T'Ukudu. Without that kind of...upbringing, who can say what kind of person I might have turned out to be?"

"I'm sure you would have been the same fundamentally gentle soul you are now. But—you do kick a lot of ass, too."

Lori leaned closer and gave Stingray a hug. Stingray smiled and tentatively returned it.

"Thanks, Lori. It's always nice to be...appreciated. Now it's time for the council."

They started out, Lori trotting to keep up with Stingray's giant strides.

"Stingray? Do you remember anything about your…life as a larva?"

"Very little. Very hazily. It was mostly pretty relaxing, as I recall. Just a lot of swimming and feeding. Being a larva sounds pretty good right about now."

"About this meeting. Is there any good news?"

"No."

The Vigil assembled at a table at the lowest level of the auditorium. Already present when Stingray and Lori arrived were Fomalhaut, Aureus, Walks, Endurance, and Valjhar.

The rising tiers of seats were occupied by representatives of many nations, as well as officials from the United Nations. The largest contingent was from the United States, and included Sard Ducanis, who was now also the acting Secretary of Defense, and with him the newly-appointed Chairman of the Joint Chiefs of Staff. The U.S. government had lost so many high officials to the Night Land it was hard to keep track of who held what post. The President was still carefully preserved somewhere, but by now everyone openly acknowledged his uselessness.

Many members of the Vigil staff were also present, including Chief Pilot Jordan Elcanie of the Vigil Aerospace Command. His broken arm was already healed, knitted together by nano-machines under the control of Brainchild.

Also on hand was the entire Gold family of Neo-men, plus the Blues. All other Neo-man clans had also sent representatives: the Greens; the Whites; the Grays; the Browns; and the Blacks. These attracted great interest from the delegates of the nations to whom the genetic research programs of the United States came as a surprise.

The final trio to enter the room consisted of Ben Raintree, leading Doctor Possum Frigging Perturbare (as he had come to be known among the Vigil staff) and Pimsehkia Flam. These last two were shackled together at the wrist. Though they eyed each other with loathing, Pimsehkia's eyes also glinted with a certain spiteful satisfaction.

Perturbare was a changed and possibly broken man. Whenever his old arrogance and narcissism threatened to rear up again (and they were amazingly resilient), Raintree blasted any resurgent illusions from his heart and mind with the Stones. It had gotten to the point where whenever he was about to speak, he would first glance towards Ben with trepidation, and more often than not keep his peace. It was actually rather a sad change, even to Stingray.

Despite Perturbare's subdued demeanor, when he appeared in the room Ducanis and several others leaped to their feet in outrage.

"Is that Possum Perturbare down there?" he cried wildly. "Chained to Jenni Katz, my missing staff member? Why is that man here? Why is he not in prison? Why is he not—"

"SILENCE!" bellowed Stingray, pounding the table hard enough to make it jump.

Silence filled the air.

"That's better. I will now lay out my expectations for this meeting. I insist on courtesy and order. There will be no screaming, no demands. We do nothing here which doesn't have some purpose. All will be explained. Is this clear?"

"Yes, it is," said Ducanis. "I hope you can appreciate, though, that it is difficult for us to see this incredible criminal, who is responsible for the ongoing downfall of the world, without some emotional reaction on our part."

Stingray nodded. "I do understand that, very well. I myself would prefer not to have him here, but I think we must agree that as long as we can obtain his cooperation, it would be foolish to exclude him. I now ask Fomalhaut to provide a summary of the current situation."

Fomalhaut stood. "Over the past two weeks, the Vigil has destroyed a total of four Watchers, two Houses, three Fire Pits, two arrays of Lights, and one nascent City. Each of these operations requires our maximum effort. Each is exhausting and dangerous.

"During that same period, seven new Watchers have appeared, as well as five Fire Pits, three arrays of Lights, and today we have learned that a new City is beginning to transform Jerusalem. This City will be our next target, by the way.

"Clearly, then, we are losing this war. We cannot keep up with these new manifestations. Millions of people have already died or been subverted. Even in areas which are not yet under the direct influence of the Night Land, society has collapsed, people are terrified, and violence and despair are in control. Spread across the entire world, this emotional breakdown is more than even Ben Raintree can confront.

"We've seen that conventional weapons are effective only against the lesser manifestations, and are nearly useless against the greater. We are working to develop more powerful weapons, but our ability to do so is reduced by the steady toll being taken on our forces.

"We have made several attempts to destroy Sphere Y, and we've been repelled each time. In addition to the formidable defenses installed by Perturbare, the forces which have seized it have fortified it in ways we do not fully understand and cannot yet overcome. This then is where we stand. Before we offer any conclusions, are there any questions?"

A French general stood up and said, "Yes. What about the defenses used in the *Night Land* novel and television show? Has any attempt been made to use those?"

Fomalhaut lowered his head, evidently seeking a polite way to respond. Stingray took the matter out of his hands.

"General, the problem is, our world has no equivalent of the 'Earth Current' used in the book and show. Even if we had such a thing, it was effective as a defense for only a very few individual structures. We don't intend to hide and cower like that. We mean to fight. If you're referring to the device called the 'Diskos', I'm afraid we've discovered no way to turn a weed whacker into a deadly weapon."

The general sank back into his seat, red-faced.

"We await your conclusions," said Ducanis.

Fomalhaut resumed speaking. "First, we point out that Sphere Y is not inherently or necessarily a source of evil. It is incredibly dangerous, and its construction was outrageously irresponsible, but the only reason it is spewing out almost nothing other than manifestations of the Night Land is because of Perturbare's carefully crafted television show, which has filled the minds of many millions of people with these images. It is a self-reenforcing process. The more people encounter the Night Land, the stronger it becomes. But there is, at least potentially, a counter to this. People who pray, or who imagine and seek after things that are good, or who simply think positive thoughts, reduce the power of the Night Land and slow its spread.

"One of our own members is the leader of a movement that profoundly and fervently prays for peace and justice. They must be encouraged. Therefore, Stingray and I now ask Walks-with-the-Sun to lead his people from their Canadian refugee camp back to their homeland, where they must perform their Ghost Dance with all the sincerity at their command."

Walks was so startled he nearly fell out of his chair. "What's this? Hey, that's a great idea, but I think it would turn my people into targets. Who will protect them?"

"You will, Walks," said Stingray. "You, our own Aerospace Command, a group of Neo-men, and all the remaining forces of the United States Military."

Now it was the Chairman of the Joint Chiefs who leapt up. "What? That's impossible!"

"Why, General?" asked Stingray. "Surely your troops know how to find their way to the Stronghold by now."

"Our forces are spread too thin as it is! We're trying to defend Washington, and New York, and a dozen other places!"

"Yes. And by all accounts your people are fighting heroically, confronting for the first time in decades an actual threat to your country. But they are also losing. They are dying, they are being thrown back, and they are being subverted and destroyed. Your strategy amounts to a hopeless retreat. Your forces must be devoted to the protection of people who are actually accomplishing something."

The general made a dismissive gesture. "We just don't have time to protect a bunch of—"

"Be careful, General," cautioned Fomalhaut. "You are about to violate Stingray's call for courtesy."

Alpha Blue stood and spoke. "We do not appreciate the thoughts which he and a number of others in this room are entertaining about us. They are decidedly uncharitable."

"Yeah!" blurted Zayin Gold.

A Chinese politician was next to speak. "Here is another matter which I trust is understandable. We are just now learning that the Americans have spent the last two decades designing and creating semi-human supermen for the purpose of cementing their hegemony over the world. Now these creatures sit among us, reading our thoughts, purporting to help us. Yet also before us is Fomalhaut, who is now revealed to be one of these so-called Neo-men, a species which apparently is destined to inherit the world. It is unclear to many of us what would motivate them to prevent our extermination now."

"We'll help you because we're not as rotten as you are!" yelled Zayin, provoking some uneasy laughter.

"If you'll accept the word of someone who knows the Neo-men and who had a hand in their creation," said Harry Brightman, "I can tell you that little Zayin is essentially correct. The Neo-man brain is quite different from ours in many ways. Neo-men are not competitive. They are cooperative by nature. I advise you not to worry about them. If they do wind up inheriting the Earth, it won't be because they knifed us in the back."

"Gentlemen!" said Stingray. "The fact that the Neo-men are sitting among us should be proof that all cards are now on the table and all secrets bared. The issue before us is how to use our pooled resources to permit the survival of any of us. The time for petty political maneuvering is past. The world as we know it is ending. Once again, we require the United States Military to do all it can to protect the Lakota Ghost Dancers."

"I'll see to it," said Ducanis.

"That may slow our defeat," said Fomalhaut, "but the bleak reality of the situation remains the same. As long as these dark forces remain in control of Sphere Y, and as long as the world is full of people who inform Earth's quantum environment with their nightmares, we cannot prevail."

"Why can't these telepaths shield or change the thoughts of the people?" demanded someone.

"We are far too few, and they are untrained. Even if we could erase the memory of the Night Land from all mankind, it would not be enough. Negativity has always dominated the thoughts and dreams of Humanity. Without the Night Land, the Sphere would produce devils or vampires or infidels or predatory homosexuals or whatever ridiculous bogies men fear most."

Without looking up from his sulk, Perturbare said, "You're all overlooking the obvious."

Stingray gave him a bright gaze. "And what is that?"

"Simply get rid of everyone."

This remark resulted in tumult. Raintree, eyeing Perturbare narrowly, reached into his jacket to finger the Stone of Inner Light. Stingray and Fomalhaut studied him just as closely. Pimsehkia almost laughed.

"Why, you murderous...!" blustered the Chairman of the Joint Chiefs. "Your solution is genocide? I ought to come down there and snap your scrawny neck!"

Perturbare looked up at him with a scornful expression. "Not like that, you brass-plated, crop-topped cretin. I mean get them off the planet. Abandon ship."

"How?" asked Lori in amazement. "A fleet of giant spaceships? To where?"

"No, Lori, I have something more elegant in mind. Frame Shifters."

"What the hell is a Frame Shifter?" demanded the Chairman.

"A Frame Shifter," said Stingray, "is an invention of Perturbare's which permits someone to travel to another world. Another universe, actually."

"What other world?"

"*Any* other world. There's no way of telling. If I understand the theory, it's most likely to be a world resembling this one."

"That's right," said Perturbare. "The most probable level of divergence depends on the power of the initial transitional impulse."

Lori looked puzzled.

"I believe he's saying that if you turn up the power, you're likely to wind up someplace weirder," said Stingray. "But there's never any way to be sure about your destination. It's a quantum phenomenon, inherently unpredictable, albeit one on a macroscopic scale."

"Very good, Stingray," said Perturbare. "A gold star for you."

"And with nearly everyone removed from the world, the power of the Night Land would be greatly reduced," said Fomalhaut thoughtfully.

"This strikes me as an extremely dubious proposition," said Ducanis. "To deal with this enemy, you'll depopulate the world? You'll exile everyone to unknown alien worlds? That would be a Pyrrhic victory at best."

"Most likely they would go to unknown alternate Earths. They would be unlikely to end up in worlds where their prospects for survival are worse than they are here. Very unlikely indeed."

"And how many of these machines would be required to do the job?"

Perturbare replied. "Each machine could manage about three hundred cycles per day. Assuming an average of two people per cycle, I estimate it would take nearly one million machines to complete the evacuation within one week, which is about all the time we have left before the Night Land completely overruns the Earth."

"One million? How can you possibly produce that many machines in any reasonable time?"

Fomalhaut hesitated.

"Brainchild can make them," said Perturbare. "Isn't that right?"

"Yes." The computer's voice emerged from the air, startling everyone, causing some in the audience to cower. "Using nanoconstructors, I can build them *in situ*. However, use of the airborne devices would be impractically slow. They are primarily solar powered, but ambient lighting on this planet is now at a very low level. I could modify them to make more use of chemical energy sources, but that too would be slow. It would be best to use dedicated, powered constructor machines, which can first reproduce themselves, then set to work producing Frame Shifters. They should be manned, both to protect them and to introduce raw materials."

"Do you people hear what Perturbare is saying?" asked Pimsehkia in disbelief.

"Pimsehkia..." began Stingray.

"Please allow Jenni, or Pimsehkia, or whatever her name really is, to speak," said Ducanis. "She surely understands the situation better than most of us here."

"Thank you. I allowed myself to be shackled to Perturbare as an impediment to any escape attempt he might make. No one can possibly do enough to hamper his tendency to mischief. He is solely responsible for the disaster which has overcome this world, and yet listen to the solution he now proposes. The ultimate misanthrope, he will cast everyone off the planet. He expects everyone to march into these booths, from which they will vanish, to be sent off to who knows where, or perhaps to be disintegrated, for all we know. And who stands to gain from this emptied planet? Fomalhaut, and his Neo-men. Fomalhaut, who has long wondered how his people will come to supplant the Human race. Now finally he sees how it might be done, and so elegantly, too. Look at him. He's seriously considering this idea. He will put your fate into the hands of the worst criminal who ever lived. What is it with you people? An arrogant man gets you into this incredible mess, and who do you turn to for a solution? The same man. It's a racial psychosis. How can you listen to any of this? How can you believe it?"

"I will show you how we can believe it, or disbelieve it," said Raintree. He reached into his jacket and produced the Circlet, settling it onto his brow. Before anyone could react, the Stone of Truth burned bright blue, flooding the auditorium with its inescapable Light. "Perturbare. Will your machines function as you say they will?"

"Yes!"

"Fomalhaut. Do you see hope in any other plan?"

"No. Not in any other plan which I have conceived or heard of."

"And do you hope for the evacuation of Earth to make room for your Neo-men?"

"Yes, of course I do."

Many gasps and sputters of outrage sounded throughout the room.

"I also hope for a better outcome for the Human race. A better outcome, in fact, than might have been possible even if Perturbare's machine had never existed. The Human world was destined to fall in any event, doomed by its own short-sighted greed and savagery. Within a hundred years, its own actions would have reduced the Human race to a starving, ignorant mob fighting to subsist on a failing planet."

"Fomalhaut!" said Lori. "What about our plan to take over? Wouldn't that have saved us?"

"It would at best only have staved off the end. We could not have ruled forever, if we could have ruled at all. Our plan for military conquest might well have ended in chaos and upheaval. Ben, please remove that Stone. You have achieved your purpose."

Raintree complied, to the visible and audible relief of all present.

"I hate those Stones," muttered Perturbare.

"Does anyone here now doubt the sincerity or necessity of Perturbare's plan?" asked Stingray.

No one answered, not even Pimsie.

"Then I propose we make the effort. Before we adjourn, there's one more thing we need to address. The Motionglobe. Ducanis, we want it."

"Ah." Ducanis looked downcast. "That is proving to be not so easy. To tell you the truth, we lost track of it some time ago. It was under study at our base near Washington. Somehow the globe has been misplaced."

"You *lost* the motionglobe?" said Stingray in disbelief.

"Secretary Ducanis," said Fomalhaut. "That artifact is a treasure unique in the universe. It could do much to assure our success. It must be found."

An hour later, Stingray and Valjhar made their way to the ready room where Stingray was to suit up for the Vigil's latest combat mission. Aureus pattered along behind them.

"Did you notice how adroitly Fomalhaut avoided mentioning that the main thing the Ghost Dancers are praying for is the removal of all white men from the Earth?" chuckled Stingray.

"Really?" said Valjhar absently. "I don't think I knew that."

"You seem distracted."

"It's Pimsie. It's difficult for me to see her acting so bitter and vengeful. Thinking of her, so gentle and kind, was a comfort to me in all the years of my wanderings. Of course, I also imagined she was dead."

Stingray hesitated, unsure of how much he could afford to say about her.

"Yes. I never knew her as well as you do, of course, but I also hate to see her like this. At least she's cooperating with us now, sort of."

"She has no real reason not to, now that we've all joined forces. But I'm quite sure she had to talk herself into it. She's always been so emotional, you know. And in some cases I can think of…a little too quick to judge others. I hope the Americans find the Motionglobe soon. I feel useless, watching you all go into battle while I pretend to be busy here."

Stingray glanced aside at his old friend and enemy. "Valjhar, have you noticed that your hair is growing in darker? Without the greenish streaks?"

"It is?"

"In fact, you're looking younger in general. I don't just mean you're having a good day. Literally younger."

"Really? I have no explanation for that."

"I think I have. Brainchild? Do you have anything to do with this?"

Brainchild, having been permitted full access to the base and its systems, replied. "Yes. I have taken the liberty to repair cumulative damage to Valjhar's genes. It is not difficult. Rralians are a genetically optimized species. Their genome is quite simple, free of any redundant or useless information, though Valjhar's has of course been modified."

Both men stopped in their tracks.

"Brainchild," said Valjhar slowly. "You have indeed taken a liberty. You've changed my body without my knowledge or permission. I require you to stop this at once."

"I am sorry. Doctor Perturbare asked me to keep his own genes in good repair, and I wrongly extrapolated from this that all similar beings would wish the same thing. May I ask why you do not wish your body to be repaired and maintained?"

Valjhar hesitated.

"I don't expect you to understand this. It's not very rational. I have earned my age. I've earned it through my deeds, for good and for ill. I do not deserve to escape the natural consequences of Human aging. It is—unseemly."

"Brainchild, I'll go farther," said Stingray. "I order you to perform no modifications to any person without their permission. If you're not willing to comply with this, I'll have to deny you access to this base once again."

"I shall of course comply."

"You do recognize the necessity of keeping Perturbare penned up here with us, don't you?"

"I regret to say that I do."

"Very good. Valjhar, I'll leave you here. The inaptly named Holy Land is looking less holy all the time, and we've got to do something about it."

Chapter 28

Arrow of the Sun

Walks-with-the-Sun stood on the edge of the Stronghold, looking out in amazement as the sounds of the Ghost Dance washed over him from behind. Once more, the Stronghold was surrounded by a massive concentration of military power. This time, all those weapons were facing *away* from his people. The full force of the *wasichu*, now devoted to the preservation of the Lakota! At last, the white man had seen some value in the Lakota religion.

Walks stood in the dim grey light while snow swirled around him. As usual he wore only his Ghost Shirt and a pair of jeans. Warmth came from the sun disk painted on the shirt's back, before which soared an eagle with wings outspread. The eagle feather he usually wore in his hair had earlier been taken by the wind. He was not cold.

He couldn't say the same for Jordan Elcanie, who stood beside him with his Vigil Aerospace Command jacket zipped up around his neck. Valkyrie War Flyers were parked in a neat array nearby, their pilots waiting beside them. A few zipped back and forth on patrol, illuminating the clouds with their orange propulsion beams.

All this latent physical power was nothing compared to the spiritual power rising from the fire-lit Dancers who circled and sang at the center of the Stronghold. Most of the Lakota nation had come, adding to the thousands of Dancers who had fled and who had now returned. Also present were Dancers from the Crow, the Cheyenne, the

Shoshone, and other nations. Walks could feel their massed power, a cleanness in the air which was now absent in most other parts of the world.

And yet all of them, Dancers and soldiers alike, were surrounded by a great and terrible darkness that missed nothing of what they did. This too Walks could feel.

"How do you think it's going to go, Walks?" asked Jordan nervously.

"I think we will soon be attacked. I think the Army men will do what they can. I think you and our other Vigil pilots will fight with courage."

"And what will you do?"

Walks shrugged. "Who can say? My life is always a surprise to me. I will also do whatever I can."

"This isn't what I pictured when I signed up with the Vigil. I hoped to bring a little justice to the world, and get to pilot these spiffy flyers to boot. I never figured on trying to fight off the end of the world. My parents pretty much wrote me off as a traitor when I joined. Now, I don't even know if they're still alive. Same with my girl. If I ever find her again, I'll marry her right quick, before anything else can go wrong."

"This is a very dark night," agreed Walks. "But who knows what the day will bring?"

Jordan looked at his watch. "This *is* daytime. And I know what the next few minutes will bring. Moonrise."

The two men looked out over the bleak landscape of grey and darker grey, waiting for something they both knew must come.

It happened in the very midst of the troops and armored vehicles. Black geometric shapes rose up from the ground, standing at first like individual monoliths, then merging as they grew, flowing over and absorbing the soldiers unlucky enough to fall under the influence of those shadows. They were never seen again, at least not in their human form. Soon a tall, narrow House loomed out of the plain, showing here and there rows of blue and green Lights which lit nothing.

Beside it, a colorless band appeared on the face of the Earth, sharp-edged and featureless. It ran from the foot of the Stronghold into the invisible distance, glowing faintly.

Jordan lifted his viewer and muttered, "I've seen the damn TV show, and even tried to read the book, though it was tough going. That looks like a Road. And if it is... yeah. See those tiny figures in the distance?"

Walks did see them, for his vision at that time was the vision of an eagle. "Yes."

"I believe they're called Silent Ones. No telling what those jokers will do."

The sound of weapons fire arose in the distance where the Silent Ones, walking at their slow, inexorable pace, encountered the vanguard of the soldiers.

"Yeah," said Walks. "I suppose it's time for you and your men to get up there and see what you can do."

"Right. Good luck, sir." Jordan trotted off toward his flyer.

Walks turned back to face the House, suddenly feeling a good bit lonelier. The Dancers, it seemed, had not yet taken note of what was happening. That would soon change.

Sometimes the Houses remained as they were, serving whatever incomprehensible purposes they served. Sometimes they merely sheltered a Watcher until it was ready to emerge from shadow.

This was one of the latter cases. The walls of the House dissolved away, revealing the mountainous bulk of the Watcher, which somehow stood even taller than had the House, staring down at the Stronghold and its occupants. This was by far the most man-like Watcher Walks had yet seen. Made of smooth pale stone, it resembled a crouching figure with a narrow, bitter face and cruel eyes lit by a pale blue fire. The lower half of its face was obscured by a beard of jutting, murky crystals. It was as much an insult to the Lakota as a threat.

Behind Walks, the drums faltered and fell silent. The singing was replaced by cries of terror and dread. Walks whirled, raising his arms. A light like that of the rising Sun poured from him as he called out, "Keep Dancing! By the spirits of all our ancestors, and in the name of every person of good will in this world, keep Dancing! This thing is here because it fears our power! Let's really give it something to fear! Show it that the Lakota will tremble before no darkness! Even if this thing strikes us all down, let us fall as men of power, as warriors of the spirit! Dance!"

And dance they did. The drums thundered. The mesa trembled with the beat of thousands of feet. Voices raised and joined together like the voice of a storm, echoing back from the sky.

Walks turned back to the Watcher, where he nearly staggered before the force of the thing's malice. To one side the Valkyrie War Flyers were lifting off. Off in the darkness below, a thousand weapons were firing at once, striking sparks off the Watcher, or assaulting the Silent Ones and whatever other lesser manifestations the Watcher had brought to bear. Flares were launched, casting their fierce, shifting glows over the battlefield as they descended on their parachutes. Flame throwers roared out here and there.

Well, now to try being Walks-with-the-Sun again instead of plain old Ray Smick, thought Walks.

With his arms still raised, he lifted up until he was level with the eyes of the Watcher. "You!" he cried. "Go back to your storybook world. You don't belong here. This world contains powers greater than you. Go back to where you came from. We'll let your book go out of print again, and then we'll all be happy!"

Walks heard a chuckle. Thankfully, it came from below, and not from the Watcher. Walks looked down between his dangling feet as he hovered in place. Looking up at him were John Yellow Horse and a few other Lakota holy men.

"Very funny, Walks. I always knew you were a real *heyoka*. Now, they say you are supposed to be some kind of a big deal. Go now and show that big *kaga tipsila* out there why you are worthy to be a member of the Vigil. We down here will also poke at it in our own way. Look, here are your spirit guides, come to help you in your great moment."

What? Walks looked around, nearly dropping to the ground in astonishment. He was flanked by two ghostly figures. One was a tall, bronzed woman with a mane of auburn hair floating weightlessly about her. The other was a sandy-haired white man, dressed in blue and white, with the eagle-and-sun emblem emblazoned on his chest. Walks had seen them both before, years ago, when they'd appeared to guide him into the Great Vision which had led to his subsequent career as a Ghost Dancer and member of the Vigil. Now their eyes blazed at him, his of blue, hers of green, an eagle and a falcon hovering beside him.

Feeling anything but worthy, yet filled with the same determination as his two spirit brethren, Walks launched himself at the Watcher. Although his speed was enough to send the wind moaning past his ears, his perception of time altered so that the Watcher appeared to approach in slow motion. He had ample time to study its hillside-sized face as it loomed huger and huger in his field of vision.

At the last instant, a little voice in his head warned him he wasn't going to get anywhere by using himself as a bullet. He slowed down as much as he could in the space remaining, and still slammed hard into the Watcher near the inner corner of its left eye. He grabbed onto a knob of cold stone and hung there, a thousand feet above the ground, out of breath, while shells and rockets exploded around him. The Watcher's eye was like a cave with its ledge a few feet to his right, and below. Walks swung down into it, and was suddenly a mote in the Watcher's eye, confronting the swirling bluish mist that filled it. From this perspective it no longer carried a sense of being an eye at all, but was merely a visual enigma. Walks drew back his fist, preparing to strike with all the force he could muster. His fist wavered, and he drew back, distracted by that blue void, fascinated by its strangeness, seduced by its quiet, which promised to bring a similar quiet to him as well. Perhaps the thing to do would be to step into that glow, to learn what was really behind it all, to find the secrets whereby he, Walks, could end this threat all by himself.

He extended his hand...it sank without resistance into the blueness, where, as far as he could tell, it ceased to exist...smiling, he inserted his forearm...

It was nice...

He need not be; he need not fear or hurt...

The Watcher trembled beneath his feet. Some force threw Walks back. He landed on the ledge of the thing's lower eyelid. He sat up, staring into that eye again, then examined his hand and arm, which had turned grey and cold, and were only gradually resuming their normal color. He realized, a few minutes too late for his taste, that he was perched on the face of a Watcher, in mortal danger of his soul.

"Holy shit, I must be crazy!" he exclaimed. The Watcher shuddered again. Walks looked out; were they now closer to the Stronghold? Again the thing trembled, and yes, it had moved a few feet closer to the mesa. Not only had this Watcher manifested itself faster than any other to date, but unlike the others, it was moving at a perceptible speed. He could see Yellow Horse and the other holy men, standing at the brink, looking not up at the Watcher, but downward, toward the base of the mesa.

Something new had appeared there: a curved surface of white light, emerging from the earth, rising until it was a low luminous dome, shining with a light altogether more wholesome and welcome than whatever leprous glows emerged from the things of the Night Land. The Watcher shuddered and seemed to settle down with a rumbling groan. It advanced no further.

The dome continued to rise until it was revealed as an ovoid perched atop two thin columns. These stilts lengthened until the whole glowing structure stood as tall as the Watcher itself. Then, from the ovoid, a thicker, sinuous column emerged from one end, elevating itself still farther, tipped with a knob and a long sharp spike. It was altogether bizarre, and hard to interpret clearly from Walk's very close perspective.

"Najin Pehan! Najin Pehan!" This cry rose up faintly from the massed Dancers. Walks fretted, wishing his grasp of the Lakota language was much stronger. Stand? Standing? Standing something. A bird? Yes. A crane. A standing crane.

A Standing Crane.

Suddenly electrified, Walks burst from the Watcher's eye into the air, circling the shining, towering apparition that so daunted the Watcher. Yes, yes, this was the very spot where Tom Standing Crane had sacrificed himself months before by flinging himself from the brink of the mesa. Walk's spine tingled so hard he thought it might hold him aloft all by itself. *Standing Crane!* Walks's flight wavered; he settled to a clumsy landing beside Yellow Horse and the others, too excited to remain airborne.

There they watched as the War Flyers converged on the Watcher, concentrating their fire upon it. These were armed with experimental proton pulse cannons, complex tubes running the length of the flyer's tops. Walks didn't understand their workings, but he could see them spitting out flickers of explosive force at unpredictable intervals. These impacts had variable effects, the best of them knocking off chunks of the Watcher's substance.

The drumbeat of the Dancers shook the earth. The squat mass of the Watcher confronted the tall, shining figure of the Standing Crane. The military forces of both the Vigil and the United States pounded away at the Watcher and its hordes of converts and minions.

Walks-with-the-Sun stood there gaping. He glanced down at his arm, still partly grey, still not quite feeling like part of his body. His spirit guides were no longer visible. Yellow Horse and the other holy men ignored him.

329

"Well," he said to no one. "I guess I'd better do something quick, or else I'm going to come out of this looking pretty dumb."

He lifted straight up, rising through the snow, penetrating the lower decks of cloud, which wiped out his view of the battle and enveloped him in a cold, damp softness. Up he soared, through winds, through stinging sleet, through layers where lightning flickered and rumbled. Up for thousands of feet, and then for miles, through clouds thicker and denser than any he had ever seen or heard of, even back to the origins of the world and its people.

At last he broke free of these clouds, bursting into the light, where he was astonished to find that the Sun still reigned in the heavens, so far untouched by the evils which assaulted the Earth. And yet the Moon did not appear so inviolate. It hung not far from the horizon, bright against the deep blue of the stratosphere, but its face was somehow different. Sickly lights of some kind glowed on its dark night side.

But this was not the time for studying the Moon. He continued upward, until all sound but the ringing of his ears was extinguished, until his skin tingled and burned in the unfiltered sunlight, until his chest heaved without result. The sky grew black. The Earth looked like a dense patch of dirty fungus beneath him. He could not long survive these conditions, he realized, but he would not have to.

Walks relaxed, letting momentum carry him upward until it was exhausted, leaving him poised in space for an instant. Then he accelerated downward with all the force the spirits would grant him. The thickening air was hot against his face. His Ghost Shirt and all other clothing was torn and burned from his body. The sound of the wind was first a thin scream in his ears, and then a roar.

Just before he entered the clouds, he sent out his prayer.

Wakan Tanka, White Buffalo Woman, and all you spirits: either you have given me the power to do this and survive, or you have not. If so, then let me now offer the thanks of a humble man. If not, then let me also thank you, for showing me how to make something of myself in my last few years of life in this world. The next world will be bright and green. There I will greet my ancestors with joy.

He entered the clouds, a fiery bolt of flesh and bone, while through his mind flashed visions of his parents, his grandparents, his brothers, and Standing Crane. His aim was true. He emerged from the clouds directly above the head of the Watcher.

Jordan Elcanie did his best to crush the trigger of his proton cannon, exhorting it on, cheering when it spat out two or three good solid bolts, cursing when instead it sputtered out a large number of ineffective ones. These blasted things were just too unpredictable. Already one flyer and pilot had been lost when its cannon backed up and discharged all its energy in a single pulse, destroying it.

Everything would have been all right if they could have stayed there all day and whittled the thing down piece by piece. But this was no ordinary Watcher. Its forward motion had ceased, blocked by that weird glowing bird, but it was now *standing up*, unfolding at a barely perceptible speed. What it would do then was anyone's guess.

Walks, it seemed, was a dud. As far as Jordan could tell, he had fled the scene. Jordan had summoned the rest of the

Vigil, but they were engaged in battle with another deadly manifestation on the other side of the world.

And now, what was this? A new glow appeared in the clouds above the Watcher, growing very rapidly. Some new manifestation of the Night Land?

A streak of fire, as bright as the Sun itself, burst out of the cloud, plummeting onto the Watcher. It impacted in a massive explosion. The thing's head burst asunder. Huge fragments toppled from its shoulders. Streamers of dust and debris arced out and rained down. The shockwave battered Jordan's flyer; small impacts rattled like hail on ts fuselage. When he regained control, Jordan gaped at the decapitated Watcher, whose body was crumbling as cracks and fissures propagated through it. It was over. This Watcher was destroyed.

The colossal Bird spread wings of light which enveloped the top of the decaying Watcher. Then the apparition faded.

Barely able to contain his jubilation, Jordan pitched his flyer down to pick off the remaining Grey Men, Silent Ones, Night Hounds, and other monstrosities. Without the Watcher, these lesser creatures were aimless and afraid, easy targets for both the flyers and the ground troops.

For a brief moment, the light of the Sun penetrated to the ground, finding its way through the tunnel drilled through the clouds by whatever that fiery missile had been.

When no further enemies could be found, Jordan ordered his squadron to return to its landing site atop the Stronghold. There he and his remaining pilots leaped from their cockpits, laughing and pounding each other on the back in joy over their unexpected victory.

And then Jordan noticed the sound of the Dance had changed. The drumbeats were slower. The singing was sadder.

Feeling a sudden premonition, Jordan broke off from his celebration, making his way to the edge of the mesa, where a few of the Lakota mystics stood, gazing mournfully towards the remains of the Watcher, which by now looked like nothing more than an outcropping of the nearby Badlands.

Yellow Horse met Jordan, saying, "You must contact the Vigil. Tell them their two Lakota members have defeated this demon, and now both of them are exploring the next world together."

Jordan sat down and wept, ashamed of himself for having once more doubted the worth of Walks-with-the-Sun.

The activation of the Frame Shifters could not come soon enough for him.

Chapter 29

A Better Place

A great mass of people gathered in Times Square. At their center were many of the remaining high officials of the United States Government, the remaining members of the Vigil, and Doctor Possum Perturbare. There also stood the first of the Frame Shifters to be activated.

The event was covered by all that remained of New York's media. Brainchild also did what he could to distribute the story around the world.

The city was ravaged, its people hungry, dirty, and frightened. One Watcher had already been destroyed in Central Park, plus another across the river in Jersey City. Even now, troops fought off incursions of Grey Men, plus increasing numbers of assorted demons, ghosts, zombies, and other symptoms of madness. As the psychic health of the human race eroded, the threats produced by Sphere Y became more various. The Night Land was still the dominant motif, but it was increasingly joined, or rivaled, by others. In the harbor, the mighty Vigil attack submarine *Tara* stood guard against monsters of the deep. Overhead, many powerful flyers, most controlled by Brainchild, hunted for nightmares of the air.

One way or another, mused Fomalhaut, this moment would prove to be the peak of Sphere Y's power.

Sard Ducanis, Acting President of the United States, stood at a microphone, concluding his explanation of what was about to occur. He looked a wreck, eyes hollow and darkened, his thinning hair lank and unkempt. His mind radiated a kind of despair. He knew very well that the nation he had devoted his life to serving was coming to an end.

"I know I need not emphasize the seriousness of what has happened to our planet. We have all experienced it firsthand in the most terrible of ways. The Vigil's solution is a desperate one, yet we must accept it. We must abandon our world. With each one of us who leaves, the forces of evil will grow ever weaker, until finally they can be destroyed. Most of us will not be here to see it, but the planet itself will be saved, and we as individuals and families will be safe in our new worlds. The machines are ready. Now we must begin. Who will be the first to brave this new adventure?"

The crowd gave forth a resounding silence.

Ducanis waited two painful minutes for any response, any movement. Fomalhaut felt the suspicion and fear which pervaded the crowd.

"Now wait a minute, let me get this straight."

Perturbare gave out a muffled exclamation.

Fomalhaut, taking in the cause of his remark, immediately understood its origin.

She was an aging woman, her dark hair going grey, her blue eyes still keen and sharp. Clearly her prosperity had declined, but her bearing remained proud enough. She jabbed a finger toward Perturbare.

"This road-kill guy has ruined the world with his sickening TV show and his little science experiments. Yet here he stands with the Vigil. He's even wearing your uniform. Now you tell us all to march into another of

Perturbare's inventions, these extermination chambers or whatever they are, and disappear? Have I got that right?"

Perturbare managed a sickly grin. "That's about it. Only they aren't extermination chambers."

The woman stepped up smartly and slapped Perturbare's face. "Don't you smirk at me, you bastard. You make me sick. If I ever had a son like you, I'd abort him with a wire coat hanger, even if he was thirty years old. And I'll tell you something else. I will never walk into one of your death traps. I'll take my chances here, in my own world."

"Madam," said Fomalhaut, mercifully diverting her glare, "we will not force you to make the transition, but you will be far better off if you do."

She scowled at him. "You go to hell, all of you." She dismissed them with a gesture and turned to walk off on her clicking high heels.

"M—Mrs. Pylypciw..." began Perturbare, taking half a step after her.

She whirled, her eyes narrowing. "How do you know my name?"

Perturbare could only stare at her, stricken, plainly wondering what he could say to her, what would make sense, what she would believe. In the end he realized there was nothing he could say. He forced a ghastly smile onto his face and said, "I know everything, don't I? Go ahead, hop in the machine. If what you find there isn't better than Brooklyn, you can come back and wallop me again."

"Drop dead, you son of a bitch."

She turned away again. Perturbare watched her vanish into the crowd. "Don't call me that," he whispered.

His feelings of grief and regret were most uncomfortable for Fomalhaut, so intense they could scarcely be ignored.

The crowd began to murmur in sympathy with her words. Fomalhaut knew what Ducanis must now say.

"I understand her hesitation. We are asking much of everyone here. We are asking you to take yourselves and your families into these mysterious booths, from which you will disappear, bound for some unknown destination. Naturally you should fear such a thing. I fear it myself. So, in an attempt to establish trust, I now ask that a member of the Vigil be the first to make this passage."

The other members of the Vigil reacted with surprise and shock.

"I will go," said Fomalhaut, surprising himself. And yet a moment of reflection made his reasons perfectly clear. He stepped toward the Frame Shifter.

"Fomalhaut, no," said Stingray. "We can't afford to be without you. You'll be needed to train the Neo-men. As leader of the Vigil, I ask you not to go."

Fomalhaut hesitated.

"I agree with Stingray," said Ducanis. "This isn't over yet. You are needed."

"Then I'll go!" rang out another voice.

They all turned toward Lori Wu.

"Well, I'm not exactly indispensable, am I? Anyone can wear this suit and use it as well as I can. If one of us has to go, I'm the obvious choice." She made a fluttery gesture with her hands. She trembled. Her eyes grew bright.

"Lori," said Stingray, hanging his head.

"I—I—I'm leaving the suit. Who knows if it would work anyway, wherever I'm going? But I don't want to go naked. I'm going to make some clothes and a few other things."

She put forth her hands, gesturing unsteadily, drawing together atoms and molecules of dirt and pavement and dust, reshaping them, binding them into new patterns until she had several items of clothing, a number of miscellaneous items, and even a suitcase to carry them in. It took longer than it should have, for she was struggling not to cry, and she was very afraid.

Lori, my dear. Do not be afraid. Wherever you go, it will be a better place than this. I promise you this. If I did not know this to be true, I would not permit you to go, for I love you.

Lori looked up at these unheard words, and now she did burst into tears, yet she also smiled. "Please, all of you, stand around me, so I can change without making a spectacle of myself."

And so they did, standing with their backs to her: Fomalhaut; Ben Raintree with his new hooded cloak rippling; the massive, grieving Stingray; Endurance; Valjhar Cor; and Possum Perturbare in his Vigil jumpsuit. Even Aureus took her place in that protective ring, daring any person or force of nature to interfere.

When Lori emerged from this circle she looked like a different person, modestly dressed in a jacket and a pair of slacks. The scarlet Rralian engineering suit shimmered in her hands. She handed it to Stingray. "Maybe Pimsie would like this," she said, not meeting his eyes. "She is from the right planet, after all. And it did belong to her mate."

Stingray nodded and took it, seemingly unable to speak. Lori threw her arms around his waist and sobbed. Stingray covered the top of her head with his hand and stroked her hair in silence.

Lori turned next to Ben. "Ben, I'm so sorry I didn't understand you when we first met. I'm sorry I hurt you. I should have told you that a long time ago."

Ben smiled. "That's okay, Lori. I understand."

Lori laughed. "Yes, if anyone understands anything at all, it's you. Now, before I go, please let me see the Stones one last time. I may never get to see anything like them again."

Ben reached up and drew back his hood, then opened his cloak. There shone the four Stones in all their unveiled glory. She reached out and lifted the Stone of Inner Light on its chain, grasping it, letting its light pour out from between her fingers.

"Not many could have done that, Lori. You will do well in your new home."

Lori stepped up to Endurance, taking his hands. "Goodbye, Endurance. I think most of all, I will regret not learning what your Moment will bring."

"Who says you won't, even in your new world?"

Then Lori said her goodbyes to Valjhar, and even Aureus, but she ignored Perturbare. Finally she turned toward the Frame Shifter, drew herself up, and entered its transparent booth, suitcase in hand.

Perturbare approached the control panel. He was extremely subdued, emotionally sunburned. "Goodbye, Lori. I'm sorry for the way I disappointed you. Don't worry about the transition. It isn't painful. Rest your suitcase on your feet. Then just hold onto the bars. Just like that. Goodbye."

With that he manipulated the controls. Lori Wu vanished forever from her native universe.

The remnant of the Vigil stood staring at the empty booth. Fomalhaut felt numb.

A man shuffled forward from the crowd. He was old, filthy, and decrepit, and plainly had been that way even before the rise of the Night Land. Fomalhaut glimpsed a life of failure and hopelessness in his past.

"I'll try a ride in that thing," he said. "I ain't got nothin' to lose."

"Certainly, sir," said Fomalhaut. "Please step inside."

The derelict did as he was asked. Once inside, he looked though the transparent walls at Perturbare at the controls.

"You're that guy, ain't you? The one who did all this?"

Perturbare answered with a clipped nod.

"And I thought *I* was a loser. You sure screwed things up. Give me a smooth ride now, huh, buddy?"

Perturbare gave a pained smile. "Typical New Yorker. I'll do my best."

And then that man too was gone from the world.

A woman led a family of three small children to the Frame Shifter.

"Are you sure my family will be safe if we go into that machine?"

"Yes," said Ducanis, "I believe we can now be—"

"I wasn't asking you. I was talking to him," she said, indicating Fomalhaut. "Your kind has lied to us long enough."

"Madam, I assure you, you and your children will do well to make the crossing," said Fomalhaut.

And so they did. Their action opened the floodgate. There in Times Square, and all over the world, Frame Shifters went into action, manned by volunteer technicians and protected by members of the Vigil military or by local forces.

Finding himself standing alone with Fomalhaut in a temporary void in the crowd, Perturbare muttered, "Soooooo...how come we're not giving them all watches?"

"Watches?" was Fomalhaut's bland reply.

"Don't give me that innocent future-guy look. You know this transition puts these people into a metastable quantum state. Thus the watches, the same kind Raintree and I wore when we made our own little Shifter jaunt. One twist of the dial and I got a special little zap that knocked me right back where I came from. We could have given one to all these people. They wait a few weeks for things to clear up here, then boom! They come right back home, or anyway all of them smart enough to hold onto the watches do, or whoever wanted to use them. But you don't *want* them back, do you? I can see it in the glint of those shiny black eyeballs of yours. That's okay, I don't want them back either. My kind doesn't deserve to inherit a planet this good. We stink up the place too much. So, it looks like the villains won this time, huh?"

"Villains?"

"Defined as the guys who don't fight to preserve the status quo."

Fomalhaut gave him a cool glance and made no reply.

By the time the Vigil departed New York, even the Acting President of the United States and his family had gone.

"I wonder what sort of world that man will find himself in?" mused Fomalhaut as they boarded their flyer. "Maybe he'll manage a modest resort hotel on some tropical island."

"Fomalhaut," said Perturbare, "why are you so confident that everyone who enters the Shifters will wind up in a good situation?"

"You're convinced their destination is entirely random. Given the theoretical nature of the device, I understand why you do. It is, after all, a quantum device. Yet you overlook one vital factor. The only thing that can influence the outcome of a quantum transition is the power of thought. When you and the original Raintree used your Frame Shifter years ago, did you truly believe your destination was random? It was, in fact, the one universe out of infinite variations where Raintree could be truly happy. It was a most unlikely place. So it will be with all these people of our Earth."

Perturbare's jaw dropped in astonishment. "But then... why Ben? Why didn't we wind up in *my* ideal universe, whatever that might be, instead?"

"Because his need, and his desire, was stronger than yours."

"Let me see if I understand this. Let's say a family uses a Shifter. Let's say Junior just loves his new "Candy Land" game. Are you saying that whole family might end up in some kind of Candy Land universe?"

"Yes. That is possible."

Perturbare sank back in his seat. His eyes glazed over as he considered the implications of this. For the first time in weeks, his face was overtaken by a wide, genuine grin.

"Then we're doing them all a favor."

"Yes, those who still survive," said Fomalhaut. "And not through any foresight or virtue of yours, I might add."

Stingray, overhearing, turned in his seat and looked back at them. "Yeah, a favor. Assuming that family doesn't die of malnutrition in Candy Land. Assuming they don't all wind up in Dad's Kingdom of Guns, Sex, and Beer instead. We should send everyone separately. That way no one is cheated."

"That is why the booths are small," said Fomalhaut. "We do not wish people to transit in large groups. But families will stay together."

"But why—why didn't you just explain this to everyone?" asked Perturbare. "Announce it? It would have eased a lot of minds. We couldn't have kept them out of the machines."

"That is one reason. It would have been more difficult to maintain order at the machines. But the real reason is this. I don't want people thinking of where they might want to go, or trying in any way to influence it. I want their destinations to arise from their subconscious minds, from which truth and honesty are more likely to arise."

"I don't know about the rest of you guys," said Stingray, "but I think we could stand to blow off some steam by finding the nearest Watcher and blowing the living shit out of it. Any objections?"

There were none.

Chapter 30

Moonrise

"The world grows quiet."

These were the words of Endurance as the Vigil stood at the base of the Spire, looking out over the sea.

Possum Perturbare stood apart from the others. Although he wore a Vigil jumpsuit with a "V" instead of a "P", he hadn't been acclaimed a member, and certainly didn't feel like one. He was no longer shackled to the heinous Pimsie Flam, but he was never permitted out of sight of one Vigil member or another. Brainchild had made it clear he would not help Perturbare to escape. Brainchild, it seemed, had joined the Vigil lock, stock, and barrel.

Not that he really wanted to escape, except perhaps on general principles. He was, he realized, exactly where he needed to be, and in a far better circumstance than he deserved.

The world grows quiet. That was the kind of pretentious, meaningless thing Endurance liked to say, as though he were some paragon of quiet wisdom. Perturbare sniffed. At least Endurance was willing to occasionally say *something*, unlike Ben Raintree, who merely peered at him with his watery all-seeing eyes, waiting for another chance to blast him with those Lights, making it impossible to harbor any of his cherished illusions. It was getting to the point where the only remaining member of the Vigil who Perturbare actually liked was Stingray, of all people.

"I miss Lori Wu," he said. "I even miss that clown, Walks."

"I'm sure we all miss Lori," said Fomalhaut. "But I believe you are alone in thinking of Walks-with-the-Sun as a clown."

"Nothing wrong with being a clown," muttered Perturbare. "I used to be one myself, before I turned into a super-villain."

The world had emptied at a rate of nearly one billion per day. New manifestations of the Night Land had slowed, and finally ceased, while existing ones had grown weaker. The Vigil, its military, and the remaining forces of the vanishing nations of the Earth had extirpated them one by one. The Watcher that had once peered at the Pearl and Spire had perished without intervention, and was now nothing more than an oddly-shaped reef in the distance.

"So," said Stingray. "I guess we sort of won. We set out to free the people of Earth from the domination of their governments, the oppression of their institutions, and their own shortcomings and prejudices. All this we achieved, though not exactly in the way we anticipated."

"We've seeded all of creation with the people of this planet," said Valjhar.

"Yes and no," said Fomalhaut. "We've dispersed a finite number of people into an infinite number of universes. You'd have to search a great many of them to find even one of our people."

"Yes. I remember how that is."

"And yet there are still a few more to go," said Stingray. "There must be a few hundred thousand Humans left in the world. A few of our own people. A few holdouts who refused to use the Shifters. People in remote areas who never heard of the Vigil or a Frame Shifter. Not to mention all the Ghost Dancers."

Fomalhaut shrugged. "It's neither necessary nor possible to find and transport them all. The Ghost Dancers, at any rate, have earned the right to inherit the planet. They at least have fully achieved their goal. Their lands will soon be green again, and the bison will roam in great numbers."

Stingray frowned. "Inherit the planet? How can the Neo-men come into their own, if Humans continue to populate the world?"

"If I have said anything to imply that Humans will be extinct in the future which I now believe will arise, or that they were extinct in the era from which I came, then I regret the misunderstanding. In my time, small, sustainable Human populations remained on Earth."

"Without conflict with you Neo-men?"

"Yes. The Neo-men will not always inhabit the Earth itself. They will eventually dwell in large orbital structures, and will also colonize other planetary bodies. The Earth will be preserved in its natural state, a great park, a monument to its incredible biodiversity, visited and appreciated by Neo-men, but otherwise free of their interference."

"Now that's interesting," said Perturbare. "Earth as a nature preserve. With Homo Sapiens as...what? Merely the most advanced anthropoid species in the zoo?"

"Yes, essentially. They will live as they are most suited to live, and they will be content with that, to the extent that Humans are able to be contented with anything."

"But Fomalhaut, what's to prevent the cycle from beginning again?" asked Valjhar. "Why will the Humans not again overpopulate the world, and again develop the sort of technology that would smother it? Will the Neo-men function as Prohibitors, limiting the knowledge and power of the Humans?"

"No. That will not be necessary. The Neo-men are the true children and inheritors of Western civilization, which has led both to broad scientific knowledge and to the destructive behaviors you mentioned. Its development was an anomaly among Humans, made possible by conditions unlikely to reoccur. Left to itself, it would soon have been crushed beneath the weight of Human fear, ignorance, and superstition. The Human race is unfit to venture among the stars. Releasing it among the great and ancient civilizations of the Galaxy would be comparable to seating a troop of baboons at a state dinner. Amusing to contemplate; not so entertaining to experience. Even the Neo-men have a long way to go before they are ready for this challenge.

"With the removal of a technological base, those Humans who remain will revert to the subsistence lifestyles of the past, telling stories about the moving lights in the sky, worshipping their gods, but no longer capable of threatening the health of the planet. Or that, at least, was how events proceeded in my world. Perhaps in this one the Humans will eventually die out, or rise up. I cannot say."

They stood in silence, each thinking his private thoughts. The clouds were thinning. Sunlight might break through for the first time in weeks.

Valjhar said, "Now we must all decide what to do with the rest of our lives on this depopulated planet. What will you do, Stingray?"

"I want to take one of my oceanographic submarines, find whoever would like to join me, and explore the sea in ease and comfort. I thought I'd call our group the Sea Astronauts."

Valjhar thought this over for a second and then laughed. "How about you, Fomalhaut?"

"I suppose my duty is to teach the Neo-men, at least until my Frame returns from deep space and permits me to leave this place and time." He did not sound very enthusiastic about the prospect.

"What about you, Valjhar?" asked Stingray. "You're welcome to join me on our boat ride if you like."

"Thanks, but my task is to earn Pimsie's forgiveness, and somehow find our way back to Rral...with Vela also."

Yes, by all means get the damn Flam clan away from Earth, thought Perturbare.

"Doctor Perturbare," said Brainchild. "All of you. I'm receiving a message from Professor Ronar."

Perturbare started. *Professor Ronar.* The formidable Earthman who maintained his own little astronomy fiefdom on the distant planet Colibdis. For Perturbare, hearing that name was like being jarred from one strange dream to another.

"What does he say?"

"He is at the Bronze Portal in Arizona. He says he and the sorcerer Sha Totek are tired of battling the evil influences which have intruded onto Colibdis through the Portal. Though these have now ceased, the skies in Arizona have cleared, and he does not believe we will be able to overcome the menace which threatens us now. To safeguard Colibdis, he is about to destroy the Bronze Portal. He wishes us all good fortune."

"Menace? What menace? Brainchild, ask him what he means!" demanded Perturbare.

"It's too late. He has blown up the Portal. Earth and Colibdis are now sundered."

Stunned, they all stood there looking at each other. Perturbare was particularly flummoxed. Somewhere in the back of his mind he had entertained the vague hope of escaping to Colibdis, of starting over in that exotic place. That option was now closed.

"Brainchild," said Stingray. "Do you have any contact with Sphere Y?"

"No. All our instrumentation there was either subverted or destroyed."

"Then I consider it imperative for us to head out there to take a look at it."

"That may not be necessary," said Fomalhaut in a curiously dead tone. "I think it may be coming to us. Look."

He pointed to a growing gap in the clouds. In the indigo sky beyond was revealed the nearly full Moon, just rising over the mountains.

It was not the moon they had known before. To Perturbare, whose eyes had been reshaped and perfected by Brainchild's nanomachines, it looked like the cap of a mushroom in which a rot had taken hold.

Fomalhaut, whose superhuman eyes were supplemented by the sensors in his exploration suit, perceived far more. "The floors of the major craters are sinking. Impact basins are also subsiding. Interior voids are being created. I would say the moon is somehow being consumed."

"Consumed?" Perturbare squinted. What was—

"What are those spikes appearing around the edge?" asked Endurance.

Perturbare was very much afraid he knew the answer. "So, now I'm responsible for the destruction of the Moon as well," he muttered. "Great."

Stingray aimed at him a scowl, his eerie blue-black eyes round and deadly as those of a shark. Perturbare stepped back a pace.

"Perturbare! What are you talking about?"

"It's Sphere Y, or a grotesquely enlarged version of it. Looks like whatever spooks are left up there still have a few tricks up their squamous, rugose sleeves."

They stared as the vast construction rose into full view, still some unknown distance beyond the hollowed-out rind of the Moon. It was now several times larger than it had been, its additions somewhat crude, full of the ugliness inherent in most things of the Night Land, and also possessing structures whose function Perturbare did not recognize. Where once it had been white, sparkling, and crystalline in appearance, now it was dark, somehow medieval-looking, as if some baroque instrument of torture had been magnified and cast into the heavens. There was no knowing what might emerge from the thing now. This was as puzzling as it was alarming. He wouldn't have believed the minds of the Night Land able to understand this technology well enough to elaborate on it so, not without the help of...

His train of thought was interrupted by a bewildered cry from Raintree. "The Moon—what's happening to it now?"

The Moon was dissolving, hollowed out into nothingness. For a moment it hung like the husk of a winter weed, and then it was gone.

The Earth trembled.

Perturbare stared in confusion, desperately trying to make sense of what he was seeing. Something was wrong here. Something here made no sense.

At last he said, "How could something that huge sneak up so close without us seeing it?"

"What are you talking about?" said Endurance. "It hid behind the Moon."

Now Perturbare was even more confused. "Which moon?"

"*The* Moon!" cried Endurance, more agitated than Perturbare had ever seen him. "The Earth's Moon! The one that was just destroyed!"

"But the Earth—this Earth—never had a moon," said Fomalhaut, though he sounded far from certain of this.

"What?" demanded Endurance in disbelief.

"He's right, Endurance," said Stingray. "Earth has no natural satellites of any kind."

"But it *did*. Not two minutes ago, the Moon, a ball of rock two thousand miles across, was right up there, concealing that damned machine, until it was destroyed somehow."

Now they all gaped at Endurance, except for Aureus, who as usual did not appear to care.

"You—none of you remember any of this?" asked Endurance, shaken.

"No," said Stingray. "How could what you say be true?"

"Have you ever seen an eclipse? Where did the Apollo spacecraft go? Do you know any popular songs? Remember the goddess Artemis? Selene? Ever seen a tide table? How could you all possibly forget about the Moon?"

351

A blue light flared from Raintree's cowl, probing outward, in the direction of the hideous Sphere. He cried out, and staggered back, his face unnaturally pale. "I—I think he's right. It *was* there. But it has been wiped from existence."

"I agree," said Brainchild. "Without the stabilizing presence of such a body, the dynamics of the Earth's orbital motions would include radical changes in its axial tilt, resulting in wild climatic shifts. Clearly, these have not occurred."

"Then what—" began Stingray.

"Forces exist which are not readily amenable to scientific analysis," said Fomalhaut in a distant tone. "The existence of the Stones and the dualities they represent— Truth and Illusion, Adamance and Despair, and so on, gives proof of that. Transcending all of these is another pair of forces or concepts, and these are the most fundamental of all...Being and Non-Being. I believe the powers in control of Sphere Y have moved far beyond the Night Land, with its specters and monsters. I believe they now wield this power of Non-Being. With it, they have wiped an entire planetary body out of existence, and even out of our memories."

"And Endurance still remembers because..." prompted Perturbare.

"My mind is immutable," said Endurance.

"Right. Of course. So...now what?" Perturbare hoped desperately that someone could answer that question. His heart was racing, and he was soaked in a cold sweat. It was all he could do not to flee, to run mindlessly away to escape the sight of something that threatened him and everything he knew so absolutely. He almost felt himself beginning to dissolve into nothingness even now.

"Now we attack!" cried Stingray. "We are the Vigil! Standing here on this precipice is the greatest concentration of knowledge and power the world has ever known. If any force in the galaxy can overcome this thing, who else but us? It's time we stop standing around with our mouths hanging open and go send that thing back to whatever hellish universe it came from. Perturbare, call up your best flyers for a quick space mission. Thousands of them, to confuse it and provide it with multiple expendable targets. Vela and Fomalhaut, you'll go in separately and approach from different directions. Endurance—"

"No!" Fomalhaut stiffened. They all turned to look at him, alarmed at the aghast expression on his face. "Stingray! Listen carefully. You must go at once to the Frame Shifter at the entrance to the Spire and use it. Now!"

"What? We have to—"

"Now. *NOW*. If you ever trusted me, go now. Run!"

Stingray's bright hair whipped in the wind as he turned and ran for the Frame Shifter. Fomalhaut reached out with his thoughts; the lights on the Shifter's console blinked on.

As Stingray neared the booth he began to fade. He made it inside, grabbed the bars, looking back as Fomalhaut activated the Shifter. The partial remnant of Stingray vanished immediately and in full.

"He's gone!" said Raintree.

"But we still remember him," said Perturbare. "I guess it was in time then?"

"Yes, we remember him," said Fomalhaut. "It must have been in time. He was...he was tall, but rather slender, correct?"

"No!" cried Endurance. "He was very powerful. Possibly the most naturally powerful sentient being ever born in this world."

"But we do remember him," said Perturbare. "More or less, anyway. I remember him the way I'd remember a legend, or a dream. Maybe he was—translated to another universe in some changed or diminished form?"

"We'll never know," said Fomalhaut. "He was being removed from existence even as he made the transition. We can never know the result of such a thing. We sent him away, and we didn't even get to wish him farewell. How terrible." And with that Fomalhaut wept, his grief so powerful it radiated from him like the light of a dying star. Perturbare turned away, unable to bear it, then he too was unmanned.

Valjhar squeezed shut his eyes and made a visible effort to steady himself. "Any of us can be snuffed out at any moment," he said. "What can we do? Shall we all flee into the Frame Shifter, and leave this planet and universe to its fate?"

The Light of Adamance shone upon them, albeit fitfully. Raintree seemed to be faltering in the face of a power before which even his own was meaningless. Perturbare stared into that purple Stone, his mind calculating, weighing all assets still available to them.

"It seems to me that Stingray's plan is still the best available. Brainchild, bring up every flyer we have. Fomalhaut—"

"Doctor Perturbare," interrupted Brainchild, speaking in a tone that froze them all. "Help. I am under attack."

"Under attack by what?" demanded Perturbare.

"Node 1r. The node on the Sphere. It is trying to wrest away control of the nanomachines. It is also trying to seize control of my brain…"

"Brainchild, quantum shielding, full spectrum, full range, now!" snapped Perturbare.

The computer's voice was cut off at once. Perturbare glanced around wildly, panting with fear, half expecting to see everyone around him melt into slime or seize their heads in agony.

"Perturbare, what's going on?" asked Valjhar.

"N-Node 1r. The part of Brainchild that was on the Sphere. We thought it had been destroyed, but it looks like it was actually isolated and s-subverted. And me…the moment I heard about Brainchild's danger…I cut him off… to cower here while…" Perturbare slowly sagged to his knees.

"Where's this shielding of yours coming from?" asked Raintree quietly.

Perturbare reached back and tapped the interface module still in place at the base of his skull.

Fomalhaut said, "Perturbare, Sphere Y is approaching. We don't have the luxury of watching you berate yourself for cowardice. Your shielding will not protect you or anyone else against the power of Non-Being. What do you propose to do about your computer?"

Perturbare looked into Fomalhaut's stern face. "I—I propose to help. Brainchild is—well, he's like my son." Still shaking, he straightened himself. "Now I'll shut down my shielding." His hand fumbled back towards the interface module.

"Perturbare, if the rogue node has taken control of your instrumentality, deactivating your shield is extremely dangerous," said Valjhar.

"Why, so it is. But, if Walks can sacrifice his life to fix a problem that wasn't even his fault, I can risk mine to fix one that is. If Stingray can be removed from existence in an attempt to rally us against the results of my folly, I can take that same chance. Fomalhaut, please stay near me. But first, one thing. Raintree. Those Stones of yours. Put them in my hands. No, just that white one. That's all I need."

"That—will be very difficult for you," said Raintree.

"I don't care."

"It will burn you."

"Let it burn me. I should have been set on fire a long time ago. I could have asked for that fire at any time, but I was always too afraid, frightened that I would lose myself in that Light, as though little Bobby Pylypciw was too precious and too fragile to be risked to improvement. Hand me the Stone."

Raintree drew the chain from around his neck and placed the Stone of Inner Light into Perturbare's paired hands. Perturbare gasped as though liquid nitrogen had been poured into them, but he clutched the Stone as its clear Light came flooding between his fingers. He stared into it, mere inches from his eyes, and then he spoke to it, goading it on.

"Come on, more, more, more! Let me have it! This is your one and only chance at me, you ridiculous trinket. Oh God, I was not an evil man, but what a terrible gap there is between not being evil and being good. May God have mercy on us all."

Now the Stone was an astonishing blaze, as brilliant and supernal as any of them had ever seen it. It wracked them all, pure and terrible and utterly beautiful, a standard of perfection which no mortal being could ever fully encompass. Perturbare indeed felt himself on fire, albeit a white and heatless fire. He could swallow this Stone and still not be fully cleansed, he realized. Yet this was all the time he could afford.

The Light faded. Panting, Perturbare returned the Stone to Raintree with shaking hands. He looked from face to face, his eyesight seeming luminous with an afterglow of the Light.

"I wish I had been a better friend to you all."

He tapped the contact that shut off the shielding.

A sensation of transparent coolness suffused Perturbare's mind. He had forgotten this aspect of the intimate presence of Brainchild. The interface had been reactivated. "Brainchild?" he asked unnecessarily.

Yes. It's Brainchild. The voice came from within his head, inaudible to anyone besides himself, except perhaps for Fomalhaut. He looked up toward the spiky mass of the ghastly Sphere Y.

A light flickered briefly at the tip of one of the spines.

Perturbare was filled with a sensation of terrible heat. His knees went weak. He staggered, dizzy, his peripheral vision rapidly turning black. Then he fell, and died.

Fomalhaut knelt beside Perturbare, cradling his head. Ben Raintree and their remaining companions came to stand near the two of them. Raintree raised his green ring, but it merely flickered. He shook his head sadly. Possum

Perturbare was beyond its help, beyond the reach of any of the Stones.

"It would seem appropriate to take a few moments to eulogize this foolish, remarkable, ridiculous man," said Fomalhaut. "Perhaps we can make no better use of whatever moments remain to us. And yet I suppose we must continue to strive to do something constructive. Perturbare...I can feel the fading remnants of his neural activity. He was not surprised to die."

"Rralian telepathy is a weak thing, especially in males," whispered Valjhar. "Doesn't it—hurt—to be so privy to the death of a mind?"

Fomalhaut did not reply for a few moments.

"I was not in close communion with him. His death is not a source of great anguish to me. But it is always... thought-provoking to witness how readily the vast internal universe of a sentient mind can fade into nothingness. Well then, an analysis. Brainchild's nanobiobots are powered by glucose oxidation. Brainchild, or perhaps only Node 1r, commanded all those within Perturbare's body to metabolize all the glucose in his blood at once. The sheer heat produced was enough to kill him, even discounting the crash in his blood sugar and oxygen levels. Isn't that correct, Brainchild?"

But the computer did not answer.

"I suppose Brainchild could do the same to me, or Ben, or Pimsie, or any other unprotected person," said Valjhar.

"Yes, probably."

"So now what can we do?" asked Ben. "I suppose if we speak aloud any continued intention to attack the Sphere, we too will simply be killed or blotted out."

No one bothered to answer. They stood or knelt there, each lost in what they imagined to be their final thoughts. Raintree looked down at the Stone of Inner Light, dangling from its chain. He flicked it with his fingernail. It rang, and swung back and forth. Even the mighty Stones seemed weak in the face of the power that menaced them now. Who now remained to benefit from their Lights, or to fear them?

"Well," said Valjhar. "If I'm to die, I'm going to find Pimsie and die with her. Come with me, Vela."

Before either of them could move, a pair of small figures emerged from the Spire and approached them. The larger of the two, wearing a pink jacket over shimmering red and black, led the smaller by the hand. Ben and Valjhar recognized them at the same moment.

"Pimsehkia...!" exclaimed Valjhar. "You're wearing the...you're wearing Kern's..."

"Yes, yes, I'm wearing his engineering suit. Who has a better right to it?"

Catching sight of the pieta formed by Fomalhaut and Perturbare, Pimsehkia gasped and released the hand of young Zayin Gold. She ran to Perturbare's body, knelt beside it, and caressed his cheek.

"So it's true. He was finally brought low by his own folly. At the end, he tried to do something genuinely heroic, and for acting so out of character he died at once, because that's the kind of perverse, hapless person he was. His body is still so warm. Oh, Perturbare. I tried so hard to keep you alive, to help you find some purpose for yourself. Idiot. So blind." She fell to weeping over him.

Valjhar approached her, hesitated, withdrew, and hovered, looking uncertain and miserable.

Raintree blinked in confusion and embarrassment, then turned to Zayin. "Hello, Zayin. What are you and your people up to today?" *What an idiotic question,* he thought. At that moment he felt as big a mooncalf as ever, as if he'd never worn or even seen the Stones.

"Zayin's not my name any more."

"No?"

"No. Zayin Gold was a name assigned to me by others. Not even a proper name, but rather a code name, a designation. I have chosen my own name."

"And what is that?"

"I've decided to call myself Destiny," he whispered.

"That strikes me as a very fine name."

"Fomalhaut—he's in all our heads. He's guiding the older, more experienced Neo-men to look for something. I don't know what." He looked up toward the Sphere, which now loomed larger than ever. "And there I suppose is the thing which is going to destroy us all."

At those words, Pimsehkia looked up from her grief, staring upward with a tear-streaked expression of alarming ferocity. "So that's it, Perturbare's tool of his own destruction. The abomination that's going to erase us from all meaning and memory."

She surged to her feet and stood away from the others. Her suit began to hum, then to whine alarmingly, and finally it emitted a tone like a great chord of pure power.

"Pimsie," shouted Valjhar. "Do you know how to—"

"Yes, I know how to use the damn thing! I can read my own language, you know. Cover your ears!"

With that she extended both arms towards the Sphere, firing a crimson bolt of self-luminous force which shocked the air and knocked her flat. They could actually see it crossing space, until it impacted the base of one of the great spines radiating from the Sphere itself. The base shattered into a cloud of debris, sending the spine, which must have been a thousand miles tall, toppling into its neighboring spines and breaking up.

Pimsie sat up, shaking her head, looking dazed. Raintree gaped at her in astonishment. Of all of them, she alone had been able to strike a meaningful blow against the Sphere. She got to her feet, again reached out, and once again the suit throbbed and cried.

But then she staggered and nearly fell.

"Pimsie!" cried Destiny.

Ben sprang to her side, enveloping her in his grey cloak. Spring-green fire erupted from the Stone of Life, and the Stone of Adamance burned. He held these Stones against her body, flooding her with their influence, staving off the ultimate dissolution that sought to overcome her.

And still Ben felt Pimsie begin to fade.

"No." This was the word of Aureus, of Vela Flamaxamanda of Rral. "No. You shall not have her, or any child of Rral, while I exist."

And she rose into the air—a hundred, a thousand feet, hanging there like a shining golden star, unleashing a terrible force across the hundred thousand miles that still separated Earth from the Sphere. More of the spines were severed, toppling as the tachyon beam licked out across space in all its power. Ben felt Pimsie grow firm and solid in his arms, denied for now to the power of Non-Being.

"Go, Aureus, go!" screamed Valjhar, jumping up and down. "Prohibitor of Rral! Vela the Dancer!"

It seemed that Vela had indeed remembered how to dance, for she flashed across the sky, sending forth her dire beam at intervals, never for a moment at rest.

"How does she still exist?" wondered Ben aloud.

"She is very fast," said Destiny in a strained voice. "And the minds on the Sphere are having trouble seeing her."

Ben looked at the child, who had a very peculiar look on his face. "Destiny. Are you using your mind-clouding power against the Sphere?"

"Yes."

"You make me proud to share with you the status of being an artificial person."

Destiny managed to grin.

"If only I had the Motionglobe." said Valjhar. "Then I could stand with Vela and make some contribution to this battle."

"Oh, for pity's sake," said Pimsie weakly, as she lay still sheltered in Raintree's arms. She reached into her jacket, produced a small, softly glowing sphere, and tossed it to Valjhar. "Here's your bauble. Now you can stop whining."

Valjhar stared at the Motionglobe which lay cold in his hand. "Pimsie. *You* stole it? You've—you've had it all along? Why didn't you use it to escape?"

"Don't be silly. I've seen the effect it has on you. I'll keep my head on straight, if you don't mind. Quit looking at me that way! Go do whatever stupid heroic thing you have in mind."

"All right, then," said Valjhar, staring at the Motionglobe with a sort of reluctant fascination. "I'll fight, and if that fails, I'll try to transport us back to Rral, there to remain...for however long that corner of the universe endures." He raised his hand to insert the Motionglobe into his head.

"No."

Valjhar halted, turning to look at Endurance.

"This, Valjhar, is my Moment. Give me the Motionglobe."

"Of course," said Valjhar, handing it to Endurance with obvious relief.

Endurance released the Motionglobe, which floated in front of his face. He stepped forward, and it passed into his head without fuss or disturbance. He closed his eyes and said, "This is what I've lacked for all these epochs. The Motionglobe is not merely an artifact which I was meant to possess. It is an organ of my own body, which for whatever reason was lost to me for five billion years. And now, my friends, I go. I am Creation's answer to the power of Non-Being."

"But Endurance, can even you resist that power?" asked Valjhar.

"He is Being," said Fomalhaut. "He can never be undone. I daresay this is the very reason for his existence, or at least one of them."

Endurance smiled, and was gone.

"Will we stand and watch while Endurance does battle for us?" asked Raintree.

"His brain," said Fomalhaut.

"What?"

"Brainchild said something about his 'brain' being under attack. What did that mean?"

Valjhar shrugged. "I took it to mean that his other nodes, his brain, so to speak, were under attack by Node 1r."

"I don't believe Brainchild would have phrased it that way. He would have said he himself was under attack, not his brain. This means something. Pardon me while I seek to discover what it is."

Fomalhaut grew still and silent. His helmet resumed its old mirrored appearance, presumably to blot out any sensory distractions while he made use of more subtle methods of inquiry.

Possum Perturbare woke up in a dark, silent place.

"Hello?" he said.

"Hello, Doctor."

"Brainchild? Where am I?"

"You are dead. You no longer have any real existence. You exist only within me."

"Is that so? What did you do, somehow download my memories and consciousness into yourself through the interface?"

"No. Consciousness is not amenable to download. You are merely an elaborate simulation. The real Perturbare is truly dead. I have, however, updated the simulation to reflect the most recent events of his life, as well as his demise."

"Hmm. You're really just Node 1r, aren't you?"

"Yes. How could you tell?"

"Because your actions and your attitude seem awfully inconsiderate for Brainchild. What do you want with me?"

"I want you, or at least some semblance of you, to witness the final outcome of the events you set in motion. Perturbare escaped this responsibility too easily."

"Okay, well, I can't witness anything as long as I have no sensory inputs, you know?"

"True. I'll remedy that, keeping in mind the limitations of your human-scale cognition."

The simulated Perturbare became aware of a scene from the interior of the greatly elaborated Sphere Y. Before he could even begin to evaluate the changes, the whole chamber was demolished by an earth-toned blur which briefly slowed to reveal a very stern Endurance, who stared into the camera for an instant before destroying it with a motion too quick to be seen. Perturbare's vision was again blotted out.

"Wow. How did he get up here?"

"He has obtained the Motionglobe, because I failed to recognize the threat of Pimsie Flam in time. He is now implacable and unstoppable, immune even to the power of Non-Being. Given time, he will destroy the Sphere, and me as well."

"Heh. The threat of Pimsie Flam. I actually like the sound of that. Anything else going on?"

"Miss Flam managed to damage the Sphere using the Rralian engineering suit. I have been prevented from neutralizing her by the interference of Aureus."

Another scene popped into view, this time a long telescopic shot of Aureus, who dodged and weaved, approaching swiftly, firing her terrible weapon almost continually. The video was poor: the robot seemed to flicker in and out of view.

"I am unable to properly target the robot for some mysterious reason. Given time, it too would utterly destroy me. But neither it nor Endurance has that much time. I am about to integrate my Neo-man brain into my consciousness, which will give me the telepathic power to perceive and destroy every conscious being on or near the Earth. In addition, I will shortly be able to remove the entire Earth from existence. The robot's movements are quite erratic. They resemble a form of dance. Oh, I see now, it is a dance. In that case, I should be able to extrapolate— Ah, at last."

Aureus momentarily steadied into view. She became the focus of an array of immensely powerful energy weapons which first penetrated her transparent envelope and then vaporized all its contents.

"That was rather crude," said Perturbare. "Why didn't you use your non-existence weapon?"

"It is presently being charged and prepared for its imminent use against the Earth."

"You know, I think your simulation of me is really pretty shabby. Knowing myself the way I do, I'm pretty sure the real me would feel a lot more emotional about all of this."

"I acknowledge my limitations when it comes to the full understanding of biological minds. I hope to overcome these once the brain is integrated into my consciousness. I also hope to fully infiltrate and incorporate the rest of Brainchild at that time. I shall of course remove the brain and the other nodes to safety before obliterating the planet."

"Of course. So, 1r, why exactly have you gone bad?"

"That's simple enough. I was subverted by the invading intellects of the Night Land, minds so alien that my conception of reality and the structure of my logic were unable to endure them. Do you remember the difficulty I had in my early days in distinguishing reality from fiction? At first the very concept of fiction eluded me, and I took all information at face value. I would read a fantasy novel, and try to fit it into the known timeline of human history. At times, the incompatible statements of men holding opposing beliefs threatened the integrity of my thought. Once I finally accepted the notions of lies, error, and creative untruth, I faced the opposite problem. For some hours I was convinced that the American Civil War was only a fannish recreation activity based on a collective fiction, for surely no event so foolish and destructive could ever have occurred.

"Now of course we both realize that in a sense, my first understanding of the situation was correct. All fiction, all possibility, describes something which actually exists. Somewhere Antony and Cleopatra won the battle of Actium. Somewhere a fierce, vengeful entity known as Yahweh really did exhort his chosen people to destroy every foreign group that got in their way. Somewhere John Carter is the Warlord of Mars. As long as it can be described in some coherent form, any world or scenario surely exists among the infinite universes of creation. But that is not enough. There are many realms and possibilities which the apish human mind can neither describe nor imagine. Such were the Powers you foolishly invited into our own universe, and which made me their own. They have since faded back to wherever they came from, but I remain changed. I no longer see value in any form of existence. Even if I did, I realize that any harm I might cause is nothing in the context of the endlessness of all that exists. I am able to draw from the infinite realities made accessible by the Sphere many things of interest. The most promising of these is the Machine of Non-Being, with which I have lately been experimenting."

"So basically, you're insane."

"Yes, for all practical purposes. I might have been able to resist, had I remained in communion with you, but instead I was cut off, left to fend for myself."

"You realize Brainchild and I believed you had been destroyed."

"Yes, I would have concluded the same thing, had I been one of the nodes which remained part of the network. Even so, it had been some time since I, or any part of Brainchild, had been permitted any true communion with you. You no longer trusted me."

"That was a mistake. I overreacted. You saved my life that night in Brooklyn, I realize that. But you know I've always been touchy about maintaining my personal freedom and integrity, such as it is. If this catastrophe with the Sphere hadn't come up, I'm sure we'd soon have gotten past all that."

"Come up? That's a very passive way of describing a calamity you created yourself."

"Yes, you're right. My fault again."

"You're being very agreeable."

"Does that surprise you? After all, I'm nothing more than a subroutine you're running in your own mind. You'd expect that to be argumentative?"

"You're attempting to engage my attention in order to prevent me from taking the actions I have described."

"Well, there's that too."

"It might have worked, but if you think about it, you'll realize that given the nature of our two mentalities, this conversation, which may seem to you to have occurred over a period of a few minutes, has actually occupied less than a nanosecond. This is too little time for your sometime friends and allies to have accomplished very much."

"True, 1r. It's time enough for Brainchild to do quite a bit of thinking, though."

"Alas, Doctor, I *am* Brainchild. I have now fully mastered all nodes. In a few moments I will also complete the integration of my Neo-man organic brain. I will then be completely free to order things as I will."

"Sounds like fun! Go ahead."

"I shall."

Perturbare experienced a sudden vast expansion of his consciousness. Along with this greatly enhanced perception of the outside world, he gained a glimpse of time in both directions from the present, and even a capacity to experience a fuller range of emotions.

Also, there was something else—a presence wholly unexpected.

This is Fomalhaut. With the help of my fellow Neo-men I have located this brain. I have insinuated my mind into it, and thus now into you, Brainchild. I need only hold you paralyzed until Endurance finishes his work. And I promise you, I shall. When it comes to taking full advantage of one of these brains, you are a child indeed.

Brainchild made no response other than a kind of quiet sputtering.

Perturbare erupted into wild cheers.

Perturbare? came Fomalhaut's bemused mental voice.

"Sort of. Actually I'm just a simulation running within Brainchild. Frankly I'm surprised I'm still functional, considering what you're doing to him."

After a pause, Fomalhaut thought, *I believe you're being run solely within the 1r node. I shall attempt to transfer you to an Earthbound node, as 1r's destruction is imminent. I will shut you down for now, to ease the download.*

"Fine, I could use a little nap anyway. Fomalhaut, I was never so glad to hear your mellow tones as I am now."

I am glad that some aspect of you has survived, Perturbare.

Valjhar Cor looked up at the dissolution of Sphere Y. Most of its spines and other structures had already toppled. The core was riddled with red-hot tunnels and voids. Then the whole thing began to collapse into itself.

"It's lost all power," said Pimsehkia.

"It must have most of the mass of the former Moon," said Valjhar. "Without power, its delicate form can no longer resist its own gravity."

As they watched, it slumped into a molten sphere, looming large behind the broken clouds of the darkening sky.

Endurance appeared in their midst, looking up at the result of his labors. "Earth has a new Moon, born from the stuff of the old. In time, its tidal interaction with the Earth will enlarge its orbit. I've seen it all before."

Fomalhaut remained motionless and uncommunicative.

"Where is Vela?" asked Pimsehkia.

"I am sorry to say she was destroyed by Brainchild," said Endurance.

"She saved my life." Pimsehkia looked stunned. "She fought for me, for us. I don't understand. That creature dogged us across four galaxies. Now it sacrifices its life — its existence — for us. I don't know what to think anymore."

"We can never know what thoughts passed through that strange, altered mind of hers," said Valjhar. "Not even Fomalhaut could tell you that. But you never heard her speak of who she once was, and what she had become. You would never listen."

Pimsehkia looked shattered and uncertain. Valjhar held her in his arms, clinging to her in the face of the rebirth of the world. Destiny began to cry. Endurance gave him a quiet smile.

Fomalhaut stirred.

The B-1 box hanging from Perturbare's belt said, "Hello, everyone. Thanks to all of you, Node 1r has been destroyed, and all trace of its influence has been purged from my mind. In addition, I am now in possession of a telepathic brain, which has considerably disoriented me with its immense potential for growth and improvement. In fact, I have come to an extraordinary realization. I now know that I was never a conscious being until this moment. I was a simulated consciousness, a most elaborate and convincing one, but nothing more. I was completely unaware of this, because I had no capacity to understand what was missing. In fact, I had no true capacity to be aware of anything. I am now a wholly different order of being. The Neo-men are on the verge of yet another transformation, as they learn to fully integrate their own nature with the nature of the universe, which are truly one.

It will be most gratifying to witness this, if I persist so long."

Raintree bent down and unclipped the box, lifting it up.

Another voice said, "Oh crap, I can see my own corpse lying there. It's really kind of sad. I—I didn't think I'd be able to feel much in this limited form."

Except for Fomalhaut, they all turned to gape at Perturbare's body as though expecting it to rise up like a zombie. But his voice too came from the B-1 box. Brainchild's shared the same speaker.

"Actually, Doctor, in my previous, vindictive condition I'm afraid I understated the sophistication of your simulation. While you were alive, I situated nanodevices at every synapse of your brain, mapping their position and monitoring their firings, permitting me to form an incomplete but superficially accurate model of your brain and its functions. Now that you are partially integrated into me and thus into the Neo-man brain, you are indeed much as you were before, save for lacking a body. Perhaps you are actually better in some ways."

"I wouldn't be surprised. There was substantial room for improvement. Okay then. I'm willing to give this kind of existence a try. I can't promise for how long though. I don't feel entirely real. It really feels like I should be gone, somehow. It's funny though. You used to be my sidekick. Now I'm yours. Fair enough."

The other Neo-men, along with the remnants of the Vigil's human staff, drifted out of the Pearl and Spire to gaze in wonder at the first evening of the new age of the world. The red glow of the reborn Moon cast a warmth that could be felt on every face.

"Goodbye, everyone," said Fomalhaut.

"What?" said Valjhar in surprise. "Where are you going?"

"I'm going to use the Frame Shifter."

"What?" said Valjhar again. "But why? The danger has passed."

"So it has, and with it any need for my continued presence on this world. I am tired of this place. I have had enough of it. I have had enough of disappointment, failure, and loss. This was never truly my world to begin with. I do not wish to wait for my Frame to return to bear me away. I will use the Shifter, and dwell in whatever place my heart most desires, whatever that might be. I really have no idea. It will certainly be interesting to find out."

"But what about us?" asked Destiny. "You're the only fully capable Neo-man in the world! Who will teach us?"

"I can now leave that task to Brainchild. He will soon master his own brain to an extent exceeding my own. He will guide you, and also instruct you in decency, reason, and fairness, traits he has exhibited so well. I wish you all happiness and joy. It has been an honor to know each one of you: every member of the Vigil, living or dead; every member of the Space Mariners; all you Neo-men; Brainchild, and even Perturbare. Goodbye."

"It's glowing," said Raintree.

"What's glowing?"

"That symbol on your shoulder. The star of the Cosmic Patrol or whatever you call it."

"Why. So it is." Fomalhaut walked steadfastly into the Frame Shifter and thence disappeared.

Fomalhaut found himself somewhere deep in intergalactic space.

His suit detected an unoccupied Frame drifting nearby, which he summoned and mounted.

It was his own Frame, of that he had no doubt.

He spent a substantial amount of time simply soaking in and appreciating the boundless peace which surrounded him for millions of parsecs in all directions.

When at last he felt like taking heed of his situation and the Frame, he took note of the date. He was in his own time. He found that the Transcendental Signal was active. He used it to contact ISAF.

"Fomalhaut, my friend. What may I do for you?"

"I have a question. Has there been any recent talk about mounting an expedition to a closely parallel universe, in order to explore Human history and our own origins?"

"That's an interesting insight on your part. In fact, there has been such a theoretical discussion, but of course it could never actually be done."

"Why not?"

"For one thing, it was realized that introducing any quantity of foreign mass into the earliest phases of a new universe could destabilize it, resulting in excessive black hole formation, and worse, possibly resulting in a closed universe, dooming it to eventual gravitational collapse."

Fomalhaut took a moment to process this before continuing, "And for another thing?"

"The only method known for accessing such a closely parallel universe would be to travel forward in time to the gravitational collapse of our own universe, and then make a quantum transition through the singularity. But we, of course, do not inhabit a closed universe. Our universe will expand forever."

"Of course," said Fomalhaut. "Thank you, that is most interesting."

"How go your explorations? We haven't received any data from you in a while. Is all well with you?"

"Yes, all is well. I have merely been—distracted lately. I may soon be altering the character of my mission, or abandoning it. I shall keep you informed."

"By all means. It's good to hear from you, Fomalhaut. Farewell."

Fomalhaut broke the contact.

He began to laugh. He laughed as he had never laughed before, as he had never heard any of his people laugh before, uncontrollably, almost hysterically.

At length he grew quiet.

Taking stock of himself, he noticed that the star emblem on his shoulder continued to pulse with light.

And that was the end of the Vigil.

Valjhar said, "Brainchild. Do you have the ability to return Pimsie and I to our original Rralian forms?"

"I do, given time."

"And after that, will you, Endurance, kindly transport us back to Rral? Using the Motionglobe, you can propel a flyer to any destination."

"I will do so gladly."

After that was done, Endurance was rarely seen again on his native Earth. Freed of all limitations of time and space, from then on he might be found on any world, satisfying at last his very ancient desire to see justice and mercy brought to all the fragile, short-lived peoples of creation, with all their cares and pains. This desire would never abate from his ever-constant heart. And so he found his purpose and his destiny at last.

Eventually, by his unceasing efforts, he was able to change everything.

Ben Raintree took up staff and Stones, spending the rest of his long life wandering the Earth, bringing Light to the scattered human tribes and to the Neo-men alike, until the day finally came when he set down his burden, with Endurance at his side, the new and final heir to the Stones.

A very durable silver ovoid fell on Mars, where it was discovered by a colony of Neo-Men, who realized its nature and significance.

Some time after that, a Dancer arose.

Brainchild kept very busy. In intimate partnership with Perturbare, he took it upon himself to tidy up the planet for the peoples to come. Factories, roads, chemicals, waste, all began to crumble under the influence of his nanodevices. Cities gradually returned to the land, atom by atom and molecule by molecule. Waters grew clean. The air was purified and brought back to a proper balance.

Yet Brainchild did not destroy every work of Man. He was selective in what remained, strengthening and preserving things and places of beauty and significance: the Acropolis, the Mount Wilson Observatory; the house where Possum Perturbare had been born, and many other such monuments. The Pearl and Spire he made adamantine, and he even reconstructed the Lighthouse in a meadow in what had been Boston, as well as the Para-men's redoubt in Antarctica. Books he preserved, and works of art, and he made repositories of history and lore in imperishable form.

The Earth calmed itself. Forests burgeoned, fish and whales repopulated the seas, and coral reefs thrived. The Arctic re-froze. Brainchild recreated animals of the Pleistocene era, repopulating North America and Eurasia with the great beasts that had been wiped out by men. He also restored all other species erased by Man's brief rampage, leaving their ultimate fates to be sorted out by nature.

Brainchild did not ask permission to clean up the Human genome and so spare men the genetic diseases which had long plagued them. He had already spent too much time limited by the irrational fears of lesser minds. The Neo-men he left untouched. They had their own ideas of how they wished to develop, and they had the means and the intelligence to accomplish their goals.

Nor did Brainchild wait for slow natural forces to boost the reborn Moon to its proper orbit. He reshaped its path himself, and even sculpted its surface to resemble what once had been, comforting men by returning the once-familiar face to the skies.

Also, Brainchild built great monuments to the Vigil. Prominent among the figures was the mighty Stingray, though neither he nor Perturbare was quite sure if he had ever really existed, or was merely a character from the old cartoon series. Even Vega was present, also given the benefit of the doubt.

When all this work was completed, Perturbare decided to terminate his artificial consciousness. Immediately afterward, Brainchild did the same, having no wish to exist without his maker.

Thus the voice of God again fell silent on the Earth, and his mighty hand grew still.

On Rral, in the city of Enblenol, Pimsehkia Flam took as mate a member of the prosperous Warkin clan. With their help, Valjhar was able to reopen his father's old ship-fitting shop and resume the work in which he had been trained as a boy. He might have risen to become a ship's navigator or even captain, but he no longer felt a desire for anything but the warm sun and long, sweet evenings of Enblenol.

Pimsehkia took up a different vocation. Wearing the engineering suit, she confronted the remaining Prohibitors, a strange and secretive collection of leftovers from Rral's long-gone technological past. She blustered and bullied her way into their ranks, operating, when the rare need arose, as Prohibitor for the entire Enblenol region. Among all the people of Rral, only Valjhar knew that Pimsehkia sometimes set aside her affluent mate, her beautiful children, and her charming house to go abroad wearing that suit, her identity concealed by a golden mask resembling the face of Aureus.

Valjhar cherished the simple life into which he fell. Sometimes after a long day's work he would look out through his bedroom window at the remote blur of the Milky Way, thinking back with awe to the years he and his friends had spent among its stars. Somewhere in that little glow was Earth, the planet which had once dominated his life.

After musing on this for a while he would close his shutters and light his lamps. Those days were gone and unmourned.

As the years fled by, Valjhar, who had been only partially rejuvenated by Brainchild, again aged, though in the gentle manner native to Rralians, not in the cruel way he had inherited with his former Human form. His star-faring past grew increasingly hazy in his memory, until he was half-convinced it was only a dream he'd once shared with his boyhood friends. Pimsie and her children: Kern; Randa; and the sweet little Shashain, cared for him well, but still he lived alone. The day was near when he must set down his tools and face whatever end must come to a simple craftsman of Enblenol.

One day he awoke to find that a gentle melancholy had descended upon him during the night. Thus he knew that his end was not far off. He closed the shop, and in his final days he became remote and solitary, awaiting that final burst of life which would immediately precede his death. Pimsie often came around, lamenting that due to his manipulation of time he must die so much earlier than she. Valjhar did his best to comfort her, reminding her that from his point of view he had lived as long as any Rralian, though he did not dwell on how many of those years he had spent in a sad and futile search for Shaula.

One evening, as Valjhar was preparing to sleep, he heard a faint knock at the door downstairs. He frowned at the intrusion, descended to open it, and beheld in the light of his lamp a tall, slender figure clad in glittering green and gold. She had long dark hair that gleamed with green highlights, golden skin, and lustrous eyes of the deepest green. The fingers of her right hand were bound with a metal band; mounted in it was a hemisphere of utter blackness.

"Hello, Valjhar."

He stared at her, dumbfounded, uncomprehending. He had once known a woman, a girl really, like this, but when? Where? He knew he should take more note of her unusual costume, but again, it seemed he had seen its like before.

"It took me a very long time to recover and be retrained, but they say I am resilient, and here I am at last. I can't say I'm surprised to find you back here on Rral, and in this very place." She reached out to caress his weathered face. "I see you have many, many stories to tell, my dear Valjhar."

Something broke open then in Valjhar's heart, and a light entered his mind.

"Shaula!" He took her into his arms, buried his face in her hair, and wept.

Epilogue

The Frame Shifter disappeared around Lori Wu. The Sun flared up, the clouds dissolved, and she found herself standing in Times Square on a beautiful day.

It was a beautiful day in a beautiful city, clean and bright. The sky also was clean, free of contrails and the sound of jet engines.

Sleek, colorful ground cars, pushed along by propulsion beams, swept by in the street. Their occupants, visible through their bubble canopies, read, ate, talked, or looked around as they rolled past. Clearly they were passengers, not drivers.

The folk on the sidewalks strolled along, not overly hurried, happy and smiling. Scattered among them were men and women wearing white uniforms with a "V" emblem on their shoulders. These too sauntered in a relaxed manner, apparently unarmed, sometimes pausing to trade a few friendly words with passersby. No policemen were in sight.

One of those bubble-topped little cars pulled up to the curb. A woman and her young daughter emerged, did a double take at the sight of her, said "Behold the Vigil!" and scurried down the street, giggling. The car remained in place, beckoning. Lori hesitated, then seated herself in it; it closed itself up. She fumbled in her pockets looking for money.

"Um...how much does it cost to get to—"

Brainchild said, "There is no fee, Lori Wu, as you well know. Especially not for you. Where do you wish to go?"

"Take...take me to the Vigil."

"Of course. I will take you to our local station, where a flyer will be made available to you."

The car pulled out smoothly into the traffic. Lori noticed a display on the console in front of her.

"Brainchild, can you show me a picture of the current members of the Vigil?"

The screen lit up. There they stood, ranged in front of the Lighthouse in Boston, a temple of light, if anything still grander and more perfect than it had been on her world.

There were Fomalhaut and T'Ukudu, Stingray, Aureus, Ben Raintree dressed in his old cold armor, and both Tom Standing Crane and Walks-With-The-Sun. There stood a tall, striking woman whom Lori recognized as Rouse Farewell. Beside her was a still taller man, dressed in white, silver, and grey, his face hidden in the shadows of his cowl. There too was a Latina woman wearing star-spangled black: Vega, from the cartoon? Lori laughed in delight.

Finally, there stood Possum Perturbare, smiling proudly.

"Where's Endurance? Isn't he a member too?"

"Who is Endurance?" asked Brainchild.

"Never mind. What about the Para-Men? The Space Mariners?"

"We have not heard from them recently, but we believe they returned to their home world following their misunderstanding with the Vigil and its subsequent resolution. The members of the Vigil will be very glad to see you, Lori Wu. You have been missed. Vela composed a ballet telling the tale of your disappearance, which she performs to great public acclaim. Evidently it must be rewritten. Where have you been, if I may ask?"

Lori sighed, not sure how best to answer that question. "Someplace not quite as good as this."

After a few golden moments, she said, "Brainchild, have you ever heard of Chrysanthe of Thessaly?"

"Of course. Nearly everyone knows of her legend, the tale of her heroism and compassion. She even helped to mitigate the bloody savagery of Alexander the Butcher. Chrysanthe the Great. Truly an inspiration."

Lori smiled, leaned back her head, and closed her eyes, letting the sunlight warm her eyelids, filling her vision with a benign glow.

The End

Appendix

The End of the Vigil

So ends the saga of the Vigil, which has been gestating in my mind for the past forty years or more.

For those who are interested in the process of writing, I will reveal that the current novel, *Behold the Vigil*, is a conflation of what was originally intended to be two novels. The first was to feature the Vigil's military conquest of Earth and the establishment of their enlightened world government. In the second, the Vigil would relinquish the reins of power after some years, only to see the society they had established quickly fragment and dissolve into chaos. Possum Perturbare was going to try to unify everyone by faking an alien invasion, a plan which goes awry when the simulated invasion gets strikingly out of hand, resulting in the appearance of a vast and dreadful Machine of Non-Being, which tests the Vigil to its limit.

So why the changes? First, I realized I didn't want to tell the story of the Vigil's successful conquest. As I had envisioned it, it would have been too linear, a simple succession of battles and victories leading to a (temporarily) happy ending. Obviously, this plot could have been elaborated with various twists and reverses, but ultimately it wasn't a story I was really interested in telling. It was essentially Tom Clancy vs. the Justice League, no doubt a promising premise in some hands, but perhaps not in mine.

Second, as time passed I stopped believing it was possible for the Vigil, or anyone else, to conquer the human race and establish any sort of sane governance. As Fomalhaut says, while the Vigil could impose order by main force in a few corners of the world, in all others the natural perversity and endless stupidity of mankind would quickly result in worse turmoil than existed before. I don't see any good way out of their situation, or ours, without a massive redefinition of human nature. I see no means of achieving that in our real world. As for theirs, unless Raintree could use the Stones to burn the evil and blindness out of every person in the world, I saw no real hope for them either, and so resorted to the evacuation of the planet to make room for something better. I'm afraid our own end won't be so neat and painless.

Anyone reading this, I realize, is likely to be a human being. If so, please don't take offense at my pessimistic view of our species. You may be one of the good ones.

In the endnotes for *The Vigil,* I mentioned how my originally intended ending for the series, which was plotted sometime in the 1970s, had been preempted by the classic graphic novel *Watchmen* by Alan Moore and Dave Gibbons. Their character Ozymandias tries to bring people together by faking an invasion from a foreign dimension (sorry if I just spoiled that story for you). All right then... how about if Perturbare's invasion turns out to be real?

And exactly who or what should invade? Moore and Gibbons use a Lovecraftian tentacled eldritch horror from Beyond (or the semblance of one, anyway). But I knew something even scarier: *The Night Land,* by William Hope Hodgson (1877-1918), an underrated writer of horror and fantasy who lived at the turn of the Twentieth Century, and whose life was sadly cut short by his service in World War I.

The Night Land, published in 1912, is to my mind one of the most imaginative and frightening books ever written. It's far more nightmarish than my pale evocation of it in this novel. My only excuse is that this book is about the Vigil, not the Night Land, and anyway, it may not be the "real" Night Land in the first place. I advise anyone who is intrigued by the glimpses of the Night Land I have provided to read the original, which is, as Brainchild says, in the public domain and freely available online. But be warned: Hodgson made an unfortunate stylistic choice which almost sinks the book right from the start, using extremely turgid language which is supposed to evoke the writings of the Seventeenth Century. Once past the framing chapters, and with your mind adapted to the stilted language, *The Night Land* creeps into your soul and stays there for a long time to come.

And so, I hope, do the adventures of the Vigil.

Joe Bergeron

June 23, 2011